THE GREY FAIRY ANOMALY

THE WEST HAVEN UNDEAD BOOK 5

THE GREY FAIRY ANOMALY

NICK SAVAGE

4 Horsemen
Publications, Inc.

DEDICATION

To everyone, thank you for the ride.
It is time to go.

TABLE OF CONTENTS

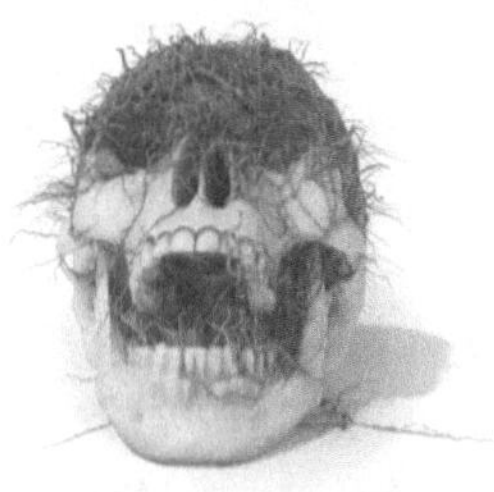

CHAPTER 1

"Given the chance,
fate answers all your curiosities
in the cruelest of ways."
~E. DeSalvo~

Rowdy patrons fill a dirty bar while a minstrel strums *some Russian drinking music in the back, providing some atmosphere to the stuffiness that pervades. The noise of both cannot drown out the raging storm outside as thunder shakes the building with each roar. The static from nearby lightning charges the room.*

Amidst the noise and raucousness, a young Vistrus, all of twenty-three years, sits alone, on the opposite side of the bar from the musician, nursing a drink. Freckles dot his face and green/blue eyes command attention from anyone he talks with. Both features he does not realize he will, one day, lose to the ravages of time.

Wanting nothing more than to enjoy a few moments to himself, he ignores the crowds around him, thinking about all the ills that plague his mind. And while time Vistrus may want, the obvious outsider, a man, walking through the door tells him that time he will not have.

No older than twenty-three, with fair-yet-olive skin and dripping wet from the rain, this stranger looks around as if expecting someone. However, the someone he spots and takes a seat a few stools down from is Vistrus. Ordering a whiskey, his eyes still search the room, though now they search for someone following him. The glass clinks against the wood bar top, snapping the stranger from his search. He inspects the glass for a moment, as if someone might have poisoned it. Deciding it is safe, he takes a sip, turning his attention toward Vistrus.

"Quite the storm outside," he says in a thick Egyptian accent, making small talk.

Vistrus offers a nod, feeling out this stranger. He suspects that this man's small talk might not be as small as it seems. So he returns with, "There is always a storm."

The man leans in, again looking around for listening ears. "It will clear one day. I always say the storm will pass when fate summons."

Vistrus huffs, offering a knowing smile. Leaning in closer to the man, Vistrus squints his eyes, marking the seriousness of his following words. "What is your name?"

Either ignoring the visual cues or not picking up on them, the man replies, "Ammar. And you, friend?"

"Vistrus. I believe that the storm will pass along the banks of Godavari."

Smiles cross both of them and the seriousness of the moment evaporates as they laugh, lifting their glasses to cheer this newfound acquaintance.

Ammar leans a little closer, but his words are no quieter than before. "It's always nice to run into someone cut from the same cloth. The roads can be a weary place, even for those such as us."

Vistrus offers a nod, saying, "Weary, indeed. But we are safe as long as things are in order."

Ammar raises a brow, confident he knows what Vistrus means but does not want to leave room for error. "Twenty-one things, if I catch your drift."

Chuckling at his newfound friend's words, Vistrus raises his glass again. "Indeed, you do." He pauses as they share a sip of their respective drinks. "What brings you to this part of the world? Or is that a topic for another time?"

Looking around, as if expecting to see someone but finding no one, Ammar turns back to Vistrus. "What are your thoughts on us?"

"That is a loaded question aimed at a wide target."

Ammar opens his mouth to speak but pauses, narrowing down the scope of his original question. "Are you one for staying hidden, feeding the fables of time? Or would you prefer to let the world know, hoping for understanding?"

Before answering, Vistrus signals the barkeep, ordering another round for him and his new friend. "It is not a simple question and, therefore, not a simple answer. I want to protect my family."

Ammar's eyes light up. "Ah, you have little ones?"

Vistrus shakes his head. "I am twenty-three. A little old now for little ones. No, I never found a woman who I think would understand our ... predicament."

"Then what was that about protecting family?" Ammar's interest in his new friend grows.

"This Body of ours ... it protects us. I want to protect them."

"A short answer, Vistrus. I think we all want to protect our family, whatever that may be."

"I want to do what is best for those like us."

Ammar huffs. "Who are we to decide what is best for others?"

Vistrus thinks on this for a moment as the bartender sets down the new round that was poured into the glasses they were already using. He turns to Ammar as a smile creeps across his face. "Something to think about."

Ammar shakes off the mood, relaxing into his stool. "Enough of that for tonight. Let's enjoy the drinks, my friend."

Smiling, Vistrus takes a long sip, turning his attention to the patrons around him. He and Ammar share passing thoughts on life, love, and existential philosophy before Ammar excuses himself, leaving Vistrus alone once again.

The late hours of the night rage on with the storm. Lightning strikes closer and more often than the drunken vagrants seeking shelter under crates and debris feel comfortable with. Their cheers of "Na Zdravi" only distract themselves for a moment from the long, wet night ahead. A few horse-drawn carriages take cautious strolls down the alley, hoping their respect and fear for the storm provide safe passage.

A back door opens, but the sound of music and drunken comradery suffocate at the threshold under the weight of the storm. Vistrus looks to the sky before stepping out. He does not relish the walk ahead of him.

CHAPTER 1

The rain intensifies as he walks away from the bar, making him question the limits of how much water can fall from the sky at once. Farther along his path, his ears pick up sounds of a struggle. Even in the chaotic noise of rainfall and thunder, he hears cries for help.

Quickening his pace, he follows the sounds a block over and stops before rounding the corner to listen, hoping he misheard, but Vistrus did not. Taking a deep breath, preparing himself for what he might find, he rounds the corner to see two men towering over a cowering man, beating him as if he were a rabid dog being put down in the most brutal of ways.

Not knowing anything about the situation, but knowing the sounds of pain and pleading, Vistrus shouts, "Leave him alone!"

The men turn to Vistrus, pointing a crude, splintered wood plank at the beaten man. "He is a monster!"

Closing in, Vistrus can make out the bloodied man as his newfound friend, Ammar. A cut above his eyes gushes blood, mixing with the rain as it flows into his eye. He shuts it, unable to see; his other eye squints, trying to both protect itself and see enough to ward off what attacks he can. Scratches and scrapes cover his arms and face.

Stopping short of the two men, to keep a safe distance from cheap shots, Vistrus says, "Monster can be a bad word. Do not call anyone that."

Vistrus's arm, shoulder, and back muscles grow, bulking up beyond measure. He lowers his shoulders, trying to make himself seem smaller than he is.

The attackers, their attention trained on Vistrus, keep Ammar at bay with the pointed ends of their weapons.

Squinting, they see Vistrus's transition, even in the heavy rains.

"Do you think the rain and dark hides your hideousness?" the first attacker retorts.

Peeking up from his grounded position, Ammar pleads, "We do not hide under beds. We are nothing to fear."

Pressing the broken end of a metal pipe into Ammar's chest, the second attacker shouts, "You say this while hiding yourselves from the world, too ashamed to show who you really are!" He releases the pressure off the pipe, allowing Ammar to clutch his chest.

Vistrus inches closer, blood dripping from his mouth. His teeth fall out, being replaced with two elongated and sharpened canines, as he speaks. "It is complicated."

Motioning for his cohort to keep watch over Ammar, the first man steps closer to Vistrus. "If you do not trust yourselves enough to show the world, how can we ever trust you?" He extends his weapon, defending himself from a perceived attack from Vistrus.

Vistrus stops inching forward, trying to turn the man's phrase against him. "When people such as you treat us this way, how can we ever trust you?"

The first man stops to consider Vistrus's words. The second pushes away any semblance of self-reflection, abandoning his focus on Ammar to turn toward Vistrus, a man they see as nothing more than another piece of filth to be eliminated.

Lightning strikes close by as thunder booms with no delay. The scene lights up, and both men see Vistrus standing there, his hair thinned and long, as if balding in patches. Blood drips from his mouth as the last of his teeth fall to the ground. He smiles, revealing fangs that belong on anything other than a human. But his bulging muscles, ripping away his clothes as they grow, give the attackers pause as they see massive, hypertrophic muscles with varicose veins pulsating with blood.

All bravado leaves the men for a moment as they summon what courage they can to offer a reply. The first attacker takes a breath, steadying himself for the moment. "We must protect what we know is right."

As if Mother Nature herself wants to hear Vistrus's response, the rain and lightning calm to a drizzle.

"Everything you are trying to protect is wrong. You can either stay willfully ignorant or learn from this and better yourself."

As if satisfied with his answer, lightning strikes even closer than the last and the rain picks up where it left off, reducing vision to a few yards.

Unlike Mother Nature, the men are not okay with Vistrus's words and turn their weapons on him. The first attacker lunges toward Vistrus, trying to connect the splintered board with Vistrus's face, but he dodges, sweeping the man's leg and sending him firmly onto the wet ground.

The other man engages with Vistrus as he parries attack after attack, not wanting to kill or maim either man. Their willingness to die for what they believe shines through in their moxie to fight an obviously losing battle.

A noise below the torrent of rain rings in Vistrus's ear. Something behind him. He swings around to see the first attacker rushing in, mania filling his face. Vistrus sidesteps, grabbing him and throwing him on top of the second man, sending them both to the ground.

Vistrus pounces on the leader, grabbing him by the throat with a need to subdue the man, not kill him.

Seeing Ammar licking his wounds, a sense of mercy overtakes Vistrus. He knows that the endless parrying will do nothing to tire the men. Subdue and control remain the only option.

Lightning flashes and Vistrus sees the madness in the first man's eyes as he rushes back into the fray. The rain picks up, limiting everyone's vision even further. No one can see a thing outside of arm's reach, even as the lightning flashes quicker and quicker: the rain, wind, and thunder mute the sounds of their blows. The storm gains momentum with each passing moment until it is so strong that the surrounding buildings' creaks resonate above the chaotic noise. And just before it seems the world around Vistrus is about to implode, the rain slows to a steady shower. The rolling thunder fades, and the moon lights the alleyway as the heavy clouds disperse in the sky.

Vistrus remains standing. The two men lie wounded but alive as the rain washes away their blood and all signs of battle, cleaning what it can of the area.

The men try to tend to their numerous wounds, looking up at the Legend and waiting to be killed.

Shaking his head, Vistrus looms over them, helping Ammar off the ground.

Ammar wipes the blood off his face and from his eye.

Turning to the men, Vistrus offers, "You are still alive because we are, in fact, not monsters. My friend still lives because you could not kill him quickly enough. The difference is all the difference."

The men do not respond but turn to each other in silent reflection of their actions. No doubt lingers in their minds that had the tables been reversed, Vistrus and Ammar would both be deceased.

Ammar turns to Vistrus, sadness painting his face with worry. Vistrus, too, shares the worries, saying, "This storm will never pass."

Ammar nods a heavy head.

They turn from the men, leaving them to nurse their wounds and find safe passage for coalescence. The Normals did not die, and that is the Legends' only concern. Vistrus supports Ammar as they make their way down the alley through the storm, walking in silent reverie over the bonds forged in battle that solidify a new friendship.

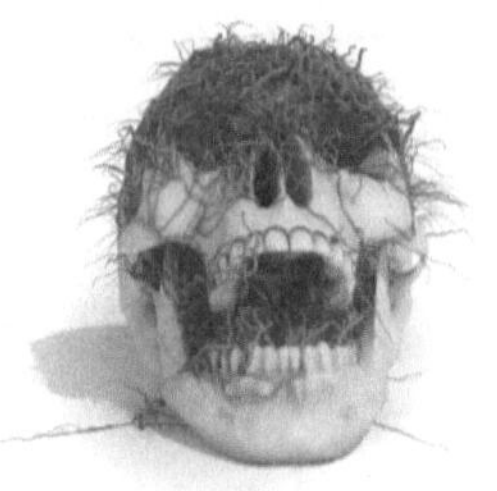

CHAPTER 2

Closing the under-sink cabinet, Vistrus collapses against it, clutching Inessa's long-hidden diary against his chest.

A soft smile that tries to repress itself inches across his face as his hands clench harder around the diary. His eyes, fixed on Eleanor who stands over him, relax as the wiry look of growing insanity dissolves. "Inessa was not crazy, Eleanor. She did not know what else to do. It was always about protecting her loved ones—her family."

Eleanor nods. "What now?"

Looking down at the book, he smiles. "We get our answers."

The spine cracks as he opens the book. Dust of years past floats off the pages' edges as he begins reading.

"I'm going to make you some tea," Eleanor says, smiling. "We could both use some."

He nods, acknowledging she said something, but she can't be sure he was listening. It does not matter either way; they may finally have their answer. Vistrus scans the pages of the diary, careful not to split the delicate spine or tear the fragile pages. He listens to the sounds of Eleanor putting water on to boil and placing loose tea leaves into steeping balls. Reading similar words to what he has read countless times, he skips to the last of the entries.

> ... What came first, the chicken or the egg? Pretend to be paranoid long enough and the act is no longer acting. Chicken. Egg. One glove, one portrait. Why one glove? Why one portrait? Why one? Egg. Chicken. It was never real. It was ever real. Words hurt sometimes. Is the drawing the egg?

Vistrus stops for a moment as Inessa's words sink in, telling him she was never as crazy as she pretended to be. A pain floods his chest as all the signs he missed flash in his mind. Every time he doubted his belief that she was fine stings him because, in the end, he did doubt her. Vistrus loved her without question, but he believed what everyone else was whispering to him; that his wife was going insane. He takes a slow breath in, taking in as much air as possible, trying to calm himself down so he can keep reading.

... I can't do this much longer. Something must be done, so no one has to know, and those that know won't be in the cross-hairs anymore.

Vistrus reads that sentence a few times, trying to comprehend what Inessa must have felt when she wrote that.

It must be me. It must be stopped. I can pretend no more. If everyone is to be kept safe, I must deal with the Adeirrig. I must stop him. I must know he knows I know he knows no one knows. But how? Will I ever know?

Those few sentences cement in his mind the anguish she must have felt upon that realization. The pain in Vistrus's chest screams to him that everything he has ever done, all the successes and victories in his life, have all been for nothing because no matter how hard he tried to be a good husband and father, his wife of too many years to count could not feel safe confiding this belief to him. Inessa felt safer pretending to be insane and watching those she loved think her mad than asking for help while she decided what to do. Inessa's realization of needing to do what she did plants not a seed of doubt, but a full-grown tree of doubt that everything Vistrus has ever lived and fought for might be wrong.

... If you find this, it means I am no longer with you ... in body, at least. In spirit, I will always be with you. But it also means my sacrifice kept you and Allison safe. I have tried in so many ways to tell you, but the hints and clues must have been too obtuse, too insane. The Adeirrig, last known Adeirrig, is still alive. I acted the way I did because I did not know who to trust. Putting you in danger was never an option. Allison needs at least one parent. All I can say is, trust no one. He killed what we now call the Council that was in place before you were part of it. His murders were why we were sent here from our homeland. The Body, as they were once called, never wanted justice, only silence. They only wanted to keep them-selves safe. After I reported what I safely could, The Body was dissolved, and The Nation was born. But their murderer is still among us. Remember, Vistrus, trust no one. Bishop is his name.

The approaching, soft rattle of porcelain teacups on saucers, along with Eleanor's footsteps, accompany a growing realization that the same man responsible for the Body's deaths is the same man responsible not only for Inessa's death but Nick DeSalvo's as well. A realization that yanks Vistrus from the pages of his late wife's diary. He slams the book shut, turning to Eleanor as she bends toward him, handing him a cup.

"I see anger has won. I assume any answers found were not what you hoped."

Vistrus forces a faint smile at her statement, watching her with suspicious eyes. Of all the people he could easily not trust, Eleanor is dead last on the list. In all the decades they've known each other, she has never given him a reason not to trust her. His wife, however, warns him to trust no one. While he could not listen while she was alive, he is listening now.

"Dead end. More ramblings indicative of her decline." He pats the book before sipping his tea.

Eleanor joins him, sipping hers. "Something will turn up, dearie. Nothing stays hidden forever."

The walls of this small research room protect the archaeological finds from the elements outside. Three carefully positioned lights shine down on various yet common artifacts resting on a table as Ammar, fully covered in a shemagh, examines them while taking great care in cleaning them off. Under the table, a wine bag rests between a briefcase and the table legs.

This makeshift room holds only the necessities for the immediate needs until the artifacts transfer to their final destination. A small chair rests at the other end of the room, a few long strides away from where Ammar stands.

Even through the whipping sands of the storm outside, his ears pick up the sounds of approaching footsteps. Footsteps he has not heard in a good many years.

The door opens, allowing gusts of sand to blow into the room as Vistrus enters, wearing his trademark high-class motorcycle-meets-business attire. After closing the door to keep the storm outside, he looks around the room, trying to find something, as if he does not know why someone brought him here.

Ammar turns to him but does not remove his shemagh. "Quite the storm brewing outside. Wouldn't you say, Vistrus?"

Vistrus squints, scrunching his face at the pointed words while trying to uncover the hint of familiarity in the stranger's voice. He weighs the man's words, responding with, "Are you In?" He hopes a response will sate his curiosity about the familiarity.

Ammar, realizing his shemagh has halted Vistrus's connection of who he is, answers, "I am in a night, chilly and dark."

Recognizing the words helps Vistrus connect the voice under the shemagh, forcing a smile on his travel-worn face. He takes a step in, responding with, "The night may be chilly but not dark."

Ammar and Vistrus approach each other and grasp the other's hand in a firm, friendly embrace.

Vistrus shakes his head. "We are inside. Take off your shemagh."

Ammar unwraps his face, laughing as he tells Vistrus an obvious white lie, "Sometimes I forget I have them on." After taking a moment to fully unwrap and fold it up, keeping it safe from contaminating the table of artifacts, he says, "Surprised you did not call me from the plane. I trust you had a good flight."

Keeping his attention on the conversation while scanning the room, Vistrus replies, "I did, but forgot my phone in the rush. As for your initial question, yes. Quite the storm, but it is always brewing."

"And it will only get worse," Ammar offers his ominous reply.

The two men step to the artifact table. Vistrus looks the items over but seems unimpressed.

"Ammar, nothing I see here is worth my time or the university's money to fly me out. This acquisition could have been digital."

Ammar, shaking his head and holding back a laugh, turns to Vistrus. "The university didn't fly you out."

Vistrus turns from the artifacts to Ammar. Frustration washes over his face. "Why the pretense? Who then?"

Ammar reaches under the table, grabs the briefcase, and sets it on the table, drawing Vistrus's attention. Before entering the combination to unlock the case, Ammar answers Vistrus, "The Nation."

Keeping his eye on the briefcase but mind on the conversation, he asks, "Which Society? Kipling? Tennyson?"

Ammar shakes his head, a sly smile painting his face. "A Council member."

Without thinking about the deeper implication of Ammar's words, Vistrus blurts out, "My Council has no authority in Cairo."

Ammar offers a wry smile, but he says nothing in response, letting the moment pass.

Vistrus joins Ammar in the passing moment, turning his attention from the briefcase to the storm outside for a moment, noting, "This passing storm is quite beautiful." Before long, he turns back to studying the artifacts, trying to find anything useful in them outside of the usual archaeological awe and wonder.

Studying them for a few moments with nothing exceptional to note, he eyes the briefcase but says nothing, a gesture not unnoticed by Ammar, who lets his friend stew in wonderment for a moment. After a long silence, Ammar brings their conversation around to a long danced-around topic. "We both know the storm never truly passes," Ammar chimes in.

Shaking his head, Vistrus exhales, not wishing to revisit this past conversation but playing into it anyway. "Is this still the game we play, Ammar?"

Keeping his attention on his briefcase, Ammar replies, "It's been our dance for more years than either care to admit."

"To keep The Nation hidden or come out to the world. Yes, I remember," Vistrus answers. His words sound tired, as if this played-out dance may finally come to an end.

"And you still want to stay hidden. Our time is near, Vistrus; I can feel it," Ammar responds back, confirming Vistrus's unspoken finality of their dance.

Vistrus, too, keeps his eyes on the briefcase, trying to study the hidden contents within it even though he can't see them. "You always feel the time is near, but never give thought to the danger fear brings." His pointed words hit with blunt edges. Both men know their stances on the topic, though opposite, have varied over the years.

Ammar responds with, "I am not that naïve. Its passing could be both great and terrible."

Vistrus breaks his stare on the briefcase, turning to Ammar. Concern paints his face, weighing heavy in his eyes. "It is the terrible I worry about, but you hold on to the hope that one day the storm might pass peacefully."

Nodding and turning to his friend, Ammar sees the tired sadness that etched itself onto his face over the decades, saying, "It's our yin and yang, Vistrus."

Vistrus does not respond, internally acknowledging the wisdom of Ammar's words.

Ammar twists the numbers on the combination lock until they all click into their proper place, unlocking it. He, however, keeps it closed.

Vistrus nods to the briefcase, finally getting to the topic of his journey. "Is this it? Why not mail it?"

Ammar smiles, lifting his chin to Vistrus. "I wanted you to see it at the site of discovery. I do not think you'd believe your eyes otherwise."

Intrigued by his friend's words, Vistrus turns his stare back to the closed case. "What is it?"

Ammar shakes his head as the lock unlatches on the case. "Not what. Who," Ammar says with a flat smile as he opens the briefcase.

Peering inside, disbelief washes over Vistrus. It takes a few moments for Vistrus to summon any words until he lands on, "This cannot be."

A seriousness washes over Ammar, leaving behind all earlier pleasantries. "Now you see why I wanted you here."

Vistrus, tempted to touch the contents as a yearning takes over, stops himself, knowing better than to do such things.

Ammar watches his friend as he studies the contents without touching it. He asks Vistrus, "Did you know?"

Vistrus shakes his head. "She ... This portrait, it cannot be... This makes her older than the Sentinels."

Ammar waits a long while until Vistrus rationalizes his thoughts. The patience of centuries lived serves him well as Vistrus stays locked in a state of awe and dumbfoundedness.

As he sees reality set back in and the obvious questions form in his friend's mind, Ammar tells him, "Found in excavation and pulled immediately. University dig."

Keeping his stare on the artifact, Vistrus replies, "Certainly was. What does this council member want from me?"

Offering a wry smile once more, Ammar breathes in before responding, "I wanted you to be the first to know. This could upend everything we've been told about The Nation. That passing storm…"

"…may pass sooner than I would like," Vistrus finishes his friend's thought, taking a moment to reflect on that before continuing. "This could endanger my life. My daughter's life. Allison has not even transitioned yet. She knows nothing about her true self."

Adding to the weight of it all, Ammar says, "This discovery means everything we know about our history is wrong."

His words snap Vistrus back to the moment. He gives a quick nod to his friend before saying, "I see no good in stirring the proverbial pot. Now, we figure out what this means for our history. But this is your find, Ammar." Ammar does not reply, perhaps waiting on more from Vistrus, who adds, "Will you tell them?"

Ammar contemplates a moment before giving a half-smile while shaking his head. Vistrus looks back down into the find, contemplating everything as Ammar closes the briefcase and hands Vistrus the wine bag. Pulling out an expensive bottle of Egyptian whiskey from the bag, he raises an eyebrow at Ammar, who says, "For the flight home. Safe travels."

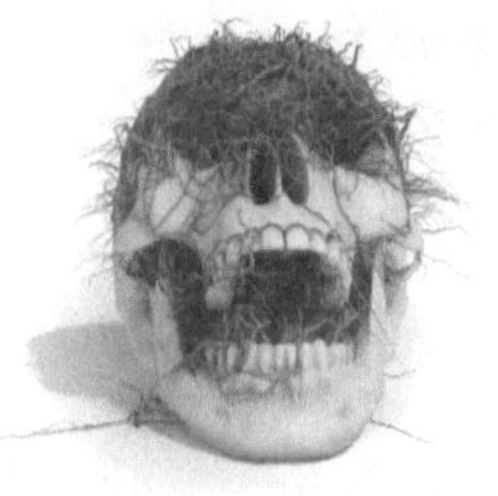

CHAPTER 3

"Whoever said it was wrong.
Time is, like, most definitely not on our side."
~B. Waldgrave~

I don't care that I'm supposed to be this Grey Fairy. The fact my parents abandoned me as a baby in some lopsided effort to keep us safe doesn't even register in my ... whatever things register on. Never mind the fact that someone framed Connor for Grandpa's murder. Nope. Not gonna talk about that right now. Not gonna ponder on the reasons someone would decide to do that. Right now, I don't even care that Max Espinoza—cop and Legend killer—came back to help us 'cause he decided cold-blooded murder wasn't as on the up and up as he thought and found some misconceived notion of redemption by jumping in front of a bullet to save Duncan.

"Hell, I don't even want to think about the time I spent buried in the ground, biding my time in—what do you call it, the Waiting—only to wake up and have to dig myself out of the ground like some zombie. Nope. Don't care. Whatever. What I do care about, right now, in this moment, is that my best friend, Allison, killed herself and not a damn one of you, us, whatever, saw it coming. Not a single one of us saw a sign, reached out, tried to say, 'Hey, we see you. What can we do to help?' And now she's dead. That's what I care about. I care about her. Damn it all to hell: this Nation, the Council, this being a Legend, and everything that's happened in this town of ours. Ha! West Haven. What the hell kind of stupidly ironic name is that?! All life in this town has brought us is death, death, and more death. I don't want it. You can have it. Screw it all. All of it can go to hell. My best friend is dead, and I want her back."

Her rapid-fire speech screeches to a halt so she can gasp a breath before finishing with, "I will find a way to bring her back."

Scarlett McAllister stares down at her best friend, Allison, lying in a tub filled with red water. Her lifeless body sits, waiting to be picked up, moved, and taken away from this house. Scarlett's tears flow but struggle against the drying wells. She has already cried so much in so little time, her body fights against making more.

The brunt of Scarlett's tirade (and father to the deceased), Vistrus Petrovsky, stands in the bathroom doorway. A man whose signature stoicism and calmness abandon him in this moment. What Scarlett's dry eyes lack in tears, his eyes compensate with an abundance. He has witnessed death before in many forms over too many years to desire to look back on, but he has never lost a daughter. Vistrus has never lost his flesh and blood before. Losing his wife was a pain he was confident he would never experience again. The gut-wrenching, nausea-inducing pain that lingers for years after the initial onset, the pain that never leaves, but, if lucky, dulls a little over time was something he was sure he would never have to repeat. Never should a parent have to experience the loss of a child. Never should a parent have to see what their child's lifeless body looks like. Here he stands, staring at his only daughter, his only remaining relative, lying in a bathtub, dead by her own design.

Scarlett turns her attention to Vistrus. "Can you bring her back? Can you do that for her? Is she something the precious Council cares about?"

Vistrus pulls his stare away from Allison. "The water is cold. She doesn't like cold water."

Scarlett, unsure what to do, lays a hand on the hot water faucet. Vistrus remains silent, so she turns on the hot water. "This should warm her."

Connor enters the bathroom, holding three glasses of ice water. "Drink. You need to stay hydrated." He hands each of them a glass. Vistrus takes a sip, holding it to his lips for longer than necessary. Pulling it away, he turns to Connor.

"Did we miss anything, Connor?"

Connor shakes his head with slow deliberation, lacking any enthusiasm or emotion—only a functional answer. "I think we filled her in on everything she missed while healing."

"Did you hear…?" Vistrus begins.

Connor nods. "Everything. She wasn't quiet."

"I think she can yell. Allison would do the same." The elder Petrovsky turns to Scarlett. "Do not let the water get too hot. We do not want to burn her. Scalding water is very painful."

Scarlett turns off the hot water, testing the bath to make sure it's not overly hot. She turns, and, seeing Connor drink some of the ice water, she follows suit.

They all sit, sipping water, unsure of what to say to one another. With each passing moment, the silence weighs heavier and heavier. Scarlett fights back tears that try to break the surface. Vistrus has calmed down, wheels turning in his mind over the events that led up to this moment and how he missed the signs. He wonders if there was something he could have done. If he had gotten Allison into therapy when she first asked or discovered the meaning of Inessa's diaries earlier. Sometimes, there are no signs, but he refuses to let that be the card he tries to play. There will be no passing the blame to the easiness of no one's fault. The fault, at least partially, lies with him and his time away from her. Away from family wrapped up in the Council, in The Nation, trying to figure out how he can make the world a better place for those like him. Now, seeing his daughter lying there, he knows he has failed.

"Brianna and Duncan need to know," Connor says, piercing the silence.

Vistrus nods. "Go. Tell them. I will tend to Allison." But as fast as the words leave his mouth, he has retreated into his thoughts.

Connor lays a hand on Scarlett's shoulder, but she pulls away.

"No way I'm leaving her. I already did that once and look what happened." Scarlett turns to Allison. "I'm right here, Al. Right here. No one is going anywhere."

"You didn't leave her, Scarlett. Being in the Waiting is not abandoning your friends. It's healing," Connor tries to reassure, so she feels she did nothing wrong.

"The only reason I came back is because no one knows where my 21 grams are."

Something in her words pulls Vistrus from his thoughts. "Scarlett, go with Connor. I have things I must do now. Calls to make." A stern determination in his voice tells Scarlett that her time with Allison has ended. She must go find Bri and Duncan and tell them the news.

Connor helps Scarlett to her feet and leads her out of the bathroom. Before he exits, he turns to Vistrus. "If there is anything you need me to do, let me know. I'll come right away."

Vistrus nods but offers no verbal response.

Connor follows Scarlett down the stairs and to the front door, but before they leave, Connor calls to Vistrus, "What do we do now?"

Vistrus doesn't break his thoughts. He thinks of many answers he could and perhaps should give, but nothing ushers from his lips. A moment of silence lingers before Connor and Scarlett shut the door behind them, leaving Allison with her father.

The door to the Waldgrave residence closes behind Brianna and Duncan as they exit her house. The calm air mirrors the motionlessness inside, and the stillness of it all holds Bri from moving toward Duncan's car. Her gaze stares past the door to the gruesome scene beyond. Though she cannot physically see the blood and death once again strewn about her home, her mind can't unsee it.

Duncan grabs her hand, trying to gently lead her from the step toward his car. "Come on, love. We need to leave." The caravan of white, windowless cargo vans pulling into her driveway and parking along the street steals his attention for a moment. "They're here. Everything will be all right."

He says those words, but Duncan is not sure he believes them any more than Brianna does. She turns from staring at the door to the vans sitting idle, waiting for the two of them to leave. "No. It won't. There's been nothing with The Nation that has ended well so far. Why would it now?" Her eyes beg him to tell her she is wrong, to find some silver lining she has missed in the chaos of the past few years. However, there is nothing he can say to alleviate her pain right now. As she was once told, "Rare are the moments for which there are no words." Now is one of those moments. It is a moment she does not want to dwell in any longer, so she starts walking to his car.

He follows behind her, saying nothing to fill the seconds until he opens his passenger-side door for her. Those seconds seem to stretch forever. Each of the vans' windows is tinted, save the windshields. All Duncan can see as he tries to sneak a peek at the drivers are people wearing hazmat suits and filtered face respirators. There is nothing visible that he can use later as identifiers, though he suspects that is not a coincidence.

After opening the door for Bri and helping her into the passenger seat, he shuts the door and gets in on the driver's side. Before he can turn the ignition key to start the car, Brianna speaks up.

"I can't go back there. I am not sure I can stay here anymore."

They both turn to see the masked people make their way inside, each carrying various equipment or chemicals. The sterile undertones of the hazmat suit parade sink into their minds, numbing them to whatever feelings are trying to surface. The couple try to turn to each other, but their gazes stay locked on the stream of people entering and leaving her house to once again cover up something she can never forget.

"That is your home."

She shakes her head but does not turn to him. "Was. No one's home should ever see that much death. There's too much … too many terrible memories for me here."

Still staring at the cleaners, Duncan finally turns on the car. "What are you saying?"

She shrugs, unsure of her thoughts. Giving her a moment to think about it, he pulls away to take her back to his home. They drive in silence until her house and the caravan of cleaners disappear from view.

"I need to leave West Haven. I've had, I don't know how many, people killed in my house, including my mother. None of it made the news beyond the fact she and Mrs. Espinoza were teachers. This won't make the news either."

"So? You have friends here. You have people who care about you. People who understand what you are going through and will have to live with. That has to mean something."

There it is—the silver lining in the macabre storm. If only it were enough.

"No," she responds, shaking her head. "It's too much." She turns to him, her puppy dog eyes begging him to say yes to what she is about to say. "Run away with me. Well, not really run away since I'm an adult. Move with me. We are getting married anyway. Let's get married in another town, live in another home. Somewhere we can start over and forget everything that's happened here."

A sad smile crosses his face before fading away. He wants to respond, wants to tell Brianna that running away from her problems won't make them go away. That it'll only delay them for a while. He knows that now is neither the time nor the place; pushing back against her grief will only add fuel to the fire burning inside her right now. So, he doesn't speak. He sits and listens to her while she rambles on. "Just imagine, Duncan. You and me living on a beach somewhere. No one else around except for maybe a bartender who runs a quaint tiki hut margarita bar. We can lie out on the beach, sunbathing all day, and surf. I'll learn how to surf. I think I'd be good at surfing. You'd be good at it. You probably already are."

He shakes his head at her words, but doesn't speak. Interrupting her train of thought might not be the wisest decision, so listen, he does.

"Or we could move to Paris. The fashion there is always fetch. Think about it, love. You and me in Paris. Nothing but beautiful Parisians eating French food all day and drinking wine while looking beautiful. It would be absolutely perfect. That's what we should do. And Paris isn't too far from Italy; it's only like a train ride away. Breakfast in Tuscany, dinner in Bordeaux. We'd live in a movie and have the perfect life free from vampires and werewolves and whatever Societies The Nation wants to shove down our throats to remind us we are some freaks unworthy of being ourselves. Free from any and all of the insane craziness that is West Haven. Ew." The words West Haven rolled off her tongue like a rotten pecan—spicy and utterly unappetizing. If ever there were words she hated more to say, Duncan would not like to find out.

Unfortunately, Duncan knows the reality of their situation. As nice as daily sand and surf or pub crawling their daily meals through Europe sounds, he knows they can't. Such flights of fancy are nothing they can indulge in. Not right now, at least. He doesn't know enough about The Nation to know if other Councils exist outside of West Haven and, if they do, how far away the next cluster of them lives. He doesn't know if the Legends in West Haven comprise a small amount of them compared to other cities or if most of them are here. As a Normal, Duncan has no basis for anything he needs to find out if he is to convince his fiancée one way or the other where they are to live.

For now, he does the only thing he can do, continuing to listen while he drives her as far away as he can from the pain she feels—past the turn to his house and onto the highway. He hopes that perhaps a night in the Windy City will help clear her mind.

Silence fills the drive from Allison's back to Brianna's. Connor's car speakers blare no music. No conversation takes place, and even the sound of his and Scarlett's breathing seems faint. Some sedated version of Connor steers the wheel, stopping at each stop sign for a full three seconds and even obeying the speed limit.

While one might think that these changes in driving habits are a sign of his coming into adulthood or some signal of maturation, his mind holds no doubt that the adjustments are temporary. This crushing weight of forlorn isolation craving company and the slow, abject loss of everyone he's ever cared about suffocates any will to move on or reason to see excitement or hope in the everyday details taken for granted.

Scarlett's blank stare watches the road pass them by. Oblivious to the world around her, she keeps replaying the moments from the bathroom in her head, trying to find a path of action she could have taken to save her friend. She searches the deepest recesses of her mind for some clue that Allison could have been saved. Thinking that instead of shaking her friend to wake up, as if she laid down to rest in a tub of cherry-tinted water, then losing her cool and vomiting, if she grabbed a towel and applied pressure sooner, Allison would have coughed herself back to life. She knows she worked fast. As fast as she could. The situation could have been avoided if she entered the house sooner. Instead of knocking and waiting, if she had run around back and tried the door sooner, Allison might still have been bleeding out when she entered the bathroom. Then she could have saved her. No. No adjustments to the moments leading up to finding her could have saved her.

Replaying conversation after conversation, looking for some sign of Allison crying out for help, Scarlett comes up empty. Her eyes keep watching the world pass her by as they drive down the roads. Scarlett blinks, bringing her back to the present.

Turning to Connor, she whispers, "How long do you think?"

Connor slows to a stop for a red light. He keeps his focus on the road, but answers with a question. "How long do I think what?"

"Allison will be in the Waiting." Scarlett's monotone response seems more automated than thought-through.

Connor presses the gas as the light turns green. He keeps his stare straight ahead, trying to form an answer to a question he'd rather not think about. But all he can see is the look on Vistrus's face as he stood over his dead daughter lying in the bathtub.

He drives for a few blocks, hoping the lapse in answer allows her question to flee her mind, but as they turn the corner to Bri's, the caravan of white cargo vans refreshes it for Scarlett. "Longer than me?" Her voice remains emotionless.

Passing the line of windowless, white cargo vans, Connor finally breaks his stare on the road to turn to his cousin for a moment. "I don't think we can go to Bri's."

"Home it is." Even the word "home" strikes no excitement or joy for her. All hope seems lost for the moment. "We can wait for Allison there. She'll be back."

The corners of Connor's mouth pull to the sides. Not in some smile, but in pain. Connor cannot summon a response upon hearing Scarlett's denial of the situation's reality. So he says the only thing he can think of at this moment: "Home it is."

Sadness pulls at her eyes, squinting them into uncertainty. "Ever wonder? After we get home…" she trails off, uncertain she wants to think about anything right now.

Connor, sensing her pain because it is his pain, too, takes a moment before saying, "Ever wonder what after we get home?"

Scarlett doesn't turn to him, opting to keep her mile-long stare out the window. Her words come out matter-of-fact and dry as soda crackers as she says, "Ever wonder what's next?"

Connor again has no reply to her words, for at the moment, she may be deep in thought, and the substance in the subtext of her questions reflects how deep she may be.

Now he can't help wondering what's next. What more could come to them? The death of those older than them is to be expected at some point in life, but at his age, at Scarlett's age, death to their elders has come too often and too soon. These young adults need their parents for guidance in times they have yet to experience. But Connor's parents are gone. Scarlett's too. Or at least they all thought they were. But no matter the age, no matter the experience, Connor can't bear the thought that someone is old enough to be expecting the loss they have endured. So, what is next? What more could come? He does not want to wonder, but can't stop the wonderment from floating through his mind. What now?

Vistrus stands in his living room, trying to remember why he came into this particular room. He had a reason—something either Connor or Scarlett said while they were here. It was something about Allison, but standing here, he cannot remember what. The picture-perfect cleanliness of the room distracts him from whatever it was he was doing. Something is off about this room and while he wants to figure out why the room being as clean as it is bothers him, his mind cannot help but picture his daughter lying in a tub of water mixed with her blood. But before he can call anyone to come get her out of the tub, he must remember what he was doing. It was simple, he's sure—routine even. But right now, his mind betrays him.

Giving up for the moment on what he was doing, he pulls his cell phone out and lights up the screen. Scrolling through his list of names, he lands on a cleaning service number, but before he can hit send, it strikes him, the why of why he came into the living room. The why also puts a sad smile on his face, as he now knows why the room is cleaner than normal. It bears a similar cleanliness to the times Allison had to cover the fact she had friends over while he was out of town on business. He always appreciated that she respected him enough to clean better than he left it, and since nothing ever broke, he let her have her secrets. But now, while she lies lifeless upstairs, he knows she cleaned before doing what she did. And he must figure out if there is anything he can do to save her.

He steps to the deep red Steinway piano that rests below the hanging portrait of Inessa, his deceased beloved. He eyes the top of the piano for any drywall dust but sees nothing, not even a day's worth of dust. Squinting his eyes as he tries to imagine Allison's motives for keeping things clean, he removes the picture from the wall to reveal a hole in the drywall. Inside sit the two 21-gram vials—one opened, the other sealed.

Vistrus's heart pounds upon seeing the uncorked vial. A part of him dies knowing that his daughter lies upstairs without hope that the Waiting will bring her back to him. Reaching into the hole, a quick inspection shows the corked vial still holds its 21 grams.

Grabbing the uncorked vial, he turns it over to see the number twenty-two on the bottom. He clutches it, tightening his grip as hard as possible around the vial, sinking to the floor. He takes a deep breath, letting out a sad smile as uncontrollable tears flow forth. The reality of everything sinks in as he clutches the vial, crying out "Oh, God" over and over while cursing himself for his failures as a parent and husband.

Even through this moment of hysterics, a notion in his mind reminds him of what he must do. After allowing himself a little time to grieve, he dials the number for the cleaning service, reporting what he must through held-back tears and sniffles.

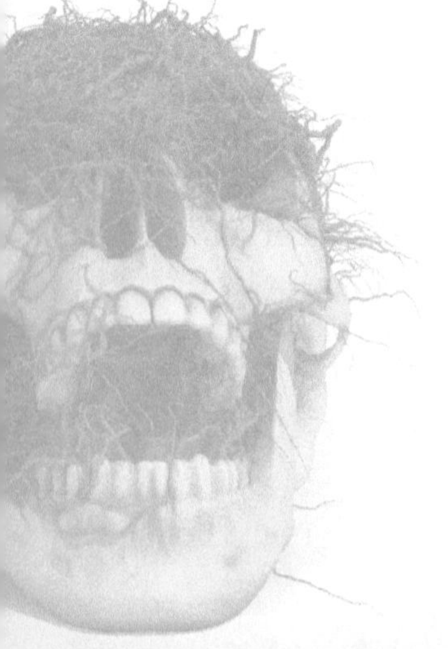

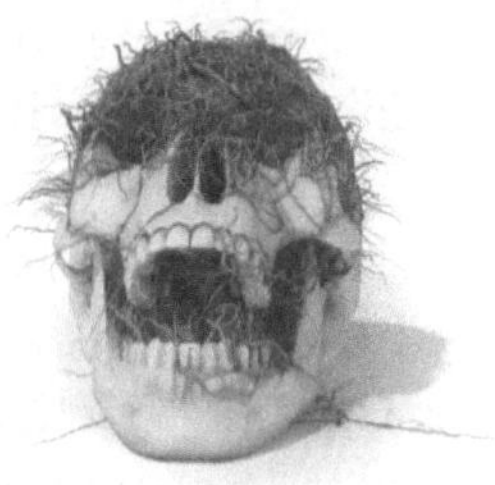

CHAPTER 4

"What comes next is always the question."
~I. Petrovsky~

The fates have a strange way of acknowledging a loss in The Nation. The wind blows enough outside the West Haven funeral home to misplace a carefully coiffed hairstyle but not enough to ruin it entirely. It seems the cosmos's way of mourning the loss of someone held close to the hearts of others. But the outside can't come in, and the peaceful breeze blowing through Connor's freshly cut hair can't keep him outside the door much longer. He takes one last look at the sky, watching the clouds float by for a moment before Scarlett interrupts his celestial bonding.

"You didn't have to cut your hair." Quiet words that were almost drowned out by the noise of passing cars. "Allison wouldn't mind."

Connor brings his stare down from the sky and to Scarlett. A meek smile disappears from him as soon as it crosses his face. "We can't pretend to be forever young, even if we look it." He stops talking as if

Scarlett might have something to say to his response, but she remains quiet. "I guess it's time to grow up a little is all."

Scarlett smiles in acknowledgment of his words. She runs her hand through his short, parted hair. A new look for a new Connor. "Well, it looks nice. I think she would have liked it." She nudges him and gestures to the door. "Come on. She's waiting."

Connor nods his head, pulling the door open. He holds it so Scarlett can enter first. Following behind her, he turns to look outside, holding onto the last possible moment of denial and hope before turning to the reality that she lies resting in a casket one room down.

Connor and Scarlett stop in front of the sign that reads:

ALLISON NASTENKA PETROVSKY
BORN FEBRUARY 5, 2000
DEPARTED APRIL 4, 2021

"Huh," Scarlett blurts out. "I don't think I ever knew her middle name."

Connor wraps his arm around Scarlett's shoulders, giving her a firm squeeze. "It's amazing all the little things we never really know about the ones we love."

Brianna speaks up, startling them from the moment. "I never knew either. Funny, huh?"

Connor turns, squinting at Bri's choice of words.

She shakes her head, waving a hand in dismissal of her previous dialogue. "Not funny, like a comedian told a joke. Funny like … just funny."

"Ironic humor might be closer to what you were searching for, love," Duncan adds, causing Scarlett to turn.

Both Brianna and Duncan dressed well and cleaned up nicely for the occasion, save Duncan's sneakers that contrast his formal wear. Scarlett stares down at his shoes.

"It's all I had on short notice," Duncan tries to defend his options of footwear.

Scarlett offers a subtle shake of her head. "Al would have approved."

Connor smiles and nods his head to the viewing room. He pulls Scarlett from the sign and conversation and toward their friend for final goodbyes.

A small group of people stand in line to pay their respects to the deceased and her father, who stands beside the casket. Connor and Scarlett make their way toward their friend, noticing the closed casket lid. Connor restrains himself from shouting across the room to find an answer to why he can't see his girlfriend one last time, but restraint wins the battle for the moment.

The four of them do the only thing they can do, which is to wait their turn to kneel at Allison's casket to pay respects. The moments that pass while they wait for the others before them to say their condolences and respects drag on for what seems like an eternity only felt before at the loss of their parents. Now, this eternity holds a new torment as one the same age as them lays to rest a few feet away. Duncan waits with them while visions of what she could look like underneath the lid dance in his head. Unpleasant visions of a friend taken too soon. He imagines Allison in some industrial rock T-shirt and freshly colored bright pink hair with black tips. He knows these thoughts are only there to console him. To Allison, it does not matter what she looks like under the lid. She has left this mortal coil and moved on to whatever comes next, something else that Duncan finds comfort in.

This moment isn't about him and his feelings, or, at least, it is about the others' feelings more. Allison's friends from childhood. Friends who understand the pain and confusion of the sudden transition into Legendary form. Friends who knew the pain she felt. If only she reached out.

Scarlett takes this time to think about what it is she wants to say to her best friend. All the small things they chatted about to pass the time: life's larger predicaments, the existential meaning of it all—everything seems so pointless now. All Scarlett wants is to laugh with Allison one more time. Point out a cute boy they could laugh at. Talk about Allison wanting to leave West Haven and not die in this town. While all of those things are simple requests, none of them can be granted and in that lack of ability to be granted, the reality of the situation can no longer be denied.

Connor, too, searches for what his last words to his lost love might be. Some sentimental words to help soothe his grieving heart, or even a joke that only the two of them would find humorous. But nothing seems to manifest itself in his head. For he knows that any solace given to him now would not offer comfort to the deceased, and that is something that does not sit well with him. A pang of guilt pours down on him that he might be relieved of this despair of Allison's death, while death offers her no such reprieve. And in that, he cannot find the words to say.

But the time to think and plan and form words has passed. It is their turn to kneel at the closed casket. The reality of her death sets in, though the urge to deny it by justifying it can't be true, since the casket is closed, pushes its way to the surface. They fight to hold back tears threatening to fall from their eyes, but the tears break through, trickling down their cheeks as they say silent words meant only for themselves and the deceased.

After an extended silence, while each of them struggles to make it through one final goodbye, they stand (making room for Bri and Duncan to say their parting words) and approach Vistrus, who waits resolutely by the side of her casket. With his hands folded in front of him, he offers a sad smile as a thanks for coming.

"How are you holding up, sir?"

"Best I can," Vistrus says, keeping his reply short and to the point. "You cut your hair. Very dapper."

"Thank you." Connor nods, understanding that words right now are best kept at a minimum. "Anything I can get you?"

Vistrus shakes his head, thinking as he does but still finishes with his motioned negative. "How are you both holding up?"

"It's hard. I thought I'd get to see her one last time," Connor admits.

Scarlett chimes in with, "Why is her casket closed? I mean, her face is still hers."

Before speaking, Vistrus takes a slow, deep breath. An act that both keeps him from saying something he would later regret and calms him down, giving him an extra moment to think. "When you live as long as we do, the last person you ever think you will see pass before you is your child. The thought never crosses your mind. She rests and will be buried. But looking at her further will only prolong the pain we feel."

The words "will be buried" burn into Scarlett's mind, etching themselves as deep as the Colorado River carved the Grand Canyon. Everything else Vistrus says fails to stick to her memory. She keeps repeating the word "buried" over and over to herself, imagining Allison as she last saw her, now covered in dirt.

Connor nods, not so much in an understanding of his reasons but in understanding that he is her father and his wishes come first in a time like this. Scarlett, however, glosses right over the subtle clues Vistrus left to drop the subject.

"So, that was it? The bathtub was the last time I got to see her? That's not how it's supposed to be."

Forcing a smile, Vistrus says through gritted teeth, "This is not how anything is supposed to be. Being an adult is learning how to handle unfavorable situations with more aplomb than you did when you were a teenager. Life can be cruel and learning that not everything is within your control is a hard lesson, but one that must be learned."

Connor notices Scarlett open her mouth to speak and cuts in. "Thank you, sir. If you need anything, let me know. I'm more than happy to help."

Vistrus nods, watching them turn to walk away. He adds, "A glass of water would be nice."

Connor nods, leading Scarlett away to fetch some water. He whispers to her, "Whatever it was you were gonna say would not have calmed the situation."

"It doesn't make sense. We all need to heal and grieve and mourn. Why is he the one that gets to do so in a way that benefits him?"

Connor shakes his head at her words, knowing she does not hear the lack of understanding in them. "Because he is her father, and father trumps best friend or boyfriend. That is why we must learn to deal better than we would have before. We aren't in high school anymore."

They stop at a watering station and fill three hard plastic cups with cold water. They sip on theirs while bringing one back for Vistrus.

"She said she wouldn't do this, ya know," Scarlett says, recalling an old memory.

"Not now, Scarlett." Connor stops her as they enter the viewing room. "We can talk somewhere more appropriate later on." He hands the water to Vistrus. "If you need anything else…" They both nod at each other.

Vistrus steps away from his daughter's casket and up to a podium a few feet away. The friends and family all settle in their seats, quieting down to hear what he has to say. Scarlett and Connor sit in the front row. Pulling a folded sheet of paper from his back pocket, Vistrus carefully unfolds it and flattens it on the podium, looking it over as he does.

"Allison was not perfect." He looks out at the crowd, holding back his emotions. "At times, her fuse was short. A live wire, so to speak. However, she always carried the best of intentions when worked up. She loved those she knew and was loyal without question. My baby girl…" His emotions simmer below the surface as he fights to hold back tears. "My little Allison was strong. Fierce." He sniffles, wiping away welled tears. "There is no apology big enough for how sorry I am that I missed whatever brought you to this." He pauses for a moment, composing himself as he stares at the prepared speech. He folds the paper and places it back in his pocket.

The crowd sits in silence, waiting for him to continue. Connor and Scarlett turn to each other. "Should I?" Scarlett asks, gesturing to Vistrus.

Connor gives a tiny shake of his head. "He'll be okay."

After another moment, Vistrus continues, "Allison was plagued by her dreams. She felt some were too real, too vivid, and they haunted her. I downplayed it. It is our job, as parents, to teach our children that not everything has a deeper meaning. To teach them that sometimes an unnerving feeling is just that, unnerving. But we fail when we fail to teach them how to deal with said unnerving feelings. So, for my failings, I apologize, Allison. You deserved better in my hands."

Entering Vistrus's home later, Scarlett, Connor, Brianna, and Duncan look around at the after-service turnout. While Allison kept her circle small and Vistrus tends to be a man of exacting words, the number of people here leaves no doubt that Allison is loved. Scarlett stops, taken aback by the crowded space. Connor stays by her side, allowing Bri and Duncan to move toward the hor d'oeuvre table.

Tapping Connor as she passes, Bri whispers, "I'll grab her a small plate."

Connor nods in recognition and points at himself, indicating he wants some as well, but offers no verbal response.

With her eyebrows drawn inward and eyes squinted, Scarlett turns to Connor. "I don't understand."

Connor keeps his eyes on the crowd of people as if searching for someone. "What don't you understand?"

"Why are all these people here?" Scarlett's words ring hollow.

Connor shakes his head at her persistent denial. "For Vistrus."

"But…" she trails off.

"Funerals, wakes, whatever are as much for the living as for the dead. At least, that's what my father told me once." Connor turns to Scarlett, whose face seems more contorted than before he spoke.

She lowers her voice, whispering, "So, are all these people Normals, and we have to pretend she is actually dead? Do they know nothing about the Waiting?"

Connor lowers his voice to a whisper as well, saying, "Scarlett, I think you're missing something, and I don't know how to tell you this, but…"

Bri and Duncan return with small plates of food for everyone.

"Here, Scarlett. Thought you might need a little bite to eat," Bri says, handing her a plate filled with Swedish meatballs and pigs in a blanket. "I didn't know if you wanted any dipping sauce for the pigs, so I didn't get you any. Thought you might not like the sauce touching your food."

Scarlett stares at the plate and nods in understanding. "Thanks." Turning back to Connor as she takes a bite of a pig in a blanket, she asks, "But what?"

Connor shares a look with Bri and Duncan that tells them this won't be a fun conversation before telling Scarlett again, "Al's not in the Waiting. I know you don't want to hear it, but I don't know any other way to say it."

The tension thickens around them. Frowning and waving a finger, Scarlett shakes her head. "Nope. It's not what happens to us. It's not that simple. We come back. I came back. She'll come back. It's what we do."

Connor takes a deep breath, looking at both Bri and Duncan as he searches for the words to say, but they both stand with nothing to offer but shoulder shrugs. Before Connor can muster up some harsh truth about life that they've all come to learn in the past few years, except apparently Scarlett, Vistrus clears his throat behind them.

Connor lets out his breath, thankful that he is saved by this metaphorical bell. Vistrus sips on a glass of red wine as he offers silent thanks for coming back to his place after the service.

"Mr. DeSalvo, there is something we must discuss." Vistrus's words are softer than normal. Almost a request instead of his usual commanding tone.

Connor nods, offering back, "Now? Scarlett is having a thing."

"I heard. As stated, not all things in life are easily learned, but best we learn them, and quickly." Vistrus waits a moment, hoping his words sink into Scarlett and the rest of the group before relenting. "Perhaps you are correct, Mr. DeSalvo. Talking today might be in poor taste." Vistrus huffs at his lack of decorum while being impressed with Connor's show of timing. "Enjoy the food. Mingle. Most are friends of mine from the museum. Normals, but nothing you four cannot handle." Vistrus nods and raises his glass in a toast before walking away.

"See," Scarlett beams with the bright eyes of youthful naiveté, "Normals. She'll be back."

Wrapping an arm around Scarlett's shoulder, Bri brings her in for a tight hug. "We'll work through this. I promise." Words that cause Scarlett to break into tears.

Connor leans in to whisper to Duncan, "I don't know how I can make her understand."

Whispering back, Duncan offers what he can, "Sometimes you can't. They need to understand on their own."

Impressed with Duncan's wise nature, Connor nods, knowing the wisdom came with a price, and the price was Rex's life. "You're a very wisdomous man, Dunc's."

A soft chuckle escapes Duncan. "Thanks. A nice Allison-ism for the occasion." After watching Scarlett cry for a moment, Duncan continues, "She'll be fine. We'll all make it through this alive."

Connor nods. "True that may be, but what's next? What do we do now?"

"Our next actions are the oldest motives: revenge. As for what we do now, we do the same thing we do every time someone shows up trying to kill you … kill them first."

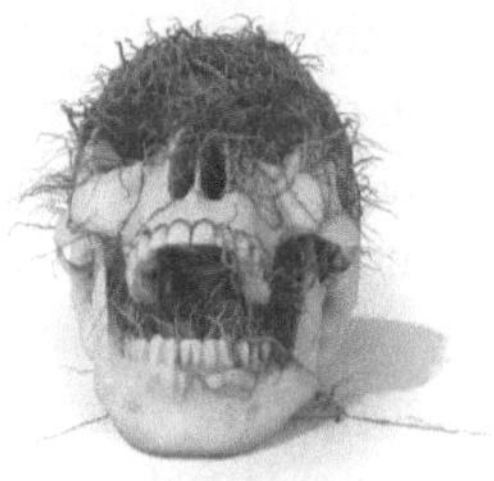

CHAPTER 5

"Within your enemy's motivation
is where you'll find their weakness."
~The Pale Woman~

Standing outside Vistrus's house, Connor stands, ready to knock on the door, but there's an unusually cold nip in the air that gives him pause. It gives him a moment of reflection that today might not be the best day to do this. But then again, Vistrus was the one who wanted to have the aforementioned talk. So, a knock on the door it is. A deep-chested "Enter" answers without hesitation.

Once inside, he sees Vistrus already seated in his red, crushed velvet, gold-riveted chair, puffing away on a Churchill. Exhaling a puff, the cloud of smoke obfuscates his face as he starts their conversation by saying, "You almost did not knock."

Connor nods, acknowledging his hesitation. "Pounding hearts are a loud noise to some ears."

Vistrus nods. "Thinking like a Legend. Good."

Connor takes a few stunted steps forward, trying to muster the nerve to face whatever the conversation ahead holds. "You seem to be in better spirits. It's only been a few days since the funeral."

Vistrus holds out a Churchill and cutter for Connor. "Better is a matter of comparison. Burying your child is the worst it gets."

Connor steps forward, closes the gap, and grabs the items. He sits on the couch seat next to the humidor and ashtray.

Vistrus adds, "Take each day as it comes. Some will be better and some will be worse. While I have seen much death in my time, the loss of a child is unlike anything you will ever experience." Vistrus strikes a match, holding it up for Connor to light the cigar.

After puffing it to life, Connor turns his attention to his elder. "Is this some sort of ritual for The Nation and those in or entering the Council?"

A hearty laugh escapes Vistrus; a much-needed moment of levity in dark times. "No," he chuckles. "I find a fine quality stogie calms the mind. It is not like we have to worry about the big 'C.'"

Taken aback, Connor looks at the cigar and Vistrus's implication. "We can't get cancer?"

Vistrus bobs his head side to side. "We can. And sure, it won't be fun, and it will put us underground. But we'll be back…" he trails off to see if Connor can pick up what he laid down.

"…As long as our 21 grams are in a vial and we go into the Waiting." A confidently spoken guess.

A slow nod from Vistrus tells Connor he is correct. "Young man, repeatedly you prove a deserved seat on the Council." He pauses, seeing if Connor will inject needless words or listen and see what else he has to say. Connor chooses silence. Impressed, Vistrus offers a half-smile before continuing, "Jack went missing and you chose to believe what your eyes saw, not what the news offered. An officer of the law thought himself above it and with no one in the Normal society to turn to, you handled the situation."

This time, Connor interjects, "With help from my friends."

"Again, you give credit where credit is due instead of taking it for yourself. Despite the high school slacker persona you projected, you are anything but. You are intelligent, thoughtful, and look to do what is right. Your friend glimpsed into our world and instead of shutting him down, you felt there was a trust that would not be broken. And again, when this friend saw our Legendary forms."

Vistrus stands, letting the impact of his words affect Connor however they may, and walks into the kitchen. Connor listens as Vistrus sets clinking glasses on the counter, pops open a bottle of whiskey, and pours it. He returns to the living room, glasses in one hand and stogie in the other, and offers one to Connor, who accepts but does not yet sip.

"When the Council wanted your head, you set out to prove your innocence. All without worsening the situation for The Nation. For that, we thank you."

Vistrus sips from his glass, and Connor follows. While the elder of the two sips without making a face, Connor winces a moment, as he does not know what to expect. After calming his face and the warmth in his chest fades, he smiles. "That is delicious. Peanut butter whiskey?"

Vistrus nods in a deliberate motion. "Splendid stuff."

"I wouldn't have thought you'd drink something that tastes like peanut butter," Connor admits.

Brows drawn together in curiosity, Vistrus asks, "What would you have thought?"

Connor chews over his words for a moment before speaking. "Something more refined. Like, Gentleman Jack."

A chuckle again escapes Vistrus. "You have much to learn. There is nothing wrong with Gentleman Jack. If you want a traditional bourbon … Widow Jane Small Batch is unbeatable." Swirling his glass and watching the caramel colors crawl down to the pool at the bottom, he inhales the aromas before stealing another sip. "But peanut butter pairs well with this Churchill. The smokiness of the whiskey complimenting the cigar is something to savor and share with loved ones."

Connor sips the liquor again, this time without contorting his face. "I appreciate the offerings, but I assume you did not invite me over for a cigar, liquor, and compliments."

"I did not, but who does not appreciate all three?" Vistrus sets his cigar on the ashtray and leans back into his chair. "The Council has lost its way. Maybe the way The Nation needs to head has changed. There has been a vacant seat that needs to be filled."

"And you think I am the one to fill it?" Connor takes a deep breath as the reality of his future is once again put before him.

"That is a loaded question. Our talk a while back about my daughter. Do you remember?" Vistrus broaches the subject with care.

The pained look in Connor's scrunched brow and squinted eyes tells Vistrus the young man does not recall.

"You came to me about my daughter's sexuality," Vistrus reminds Connor.

"No, I didn't," he defends, shaking his head.

"You said she belongs with you and that no one should stand in the way of that. It was quite uncharacteristic," Vistrus adds.

"It was uncharacteristic because it wasn't me. Al can be with whoever she wants. Whomever. Whatever. She belongs to no one." He sits up a little straighter, tightening his posture. "Frankly, Mr. Petrovsky, I am a little miffed you would even think that was me."

Vistrus nods in acknowledgment of this mistake. "Wrong, I may have been." He sips his whiskey, debating his next choice of words. "I am over three hundred years old, Connor, and have made mistakes. I do not understand how I missed that the person I talked with was not you."

Connor sips his whiskey, following suit of Vistrus's previous stall, choosing his words while he savors. "You have never seen an Adeirrig. No matter how long you live, there is always something new."

Vistrus contemplates the statement for a while as both men sit in silence, enjoying their cigars and alcohol. Noticing Connor's comfort in the moment, Vistrus takes a while longer for himself, enjoying the company of someone so close to his daughter. As with all good things, this moment, too, must end. Vistrus exhales a cloud of smoke. "The past few years have given you wisdom beyond your age. You have learned when to hold your tongue. When you speak, your words have meaning. Not everyone is so blessed. You absorb the world around you, taking it all in. All these things make you better than you were yesterday, and continuing to practice will only continue bettering you. For those reasons, I believe you are fit to fill the Council here in West Haven."

"Convincing the others won't be easy. Not after the whole framed-for-murder bit."

"True."

"And there's that World Health Organization building, a not-so-secret secret facility in our back-yard. That won't end well for anyone in The Nation or on the Council."

"It will not. But it may hold a light at the end of the tunnel. If you can find the why behind why they are in our backyard, it may just be the 'in' you need."

"As well as put to rest any suspicion we have."

"Or confirm." Sipping his whiskey, Vistrus con-tinues, "But this is a test to see what you can do. While you have proven yourself before, you need to do it again."

"I don't understand why. If I already have…"

Vistrus cuts him off, saying, "Because as someone who will be sitting in a position of power, you will always have to prove yourself. Repeatedly. If you become complacent, thinking that you have nothing to prove, then you have nothing left to offer and no reason to be a leader."

Connor understands the enormity of the task before him. An understanding he punctuates by downing the rest of his peanut butter whiskey in one gulp. "It can't be that pointed of an answer."

"When someone in power becomes complacent and has nothing left to offer, their lust for power does not diminish. Corruption takes seed because, in that, they can manipulate their people and the system that placed them in power. Manipulating the system gives them more power, and more power leads to wanting more power."

"Power corrupts. I've heard that before."

"It is not that power corrupts. Power causes greed to grow. Greed leads to more power. Power is the tool greed wields in its path of destruction."

"What if there was no greed there before?"

"People who are not greedy do not seek power. Do not mistake power for charisma nor gained power for natural strength."

Connor nods. "And this is why I will have to repeatedly prove myself."

A smile escapes Vistrus. "While I may have failed in being a father, life offers second chances sometimes. I cannot offer you help with this task. But I will be here for guidance."

"Is this something I have to do alone?"

"I cannot answer that. Such questions are for you to answer. I assume you have people you trust and who stand by your side."

Connor nods, remaining silent in his answer.

Continuing, Vistrus says, "There is one more thing."

"About the WHO?"

Vistrus shakes his head. "A test of a different sort."

"What kind of test is this?"

Sitting in front of a blank Word document, Connor stares at the computer screen, uncertain of his next move. His mind keeps flipping from thoughts about infiltrating the government entity known as the World Health Organization and the whispering musings of the mysterious pale woman, who offered answers to questions he never asked, implanted in his brain. There is a constant back and forth between the two that he can't connect, something in each of those that he can't figure out. Trying to push the pale woman out of his mind for as long as he can, his fingers hover over his keyboard, ready to type.

Covert Plan To Sneak Into the WHO

As quickly as he types it, he deletes it. After a moment of contemplation, he settles on a more coded title.

CPTSITW

Chuckling at his juvenile covert tactics, he leans back, unsure what to do next. He sits, tapping his head against his chair's headrest to the beat of whatever Taylor Swift song Scarlett just turned on in the other room. Continuing to tap his head against the headrest, he listens to the forlorn lyrics about love and loss and how she knows it will all happen again. But before he can delve too deep into either the meaning of Ms. Swift's lyrics or his master plan that will cement his seat on the Council, his door swings open.

Scarlett prances around the room with wide, wild eyes, looking around as if stalking some prey. She sings along with the song, though to call it singing is playing fast and loose with the definition. Connor smiles, amused at her seemingly pleasant mood.

"What's with the ants in your pants, as Mom used to say?" Connor queries.

Scarlett stops jumping around, opting to dance in place instead. She stops singing along so she can answer his question despite being out of breath. "No ants. Just … not going to … let myself … be sad."

"It's nice to see you've accepted reality as it is." Connor attempts to acknowledge her growth.

"No reality," she says, adding a bounce to her impromptu dance routine. "Nothing to accept. She'll be back." Before Connor has a chance to respond, her eyes glimpse his computer monitor. "What's Cop Tease I Two? Or is it Cop Tease It Double You? Oh, no, wait … Captain … something. That's all I got."

Connor shakes his head at her energy. "Neither. It's an acronym. Doesn't matter since I'm not making any progress on it."

Her bouncing steadies back into one spot as she slows her dancing. "Something I can help you with?"

"Nothing to help with. I can't focus long enough to make any progress."

"What's on your mind? What's keeping you from focusing, Cos'?" She waves her hands at him like she is casting a spell. "Focus *perfectus!*"

"Points for effort, but no go. I can't stop thinking about the pale woman." His words stop her dancing.

She relaxes her wild eyes and settles into a standing position brimming with potential energy. "From the woods? If you need to talk, I got nothing but time."

"I don't know where to begin." He looks around the room, trying to find a catalyst to start his thoughts in the correct direction.

Noticing his inability to start things off, Scarlett offers the only thing she can think of. "Start where your mind is stuck; it's as good a place as any."

"It was right by that giant, old weeping willow tree. She was there. I was walking back to the woods after talking with the Council. It was so surreal."

Turning a corner down a side street of brick town-houses across from a single-family home, a voice whispers out to Connor as he passes a giant weeping willow tree. "Are you ready now?" The pale woman steps out as he stops and turns toward the tree. "Do you think the Council will find you innocent? Or are your thoughts screaming to you that they don't care?"

"I remember thinking that she had a point. Something didn't feel right. I mean, besides the fact this lady was hiding behind trees and whispering promises to me. But she had a point: The Council didn't care about me. And while that was appealing, I still didn't know her name, but she made a point that names didn't matter. What I was looking for then was a reason to trust her … or anyone, really. And give it to me, she did."

"Give it to me, she did? You telling some noir detective story?" Scarlett giggles.

The pale woman takes one step closer to Connor. "I can give you no other reason than those I offered before. Let me show you what The Nation really is. All it encompasses and the future it holds for you. A future where you no longer have to worry about hiding. One where you may find yourself at the head of the table instead of hiding under it."

Hesitant about the obvious temptation too easily within reach, Connor asks, "And what do you expect in return?"

"That you listen to me. Trust what I say without question, and I will show you everything you have not been told; answer all the questions you haven't thought to ask. I will show you the meaning of life itself."

"And she walked off behind the tree to the back of the house. I followed. Everything seemed so beyond my control."

Scarlett leans in as if listening to a scary campfire tale intended to keep children from wandering off. "What happened next? What'd she tell you?"

"I'm getting there, Scar."

Following her in the shadows of night would have been far more difficult if not for his Legendary eyesight. Perhaps this was a test to ensure he was who she thought he was. Maybe she was testing how far he would follow. Maybe she was walking through a shadowy spot to get to where she needed to. And where she needed to get, she got—a large, 12x12 metal shack meant for lawnmowers and other lawn care equipment. The inside was used for anything but, though. Intentionally dim lighting that refused to cross the threshold to the outside was the only illumination in there. Decorations and furnishings were just as sparse. A small desk of contemporary quality made from compressed wood manufactured by the lowest bidder and available at any big-box store sat against the side wall. Along the back wall was a small loveseat covered in plastic, usually reserved for furniture owned by Chicago Italians back in the 70s and 80s or carpeted stairs. The entire atmosphere lent itself more to someone wanting to move to the forests of Montana and mail explosives to titans of industry than to a Legend trying to expose the truth. But desperation grows quickly in trying times.

"This way." The pale woman gestures to a small hatch in the corner next to the couch. Opening the hatch to reveal a narrow staircase, she descends. "Right through here and all your questions shall start to be answered."

"I know what it looks like. Hell, even then I knew what it looked like," Connor begins before Scarlett interjects.

"Yeah, like an episode straight out of *Criminal Minds*," Scarlett jests.

"Exactly, but I didn't care. I mean, I did. I wanted to prove my innocence and any insight into the Council might have helped. This was nothing more than a means to an end, but the things she said ate at me."

Following the stairs down, Connor enters some remnant of a World War II fallout shelter. The type of place that no one would know about unless they owned the property and, even then, might have never found. The harsh, fluorescent lighting serves a far more functional purpose than decorative, illuminating pictures of all the current serving West Haven Council members. On the same wall to the right of those pictures, but separated by a strip of black duct tape, are pictures and sketches of deceased Legends, including Ken DeSalvo, Sylvia Waldgrave, and Nick DeSalvo. Below those are pictures and lithographs of others Connor does not recognize.

"Who are they?" Connor says, indicating the pictures beneath those he knows.

"Ones who came before those who serve now."

Connor shakes his head, thinking. But I've been told … I know… Vistrus … was one of the first. *He looks to the sky past the concrete ceiling, trying to remember all he's been told. "The Council was founded when Vistrus and his wife moved here."*

The pale woman gives a slow, deliberate head shake. "Before the Council was the Mind. There is so much hidden from us, we can no longer trust those who lead."

"She told me things. Things like where the symbol for The Nation came from. That, before it was what we were taught, it was six wavy lines, each representing a different Legendary society. Things that we were never told," Connor tells Scarlett, sounding more like he's telling folklore about one-eyed pirates than truths about their nature.

"What else did she say?!" Scarlett's interest grows, though she isn't sure if it's more morbid curiosity in an engaging story or interest in a possible truth about who the pale woman might be.

"Why are you telling me all this?" Connor asks with growing suspicion as he inches toward the stairs leading to the outside world.

"Because you deserve to know."

"Why me … specifically?"

"You are positioned to fill the vacant seat. You deserve to know the seat you will fill. The lies you will tell. This is something not to be taken lightly and not to get involved in half-cocked."

"Why do you care?"

Before speaking, she pauses to cherry-pick her words. "This tiny amount that I told you is a lot to absorb, so there's no need to push further today. But sharpen your metaphorical axes … you never know when you'll need them." With those words spoken, she nods to the stairs behind him, indicating he can freely depart.

"That was it for the time. But it wasn't the last we spoke," Connor says, turning to his cousin. "If only I can connect why my brain circles back to her while thinking about this." He gestures to the computer monitor that has since gone to sleep.

"You'll figure it out, Con. I trust that you and the cop tease," she motions to his screen, "can piece it all together." She hops up, having sat on his bed during his story, and bounds to the door as her abundance of unbridled energy returns. "If you need me, I'll be around." Without waiting for a response, she turns and exits, singing along to whatever Taylor Swift song plays on the stereo.

Connor turns back to his computer screen and wakes it from sleep. While the computer monitor may have woken up, his mind, on the other hand, has not.

Though now, he can't help but think about the man in the red tracksuit. Sure, he now knows who it is, but now it makes him think why Bishop didn't make a move. Connor doubts he was that good at losing someone in the woods; after all, it's not like he's a woodsman with years of tracking experience. But some nudging notion of unknown origins brings an encounter to the front of his mind, pushing out the pale lady for now.

Approaching his makeshift shack in the woods, holding his evening's grocery purchase of Pop Tarts®, a noise alerts his senses. A snapping noise that, on any other occasion, may have seemed as innocuous as the buzzing of a fly by his ear, sounded a tad too loud for any of the forest's inhabitants to make. No squirrel, chipmunk, or raccoon would have made such a heavy snap, followed by deliberate silence. No. This noise was accidental. There were no noises preceding the snap and nothing since. No scurrying footsteps and moving leaves and branches from a falling pine cone. Nothing. Just one snap.

Being careful to take cover in the night's shadows, Connor scans the forest for the source of this suspecting snap. Patience favors the patient. So he waits. Even at the risk of his rumbling stomach betraying his location, he leaves the breakfast pastries alone. He watches the man he now knows is Bishop skulk around and unsuccessfully break and enter into the shack Connor has claimed as his after first breaking and entering.

The man walks off, and Connor records him on his cell phone as evidence.

Before the memory can play out and show its connection to Connor's current conundrum, a banging sound from the other room snaps him back to the present.

"Are you all right, Scarlett?!" he shouts, standing from the computer chair.

"What?!" Scarlett asks as her mind pieces together his words. "Yeah, I'm fine. I fell off the couch dancing! Such a klutz!"

And with a smile, he sits back down, knowing while the moment may have passed, everything seems five by five for now.

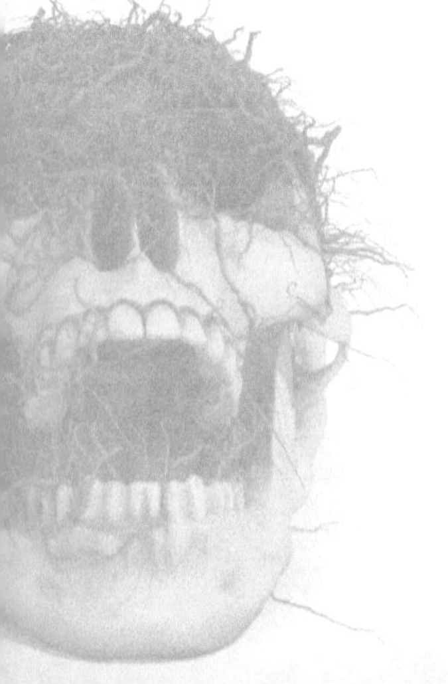

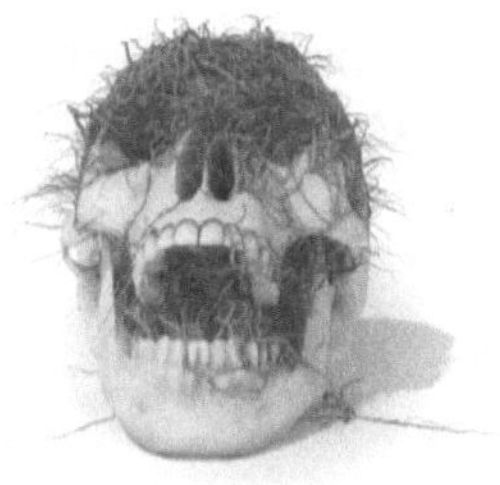

CHAPTER 6

"Never mistake obsession for love."
~N. DeSalvo~

*E*ndless fields of emerald grass and various wild-flowers surround a young woman whose eyes match the vivid green around her. Her dress flows about in the gentle breeze. An air in the moment of perfect happiness makes her feel content to be where she stands.

The man with her, on the other hand, seems nervous as he pulls a woven blanket from a wicker picnic basket to spread out on the ground. His arms shake as he opens and fluffs it, but the young woman does not seem to notice. Her attention focuses on the sights around them: the fluffy clouds drifting through the sky and the foxes chasing hares in the distance.

After a few moments of setting up a modest meal for the two, complete with wine and wood goblets, he motions for her to sit with him. His nerves calm down, but the forlorn look on his face shines a dark-lighted contrast to her fancy-free demeanor.

"Aoife," he says her name, but her attention is elsewhere as she joins him, taking her seat on the blanket.

Her attention turns to the food being plated and placed between them.

"I thought an afternoon away would be nice." His words ring with meek tones, unsure if he can deliver said afternoon. It does not matter since her attention is still not on him. "Aoife? Are you with me?"

Her daydreaming ends, and her eyes meet his, causing her smile to fade. A change in emotion that sends self-doubt coursing through him. His furrowed brow lends uncertainty to his question. "Is everything fair with you?"

Forcing a stunted smile, Aoife nods. "Of course. A day lovely as this, how can anything not be, Easpag?"

The pointedness of her words escapes her, but the pain inflicted by them forces a winced smile from Easpag.

"I made some goat cheese fresh for today. I purchased the crackers at market, but I made the cheese." Thick desperation coats his words.

Cocking her head to one side, she offers an honest and perplexed smile. "Is there something on your mind?"

A wave of relaxation washes over him, feeling like he finally has her complete attention and an opportunity to confess the reason he brought her out here.

"Aoife, darling, I know there has been turmoil in your mind. Two men tugging at your heartstrings does not an easy decision make. I can say no more than I have before. You know what you mean to me." A timidness and uncertainty in each word betray the confidence he attempts to exude.

"Oh, Easpag." She offers a playful laugh in an attempt to lighten the mood and calm his nerves, but it only serves

to add an uncomfortableness to his anxiety. "This is a lovely day. I am glad you are with me."

"But are you with me, Aoife? Your mind has been wandering the plains all day. Fancying yourself with every color flower on this green earth and every furry creature that crosses your path."

She reaches out, grabbing his hand with a gentle squeeze before placing her other hand under it. "Dear, dear Easpag, I am with you. Even when I am frolicking in joviality, I am prancing at the day you presented."

"And I do offer you what your mind needs. I know Nioclás offers you much as well. I know your heart longs for him and my place is but a hut to his palace in you. But I try to be a good man."

"You are a good man, Easpag. No one has ever thought otherwise. Don't try so hard. Be yourself; it's all you can do. Let the rest of the leaves fall where they may." She releases his hand to place some cheese on a cracker so she can sample his offering.

He nods, sheepish in his motions as he rummages through his basket. "I will no more try to convince you that my heart is all you need and the least I can offer. I know you have already told me your choice. That it is Niolcás you shall wed. Try as I might, in the end, I am a friend. One who could offer you the moon and stars above, but the meaning within that gesture would be vague. So, instead, I offer you this." He pulls out a white glove and an amulet from the basket. "These represent everything that I control in my life. Now, they are in your hands."

Confusion mixed with gratitude wash over Aoife as she holds his gifts. "I am at a loss for words."

"*Then say nothing. Take them. Consider it my last attempt to sway you. My last gesture that you may make room in your heart for me. But even if you do not, keep them. Hold them close and remember me.*"

She turns her gaze to him, seeing his soul in a light that she has never seen before—in a light he has never shone it in before.

"*I know that you may not always be Aoife. One day I may wake and hear rumors of a woman who looks like you, acts like you, maybe even sounds like you, but called Naimh or Ciara or some English or French derivative, such as Eleanor. I know that no matter what you are called in some other life, you will always be my dear Aoife. And no matter the life you lead, if you hold these close, I can be there for you when the time needs.*"

A tear trickles down her cheek as she stammers through her words. "*Thank you … Easpag. This means more than I can say, my friend.*"

The distant bang of a hunter's rifle followed by the baying of a wounded buck pierces the moment with a palpable unease. Now, all Easpag can think about is the sound of the gunfire. The ruined moment of his last chance to win his love because of a hunter not too far off, trying to catch a meal for his family, turns his hopeful mood sour. His mind floods with thoughts, terrible thoughts of snatching the gun and turning it on the unsuspecting hunter—this hunter who stole his final act of wooing. No more shall Easpag have a chance to prove he should hold a bigger place in her heart. No more shall he try to be with the one who holds his. The moment has passed. She had already stated her choice, but he had to try one last time, only to have this perfect day ruined by buckshot and hunger.

Aoife sees the transformation in Easpag from hope to despair, and the face it paints is not one she wishes to remember. She knows that her choice words ending her last sentence, "My friend," were not the wisest when trying to let someone down gently. If ever there is a way to recover, she hopes her next words are them. "Easpag, as said last time we met, 'maybe in another life.' Maybe then we will work. I might be yours. But, please Easpag, do not think I do not want you in my life. A part of the joy I feel is because of you. Because of your kindness and your gentle soul. Never have I met someone like you, but I must go where my heart leads. At least for now."

She stops her words, noticing the glossed-over eyes and mile-long stare. She knows his mind is anywhere but here. And the tensing jaw tells her wherever he is, it is no place he should linger.

"Easpag," she says, trying to bring him back to the moment. "Easpag, please, come back to me. Do not wander off to dangerous places. We will always have a place in each other's lives ... so long as you would like to."

Easpag stands, offering a sad smile. "Aoife, take care. Hold my effects dearly. I love you, but I have to go."

With his parting words, he walks off. Aoife watches his gait hold an anger and madness that he has never shown before. She strokes the amulet in her palm with her thumb. Rubbing it over and over as he steps farther and farther away, knowing the man who left her in this field is not the same man she came here with. A part of her knows she contributed to that, but she wonders if there was anything she could have said to end things on a higher note, short of telling him he was hers. As he walks away, she realizes he already is hers. His love belongs only to her, and hers to two men. While he leaves a changed, angrier version of himself, doubt creeps into her mind that she is as thoughtful and gentle a person she woke up thinking she was.

Bri and Duncan sit in Connor and Scarlett's living room. No television drones out the hourly news in the background, nor does the stereo supply a soundtrack to this moment. Only an uneasy tension fills the silence between words while each of the four scours their minds for the right words to say that can provide comfort to healing wounds or substance with a way to move forward.

Duncan itches with a need to talk about where Bri and he can move. The need to not sound like he cares about the money she has in the bank prevents him from speaking. She knows he knows it's there; the nest egg her mother amassed made a welcome surprise during the dark times dealing with her death, and, topped with what The Nation had provided in support after Sylvia's death, they'd both be taken care of for a long time. Bri never talks about either of those things. They are things Bri views from the peripheral. But he knows, and she knows he knows. However, right now, in front of Connor and Scarlett, Duncan thinks this isn't the right time.

Connor wants nothing more than to say something that will give Scarlett a little solace, not only over the loss of her best friend but over everyone she has lost and not had time to mourn. Everything that comes to mind sounds clichéd and trite—nothing more than maxims acting as a balm over itching skin. To him, nothing that will make any meaningful impact in her current state of denial and grief. So, he does all he can do—continuing chewing on his words.

Scarlett, too, stews in her thoughts of Allison and her return, unable to rationalize the loss of her boyfriend, her best friend, her adoptive parents, and the death and resurrection of herself all before hitting a quarter of a century. She forever fights against the reality to which she surely will succumb. A cause that may be lost, but the fight is all Scarlett seems to have left. So, she fights, holding nothing more than hope in her heart and a twinkle in her eye that she holds the power to will fate to her side. But those thoughts do not form words for conversation. At least, not words that will yield responses of agreement and words of further encouragement. So, she sits, further stewing in her thoughts.

Even Brianna seems at a loss for words. The corners of her lips repeatedly twitch, each time sending her shoulders forward with intent to speak, and each time the thought of being the one to break the silence sends her back in her seat. To Bri, the thought of speaking has never bothered her, but at this moment, she wants to find the right words to say. A thought that, in and of itself, is new to her. Leading her to think that, perhaps, she has matured over the last few years.

Their motivation to break the silence abandons them as fast as it comes. The silence of four people, all wanting to speak and not knowing what to say first or who should speak it, continues to drown and carry away in its tide any budding thoughts in their minds. But tension can only hold so much weight for so long until it snaps. It must be someone who breaks the tension of silence and, even after realizing she may have matured, Bri knows it shall be her who draws the short straw here.

"So, like, what are we going to do exactly?" Bri poses the question, though, speaking her mind, she realizes she does not know exactly what she means or why she said that.

The other three of them look at each other, trying to bring to light a more vivid picture Bri painted with vague words, but none of them seem to know the meaning behind them.

"Dear, my love, what do you mean?" Duncan gives a gentle nudge, hoping for clarification.

Bri bobs her head, searching for the words that will shed light on her dim thought. "I mean, us three," she says, pointing to Connor, Scarlett, and herself. "We are parentless. Isn't that supposed to be a late-life occurrence? Something reserved for the elderly? We are all, like, early twenties and are floating around this world with no one to guide us." Bri turns to face Duncan. "And I love you, babe, but we can't exactly ask your parents about things that aren't part of their world. Ya know?"

Duncan nods in agreement. "Wouldn't be wise, I'd say."

"We wait," Scarlett says, as if she has this all figured out.

"We wait?" Connor parrots, raising an eyebrow.

"Yeah," Scarlett continues all matter-of-fact-like. "We wait for Allison to come home, and Vistrus will be our guiding light. He's still here."

Connor rests a hand on Scarlett's shoulder. "I don't think we have to wait on anything. He'd be there for us, with or without his daughter around."

"But, I mean, like, also, what are we going to do?" Bri brings her initial statement back around. "We don't have gainful employment, no real future here in West Haven, at least not one that I can see, and it just all seems so muddled."

Connor nods in agreement. "I can see your point. This is the first time in more years than I'd like to admit that things still aren't calm."

"Yeah, but in all reality, will they ever be calm again?" Duncan poses the question, and all eyes turn to him. "I mean, with you three being what you are … Legends, will you ever have a chance to breathe deep? Won't there always be someone, somewhere, trying to beat you down or expose you in some unflattering light, making you a scapegoat for some agenda that, in the end, will only fuel a fire that tries to burn you down and bring you out of hiding when said fire never would have existed in the first place if it weren't for whoever started it out of some misguided notion to better the world?"

His words weigh heavy and knock them all deeper into their seats and couch cushions as the meaning twists its way into their souls. But after a few moments of a return to silent contemplation, Connor possesses no hesitation in speaking first on the matter.

"Yeah, no, yeah. You're right. But that doesn't matter. The next, unknown combatant, enemy, foe, whatever … is not one we need to be worrying about. Right now, we have to figure out how to deal with the man in the red tracksuit. The man who killed Gramps and framed me for it. The man who knows why the WHO decided to build a center on the border of a haven for Legends—"

Bri blurts out, interrupting Connor's grand oration, "Oh, West *Haven*. I get it now!"

Having lost his momentum, his shoulders slump as he sums up, "We have to deal with him."

"One more for the road, eh?" Scarlett says with a budding smile.

"What?" Bri asks, coming out of her own internal thoughts.

"One more baddie. One more guy to finish off what started with Jack's arrest and subsequent kidnapping a few years ago. I mean, I don't think he'd be opposed to it." Scarlett seems lost in her words as they fly forth from her lips. "It's funny. I remember once, Al and I were sitting in the cafeteria and the school counselor, Ms. Hsu, started trying to be all Miss I'm-here-for-you-whenever-you-need."

"And?" Duncan prods.

"I'm just spit-balling. But if Vistrus is one light in a dim world, maybe she can be a second? Having two lights will brighten it up a bit more," Scarlett finishes her thought, scrunching her lips to the left side of her face.

"While I like that thought, Cos'," Connor adds to the momentum, "we still need to know what Vistrus and possibly some rando school worker will be shedding light on. That's assuming one, she'll remember any of us, and two, that she wants to help if she can. There's a lot going on in that brain of yours, and while I think therapy would be beneficial, I am not sure regressing to high school is the way to do it."

"Well, Allison would know. She visited with Ms. Hsu a few times," Scarlett says, as if Allison will be by any moment to weigh in on the matter.

Connor clenches his fists, taking a deep breath before releasing it into a torrent of words. "But Allison isn't here. She's not here, and she's not coming back. Why? 'Cause she died, just like Jack and his parents and Mom and Dad. But unlike them, she killed herself and it sucks … worse than anyone can know or say. But that's the reality of the situation and the sooner you get that through that thick skull of yours, Scar, the sooner you can move on with your life and deal with the loss. Stewing in denial has got to be one of the most unhealthy ways to deal with anything in life. And this, especially this, has got to be dealt with in a way that allows for healing and moving on."

"Moving on? Is it that easy for you? Just move on like she never existed? Like she was never a part of our lives? Sorry I didn't mourn everyone sooner. Things were nonstop if you don't remember. Then I was underground. I didn't have time to mourn or come to terms with any of this. I wake up, claw myself out of the dirt, and find another person in my life has left." Scarlett's voice rises with her anger. "So tell me, Connor, how did you deal? Huh? How long was her body cold before you moved on? Was she still lying in the tub and you were ready? People don't move on that easily! You think I don't know she's dead?! You think I want this to be the reality I come back to?! It wasn't even a day of coming out of … of whatever The Nation calls it—the Waiting—to find that my best friend off'd herself in a way that no one should ever have to find?! Do you have any idea what sort of hell I came back to?! I am still not sure I'm not dead, being forced to bide my time in some hell version of where I lived, or some third option I can't even comprehend yet. What kind of world allows for someone to do that to themselves? What sort of world allows people to walk around so blind to the pain of others that they get to a point where a razor blade is their only option? It has to be hell I climbed out of the dirt to because no sane person could ever call this world anything but."

Connor wants to respond, but her words have sucked the air out of his lungs. He exhales, knowing that in all his grief, he failed to acknowledge how her experience in the Waiting and waking up might have affected her views on this ordeal. But even as the realization washes over him, her words demand a rebuttal.

But before Connor can respond, Duncan holds up a hand, signaling his wanting to say something. All eyes turn to him. "Scarlett, I might be out of line here and I may be wrong, but I don't think Connor is hunky dory. He still grieves for everyone he lost. We all are still grieving in our own ways. No one is moving on as if Allison or their parents or Jack and his family never existed, certainly not Connor and especially not you. That is not what anyone means when they say moving on. But life goes on. And we must learn to live without them while keeping them all in our hearts and their spirits in our actions. Remembering Allison and Jack, how they lived, how they made you feel, is how you move on. Bri remembers that her mom wasn't perfect, but she remembers the lessons her mom taught her, no matter how unconventional or emotionally draining the way was. All of these ways are how we keep the departed ones alive.

"It's hard, and it sucks, and there are days you want to do nothing but sit and cry. And some days, that might be all you can do. There will be time for that brand of grief, I promise you there will. When you have those moments for that kind of grief, you will take them, sometimes without even realizing you are. Right now, though, there is a man out there. A man who wants nothing more than to expose you, exploit you, and either weaponize or neuter you. *He* needs to be dealt with. Then, you will have time to grieve and sit around sharing stories of Allison and what a wonderful, angry soul she was or Jack and how he made you feel loved."

His words about Allison cause Connor and Scarlett to smile, releasing a small chuckle as they do. Duncan and Bri join in the budding laughter as they think about Allison and her short fuse.

"She was a firecracker," Connor says.

Continuing the laughter in the moment of levity, Duncan adds, "I may have known her the shortest, but that girl was scary fierce."

Bri chimes in, "You're telling me. It was my mother, but damned if Al was going to let anyone hurt me."

Scarlett laughs, adding, "Ms. Espinoza didn't stand a chance."

Connor smiles. "No one stood a chance when that girl got angry."

Scarlett shakes her head, bringing herself back to the reality of the moment. "Don't think I'm cured or that this will be the last time I fight against the reality of it. But there's still the matter at hand."

And the remains of their joy flicker out as reality sets in for the rest. Bri's first question that broke the silence reforms in her head, this time worded with clarity. "What are we going to do about this Bishop?"

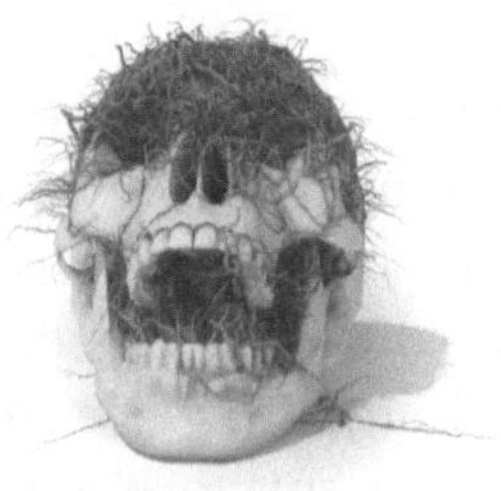

CHAPTER 7

"Sad, little men are ofttimes the loudest
out of need to placate their own inadequacies."
~N. DeSalvo~

A cool, sometimes brisk breeze always seems to accompany Scarlett on the days she visits her parents' tombstones; this time is no exception. But her stride is a little less solemn. The melancholy that washes over her seems pale compared to other times. Perhaps it is because of the news she received. That while she always had her cousin Connor, Aunt Tracy, and Uncle Ken, she now knows she has always had more. While she has yet to meet them and introduce herself face to face, she knows they are there. A family that loves her. News she still hasn't told Brianna. How can she tell her friend that while one mother was stripped away from the world, another returns? That seems a little uncouth the more it tumbles through her mind. No matter now, her walk to visit her parents' seemingly empty graves comes to a finish as she approaches.

Noticing a small envelope propped against her father's headstone, she looks around the cemetery, hoping to see the man she's ever only noticed in her peripheral vision before. Proving fruitless, she turns her efforts toward the envelope, squatting down to grab it before falling into place against his stone.

The nondescript envelope would not have caught her attention had it not been placed against her parents' headstones. White, sealed as if meant to be mailed, and something that looks like it came from a pack of thirty. Nothing cryptic or magnificent. A tinge of disappointment hits her upon realizing a moment, like she imagines this will be, would have been better met with a cool parchment or velum envelope. Something old, musty, and fragile to deliver whatever news might be waiting inside for her seems a more appropriate delivery device. Nonetheless, this plain, white, mass-produced commercial item waits to unveil its contents.

Scarlett,

How to begin? Years of watching you visit us, never able to say hello, never able to tell you we are safe, that we are not dead is harder than I can ever put into this letter. I know you've seen me trimming trees, cutting the grass, or offering funeral services near you when you visit. I have listened to every word or almost every word you've said and cannot apologize enough for missing the days I did. And I especially can't apologize about the day you ended up in the Waiting. It's never fun to experience, no matter how many times.

CHAPTER 7

And the first is always rough. There's no proper way to prepare you for it. Though, I guess, I could have tried had we been there for you.

But to that point, Scarlett. We weren't as young as we were naïve. It used to be easier being what we are. Easier to hide, easier to live, and easier to be ourselves. But now, with cameras everywhere, it seems that each day is harder and harder to be who we are. Your mother shouldn't have been able to conceive you. It wasn't supposed to be. We didn't know what to do. As I said, we weren't as young as we were naïve. We made plans and made them fast against surveilling technology that was advancing even faster than we could think. At least, it seemed that way. But we didn't have the answers to anything that was happening around us. We didn't have them because we didn't know what the question was that needed answering. But we sure weren't going to approach the Council with it. Ask V about it. The distrust and discontent have been brewing for a long time. But he didn't know about this. He's as innocent as you are. Had we been there for you, maybe we could have prevented all the death that's surrounded you and your friends. Had we been there for you, we might be dead as well. I know the irony of that statement is not lost on you. But we didn't know what to do, and doing nothing was not an option. We made a decision and looking back, it may have been the wrong decision. But there is nothing that can be done about it now. Back then, it seemed like the only option to keep everyone safe. Now, the only people it has kept safe are those still being hunted. I do not enjoy the implications of the words I wrote. But you are an adult, and we can't lie to you anymore. Looking back, we never should have lied at all. But hindsight is always 20/20. The events of the last few years are all connected, as I'm sure you have pieced together. This means those that hunted James, Lucretia, Ken, Tracy, Sylvia, and Nick will not stop until you are killed.

This is the worst possible way to introduce yourself to your grown child, who thought you'd died long ago. I am beyond sorry this has to happen this way. I cannot be around when you read this. If you search your surroundings, I will not be here. If you see me, know that it is not me. Do not approach that version of me. When... if we ever get to meet, assuming we make it through all of this, you will have no doubts it is me. When we do meet, I will explain everything in person and explain it better than I tried to in this letter.

Know this. Your mother and I have not been sitting back, idly watching as you grow. We have been paying attention to the world around us, hiding in plain sight as Normals instead of who we are. How to deal with the WHO and the shadow organization operating within its walls is in your hands. Yours, Connor's, and your trusted friends.

That is a heavy burden to bear and one I would not envy if I were your age. I will help any way I can, but exposing myself now for who I am, or your mother exposing herself, would only give them another target to reach you through. So, I offer this: Anyone thought of as evil or an enemy never looks in the mirror thinking that about themselves, but to someone, I am evil; I am the enemy. Same for you. In someone else's eyes, you are the enemy. If you want to defeat the enemy, you must understand your enemy. Know them and the motivations behind their actions. You don't have to agree with why they do what they do, but you must learn why. It is within that why that lies the key to finding and then exposing their vulnerability. Find your enemy's weakness, and there you'll find the way to defeat them.

Again, there are no words to express our regret, sorrow, and sadness at the choices we made. We only wanted what is best for you. Perhaps we should have taken action and not left you to clean up a mess that was made decades ago.

Love,
Your father and mother

Scarlett turns from the letter, breaking herself from the tunnel vision focus. The world around seems quieter than before. The wind still blows and the distant traffic still sounds, but right now, it's muted against the tide of feelings swelling inside her.

Unsure of what the letter truly means, all she can take away from it is that the mountain of death that has been the last few years of her life, culminating in Allison's suicide, could have been prevented had her parents not been so cowardly. That her life could have been different had they not let some freak incident of their genetics scare them so badly hits her like an aftershock of the letter's first quake. A rage fills her, knowing that had her parents and those involved possessed more backbone for doing what is right instead of thinking what seemed less confrontational, or perhaps easier, was right, Allison might still be alive, and all the past few years would not have been the hellish nightmare they were.

But even in her anger, Scarlett knows she should not discard this letter. Though, she doesn't feel it deserves the respect its author might feel it should get. She crumbles the pages and shoves them in her pocket.

Standing from her spot and adjusting her clothes, the envelope slips from her hands as a breeze steals it from her. She doesn't chase it down, figuring maybe her father will see it while doing maintenance and know she received his apology.

Looking down at the headstones, she squints her eyes as newfound regret fills her. All the years of visiting these graves, hoping that one day she would uncover the reasons behind the lack of information, or learn a little about who her parents were, she can't help feeling that it might all be a waste now knowing they never were there. But what other answer to her lifelong quest would have better sufficed? That they were buried and decomposing six feet under? At least, this way, they are alive. But being alive means still having to deal with the consequences of their actions and eventually, hopefully, meeting the people you thought were long dead and the awkwardness that comes in that moment—the uncertainty of what to say to someone you've already said everything to, at least in your mind. She will have to find a way to separate everything and deal with it when the time comes. For now, she huffs a little indignation.

"One day. Ha." She shakes her head. "Now I know."

Oil lantern sconces illuminate the smiles on the patrons' faces as they imbibe, enjoying a moment free of work and worry. One man, however, seated at a corner table and hiding in the shadows, nurses an ale. The scowl on his face refuses to relent, even as he sips his liquid medicine. He watches as Aoife and Nioclás share a drink, laughing about something unheard. The man's angered imagination runs wild as some new paranoia whispers in his mind that they shared a laugh at his expense.

The scowl fades for a moment. Shaking his head in disbelief, the shadows betray his attempts to watch discreetly from a close distance—Easpag. Pushing away the budding paranoia, he exhales out every ounce of air his lungs hold, calming himself.

At the bar, Aoife smiles, gazing into Nioclás's eyes before he turns to the barkeep, whirling a finger that signals another round is in order.

"Nioclás, do not jest. He is a good man," Aoife defends *against a jab at Easpag. "It's just…" her words trail off, lost in her thoughts.*

"Just what, my love?" Nioclás urges.

"You are relaxed around me. He tries so hard to show me he loves me, and the gesture is nice," she continues. *"But it's so intense. Like a faerie fire consuming a bog. I don't know what would remain if I stayed."*

"So, I am some boring, safe alternative to him?" Nioclás jokes.

"Not at all. You make me feel at ease. Safe in a way that lets me enjoy life and not worry about appeasing some deep insecurities. But he's a good man and knows I choose you. I can't be what he needs and what I am is what you want. There's no making him understand the difference between the two."

"Ní dhéanfadh sí sin domsa. Not me. She loves me, I know she does," Easpag mutters in some futile attempt to delude himself that he still holds a chance.

A tightening in his chest clamps harder while watching them continue laughing without a care in the world. Squinting, he notices Aoife's relaxed body language in this moment. His heart beats harder with a desire that she should be that relaxed around him. A difference between him and Nioclás that Easpag cannot understand.

Gulping down the last of his ale, he slams the mug onto the table, but the clank is lost in the rambunctious noise of patrons' fun. Wanting to stand up, a weight holds him down, keeping him in his chair to stare at the love he cannot have and the man who stands in his way.

Finishing the round of drinks, the bartender raises an empty mug in a motion that asks if they would like more. Nioclás shakes his head, declining more alcohol. He turns to Aoife, cupping her cheeks in his hands.

"I am glad that I make you feel relaxed and safe. There is no other way I'd want you to feel around me," Nioclás *whispers before planting a kiss on her lips.*

After a momentary public display of affection, she takes a turn to speak. "You accept me for who I am. You put no pressure on me to choose. Made no ultimatum. Only that you wanted me to be happy."

"Do you think he does not want the same?" Nioclás *ponders.*

"Perhaps. But it's not what he said. He said he wanted me to be happy with him," Aoife answers.

"That's the same thing I said." A hint of confusion coats his words.

"Similar, not the same. The devil's in the difference, but the difference is everything."

Easpag watches them exchange words and smile the whole time. "I am worthy of love, am I not?" Another utterance to delude himself that things may still end the way he wants.

But the sprouting paranoia again whispers to him he must take what he wants; that yes, he is worthy of love, and Aoife will one day see him in the way he desires. The swelling anger pushes him out of his seat, standing him up. His body shakes as he holds words in his mouth better swallowed than let out. After a moment of choking on the words he has been trying to chew and swallow, the shaking stops as they slide down his throat.

*He watches them both. Aoife laughs while Nioclás con-*tinues chatting away. After a moment, Nioclás leans in, giving her a passionate yet brief kiss. He grasps her hand in his and a smile widens on her face. An idea strikes *Easpag—he needs to give her something of his, something that she can hold to remind her of what she is leaving behind. Something that will make her happy when she holds it and cause her to rethink if she made the correct choice. He shall give her something to hold in her hand for all her life.*

"She will love me yet." A final utterance as he slinks out the door.

"This isn't something we have to do right now, love." Duncan tosses some ice into a couple of glasses before filling them with home-brewed iced tea. "This isn't supposed to be stressful in a detrimental way. It's supposed to be good stress."

Walking back into the living room, the visible strain on Brianna's face makes him think her insides are trying to make their way out. Out-stretching a hand, he offers her one of the iced teas.

Taking it, she forces a smile. "Good stress? How can stress be good? Stress, any way you cut it, is bad."

Duncan chuckles. "Any way you cut it? Interesting choice for this situation."

Slapping his arm, she responds, "You know what I mean. But stress sucks."

"Sure, but this shouldn't be anxiety-inducing. It should be more like a hard workout. Hard and sweaty, but in the end, you feel better for having done it."

Bri's stress slips away at his words. "I'll give you a hard and sweaty workout."

Duncan tilts his head at her twist of his words. "Will I feel better for having done it?"

Laughing, she continues, "You for sure. Me, about half the time." She laughs harder.

"Ouch. Wounded pride, love." Kissing her on the crown of her head, he adds, "See, fun stress."

Taking a deep breath in to reset herself, she turns back to the task at hand. "Then why is *this* still so stressful? Nothing looks like home."

"That could be your way of telling yourself moving isn't what you actually want…" He pauses for a moment, but those words only worsen her panic, causing her to shift in her seat. "Or it just means nothing looks good to you. House-hunting is not a simple decision and not one that should be taken that way," he finishes, settling in beside her.

The last of his words appears to tame the growing beast inside Bri, if only for the moment.

"I didn't think it would be so hard," Brianna relents.

"What did you think it would be like?" He sips his tea, awaiting her response.

She ponders that thought for a moment before answering. "I don't know. I imagined it would be you and me going to open houses and some Realtor® ushering us inside with some grand, sweeping gesture.

We'd walk through a bunch of quaint houses and condos, imagining our life together room by room. Stupid, I know."

Wrapping his arms around her, he gives her a gentle squeeze. "There's nothing stupid about painting a Norman Rockwell picture for yourself, for us. It's sweet, and I wish I could give that to you."

"Instead, it's scrolling a phone, looking at photo after photo of some random house in some random neighborhood. I don't know how the other houses look. If it's noisy or quiet. It's not like these listings are advertising the freight trains that run behind them."

"But they do mention that the windows were recently updated. So, that's nice, yeah?" he encourages.

Nodding, she adds, "Yeah. There's that." Bri lets the moment marinate in her head for a minute before continuing, "None of these are home."

"No. They are not. Home is wherever you want it to be. Right here can still be home, even if it takes a while to get back to it." A bit of solace to soothe an aching heart.

"What if it never returns? That's why I want to leave."

"Then we find a house we like, get approval for a mortgage, and put in an offer." He simplifies the process for the moment's sake.

"When do we put this one out there?" she asks, eagerness creeping in.

"Once we put in an offer," he says, smiling. "Or at least once we start finding houses that call our names." He watches as she offers a meek smile on the subject before returning to scroll the never-ending list of houses. "On that note, how much do you have in the bank for a down payment? It can help us get lower rates." He knows she has more than enough for a twenty percent down payment, with the nest egg and contributions from The Nation, but he couldn't bring it up before. The time never presented itself before now.

"How much do we need?"

"Depends on how much the house is. On a two-hundred-fifty-thousand-dollar house, ideally, we'd want to put down fifty grand. In other words, twenty percent."

She does some quick mental math in her head, then responds with, "We have enough. But it may be all we have. I don't remember exactly how much is in the bank."

"Plus, whatever we get from this house, too. But you don't want to spend all of it. Keep some for any repairs and stuff."

Brianna smiles for the first time today. She relaxes on the couch and sets the phone down. "We got time, right?"

"The best way to look at this entire process is as a distraction."

"A distraction?"

"Yeah. A distraction from everything going on with the WHO and their grandma."

The harsh light of day that is her world as a Legend hits with blinding force. Any thought she had of picking her phone back up to scroll houses has abandoned her.

"What do you think about everything?" Her words sound like an innocent question, but he can sense the leading undertones, hoping he says what she wants to hear.

"I think that of everything we've done and everything I know about you and them as Legends, this is perhaps the craziest idea I've seen you guys come up with. But … I also know that each of you is smart, determined, and has been through more in the last few years than many go through in a lifetime. So, I say, hell yeah, and I want in." An unintended smile crosses his face, like a kid seeing giant supplies of ice cream all for the taking.

"But when we talked about it—" she starts before being interrupted.

"You all decided that as a Normal, I have too much to lose and not enough strength if I have to fight a Legend." Bri opens her mouth to speak, but he continues, not letting her. "If something happened to you and I didn't do everything in my power, as limited as that may be to you, to stop it, then I'd have nothing left, anyway. Sure, I don't have the strength you all have, but for lack of the condition, I consider myself one of you one hundred percent. I've seen what Legends can do, and I've seen what Normals can do. There's not much left in this town that's gonna shock me. So yeah, I want in."

Bri thinks about it before the second smile of the day crosses her face. "All right. I'll let them know you put your foot down. You want in."

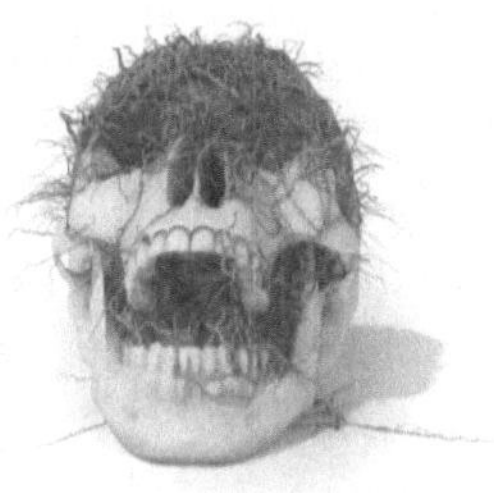

CHAPTER 8

"It's never one thing that leads to this."
~ A. Petrovsky~

A small crowd, dressed in formal peasant wear, gathers in the area known as the Bridges of Ross in Éire. Chattering fills the air as a well-dressed Nioclás stands in front of an officiant, both of whom watch Aoife walk toward them. The crowd hushes as they lay eyes upon her long, flowing, forest-green dress with brown accents. A dress that is both heavy enough to keep her warm on this spring day and elegant enough to have silenced the crowd. Her eyes catch her soon-to-be-wed standing in a kilt, *a traditional formal Irish jacket called an inar, and a shirt, all wrapped in a cloak known as a brat. His handsomeness almost stops her in her tracks, but she catches herself and continues walking.*

Despite a cloudy sky, the rain has staved itself off for the day's event. The nicety of Mother Nature providing as ideal conditions as they could hope for is not enough to keep away a man with growing anger in his heart. In the distance, far enough away to go unnoticed, yet close enough to spy on the event, is Easpag, watching with squinted disdain as the happy couple settles into their places.

The officiant, his back to the seas, looks out over the crowd as they stare back and begins the ceremony as a slight breeze blows over them. "Love comes in many forms in many ways." His thick brogue coats his speech in tones of melancholy happiness that dull the soft "th" sounds in his words into hard "t's." "Some love burns hot, like a fire engulfing everything in its path."

As he says this, Easpag listens in. Even at a distance, his ears pick up every word being said. Words that sting him like needles digging under his skin, searching for a vein.

"And much like a raging inferno, that love will dwindle eventually, leaving nothing as it once was. Everything will change." The officiant pauses, looking out at the crowd, then at Aoife and Nioclás. "There is nothing wrong with love that burns so strongly. If both people burn with such a fierce intensity, who knows what could be accomplished?"

Those words resonate in Easpag's mind. Words that set in like stone, making him wonder what can be done, or what he could have done, to make her feel the same.

As he continues the ceremony, the officiant says, "But that is not your love. Some love never finds roots. Wandering free from person to person, looking to spread its joy and find inner peace with each encounter. A way to never commit to any one person beyond themselves. And some people find contentment in this brand of love." He stops to look at the happy couple.

Nioclás and Aoife gaze into each other's eyes, thinking thoughts of the future and the life they are going to share. Each knows *that with their Legendary condition, the years are limitless.*

The officiant looks back out at the crowd, smiling as he continues, "But that is also not the type of love that defines yours. Your love burns strong but steady. Yours does not demand change or push you from others. Your love gives you the choice to stay, the choice to go, the choice to grow. Yours is a love that is built of endurance. One that is built on friendship and understanding. I look at you, and I see two people who will better the other. Two people who will support each other in every way they can and help one another become the best possible version of themselves that they can. No ultimatums, no limits on what each of you can do. I look at you both, and I see two people who were meant to spend their days together."

Easpag's heart races and pounds as the officiant continues the speech. Each word spoken drives a nail through his heart because, to him, he should be the one standing beside Aoife, not Nioclás. He should be the one to grow old with Aoife and tell her what's best, not Nioclás. But Easpag promised Aoife that he would let her go. In this life and the next, no matter what name she chooses to go by, he would leave her in peace. So, right now, he turns his back on the ceremony and walks away, even as his inner conscience whispers other options.

The officiant finishes their vows, ending the ceremony so Nioclás can kiss Aoife as his wife for the first time. Pulling back, he holds his face close to hers, whispering, "I thank the stars above that I am the lucky one, Aoife. Thank you."

"You are my best friend. My heart might be big, but you're all I need, Nioclás."

Ammar settles into a shiny, new leather wingback chair in Vistrus's office. Vistrus pulls out his desk chair, swiveling it to face his longtime friend. They each hold a cigar lit moments ago.

Digging his back into the chair, Ammar smirks, looking at the design and stitching. "This is quite comfortable. New, I take it?"

A ring of smoke encircles Vistrus as he says, "I think it is quite comfortable. That is why I bought it. And yes, arrived the other day." He takes another puff from his cigar before letting it rest in a polished ceramic ashtray. "That is not why I pulled you away from your vacation."

Ammar chuckles. "I flew in for Allison's funeral, Vistrus. I would not call that a vacation, but I understand. What's on your mind?"

Vistrus opens a desk drawer, lifts up a false panel on the bottom, and pulls out a clear bag containing a stone panel covered in detailed painting.

Recognizing the piece, Ammar sits more upright, taking a puff of his cigar. "I thought you'd given up on that. I haven't heard from you since you returned from the dig. What, four years ago?"

"Apologies. It has been some time, though, I have not given up on anything," Vistrus says, setting the bag on the desktop.

"It wouldn't be you to forget such things." Ammar leans forward.

"I was waiting until I had more pieces that fit into this," Vistrus defends.

Still leaning forward, but at a bit more attention, Ammar asks, "You found something?"

Vistrus nods. "I believe so. And I have you and Allison to thank."

Ammar's head tilts a little to the side as he arches an eyebrow. "How so?"

"Shortly after we met in Cairo, Allison also encouraged me to read my wife's diaries, thinking they could shed insight into her dreams. It provided many answers to something I did not know I was looking for."

Ammar shakes his head, indicating he is not quite following. He turns to his cigar, hoping a puff will impart some understanding of his friend's words. After a moment of enjoying the smoke, he releases, saying, "What more did you find?"

"She had not gone insane. I now know as much." Vistrus hesitates a moment, unsure of what detail from his reading might provide further context.

"But?" Ammar urges.

Vistrus shakes his head, still lost in his thoughts. "I have read each diary cover to cover. Mundane entries of daily life fill most. Of course, as she started to … protect us … the entries reflected that speech pattern."

"And?"

"She lived a double life. I know she loved me, and I know it was to protect me. But she lived a separate life I knew nothing about."

Ammar waves a dismissive hand at the stone panel. "And for many more centuries than you knew, apparently."

"She never mentioned that part of her life in any of her entries. Outside of an investigation into an old Council … or whatever she said they were called, and everyday ramblings, the only things she wrote were various poems, all with the same title, 'The Grey Fairy Anomaly.'"

"What do you think it means?"

"Nothing that I can figure. The poems all were just that. Poems, or so it seems. But to the point of the stone."

Nodding, Ammar adds, "Yes, to the point."

"It means we know nothing about our history before the Sentinels. That is thousands of years."

"A dark ages for The Nation. Interesting."

Both men sit, contemplating the implications of Ammar's discovery and recent events.

"Everything does not always tie together with little bows. Sometimes, things are what they are … random," Vistrus says after an extended silence.

"That's it?" Ammar starts. "She had an entire lifetime or three before you, and you're okay with it?"

Vistrus turns to his friend. "What choice do I have?"

Bishop walks down the suburban sidewalk, approaching Eleanor's home with hope in his mind that even after all these years, she may still carry a torch for him, even if it only glimmers. The closer he gets, the more he thinks the timing is not right, that something will ruin the moment if she sees him. Still a few houses down, he hears movement in the backyard, accompanied by light singing. Her voice, forever recognizable to his ears no matter how much time has passed, brings him a sad smile. Walking up the side of the

house toward the back, he realizes she might not be alone. But she might be. If she is, then he can be himself, but if she isn't, he might not be a welcome sight.

A quick decision sends pain shooting through him, causing him to double over while clenching his teeth to prevent himself from screaming. Standing tall again and shaking off the pain, he checks his reflection in the window—a nearly perfect mimicry of Connor DeSalvo.

He rounds the corner disguised as Eleanor's grandson, listening to her sing a verse of "Greensleeves."

"Your vows you've broken, like my heart/Oh, why did you so enrapture me?/Now I remain in a world apart/But my heart remains in captivity."

He hears the words she sings, and they sound as if she sings them specifically for him. As if the songs she sings when alone are her way of holding onto a life that could have been if only she had chosen a different path—a different man. Oh, how after all these countless years, he still wishes to hold her in his arms, wishing to be the one she tells her thoughts to, the events of her day to. But no, he can't find the courage or will within himself to walk up to her as himself, so he approaches hidden in the guise of her grandchild.

Wanting to speak, he needs her to know it's him within the guise without giving away a secret he has kept since his beginning. Perhaps a small hint at a moment they shared not too long ago, compared to other moments she has long since forgotten.

"It's a little early for Christmas music, Grandma Eleanor," he says, approaching from the side gate.

A hope resides in his words that she remembers the tune she sang at the nursery, the worker who made a similar comment, and then that she ran into him. She still cares. He knows she does. All he needs is a reason to come forth. A reason to change the past and claim for himself the life he should have had centuries ago. But her glance in his direction and the smile on her face do not express the excitement of long-lost loves reuniting after countless time apart. No, it is a familial smile an elder gives a young one. And the smile, paired with her inability to see him for who he truly is, kills any lingering hope that started pushing through.

Shaking her head as she stands, she says, "You youngins all think it's about the holiday."

Seeing her squint to see him, he steps out of the direct sunlight. He sees her smile turn to something of concern, and she looks him over. "Looks like you caught something. Go grab yourself some water."

Shaking his head and double-checking his reflection in the window, he can't help feeling the warmth that she is forever the maternal figure, wanting to care for everyone in her life. But no amount of water will cure his sickly condition. The one thing his Legendary kind never could mimic a hundred percent was the color. No matter how perfect every other detail was, there was always an underlying pale or sick look to their complexion; it was the only thing that never matched the original.

The Adeirrig went into hiding long before the scientific advancements were available to figure out the genetics behind what made them unique within The Nation. Bishop always attributed the inability to create a perfect color match to a lack of time around those he mimics. But for now, he needs a response that would be something Connor would say. If only his abilities allowed him to think like those he mimics.

"I feel fine. I'll grab some drive-through after I leave." *A response he hopes leaves it at that. And, by her next questions, seems to have accomplished just that.*

"What brings you by this afternoon?" Eleanor asks, eying him for a clue to his visit.

Butterflies flutter around in his stomach. Some puppy love pangs, reminiscent of his teenage years, cause him to fumble a response. Instead, he looks around as if the answer to her question hides in the garden. Unable to think of a suitable response, he uses her observation of his looking ill as cover. "Must've forgotten. Blame it on the sick."

While sick he might not be, he can't help but wonder if her inability to pick up on his hint of their encounter at the nursery while picking pavers might be a sign that he does not hold the place in her heart that she holds in his—that, perhaps, she has moved on and never gives him a thought.

Squatting back down to return to her gardening, a silver amulet set with amethyst and sapphire stones falls out from her top. She fumbles, trying to catch it as it swings, but manages to tuck it away once again.

Hope springs eternal for Bishop, taking the momentary escape of the amulet to bring up something that if he were here as himself might be a sensitive subject. A moment to pry into her thoughts and see if she does still carry a torch.

"Nice necklace." He keeps his tone casual, not wanting to raise either suspicion, alarm, or put her on the defensive. A moment of relaxed conversation that gives him a reason to take a seat at the patio table as he hopes she speaks of long-lost love and how things could have and should have been.

"Thanks. It was a gift." Simple words are sometimes sharper than swords as her response stabs his hopes.

Hoping to draw more of her thoughts on it, he thinks for a moment about how Connor might respond. "From Grandpa?"

Eleanor continues pulling weeds, but her stare grows a mile long, looking into the long past. A wistful, yet sullen expression glosses over her. "No, this was given to me by someone I knew long ago. An old…" she searches for the right word to use and his heart races, hoping to hear the word he has longed to hear for too many years to count, "…friend."

Again, she twists the knife she does not know she wields, plunging it a little deeper into his heart.

"Friend, sure." Accusation coats his words. A mistake, perhaps, or an unconscious truth. Either way, Eleanor does not let that slide.

The words from who she thinks is her grandchild rocket her back to the moment. "Young man, you might be an adult, but do not forget that I was young once, too. Your grandfather might be the love of my life, but he was not my first."

While those words would have made the real Connor DeSalvo sit farther back in his chair, it renews all hope that was murdered in earlier conversation. That Nick was "not her first" means that she did love Bishop. And if she once loved Bishop, she can learn to love him again. Now, if he can only get her to admit her love, then he can reveal himself.

"This other friend, who was he?"

Smiling, she turns from her gardening. The smile, though, is more obligatory than wistful and yearning. "Just someone from another life. Someone who would have made for a far different life had things been … well … different."

Hope will always live in places one sees it. Sitting up straighter in his chair, Bishop takes a deep breath, knowing that this moment could be the moment that she admits every-thing he ever wanted … if only he says the correct words. Evident deliberation in each word shows in the slow pace he speaks them. "Do you ever wish that life was with this mystery man?"

He could not have chosen better words to cut right to the root of everything at stake. Shaking her head, she drowns any signs of hope that remained. He no longer feels that this will end in a way that benefits him. No. From this moment on, anything can only further add to his pain.

Finally answering him, she says, "Life works out the way it does. I am not one to reason why. At least not anymore."

He can feel tears start welling up, and the last thing she needs to see is someone she thinks is her grandchild crying over something unrelated to him. Searching for a reason to leave, he hears a car approaching. He stands up, giving a sudden declaration. "I have to go."

As he turns to leave, Eleanor asks, "Do you remember why you stopped by?"

He faces her for a moment, shaking his head. "No. But it is always nice to see you."

He exits the gate and walks behind the neighbor's house, hiding from the car parked in front of Eleanor's house. As he waits for the opportunity to leave without being seen, he goes over all the ways he imagined that conversation taking place, but can't seem to figure out how he never imagined it taking place the way it just transpired.

CHAPTER 9

"Hatred plants roots in individuals
ill-equipped to deal
with uncomfortable situations."
~D. Elias~

Blaring through the speakers, The Offspring's "The Kids Aren't Alright" sets a peculiar mood for tonight's drive. Connor, Scarlett, Brianna, and Duncan all sit in silence, absorbing each word Dexter Holland sings, like if they listen hard enough, a hidden message holding the answer to the meaning of life will decode in their brains. But as he sings, a reminder hits them at ninety decibels that the cruelest dream is, in fact, reality.

Reaching over the center armrest console and turning down the volume, Duncan brings everyone back to the stark reality of the moment. "We have our plan, sure. But we assume that the building is built. It hasn't been that long since they announced it."

Scarlett lowers her visor and opens the makeup mirror to see him. "So?"

"So, what are we expecting to find in what should still be a construction site?"

Connor chimes in, "How did we never think of that?"

Ever the quick one to catch on, Bri pipes up, "I don't get it."

"How much incriminating evidence do we expect to find in a research facility that is still being built? I think that's their question, Bri," Scarlett clarifies.

"Oh, yeah, no," Bri starts. "I've seen it."

"When?" Duncan asks.

"Driving around, looking at houses," Bri says with a casual nonchalance.

Connor peeks at them in the rear-view for a second. "You lookin' to buy?"

"Yeah," Bri says, keeping her reply short and unspecific.

"Just browsing. Seeing what's on the market, but I think it's more an idea to entertain than something too serious right now," Duncan offers a bit more than a one-word reply.

"Any towns in particular or wherever?" Scarlett asks.

But before Brianna or Duncan can answer, Connor cuts in, "To the point, what do you mean you've seen it?"

"Well, I was driving about, no real destination to go to, looking at houses. I happened to pass by it. It's there." Again, her response doesn't offer much clarity to their confusion.

"Built? Finished? Functional?" Scarlett asks, turning around in her seat from staring in the vanity mirror.

"Yeah, I guess. Some windows still have that clear stuff over them that waves in the wind, but lights work and stuff." Her words hit them, making this more real than when hatching the plan.

Everyone is staring at one another, except Connor, whose eyes are on the road. "And not a moment too soon to learn of this." Everyone turns their attention to him as he nods his chin, motioning that they look out the windshield. "Look."

Their eyes land on a building that looks like it should be the under-construction floor for the Nakatomi Plaza in *Die Hard*. But here it is, in West Haven—four stories of offices and research labs that couldn't wait for construction to finish. No. Here they are, doing whatever it is that they do while the workers finish installing the windows, flooring, acoustic ceiling tile, and whatever else needs finishing up.

As they approach, the parking lot comes into view; only a few cars dot the abundance of lined parking spots. Pulling off into a parking lot of a mini-mall housing a 24-hour greasy spoon, Connor offers up, "Last meal, anyone?"

"What's that supposed to mean?" Scarlett scoffs.

"I mean, before we head in and do what we do, anyone hungry?" Connor says, mocking her tone.

Duncan looks at Bri, who shakes her head. He nods, adding, "How about this? We make it out of a government facility alive after breaking in and the experience, for whatever reason, gives us the munchies, then we grab a celebratory burger or Denver omelet. But until that time, we concentrate on the task at hand: finding out why the WHO wants you dead ... or neutered. "

Connor nods. "Let's walk there. We don't want my car in their lot, setting off any alarms."

"Why would your car set off an alarm if there are other cars there?" Bri asks, batting her innocent, vacuous eyes.

"Dear, I love you so, so much. But he means an unfamiliar car. One that might not have a parking permit or such in case night-time security drives by." Duncan eases the blow.

And the light bulb turns on inside her brain. "Oooooh. Yeah. That makes sense. I remember the plan now."

"Everyone remember what we talked about?" Connor moves the conversation to the night's plan.

"Yeah. Dinner celebration," and Brianna brings it right back to where they were.

"No," Scarlett says, trying to control her impatience. "He means the plan to get inside and once we're in."

"Oh, that. Yeah. All kosher." Bri smiles.

"Questions, thoughts, complaints?" Connor offers up one last time.

They all shake their heads, ready to take action.

Connor hits the trunk release button before turning back to everyone, nodding one more confirmation. "All right, then. Let's go."

Chain-link fence surrounds the property housing the WHO's newest building. An oversized backpack rests at Duncan's feet as they stare onward.

"We sure we're ready to do this?" Scarlett asks, unsure of herself.

Connor shakes his head. "I'm not running forever from some old man trying to kill me for whatever reason. And that reason is inside that building. It's now or never." He turns to Duncan, pointing at the backpack.

"Sure it's not now or sometime later?" Scarlett jests, trying once more to sway them to another time.

Bri turns to her. "This isn't about us. I mean, yeah, it's about us. But more than that. This is for everyone who's been slaughtered like pigs in the last few years."

Connor's face contorts, thinking about his parents in relation to Bri's metaphor. "Word choice matters, Bri."

Bri turns to him, her boldness growing. "Sorry Con, but my mom, too. Your parents, Mom, Jack … everyone that's not able to be here tonight. This is what we're doing this for. Sure, we might be arrested. We could be maimed or even killed. But staying out here, hiding from it all, is what led to this—to us standing here. I sure as hell am not gonna not go in. Whatever answer we need is in there. If nothing else, maybe we'll find a moisturizer they're developing for Legendary skin. Mine's not been as soft and smooth since I first went *Walking Dead* mode."

Duncan laughs, shaking his head. "So close to that being a great motivational speech."

"Where'd I lose it?" Bri ponders.

"Moisturizer. Not sure that should be your driving motivation, love," Duncan offers. "But we still love you just the same."

"Well, Legendary lotion or not, there's something in there that we need and I, for one, don't want another dead body on my hands. At least, not a dead body of someone we know." Bri turns to Scarlett. "So, Scar, get your act together and, as Alli would say, Betty White up."

Scarlett takes a deep breath, steadying herself. She nods faster and faster with each succession, psyching herself up. "Yeah. Yeah." She nods a few more times. "All right. No more excuses. Let's find the Jergens they're hiding and give Bri the smooth skin she deserves."

Connor and Duncan both stifle their laughs.

"Whatever works for you, Cos'."

Duncan unzips the bag, grabbing black cloth gloves for each of them. They put them on, and Duncan pulls out a pair of metal clippers. He snips away at the chain-link while the others keep watch.

After watching for the security car to pass out of sight, they skulk to a side door. Connor reaches into his pocket and pulls out a set of lock picks, handing them to Duncan.

He takes them, ducking down to eye-level with the lock. Before he can begin, however, Scarlett whispers. "You sure you got this?"

Duncan looks up at her. "Been practicing ever since we planned this."

But after a few moments, he still doesn't hear anything within the lock to indicate he's opened it.

"What's wrong, baby? Performance anxiety?" Bri jokes.

"No. Not performance anxiety. I don't know what's wrong."

"Hold on," Connor says. "It's a new building." He reaches for the door handle. "Maybe…" he pulls on it, opening the door, "…it's not locked."

Duncan stands up. "That was anti-climactic."

"I'll take not having a climax tonight. No climax is good," Bri blurts out.

"Not the same thing," Scarlett advises.

A low noise rumbles in Connor's ears. "The car's coming back. Get in."

As the last of them enter, the patrol car comes around the corner. Duncan pulls the door shut, hoping security does not see them breaking and entering.

"Now what?" Bri asks in earnest.

They look around the halls, the smell of new construction and fresh carpet assail their noses. "Should we split up?" Scarlett asks. "Isn't that why we brought the walkie-talkie thingies?"

"Why?" Bri gives her one-word reply.

"Why what, babe?" Duncan pushes for clarification.

"Why split up? Sure, we'll cover more ground, but safety in numbers and all," she offers, keeping watch down the hall.

"Because we'll cover more ground. Not only do we not know this building, we don't really know what we're looking for. So take what you think is important, and if one of us gets caught, we can warn the others and hopefully leave with something," Connor explains.

The group starts swaying, ready to tackle what lies ahead. Duncan looks around, eyes darting, trying to see what lies in the dim halls. Bri bounces from foot to foot, trying to psych herself up while Scarlett fidgets with her hands, unsure of their abilities. Connor controls his breath, head bobbing while trying to stay as calm as he can while adrenaline pumps through him.

"Duncan." Connor nods to the backpack, and Duncan gets out four small walkie-talkies and headsets for each.

Donning her set, Bri jokes, "I feel like one of those operators. How may I direct your call?" The other three shake their heads, smiling.

"Channel four. Make sure it stays plugged in. We don't need to attract attention with squelching, squelches … whatever. Be safe."

Scarlett stops them before anyone has a chance to walk off. "Who's going with who? We need to stay in pairs."

"Whom," Bri blurts out.

"Whatever. You know what I mean," Scarlett dismisses Bri's interjection.

Connor points at Duncan and Bri. "Since they bump uglies, they go together."

"Bump uglies? Really?" Bri mocks disgust.

Duncan offers a half-smile. "He's not wrong, just saying."

Bri slaps his arm. "Let's go, Duncan. It's not like you'll be seeing my ugly tonight."

Smiling, Duncan adds, "It's anything but ugly, beautiful."

As they turn to go their separate ways, Duncan stops and whispers to Connor, "We need a code word, phrase, noise … something in case we need to alert the other pair to leave or we get busted."

They think a moment, but no one says anything, causing Connor to scrunch his face in frustration. "Anything, something, anyone?" Connor urges.

"Blue pineapples," Scarlett blurts.

Connor turns back around, whispering, "You heard it, blue pineapples."

Walking down the halls, the dim light provides an ominous setting for their government theft. With each door they pass, Connor and Scarlett's hearts both jump in anticipation of stumbling upon someone. But as they pass empty office after empty office on the ground floor, it begins looking like this venture might prove fruitless. Each office they pass is set up identical to the last. A generic low-end office chair from a big box office supply store and a matching desk. Even the scent of fresh-laid carpeting permeates each room. The only noises are the flapping tarps covering the windows, still waiting to be taken down after the walls received their final coat of paint.

After walking the halls to the far side of the building, Connor stops before turning the corner. He sees the hallway open up into the darkened, sprawling lobby. Peeking his head around, the reception desk does not even have a night guard posted.

"Something's not right," he whispers.

Scarlett holds her hands palm up, shaking them, not wanting to add unneeded noise.

"I don't know," he continues. "There's no guard at the desk. If this is some big government building, I'd think they'd want a guard to keep things safe. "

She nods, realizing he has a point. She again turns her palms up, this time adding a shoulder shrug while pulling her lips to the side.

"Outside, we saw lights on. But this floor is abandoned. We've been through half of it and haven't even run across one security guard. No security on the entry level?"

Scarlett points her finger to the ceiling, then to the floor, shrugging.

"You can talk, ya know. Just keep it quiet," he assures her.

"I think you're right. Next floor up, or maybe down?"

"Down. I think. If you're running a secret operation, lighting up the tenth floor isn't gonna keep it secret long."

Scarlett points down and nods. "Better quiet than caught."

Connor presses the talk button on the walkies. "Heading to the basement. Taking stairs."

"Blue pineapples? What does that even mean?" Bri whispers to Duncan as they head down the hall.

Sneaking past an open door, Duncan takes a quick peek inside but sees no one. "Just something to say. I don't think it has any special meaning."

Stepping into the office, he sees the translucent, plastic sheeting covering the windows rustle. Holding out his arm to stop Bri, he puts a finger to his mouth. Pointing at the moving curtain, he tiptoes closer to it. Bri taps his arm. Stopping and turning to see her, she points her index and middle fingers on her right hand at her eyes, to the sheeting, then back to her eyes while mouthing, "There's no one there."

Duncan taps his temple, mouthing, "I can see no one is there, but it's moving."

Turning back, he finishes tiptoeing to the sheeting, pulling it aside.

Nothing.

They both look down to see a floor vent. Duncan squats, placing his hand over the vent, feeling the air rush out of it in a futile attempt to regulate the room temperature. He stands up, moving away from the windows and letting the sheeting fall back into place.

Upon opening the desk drawers, finding them empty, and shutting them, Duncan turns to his fiancée, who stands in front of an empty closet. "I don't get it," he whispers.

"That this office is empty?" Bri observes.

"Not just that," he says, looking down at the carpeting. "No wheel marks on the carpet. Nothing out of place. It's not just a new office. I'd say it looks … staged."

"It could just be unoccupied," Bri counterpoints. "I mean, the building is still being built."

"Possibly, but why the lights on the upper floors?"

Duncan heads back into the hall, passing a few more offices, all empty and all the same. A few doors from the end of the hall, Duncan notices a door labeled "Security."

He wags a finger at the door. Bri stares at him, confounded by his use of silent signals. She listens, trying to focus her senses but hears only low-frequency hums. Joining his Navy Seal-like attempts at hand signals, she waves him into the room.

Three security monitors span an extra-wide desk that faces the door. There are two empty rolling chairs keeping watch over the monitors.

"Keep an eye out," he whispers, motioning for her to stay outside the door.

Nodding, she stands watch while he sneaks a peek at the monitors. The screens are split into twelve different cameras. Around a quarter of the cameras display nothing but static, while others keep watch on darkened offices. Judging from what he sees, none of the security cameras secure floor one. He does notice a few cameras keep watch over a laboratory, an office, and a hallway. None of the feeds are labeled, but the lights are on. He does not see any activity happening.

Connor's voice sounds in his earbud. "Heading to the basement. Taking stairs."

He presses the button to respond. "Hear that. We're gonna be moths and head toward the lights."

Outside the room, Duncan spots a door leading to a stairwell. "Up for a walk, my love?"

At the bottom of the stairwell, Scarlett and Connor stand in front of a door labeled S1.

"S1?" Scarlett ponders aloud.

"Sub-one, I assume," Connor explains as he rests his ear on the door, trying to listen to what's on the other side. His sight periscopes as his senses focus and heighten. The sound of his heartbeat pounds above the sound of Scarlett's. Their breaths make wavelike sounds below the echo of moving air on the other side of the door. He pushes the heartbeats and breaths aside, leaving only the moving air. He tries to hear movement, feet, talking, anything, but only hears the air and a low-frequency hum.

After a few moments, he shakes his head. "Nothing," he says, turning to Scarlett, who seems lost in thought.

He goes to grab the door handle, but Scarlett stops him. "If it's sub-one, as in basement one, doesn't that mean there's a second basement?"

Connor huffs, nodding his head. "Only one way to find out."

He turns the handle, opening the door to a dark room. The light from the hallway illuminates it enough that his still-heightened senses see as if it were lit. "Come on," he says, waving her in with him.

"I can't see much," Scarlett protests.

"Concentrate. You gotta have some weird powers or whatever we call them," Connor encourages.

She steps into the room, and the door behind them closes, engulfing her in complete blackness. "Now, I really can't see."

"Are you trying to see?" Connor asks, walking to a cluttered table with metal handles soldered to its top.

"Yes, I'm trying to see. Sorry, I don't have cat eyes or whatever. If you haven't noticed, I don't have much of anything," she continues her protest. "Can you flip a light on?"

Scanning the corners of the room for security cameras, he sees nothing. Looking at his cousin, he notices a switch next to her. "Reach left; it's right there."

Fondling the wall for a moment, she finds the switch and flips it, illuminating the room.

Scarlett stands speechless, her jaw dropped open.

"I know what you mean, Cos'. This is heavy," Connor speaks for her, shaking his head at what's before him. "I never thought I'd say it, but I'm glad Jack's not here to see this."

Still slack-jawed, Scarlett nods. She shakes herself out of it, closing her mouth. "I know what you mean."

Scarlett steps over to Connor as they survey the equipment. Modified tables stacked on top of each other. Along the walls, cuffed chains overflow out of metal bins, hanging down like drunken vagrants. Dozens of vital sign monitors huddle in a corner like scared raccoons. The far wall from the entrance bears a door with a stairwell plaque. Metal tool cabinets rest on both sides of the door.

"What happened to Jack wasn't a one-time thing, was it, Con?"

He shakes his head. "And that blond guy was no lone gunman."

"What do we do?"

Connor points to the stairwell door. "See how far down this rabbit hole goes?"

Bri jogs up the ninth to tenth floor while Duncan turns the corner to the final ascent. Bouncing on her feet, waiting for him, she pumps her arms. "Come on, Duncs. Looks like you need to do a little more cardio."

Duncan smiles at her energy at this moment. "I'm fine, my love. Just don't see a need to make it a race. Conserve energy if we need to run."

Her bouncing calms from a rapid boil to a simmer. "Like, how will we know when we find what we're looking for when we, ya know, don't know what we're looking for?"

Duncan finishes the final stairs, stopping in front of her. He cups her cheeks in his hands, planting a kiss on her lips. "That, my love, is the fun in all this. We will know when we know."

She pulls back, but then leans in, planting one back on him. "But what if we walk through and don't know?"

"We'll have to see how this all plays out. How bad can it go?" He turns the handle, opening the door to the tenth floor.

The light spilling into the stairwell from the hall, accompanied by buzzing lights, contrasts the abandoned facade of the first floor.

Turning to Bri, Duncan whispers, "Why have an empty lobby? One security guard at the desk might have kept us out of here."

Bri looks around, hoping his question is rhetorical. "This way." She nods her head down the hall.

"Why *that* way?" Duncan points in her direction.

"Why not?" She shrugs, walking off.

Upturning a hand, he mutters, "Good enough for me."

The first room they come across is a break room. A simple office table with four mesh chairs, none of which are pushed in. Next to a sink stands a fridge/freezer combo. They assume the couple of cabinets on the walls hold cups, plates, and utensils. A drying rack next to the sink holds a few dishes and hard plastic cups.

Bri points at the room, shrugging. Duncan shakes his head, mouthing, "Why?"

Unable to think of a reason to waste time in the break room, they move on.

"At least we know people are here," he whispers.

They pass a door labeled, "Supply Closet."

Bri stops, but Duncan motions for them to continue.

The drywall turns to windows as they approach some room. A quick peek into the windows shows an empty lab. Feeling more secure, Duncan peers inside at lab tables with installed Bunsen burners, on top of which sit Petrie dishes and numerous other bio-logical-based equipment. Microscopes line the walls below glass cabinets, filled with vials of various colored liquids.

A squelch of a radio down the hallway distracts them. Duncan tries the handle, finding it unlocked. An approaching voice causes him to open the door, pulling Bri in with him. They shut the door and hide behind a lab table, hoping that whoever approaches passes instead of enters.

Another squelch and unintelligible response later, the person passes, leaving them to their devices. After they feel certain they are safe, the couple slowly stand up, watching the windows for anyone passing by.

"This is what you meant by, 'we'll know,'" Bri notes, looking around.

"It doesn't make sense, babe. Why have news stories detailing a fight between a new park and a WHO headquarters if the building is already half-built?" Duncan says, taking in the extent of it all.

"I could be wrong, but I'm pretty sure this building was supposed to be a new lab, or production spot, for some cosmetics company." She says this as if memory spews from her mouth, and she has no real control over her words. She spies a notebook sitting next to a microscope. A piece of masking tape across the cover bears the words: *The Grey Fairy Anomaly.*

"Why didn't you mention this earlier?" Duncan asks, picking up a residue-filled beaker and examining it.

Bri shrugs, still entranced by the notebook. As she flips it open, a voice interrupts, causing her to drop the book back on the counter close to where she found it.

"May I help you?" a man asks.

Bri stares at the man, unsure why he looks familiar. Her mind flips through old memories trying to place him, but comes up empty.

Duncan shoots a look at Bri before turning to the man. "We're new. Getting a feel for everything before starting."

"You're new? Here?" The man plays into Duncan's excuse.

Bri pipes up, "Yeah. We were just brought on to help with research. Thought it'd be fun to scope out the place."

The man's attention turns to Bri. A look in his eyes tells Bri he recognizes her. She hopes he does not remember from where.

"Are you In?" the man asks her.

Bri freezes, trying to remember everything her mother told her about moments like this before her passing. Bri knows there's a proper answer, but can't remember what to do if she doesn't want to answer. Her mind reaches for the memory, but it's just out of grasp.

In a panic, she says, "I might be. We all might be. But in *what* is the question, isn't it? Who's to say what we are all in? Are we in trouble? In danger of an existential crisis? Are we in love? I am. I hope you are. We are all in something and *that* truly is the question. To be in or not to be in. I think that Shakespeare was on to something there."

An amused smile crosses the man. He takes a step farther into the room, causing Duncan to step toward Bri and Bri to step back from the notebook.

"I think the response you were looking for was, 'I am in true, whate'er befall.'"

Bri tenses, remembering where she knows this man from. Holding onto the hope she can weasel her way out of this, she responds, "It is the east, and Juliet is the sun." The man chuckles. Bri continues, "I mean, I can dig poetry, but really don't know much. I do love me some T. Swift, though. I could talk about her all day."

The man takes another step forward, his smile turns sinister as his eyes narrow on the two of them. "And I would have responded with, 'I feel in when I sorrow most.'" He takes another step in. Duncan now stands in front of Bri, shielding her. "You aren't new. You are that girl who interrupted a council meeting with your eye in a thermos of milk."

Duncan looks at Bri. "Eye in milk?"

Bri pulls Duncan a step back with her. "I didn't know what to do and now is not the time."

Duncan slides his hand to his waist, trying to discreetly press the button on his walkie. "I feel nauseous, man. Can we just leave before I have an accident?"

"An accident?"

Duncan depresses the button, saying, "Yeah, I feel like I did that time I blew pineapples."

The man cocks his head to the side, adding, "I think you'll be fine." Turning his attention to Bri right behind Duncan, he continues, "Why don't you both come with me? This is all way beyond you."

The man's face sags for a moment before returning to Normal, betraying his words.

Duncan keeps his finger on the button. "I'm telling you, blue pineapples might come up." The urgency in his voice rises. "Blue pineapples, man."

The man turns to Duncan. "Why do you keep saying that?" He spots the earpiece in Duncan's ear. "Oh, I see. You have others running through the building." Closing the gap, his skin again sags before sloughing off. In a few steps, the man transitions into the full Legend form of Tennyson Society.

He reaches for Duncan but misses as Duncan rolls out of the way. By the time he stands back up, Bri, too, has transitioned. Her slacked jaw rests in what has become a bag of skin hanging off her face. Her left eye bulges from its socket, teetering on popping out from a good breeze.

Bri reaches for the notebook, but the man grabs her, throwing her onto a lab table. Unfazed, she sits up, but the man jumps on top of her, preventing escape.

Duncan grabs the residue-filled beaker, hurrying to protect his fiancée. Bri struggles under the man, who grabs her jaw and yanks it down. Her skin pulls apart as if it were some macabre melted mozzarella on a flesh crust, and her blood, the sauce. Seeing this, Duncan releases a war cry, causing the man to turn and face him, and he brings down the beaker, smashing it into the guy's face—broken shards of glass embed into the man's skin.

A primal scream escapes the man as his skin starts bubbling from the residue. He rolls off Bri, and she gets up and runs to Duncan. Instincts take over as he swipes at his face, ripping open more flesh for the residue to interact with, worsening his condition. Bri and Duncan stand, unable to look away from the chemical reaction, but the man gains control and stands up. His skin sloughs off in further decay, removing the residue.

"You don't get it," he says, stalking closer to them. "We don't matter. What we can do, what we can be, is irrelevant."

Duncan spies another residue-filled beaker next to a butane lighter stick. Ignoring the man's words, he whispers to Bri, "Distract him."

She side-eyes him, trying to respond as her completely dislocated jaw hangs in its skin bag, "Ho…?"

Thinking fast, he sees her jaw tangled in strings of skin. He grabs it and chucks it at the man but misses. As it passes him, it hits the Bunsen burner handle, filling the room with gas.

A laugh of mockery escapes the man, who turns to see how far off the mark Duncan's aim was. Clenching his fists, wanting to swing, he spies a long-necked butane lighter sitting by four more residue-crusted beakers.

The man lunges for Bri, swinging her back against the table with the gas-spewing Bunsen burner. Still holding onto her, he goes to lift her by her arms, but her left arm pulls away from her decaying body. Using her good arm, she grabs his face, ripping off any remaining flesh and muscle, revealing only bone structure dotted by two yellowing eyes.

Bri spies Duncan closing in behind the man standing in front of her. She ducks and rolls out of the way. The man turns in time to see two residue-crusted vials smash against his facial and skull bones. Broken glass rains down as Duncan tackles the man back onto the table. A crunch of breaking bones rings out as a Bunsen burner pierces the man's skull. The chemical reaction of the residue against his body sparks and lights the flowing gas. Duncan and Bri duck for cover from the burst of flame. The man, however, ignites as the flame burst catches on the unlit residue, clothes, and hair. The impaled burner holds his head and neck in place, preventing his twitching from freeing itself.

"This can't be good," Duncan says, watching the man burn.

Bri tries to speak but can't. Her frustration grows in her inability to communicate now.

Thoughts race through Duncan's head as he watches smoke rise from the man.

Before he can take any action, the smoke alarm triggers, and the sprinklers activate.

Duncan grabs Bri's good arm and leads her to the door. She stops and swings her limp arm toward the evidence they need. She starts toward the notebook, but the sounds of approaching radio noise and yelling make Duncan pull her away from their goal.

"We can come back. We know what we need," he says, relenting on succeeding.

They duck out of the room and around the corner in time to see the approaching security guards see the fire still blazing in the water. Not wanting to watch the scene play out, they head down the stairwell, hoping they run into no one else.

Scarlett and Connor descend the stairs to the second sub-level. The lights in the stairwell change from fluorescent with emergency backup lights to only emergency backups. The walls, no longer bearing paint, and the concrete holding any cave-ins at bay already show signs of cracking. Not even the stairs hold safety markings on the first and last of each floor; it seems OSHA does not know or acknowledge this part of the building. The door they stop at has the same machine-engineered quality as the last—S2.

Connor presses his ear against the door, again hoping for a clear-to-enter quiet from the other side. Again, he gets what he hopes for.

"Are you sure we need to see this?" Connor asks, hand on the handle.

"What choice do we have?" Scarlett says, sounding almost defeated. "We need to find what we came here for. I hope that Bri and Duncan are having more luck."

Connor nods, opening the door to another storage room. Emergency lights add minimal illumination, but enough that Scarlett can see rows upon rows of boxes stacked floor to ceiling.

The pair walk the rows, reading the boxes.

"They have everything," Connor observes.

"Enough to stock a hospital," Scarlett adds.

"Or ten hospitals. Why does a research lab need…" Connor counts three stacks of boxes before finishing his sentence, "…twenty-four boxes of thousand count twenty-five-milliliter vials? That's twenty-four thousand vials."

"And a lot more millimeters," Scarlett appends his statement. "Look, an entire stack of hazardous waste disposal bags. Another of … cheap cots, two stacks. More vital monitors." Her frustration grows with each reading. "Syringes. One, two, three, four stacks, ten high with seven-fifty in each box. That's I-don't-know-how-many hypodermic needles. Bed straps. A box of straight jackets?"

She wipes a tear away.

"I don't get it, Con."

"Neither do I," Connor offers.

"I mean, I really don't. What do they have planned? What do they think makes us such a threat or so important that they are going to need all this stuff? I just don't get it. I mean, I'm normal, not some freak. None of us are. And maybe if we could have gotten Al to understand that, she'd be here with us instead of buried six feet under."

"Scar, some people just don't understand," Connor tries to soothe her while he eyes boxes of various other chemicals: bleach, ammonia, naphthenic acid, palmitic acid, sodium, and chlorine tablets, to name a few.

"No, they don't. And right now, I'm one of them. What kind of threat do we pose that they need boxes upon boxes of sulfuric acid … hydrochloric acid and who knows what else sitting in a basement, completely unattended? I haven't even changed or transitioned or whatever it's called, and somehow, I'm the reason for everything that's happened? This is ludicrous. No, not ludicrous. Completely bonkers. They have no right coming after us because they don't know or are scared."

Connor decides to open some boxes to see if they are what they say they are. He starts unpacking some chemical containers, lining them up near each other.

"I mean, what kind of person can pass judgment on me? Do they know me? Do they know I exist, or are they forming some opinion of me based on what limited knowledge they have of people who share some of my characteristics and think I must be like them? Screw this. I am mad!" She finishes her tirade with a solid foot stomp.

"Are ya mad? We could do something about this." His offering catches her attention.

She turns to him, seeing the various containers and items lined up. "What ya doin', Cos'?"

A sly smile escapes him. "Do you see any … gels like used for ultrasounds or anything?"

Searching a few stacks down, she spies a box. "Will petroleum jelly work?"

"Bring me the box. I'll need cloth … some gauze or cotton wraps."

She sets down the box next to him and heads off to find the wrappings. "What are we doing?"

"One might say, 'Giving them a reason to fear us.'" Scooping out jelly from the jars, he coats the cotton wrappings in it, making numerous gel starters.

"What would someone else say?" Scarlett asks with a bit of hesitation.

"That all is fair in love and war," Connor responds, opening up a box of sulfur samples.

"I don't sense the love," she replies, returning with some cotton wraps. "These?"

Tearing open the box, Connor smiles. "Perfect. All I need is a way to start a fire. Did you happen to see anything we can use?"

"I'll look." She looks down in disbelief at this moment, heading off again.

"If you're not sensing any love, then this must be war."

"But what is the point of this? Destruction for destruction's sake?"

"No. To set them back on whatever it is they are planning."

"But we came here to find evidence of some greater scheme."

"Maybe Bri and Duncan found it. Let me ask." Connor presses the talk button on his walkie. "Hey, guys. Any luck?"

He waits a moment, but no response comes.

"Duncan? Bri? Do you copy?"

Again, no response.

"We must be too far underground. Maybe you're right," Connor relents, standing up. He heads down the aisle, scanning the contents of each box. He sees one labeled "stick lighters." Opening the box, he shoves the lighter as far into his pocket as it will go.

Scarlett turns the aisle and stops before asking, "What's next?"

Before Connor can formulate a response, the fire alarm triggers. "Up and out the way we came in. We can't get caught."

Scarlett starts to the door, stopping after seeing Connor did not follow. "What are you doing?"

"Cleaning up evidence. Don't want anyone to know we were here."

She nods and heads into the stairwell. Connor places the petroleum-covered cotton wraps on a couple of cardboard boxes, lighting them. Before heading out, he grabs a bottle of bleach and a bottle of ammonia. In the open door to the stairwell, he dumps the bottles into the room labeled "S2," drops them, and runs full speed up the stairs.

Bri and Duncan run out the back door to the building, watching a patrol car turn the corner away from them. Without stopping, both dash to the fence they snuck in through. Duncan stays a few paces behind his fiancée, ensuring her safety.

Bri stumbles across the parking lot, but her pace quickens and steadies as she gains control over her Legendary state. From behind her, Duncan sees the dislocated arm draw back into the socket as if it were being sucked into a vacuum hose. Even her skin swaying like a turkey wattle off her face tightens up. While she does not scream, he can hear her whimper in pain as the sound of rapidly replenishing bone returning to its Normal state reminds him of the one time he heard corn growing in a field.

Reaching the fence, she turns to him, only making eye contact for a split second until her eyes dart downward. "Thank you," she offers.

He looks back to ensure their safety before lifting her chin with his finger. "My love, there's never a need to thank me."

"It seems that I always have people doing that for me." Her eyes still can't meet his.

"Doing what? Protecting you?"

"Killing someone." She pulls back from him, hanging her head.

Pulling her close, he wraps his arms around her. "I will always protect the people I love."

"Even when I look the way I do sometimes?"

Her eyes rise to meet his. They stare at each other for a moment, not saying a word.

"That does not matter to me. Who you are as a person is infinitely more important than what you look like. Beauty standards have always done far more damage, preventing focus on possible accomplishments, than anything it has done to improve outward appearances."

Before Bri can respond, a hand grabs Duncan's shoulder. He spins to defend himself only to see Connor heaving up and down, about to pass out, and Scarlett on the verge of tears from being so out of breath.

"We need to leave ... now!" Connor urges.

They all escape back through the hole in the fence and make it back to the car.

After storing all the walkies and accessories in the trunk, the girls eye each other before turning to the boys. "We're hungry," Scarlett says, nodding to the 24-hour Greek diner.

Connor shrugs. "I could eat."

Duncan nods in silent affirmation. "Anything else we need to leave here?"

Brianna waves a timid hand. "Am I all good or still...?"

"...*Night of the Living Dead?* You're good," Scarlett says, giving her a once-over.

They all pat themselves down, making sure they aren't carrying any evidence on them before walking to the restaurant.

Sitting in a corner booth still covered in wet crumbs from a lackluster wipe-down, the four friends pick at fries between bites of their burgers. The burgundy leather seats and dark wood trim have seen better days, but the rest of the place looks fairly well-kept. In the center of the restaurant, near the host stand, sits a huge display case filled with a plethora of home-made Mediterranean desserts.

In front of the four sit empty soda and water glasses. High school students fill the tables and booths surrounding them. While they never frequented this place while in high school, the theater and band kids made sure the late-night business was secured. A frazzled waitress reaching the end of her dining career swings by the table with pitchers of soda and water. After refilling the drinks, she leaves the pitchers for them.

Tapping more ketchup from the bottle onto her plate, Bri scans the crowd for the hundred-something time. "Are we sure this is a good idea?"

"For the thousandth time, love, we're fine. We've been here for an hour," Duncan says, chomping into his burger.

Connor adds, whispering, "Plus, we blend right in."

Scarlett gulps all her water, releasing an exaggerated, "Ah." She refills her glass, adding, "Now that we've determined … again … that the men in black aren't coming for us, can we talk about what we found?"

Bri sighs, relinquishing her paranoia to defeat. "Fine. You first."

"Boxes. And I mean boxes. More than I could count," Scarlett dives in.

"But that's the thing," Connor interjects. "The boxes weren't anything unusual for a research lab or hospital that I know of. It was the quantity. It made me think, while we were running up the stairs, that I don't think the WHO knows what we think they know."

"What the hell does that mean?" Duncan asks, chuckling.

"I mean…" Connor trails off, gathering his thoughts. "Okay, work with me on this. The government is the entire entity, but it has parts. And some of those parts work without the parent body's knowledge or control."

"Like black ops?" Scarlett asks, dipping a fry in ketchup.

"Something like that, yeah," Connor says, pointing a fry in her direction.

Duncan raises a finger. "Like, a rogue branch of the WHO is out here doing shady stuff and passing the buck on anyone who can take the fall. That makes sense."

"Why?" Bri pipes in, sipping her soda.

"Why what?" Connor tries to get some clarification.

"Why any of it?" she amends.

"Crowd control," Duncan starts. "If you can control the masses, you can do anything you want. Sure, Normals such as myself get controlled by entertainment. Back in the day, it was a gladiator arena; nowadays, it's sports. But you guys," he says, waving a finger at them. "You guys are more of a threat. That's what the cure is being worked on for. Control."

"But who are we threatening?" Scarlett's words drip with naivety.

"No one … yet. And you might never intend to threaten anyone. That is until they want something from you that you are unwilling to part with. So, take away something now under the guise of safety and country, and when they want more, you'll be powerless to do anything about it," Duncan finishes with a fired-up gaze.

"Are you a conspiracy nut?" Scarlett blurts.

"No, and no offense taken," Duncan responds, picking up the last bite of his burger. "But I do think that while the government as a whole isn't some organization trying to make us slaves, there are those that think drone workers are better than critical thinkers. I intend to stay critical."

"Say he's right," Connor interrupts. "We still have to find what we went there for. Proof of all this conspiracy. While we know one is going on, we need proof."

"I think we found it," Bri says. "But we couldn't get it."

"Then we'll have to go back in and grab it," Connor says, as if they can stroll through the front doors.

"That might be a problem." The sheepishness of Duncan's words sits poorly with Connor.

"Do tell."

"Two reasons. One, the lab was on fire, and I don't know if what Bri found was destroyed." And with his words, the image of the security monitor overseeing the laboratory flashes in his head. "Three reasons."

"That's not better than two," Connor notes.

"That first one. The second is the lab had security cameras, and we were in there," Duncan continues.

Connor takes a deep breath, realizing the severity of the situation. "And three?"

Duncan hesitates, sharing a look with Bri before turning back to Connor.

"Come on, Duncs. How bad is three?"

"I killed a Legend," he admits.

"You killed a what?!" Scarlett shouts, garnering the attention of nearby tables.

Thinking quickly, Duncan says, "A twelve-point buck. I tell ya, it was huge."

Connor looks around, seeing the crowd's eyes still on them. "She's not a big hunter. Doesn't eat venison."

At that, the crowd returns to their meals, ignoring them for the time being.

"A Legend," Duncan brings his voice down. "He tried to kill us."

Bri chimes in, "He is, was on the Council."

"What the hell are we going to do now?" Urgency and panic coat Scarlett's words.

"I think that notebook I found is the answer," Bri deflects the question.

"Another notebook to obsess over? How can you be sure?" Connor tosses a fry into his mouth.

"It had the words *The Grey Fairy anemone* written on it."

"What do anemones have to do with this? Are you sure it said anemone?" Connor asks.

"Maybe it was something else, but it had the words *Grey Fairy* on it and that's gotta mean that's the goldmine." Bri's words carry more confidence than the last.

Bri and Duncan relay the events in the lab and their escape. Both Connor and Scarlett sit flabbergasted at the death of the councilman.

An idea comes to Scarlett, lighting up her face until a starker realization overwhelms her. "What if he was there for the same reason?"

Duncan shakes his head. "He said you were irrelevant. I don't think someone who's trying to expose corruption that could harm you would say something like that."

"Then why was he there?" Scarlett begins. "I mean, if he was working for the WHO, or at least some black ops section of it, what was he telling them, or not telling them, that all the supplies in the Midwest were needed for more research?"

"If we're irrelevant and they have a working cure, or at least something closer to what they want, then what is their endgame?" Connor ponders aloud.

"And who's running the black ops branch of the WHO?" Scarlett adds.

"And how are we going to protect my baby if he's on camera doing what he did?" Bri adds.

The weight of the night's events crushes all further thoughts in their minds. A quiet overtakes the table that seems to deafen the entire restaurant for the remainder of their meal. All they can seem to muster are fleeting glances at one another, trying to gauge everyone else's thoughts while not wanting to speak about their own.

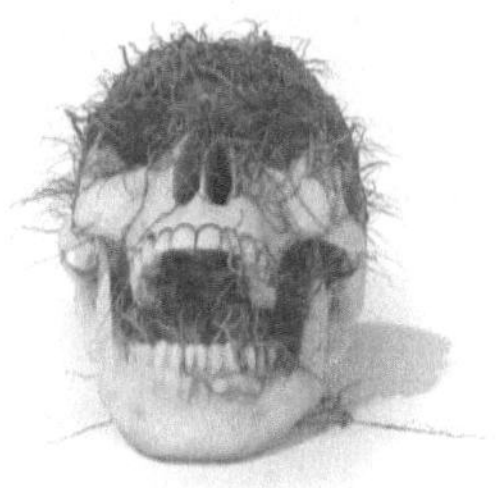

CHAPTER 10

*"It's a fine line that separates love and hate.
Be careful which side you're on."*
~E. DeSalvo~

Standing against the trunk of the Kentucky coffee *tree, green eyes watching the goings-on inside the Waldgrave home, Bishop listens to the television droning in the background of their living room, playing a news clip of a missing young man named Robert Burns. His thoughts turn inward. He thinks about how resolve can transform into obsession and how that obsession can be all-consuming. He stands against the tree, hiding from the world around him, denying that his resolve for the woman he loves has turned into an obsession. Mantras, or whatever word can be bastardized to fit him at this moment, float through Bishop's mind, deluding himself that he still stands on the right side of resolve—that he would have realized had he turned.* Young women strike the fancy of young men all the time, *he tells himself.* Her repeated rejections only present an opportunity to try again, differently.

Eleanor's repeated no after no pound his brain, pulling him further into his thoughts. Her endless rejections harden his heart. But a callous hardening can be mistaken for hardened resolve and determination to turn her no's into one final yes.

A conversation between mother and daughter, Sylvia and Brianna, rings in his ears, pulling him from his thoughts. Their casual chatting turns sour as they argue about dinner, the book club, and the subtle manipulation of a functional alcoholic toward her daughter. But, as he listens, all he can think about is why he is here, hiding against the tree, camouflaging against it with bark-like skin.

A thought floats through Bishop's voyeuristic mind. I will get what's mine. If she won't listen to me, I'll make her listen. *Looking down for a moment, while still eavesdropping on the conversation, a rolled-up parchment reflects the moonlight.* They want to hide from the world. But the world will know and once they know, there will be no hiding. No denying what should have been.

She never said, "Not in a million years." No. It was always, "Ask me again, later," *he continues deluding himself. So he argues the two sides—though the difference might be subtle, it is all the difference. The mantra,* "I am a good man," *sounds in his mind over and over again. And only well-intentioned, good men get love-struck. Good men do not misread signals and, as lonely as he might feel, he would never miss in her "ask me again later" any hidden undertones signaling for him to stay away and move on. For if he refused to see those signals, he would be a wicked man, and he is not a wicked man. So he tells himself as he stands against a Kentucky coffee tree.* No. There was never a line, *he continues thinking.* I would have seen it. I would have seen it and stopped myself before crossing it. This is not some butterflies-in-the-stomach, puppy dog love; this is love. True love that fills my soul with hope for her companionship. I have shared my hopes and bared my soul. This is why I do what I do.

The argument inside the Waldgrave residence heats up, giving the perfect opportunity to plant the parchment where one will surely find it. Scurrying to the front door, the argument inside further intensifies, moving closer to the door, leaving the voyeur less time than anticipated, causing him to drop the parchment on the porch.

Back at the tree, the voyeur listens as the fight culminates and the door opens as Brianna rushes out. Holding tightly against the tree to keep himself hidden, the voyeur watches as the mother and daughter end their feud with resentful words and Brianna's driving off. Sylvia finds the dropped parchment and reads it, sending fear rippling across her face. Heading inside, she works her way through the house; the voyeur listening as Sylvia turns on light after light, looking for any sign of an intruder or who may have left this note.

Taking advantage of the bright lights inside, the voyeur limps a few steps away from the tree, revealing he disguised himself in a female form. As she walks farther away, her bark-like skin and limping gait both smooth out. As they do, the female form shifts to a much larger male figure of lumberjack proportions with broad shoulders to match.

Thoughts flow through his head of exposing The Nation and all five Societies, as Sylvia's panicked voice fades from his ears. As silence falls over his ears, his thoughts turn toward the only woman he has ever wanted and how she has only ever refused. Time and time again, she rejected his pure and chaste offerings—said no to his advances, his amorous offerings—but she said he should keep asking, keep pursuing because the future is always uncertain. So pursue he shall.

But here, now, all he thinks about is the centuries alone with Eleanor just out of reach. He does not realize that time has the uncanny ability to warp even the purest of minds, washing it with the most abrasive scrub of all, isolation and self-delusion. As he walks farther into the night, his mantras morph from, "I'm a good man" into, "If only she chose me, everything to come could be avoided. I only need to find a way to work myself inside their circle."

Picture after picture of Scarlett and Allison spill out of the printer in Connor's bedroom. Tears stream down her face as she lies on her cousin's bed, holding a handful of pictures. On the floor, next to the bed, sits a half-empty bottle of cheap Merlot. Next to it, an empty bottle from the same vineyard lies on its side. Lost in thought, she does not hear the front door open or the laughter that follows. Her long, sorrowful face tightens, thinking about her friend. Though Scarlett stares at pictures of happier times, she only imagines the terror and pain Allison must have felt in her final moments. The agonizing weight of everything suffocating her to the point of ending it all does not sit well with Scarlett. Thinking about Allison's final moments and whether she fought against the dying light or went willingly until the bitter end fills Scarlett with newfound rage.

Pulling herself out of bed, she grabs the new pile of pictures, but before she can lie back down, the door opens as the sound of fading laughter attempts to drown the melancholy in the room.

"What up, Scar?" Connor says, turning back to Duncan, shaking his head.

"My printer's out of ink. Had to use yours." Scarlett's noncommittal reply holds undertones of her rage as she forces herself to stop crying and wipes away her tears. She plops back down on his bed as more pictures print out.

Deciding not to press the issue at hand, he changes the subject. "Well, Duncan and Bri are here. We're gonna go grab a drink," he says before eying the bedside bottles. "Looks like you already started."

"Whatever," Scarlett dismisses his notes of concern.

Duncan and Bri enter the room, sharing a laugh.

"What's taking so long?" Bri says, turning from her fiancé to see Scarlett. "Hey, Scarlett. Didn't know you were home." Looking at the pictures in Scarlett's hand, Bri bounds next to her, taking a seat. "Oooo. Gonna make an album or deck out your vanity mirror?"

Scarlett shrugs. "Haven't thought that far. Just needed something I could touch. I need to feel something."

Oblivious to Scarlett's pain, Bri says, "Well, come with us. We're, like, gonna grab some drinks."

Scarlett reaches down, grabbing the half-full bottle. She holds it up to show Bri. "I'm way ahead of you." She chugs a bit before extending it to Bri. "Have at it."

Bri tosses a glance at Duncan and Connor, nodding her head at the door. Duncan picks up on Bri's cues.

Scarlett pulls the bottle back to her, taking another swig.

"I think maybe we should order a pizza. My treat," Duncan offers.

Connor nods. "Let's go do that."

Both men exit the bedroom, leaving the two women alone.

Bri grabs the bottle from Scarlett, taking her offered drink.

"This is … not good, Scarlett. You couldn't find anything better?" Bri tries to start some semblance of conversation.

Scarlett shrugs. "It's all I had on hand." She motions to the empty bottle. "And that one. But you missed the opening act."

Bri puts her arm around Scarlett and both of them sit, passing pictures back and forth for a long while, silently reliving old memories.

As Scarlett sets the last of the pictures down, Bri breaks their silence. "I know Allison had … mixed feelings about me. I'm not sure I have the right words to make your pain go away. But I do have some news that should cheer you up."

Scarlett raises a suspecting brow. "What might that be?"

Bri hops up, grabbing Scarlett's free hand. "Come on," she says, pulling Scarlett up from the bed. "Con should hear this."

"Oh, God, are you pregnant?!" Scarlett says, with no mixed signals that she thinks that would not be a good thing.

Bri stops long enough to turn to Scarlett and say, "No." She leads Scarlett into the living room.

Duncan and Connor choose seats on opposite sides of the couch, each holding a beer bottle. "About forty-five minutes."

"What you'd get?" Bri asks.

"Half pepperoni and mushroom, half peppers, onions, and jalapeños," Duncan says, smiling.

"No apps?" Bri pouts.

"I got some garlic knots. I wouldn't deprive you of your carbs," Duncan finishes.

Bri sits on Duncan's lap while Scarlett plops down on the floor, cradling the wine bottle as if it were a small child.

"So, what's this news that you had to drag me away from my solitude for?" Impatience and petulance coat Scarlett's words.

Bri and Duncan share a look, debating if this is the best time to share news.

"Go for it, love," Duncan encourages her to share the news.

Bri turns to Connor, who waits to hear the news, and to Scarlett. Bri wonders if now might not be the best time to share, but they are all here. So, after a quick deliberation, Bri begins.

"Duncan and I have been looking at places to live," she starts.

"I think you mentioned that," Connor interjects.

Scarlett stays silent, swigging the merlot.

"We found a place! We weren't sure when we should say something, but, ya know, I think it's as good a time as any," she beams.

"Congrats. Where?" Connor asks in earnest.

Bri answers, "Morton Grove. It's this cute—"

Scarlett stands, interrupting Bri. "Great. Leave me. Leave all of this behind."

Connor stands, stepping toward his cousin. "I don't think it's like that, Scar. Morton Grove is twenty minutes from here. One town over."

Scarlett swings her bottle with her words. "That's not the point, Con-nor."

Sensing the rising tension, Duncan taps Bri to get off his lap, and he rises. "Maybe now wasn't the best time to share this."

Scarlett waves him off. "No. It's the perfect time. What time could be better? Leave town. Not far enough to abandon us altogether, but far enough that you can pretend none of this is real." With her last words, she makes giant circles with her free hand. "Pretend The Nation is all just some game, and that you didn't just off someone to save Bri."

"That's completely unfair and also not why we're moving." The joy Bri feels fades. "I just think that enough people have been killed in my house and this town the past few years that it doesn't feel like home."

Scarlett pulls her lips away from the bottle after taking an excessively exaggerated swig. "Whatever. Move. Stay. Nothing changes. You're leaving. Allison's dead. Your mom's still dead. Moving won't change any of that. All you're doing is playing make-believe. Move into some shiny, new place. Pretend everything is all hunky dory and that your bride-to-be isn't some Legend who will be around, looking like she does now, long after you've turned old, gray, and finally die. Don't get me wrong. We all die. Some just much sooner than others."

Connor grabs the bottle from Scarlett's hand, but she reaches out to take it back.

Shaking his head, Connor pulls the bottle farther out of her reach. "Oh no. You've had quite enough."

Waving in her stance, Scarlett admits her defeat. "But it's true."

"No. It's not," Duncan adds, joining the fray. "Not all of it." He takes a step to Scarlett. "How long did it take for you and Connor to have this place feel like home again? How much help did you get to make it seem like a place you want to come back to?" Scarlett thinks, but says nothing. "The fact you can't answer doesn't matter because any help is more than she had. Sure, she has me. I may have been able to convince her had it just been her mother who died there. But it was a bit more than that."

Scarlett's tears start up again. Clenching her fists, she searches for words that elude her before they can begin to form.

Connor tries to put his arm around Scarlett, but she pushes it away. He speaks, anyway. "Scar, I think they have a point. That's a pretty high body count for any house."

"Then you go live with them, too. Just leave me alone!" Scarlett shoves Connor away, almost knocking him over, before running to her room and slamming the door.

Connor, Duncan, and Bri stand in the living room, not knowing what to say. Before anyone can make a move, loud music blares from Scarlett's room, causing the three to share a look.

"I can go check on her," Bri offers.

Duncan shakes his head. "I think you and I are the last people she wants to see right now."

Connor, unsure of the moment, offers, "I'm so sorry, guys. I did not see that coming."

"Should we do something?" Bri asks, pointing to Scarlett's room.

Scrunching his face, Connor shakes his head. "Let her stew. She's having a hard time with Allison's death."

"I don't think any of us are taking it lightly, Con." Brianna's tone harbors hints of defensiveness.

"Pretty sure he meant harder, love. As in, she's taking it harder than we are. It wasn't an implication that we are fine with it." Duncan's words calm Bri's defenses.

"Well, fine," Bri huffs, unsure if she believes her man's words. "Then what about the pizza? She needs to eat."

"If she gets hungry, she can come out," Connor responds, checking his watch.

"We'll be sure to leave her a couple slices, babe," Duncan adds before Bri says something to worsen the situation.

Bri parts her lips to speak, but the doorbell sounds.

"I got the tip," Connor says, pulling out his wallet as he heads to the door.

Bri turns to Duncan, adding, "Think she'll be all right?"

Duncan nods. "In time."

Aromas of slow-cooked marinara simmering in a large pot on low flame waft through the kitchen. Eleanor stands next to it, stirring occasionally and tossing in pinches of various spices while talking with Vistrus.

Pouring himself a top-off of red wine, he sips it. "I still cannot connect the two. Inessa would never lie to me, or so I thought."

"The lies we tell to protect our families are not told with ease; they weigh us down. Burdens come in many forms. It doesn't mean she loved you any less." She dips her finger in the gravy, sampling the seasoning. She decides not to add any more, so after adjusting the heat down another pinch, she joins Vistrus at the table. "Whatever parts of her she hid from you, I am sure she did so to protect you and Allison. I never once saw an ounce of anything that couldn't be described as love between the two of you."

Swirling the wine in his glass as he does the words in his mind, Vistrus lets them both settle. "Perhaps. But I cannot piece together her investigation into the former Council and the murders over the last few years."

"Step back, Vistrus. Try to see the bigger picture. You might be missing more pieces than you think."

"That alleviates my worries little, Eleanor." He sips his wine, thinking about what he might be missing.

"We are Legend, Vistrus. What is a hundred years to a Normal can be very different to us." She pauses, gets up, and heads back to check the gravy. "Maybe this goes back further than her being sent here."

Vistrus stares at his wine, trying to divine the meaning of her words, but he cannot. Defeat in the moment leads him to finish his glass in one gulp.

"Perhaps. But if that is the truth, how far back does this go? As far back as all the secrets she has kept? Further?"

Neither attempt an answer to his posed questions. Eleanor stirs the gravy while Vistrus pours more wine.

"When someone doesn't have a definitive answer, but knows there's more, the only thing they can do is stir the pot and see what rises," Eleanor says, tasting the gravy again.

"What do you know of the Sentinels?"

"Raymond and December? Lovely people. Why?" Eleanor keeps her reply suspiciously light.

"Could they somehow have betrayed us?" His words trail as if not wanting her to answer, but that putting the words out there was enough.

"Being the wife of the Council head has afforded me much in my time in West Haven. I have a theory I am working on, but do not wish to share yet." She stirs the gravy one more time before grabbing a wine glass for herself.

"Care to share anything I might be privy to?" Vistrus hopes for her to elaborate on her words.

"Not yet. Putting things out into the universe that are ill-formed can lead to bad things. But when I feel the time has come, I will." She sits at the table and pours herself a small glass.

"Then do you have anything useful to add at this point?" His words come out a tad harsher than he intended, but he does nothing to soften their blow.

A small laugh escapes her. "Young man, everything always has something useful to add. Whether you can find the use is on you, not the one who spoke."

Vistrus nods at a point well-taken.

She continues, "Much like the all-important prophecy not being as prophetic as you thought, this might go back further than you can see."

He tilts his head, trying to understand the message hidden in her words.

"I could be wrong," she adds, undermining her contributions. "Just something to think about." Eleanor stands again and heads to a cabinet, grabbing a box of pasta. "Want to stay for dinner? This is a lot of pasta gravy for one old lady."

Vistrus stands, pushing in his chair. "I appreciate the offer but have many things to take care of. Another night."

He wonders how far back he may have to go to find what he needs. How far back will he need to dig into his late wife's affairs to see a clear picture that pieces together all these events slowly destroying their lives? While all these weigh on his mind, his curiosity pokes at whatever Eleanor might be working on that is still too ill-formed to tell even him. Ponder as he may, he has to go see someone about a dead fairy.

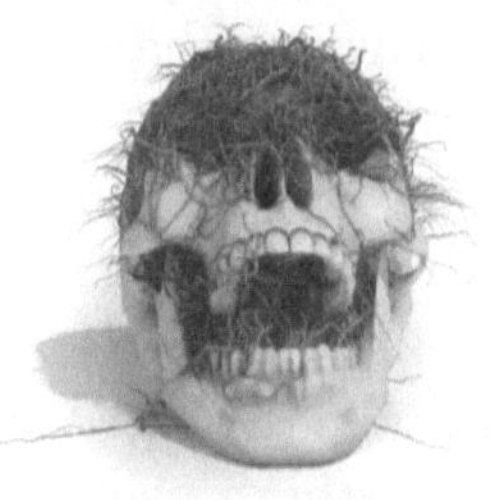

CHAPTER 11

"Never ask a question you don't
want an honest answer to."
~K. DeSalvo~

Heavy winds outside Connor's bedroom windows batter tree branches against them, stirring his sleep. He tosses and turns, but even the storm
does not wake him. With a momentary break in the
wind, Connor turns over, pulling his blanket in tighter.
The winds resume, causing Connor to stir once more
without waking.

Walking through the woods, back to where he once hid
while proving his innocence, a branch snaps behind him
as a female voice sounds from the same direction. "I want
to show you what's out there, show you what The Nation
really is. I want to show you what The Nation has been
hiding from you, from your family, from all the Councils in
every city that holds Legendaries so sacred."

A now-familiar female, whose prominent cheekbones,
pale skin, and gray eyes still haunt Connor's dreams,
emerges from the tree line.

She steps forward, continuing, "I want to show you the truth."

Measuring the weight of her words and if trust can be had, he inhales deeply before asking, "Are you In?"

Pausing at his question, she contemplates her answer. "I am in the existence between the essence."

This scene has played out in his dreams time and time again after their meeting that night. In his bed, he pulls the blanket tighter.

"And the descent falls the shadow." Connor stuns the pale woman with his reply.

Stirring herself from her thoughts, she steps a few inches closer. "Why respond with a Society that is not yours?"

In all the times he has dreamed this exact dream since it first happened, he has never replied with anything but what he first said.

"Why use a reply that I assume you know I know isn't part of the current Societies? But, more importantly, why answer a question you know I should not recognize the answer to?"

This night, the winds may be stirring something within him. The windstorm raging outside might allow him to finally find the answer that he wanted to give so long ago.

"You are not as you seem. I know you from somewhere. I can't remember where, though." These words have never been part of this dream. Something new in the dream causes him to toss in his bed.

She smiles, saying, "This is why I must show you the truth that awaits. Perhaps even The Nation does not know of every existing Society. Or maybe it was a test."

"*Of my general literary knowledge, or specifically my love for T.S. Eliot? Either way, tests are stupid.*" He pauses, studying her. "*Who are you?*"

She does not answer.

Connor watches as the pale woman's smile grows. "*Let me show you.*"

The branches beating against the window push him into a deeper slumber. Instead of his mind waking him, forgetting what came next, his sleep deepens.

"*So, show.*" *He crosses his arms in disbelief at her claim.*

"*I can't show you here. Come with me. All will make sense.*" *She waves him toward her and turns to leave, but he does not follow.*

"*I'm not following you anywhere. Tell me what you know. Maybe I'll find interest.*"

She stops, a condescending smile on her face as she turns back to face him.

"*Things are in motion. They always have been, but no matter how low the flame, a pot will eventually boil.*"

"*You can always turn off the stove.*"

She shakes her head. "*Too late for such niceties. Legends play with things they should not. 21-gram vials hold no place in the natural order of things. That is a luxury Normals do not have. Believe me.*"

"*What does this have to do with anything?*" *His impatience grows, tempting to wake him, but he resists.*

"*The Nation has become a cancer, and Legends are going to suffer.*" *Her words placate his impatience.*

"*And you think I can do something about this? I don't know enough about The Nation or the West Haven Council.*"

"*But you are smart. You know when something is out of place, even when it looks like it should belong.*" She steps into a shadow.

"*And you think I can seek out the cancer in The Nation?*" He raises a brow at the burden she implies is on him. "*Right now, the only thing that seems out of place is you.*"

"*Things change, Connor DeSalvo. You shall see.*" She steps back, farther into the shadow, but he does not follow.

"*That's it?*" he calls after her.

"*There's always more. I will see you soon.*"

A clap of thunder shakes his house as rain pours down, startling Connor awake.

"*There's more to this than I have time to explain now,*" Bishop says, watching the faces of four Council members stare at each other in disbelief. They look around the basement lit by dimming sconces, as if the answers lie in the shadows. "*The Nation wants this to remain between you four and me. If we move forward, there will be no acknowledgment by anyone that we even exist. We will be a secret within the secret society.*"

The representative of the Frye Society, the one who would eventually be killed by a Normal named Duncan Elias, raises his hand but does not wait to be called on. "*Nick does not know about this?*"

Bishop shakes his head. "*Neither does Vistrus. And if we are to move forward, it is to remain this way.*"

The Frye representative turns to the others to gauge their reactions before saying, "And what is the purpose of all of this, again?"

Bishop inhales, calming himself because he knows time runs short right now. His ears pick up the distant sound of a horse's hooves clacking against stone. "Because the truth," Bishop catches his words, giving him pause for a moment, "The Nation can't remain hidden forever, and we must do everything we can to protect not only ourselves, but we must have paved the way to protect and do what we feel we must for the ones we love. This is about seizing the opportunity to make sure things are as they should have been when all else seems lost."

He watches as they turn to each other, grumbling half-baked thoughts on this idea of deep secrecy. His ears pick up the upper-level door open and the weight of it shutting.

"I must go. There is no need to answer now. But without the utmost secrecy and dedication, this will be for naught. Think about your future."

Bishop turns and exits before anyone else has a chance to speak. The sound of descending footsteps causes Bishop to transition into a near-perfect match for Nick DeSalvo. While he would rather not run into anyone, he knows he cannot run into the new member, Vistrus, or the man he replicates. Spotting a pile of wooden crates, he sneaks behind them and ducks, hoping that whoever walks past does not pick up his heartbeat.

A few moments later, a younger Vistrus Petrovsky steps through the stone archway leading from the stairs to the basement. Without hesitation, either from not hearing the heartbeat or thinking it unimportant, he heads toward the other members.

Plastic tarps still cover the broken windows in the Waldgrave residence, the only remnant from the latest addition to the body count under this roof.

Duncan nods his head at the tarps. "Any leaks with last night's storm?"

Bri shakes her head. "Sealed tight. Not one drop."

Brianna and Duncan sit on her couch, cuddled into each other while watching reruns of *How I Met Your Mother*. She snuggles farther into him as the character of Lily exits a taxi.

"This part always gets me," she says, gripping Duncan's arm.

"Because of your mom?" Duncan goes for the obvious answer.

She shakes her head, turning to him. "Marshall, well, the actor, didn't know what this scene was about. He was told the news was something good, and they hit him with that. His reaction is a hundred percent real."

Duncan pulls Bri into him tighter, as if trying to become one. "I never realized you gave things that much thought."

Bri turns to him with an upturned eyebrow and scrunched lips, letting him know the sting of his words.

"That's not what I meant. I know you aren't the image you portrayed when we met. It was just that, an image. But this is pretty deep." He hopes his recovery sticks the landing.

Letting out a huff, she shrugs. "Doesn't matter how shallow someone is or pretends to be. One day, life will throw something at you that stops you and changes you somehow some way."

"Sorry it had to be something so … life-changing." Duncan's soft words are all the apology she needs.

Turning back to the show, she adds, "Me too." She lets the subject drop for a moment, but the wheels keep turning in her mind. She squirms in her seat, unable to find comfort.

"Something still eating you, babe?"

"I think … if I had to really pinpoint the moment that defined me, it happened long ago," she says, calming her squirming.

"Where is this coming from?" Duncan turns her toward him. "I didn't mean for my words to come out the way they did."

Shaking her head again, she waves him off. "No. It's not you, your words. It's … when I was younger, like middle schoolish … I heard Mr. DeSalvo tell my mom something, and it stuck with me." She pauses for a response, but Duncan waits for her to continue. "Has anything like that ever happened to you?"

Thinking about her words, he returns to the moment, saying, "I remember when I was around five or six, a water pipe burst one winter. Our basement flooded and my mom, dad, and the neighbors from across the street who came to help were all sorting through what they pulled up to see if it could be saved. I don't know why it stuck with me, but there was this old painting of an aging, decrepit rockstar sitting on a barstool playing an acoustic guitar. While I was too young to understand the meaning of it, the vision stuck with me. It made me feel sad, though I never could figure out why."

She stares at him, seeing a side of him that usually stays hidden. She leans in and plants a quick but passionate kiss on him.

"I'll say this, love. A person doesn't have to have only one defining moment in their life; that's the beauty of it all. We can constantly redefine who we are. Whatever you overheard, it doesn't have to be the motivation behind every action you make."

A ringing doorbell interrupts their perfect moment.

"Expecting someone?" Duncan asks.

Standing up, she responds with, "Was about to ask you the same."

"Any idea who it could be?" he says, leaning forward, trying to see through the closed door.

"Let's find out." Bri peeks through the blinds covering the window to see Vistrus standing there with a look on his face that could only mean business. She looks past him, but no one else can be seen.

"I can hear you, Ms. Waldgrave." Vistrus's stern voice sounds through the door.

Opening it up without further delay, she smiles, welcoming him inside.

"Is everything okay, Mr. P ... trovsky?" she finishes his name after he shoots her a displeased glance.

Stepping past the threshold, he stops and wipes his shoes on the front door mat. "Is Mr. Elias here?"

"In here." Duncan's voice rings out from the living room.

Vistrus squats down to take off his shoes, but Bri quickly stops him. "Thanks, but no need." She waves him into the living room.

Vistrus looks around for a place to sit, finding a recliner positioned in a way that faces both the couch and television. Sensing the seriousness of Vistrus's visit, Duncan straightens himself in his seat. Bri sits with space between her and her fiancé.

The silence while the two wait for Vistrus to speak suffocates them. They both know the reason for his visit, and it seems no one wants to breach the inevitable subject. Taking a few deep breaths while finalizing his thoughts, Vistrus finally speaks.

"Can you explain what happened?" Vistrus cuts straight to the point.

Duncan, not wanting to revisit the event, plants a half-smile on his face, saying, "Well, the doorbell rang, and we answered it."

Sucking in some air, Vistrus slaps his thigh. "This is not a matter to be taken with such nonchalance or levity."

"What do you want me to say?" Duncan's tone does a sharp turn to serious.

Squinting his eyes, trying to find the truth in Duncan's, Vistrus responds, "You killed a man."

Duncan turns to Bri, knowing why he did what he did, but unsure if the truth will set him free. He takes his time, weighing how he wants to respond, hoping Vistrus's patience will match his indecision. Finally, his words come to him.

"He was a Legend," Duncan says.

Vistrus nods. "He was."

"How did you find out?" Duncan asks, again turning to his beloved with a rueful expression.

"Did you think a place such as that would not have security cameras?"

Vistrus's words hold more empathy than accusation. An unexpected niceness at this moment.

"We needed something." Duncan leaves his reply short and to the point.

"Did you find it?" Vistrus avoids the original question for now.

"Possibly. I think." The defeat coating his words inspires no confidence in Vistrus.

"What happened?"

"She found something…"

"…a notebook." Brianna speaks for the first time since she sat back down.

"A notebook?" Vistrus questions her words.

She nods. "It was labeled: *The Grey Fairy Anomaly.* I figured that was it."

"What is it?" Vistrus prods.

"Whatever it was that—"

Sensing Duncan might say something he does not want to hear, Vistrus holds up a hand. "Stop talking." Duncan stops and tightens up. Bri sinks into her seat, trying to hide. "From what I was told, the cameras were blurry until you separated from whoever you went in with. Do not tell me who, even if I know. The blur stayed with the others, and that keeps them safe."

Relaxing from his sudden interruption, Duncan continues, "We went in to find something. All we knew was that we would know it when we saw it. She felt like that was it. I believe her."

Nodding at his words, a smile almost forms on Vistrus. "Then what?"

"He came. He saw us. He attacked. I had to do something."

"And something you did. But you killed a Council member, Mr. Elias."

He sees Brianna shaking her head.

"Do you have something to add, Ms. Waldgrave?"

Pursing her lips while thinking, she says, "He wasn't the same man who helped me when I lost my eye. He was really mean."

"Mean is not a reason to kill," Vistrus scolds. "I have been tasked to deal with this situation. I need to know how."

"How?" Bri blurts out. "We defended ourselves…"

"…while trespassing…" Vistrus interjects.

"…because he would have killed us," Bri finishes.

"If an intruder enters your home and you kill them, should you be charged with their death, even if they intended to harm you?" Vistrus poses the hypothetical.

"Never ask a question you aren't prepared to hear the answer to," Bri replies.

Her words take him aback. A familiarity in them pulls him from the urgency of the moment.

"Where did you hear that?" Vistrus asks, leaning forward in his seat.

She shrugs. "A long time ago. It stuck with me."

Calming his tone, he continues, "What I need to know about is did you get it?"

"What about the tapes?" Duncan interjects.

"They said the cameras went dark," he admits.

Duncan looks at Bri, trying to invoke an answer from her with his stare. Finally, she nods in Vistrus's direction.

Duncan shakes his head.

"The fire was getting really big," Bri admits. "Like really big."

Duncan stands, unable to sit any longer, and paces the room. "So what now? Are you gonna turn me in to the cops? Am I gonna be some sorta scapegoat for the WHO? Some guy made out to be a crazy, conspiracy nut to keep the truth from getting out? 'Cause I wouldn't tell anyone. I love her too much to say nothing."

"Sit, young man," Vistrus commands. Duncan shoots back into his seat. "No one is turning you in. I know the lengths one will go to protect those he loves. As said, I have to deal with this. I need a story to tell. And while some of this is beyond you as a Normal, I think you already know the basics."

Relief floods both Duncan and Bri, feeling safe for the first time since he entered her home.

"So now what?" Bri asks. "Do we just lie low?"

Vistrus shakes his head. "No, and yes. I need you, Mr. Elias, to lie low until you know it is safe to show yourself. Keep an eye on the news, and you will know. But while you lie, figure out how you are going to complete your mission."

Duncan, still bathing in relief, asks, "What are you going to do?"

Standing up from his chair, Vistrus responds, "Clean up this mess. Another one is always around the corner."

The gentle breeze rustles through the streets, playing with the trees, a comforting gesture after last night's vicious storm. Eleanor looks to the sky for answers to everything unraveling around her, but finds no cosmic solace today. Even the framed portrait in her hands offers little comfort. Painting a smile on her face, she enters Connor and Scarlett's home.

"Hello?! Scarlett, are you home?" Eleanor looks around at the empty home, seeing no one. "I did something I want you to see." She steps inside and wanders the living room and kitchen, finding no one. "Scarlett? We should talk, dearie."

A sneeze from Scarlett's room betrays her location, and a few steps later, Eleanor knocks on her door.

"Yeah," Scarlett replies with all the lethargy of a young teen recounting the mediocrity of an uneventful school day to a parent they'd rather not be conversing with.

"May I come in?" Eleanor's calm tone gives Scarlett wiggle room to avoid conversation if she desires.

In a tone matching the nonplussed previous reply, Scarlett utters, "Whatever."

Opening the door, Eleanor finds Scarlett lying on her bed, staring at pictures of her and Allison.

Easing toward her grandchild, Eleanor peeks at the pictures sprawled out on Scarlett's bed. "Doldrums got you?"

Scarlett turns her attention to her grandmother, tossing the three pictures she holds onto the bed.

"Doldrums, huh? That's an interesting spin on it." She notices the framed portrait Eleanor holds but says nothing of it. "Just trying to figure out what I missed, what we all missed. Allison promised me she wouldn't ever do it."

Eleanor points to the bed, motioning a desire to sit. Scarlett waves her permission, sitting up to make room for Eleanor, who, resting the frame against the bed, sits next to Scarlett and places an arm around her. Scarlett looks to her elder for answers with silent pleas.

"We all make promises we intend to keep. Life can sometimes make us do things we never thought we would," Eleanor starts. "We all want wine and roses, but sometimes we get vinegar and thorns."

"That's it? The wine that was my life has soured to vinegar. Those are your soothing words?" Scarlett turns her gaze to her feet, comparing their size to her family matron's.

"Oh, dear. No. But even so, vinegar is great in so many foods."

Scarlett pauses her foot comparison to turn back to Eleanor.

Continuing, Eleanor says, "But food metaphors aside, my visit is to give you this. Last time I tried, things happened." She looks down at the framed portrait resting in her lap.

Scarlett turns her attention to the piece. "This again?" Scarlett waves off the portrait. "I think your age is finally catching up with you."

Eleanor lets out a woeful huff. "If only things were so. Scarlett, things may get worse before they get better. In life, that's always the way things can go."

"That's a joyful outlook," Scarlett jokes.

"It's not meant to be anything but truthful. Just because it can get worse doesn't mean it will. Life works out the way it works out. But with this," she gestures to the picture, "accept it as a gift."

"A drawing of myself? A gift?" Scarlett's words tell Eleanor that understanding is not a friend of hers right now.

"Just accept it. Put it up on a wall and if anyone asks—and I mean anyone, Connor, that Bri girl, or her friend—you tell them I had it drawn up for you as a surprise."

Scarlett, still missing the point, catches the urgency in her grandmother's words. "Had it drawn up? Like commissioned?"

Eleanor nods. "Whatever you remember from when I first showed this to you, forget it all. It was a commissioned piece."

The weight of her words sinks into Scarlett, who nods. "Understood. You came by to give me a gift."

"And to see how you are holding up. But I didn't have to ask any questions to get my answer." Eleanor pauses to see if Scarlett wants to say something, but she remains silent. "If you want to talk about it, I'm here. I can understand what you are going through."

Scarlett opens her mouth. The expression carved into her face screams it will be sarcastic, but no words usher forth. Instead, her expression melts back into the sadness painted on it from earlier. "I am sure you do."

Both ladies sit in a comforting silence for a few moments while Scarlett stares at the framed portrait before her. She studies the lines drawn into her forehead and the growing crow's feet around her eyes. The almost perfect placement of each freckle makes her wonder how someone drew this so many centuries ago and why the picture itself is so important.

Scarlett turns to her grandmother, who also studies the drawing, looking for hidden answers that are not there.

"Grams, where did this come from?"

Eleanor weighs the honest answer versus the unnecessary burden it will place upon Scarlett. Pulling her eyebrows together, thinking of how she will word her response, she kisses Scarlett on the forehead. She cannot bear the thought of telling her, with as much as she is going through, that Vistrus gave this to her without relinquishing the full details of how he came upon it. However, the details she knows would lend no comfort to a young adult dealing with fresh death.

"The years may be catching up to me, after all. It was a gift, but from whom I can't remember."

Scarlett senses Eleanor withholds some information from her and while she can't understand why, she can feel that pressing now will not yield anything fruitful. So, she lets the answer rest where it falls.

Eleanor, on the other hand, knows that the truth can only stay hidden for so long, but until she can fully understand the significance of it, she will try to keep it hidden as long as she can.

Vistrus stands, and a spotlight shines down on him, drowning out the faces of those seated at the table ten feet in front of him. Silence fills the room, save for the breathing of the High Council members and the low hum of electricity in the background. No distant sounds of cars whizzing by, elevator doors buzzing open and closed, nor idle conversations play out. Another Council means another secret room, but unlike the one currently used in West Haven, this room's secrets hide not in plain sight but as far from society as these members deem necessary. The spotlight reminds Vistrus that even a secret society has secrets of its own to protect.

"Duncan acted in self-defense," Vistrus says, keeping his replies short.

The shadowed faces turn to each other, whispering too low for even Vistrus's ears to pick up. After a moment of quiet conversation, the middle face speaks. A thick Russian accent coats his words. "You've said as much. What we do not understand is why he trespassed in a government building and with a member of The Nation, no less."

Projecting a confidence that only comes with the centuries behind them, Vistrus says, "I cannot tell you why at this time."

A man with an Eastern Russian accent speaks. "But you do know why, don't you?"

"Yes."

A chuckle escapes the Eastern Russian. "But you will not tell us?"

"No." Vistrus keeps his replies short. He does not know who he can trust, and one extra word might reveal too much.

The man in the middle turns to the Eastern Russian, holding up a soft hand to silence him before turning to Vistrus, saying, "You want us to protect a Normal and throw one of our own to the side as if his life matters less than this ... Duncan's."

"Yes. Normal or Legend, life holds value," Vistrus says, again keeping his words succinct.

"But in this case, a Normal's life seems to be worth more than a Legend."

Vistrus squints, struggling to see anything other than silhouettes under the spotlight. His eyes can't seem to adjust, leaving every council member cloaked in shadows.

Relenting to his lack of sight, Vistrus continues, "No. But Duncan's actions hold higher importance to the continuance of The Nation than one of the West Haven Council members did."

A female, seated on the far left, clears her throat. "You have traveled many miles to give us so little." Her accent brings back childhood memories of elderly Russian women selling bread out of carts. "How do you expect us to understand your side, let alone grant your request if you refuse to give us further details as to why we should?"

The Eastern Russian interjects, "Yeah. What importance lies in the murder of a Council member when a Normal knows about The Nation?"

Vistrus lets the silence stew for a moment, trying to listen to heartbeats, teeth grinding, or any other tell that may give him a clue as to who he can trust or which way they might be leaning. But Legends as experienced in life as they do not easily give away their secrets.

Running his hand through his hair, Vistrus speaks. "I cannot tell you now. But I will say this. Give me a week and think about what I ask. When I return, ask me anything and I shall answer. Before I go, however, know this: Duncan asked a Legend to marry him, knowing she will long outlive him. He guards our secrets and our society as if he were one of us. These things he does, he does not do only out of love for his betrothed but because he feels it is the morally just thing to do. When was the last time the mighty Nation acted thus?"

They meet his words with immediate, muddled protests as they all speak simultaneously, drowning out the points they want to make. The middle member stands, holds up both hands, and shouts, "Silence!" Other members quiet down like school kids afraid of detention, less they talk. Sitting back down, the middle member leans forward in his chair. "Your point, while ... pointed and offensive ... has merit. We shall discuss this in one week. Safe travels until then."

The spotlight dims and lights on the ground lead the way to Vistrus's exit. Before he passes the threshold out of the chamber, he turns to the Council table, only to find it empty. He smirks, knowing the pomp and circumstance they stand on dies a slow death.

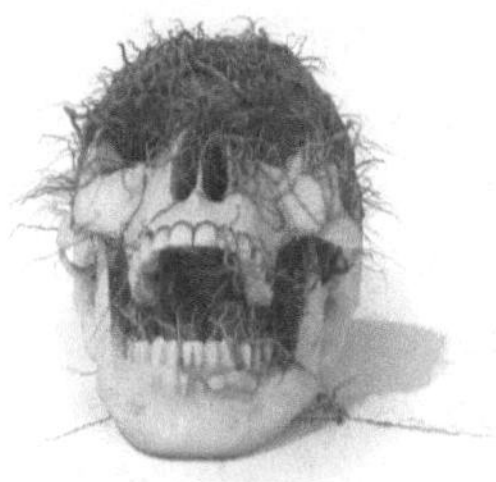

CHAPTER 12

"The answers you find might not
be the ones you want."
~C. DeSalvo~

Credits begin rolling on *Some Kind of Wonderful,* prompting Duncan to grab the remote off the bedside table and scroll for another movie to watch.

"I can't believe you've never seen that movie," Duncan says, still shocked at Bri's cinematic short-comings. He pulls the sheet down, rubbing his hand over a bite mark on his bare chest, massaging it. "Arguably the best John Hughes movie out there."

"Well, I have now. I enjoyed it for sure. You think I could play the drums?" Bri asks, rolling over to cuddle with Duncan. She replaces his hand with hers, rubbing his chest. "Does it hurt, dear?"

"No, to the drums. I think you'd have fun for a week, then wonder why you spent a grand on them. Yes, it does. You bit me pretty hard." He lets out a chuckle, rolling on top of her before planting a passionate kiss.

"Are you ready for another round?" Bri smirks, looking down between the sheets.

Duncan shakes his head. "As fun as the never-ending Netflix and chill sessions are, aren't you getting a bit cooped up?"

Bri's face looses the excitement it held thinking more fun was on the horizon. Her lips squish to the side, relenting to the fact that she, too, would like to do something outside the bedroom with her fiancé.

"Are you getting bored of having sex with me? We aren't even married yet." Her words start as a joke, but something in them makes her start to think that perhaps she isn't joking as much as she wanted to.

Duncan sits up against the headboard, while Bri resists running her hands across his chest again. She spies the bite mark that is a bit too deep for her liking.

"Sorry, I bit you so hard."

He chuckles, shaking his head. "It's all good. The moment felt right. But that's just the moment."

Now her previous comment digs deeper into her. Before she can stop herself, she begins reading deeper into his words than she knows she should.

Duncan looks at her and grabs her hands. He pulls her to him but stops her short of a kiss. Staring into her eyes, he says, "Love, relationships, marriage … whatever isn't about 24/7 sexy time. It's about being with each other, even if we're doing nothing or different things. To me, it's about having someone to share silence with, in a comfortable way. Not always feeling the need to talk or do something or do … each other. We've been at it since Mr. P told me to stay indoors. Don't get me wrong; I love you and the super sexy times, but I can only handle so much. And, honestly, I am cooped up beyond anything I've ever felt before. I don't know how much longer I can stay in the same eighteen-hundred square feet."

All of Bri's worries melt away. The assurance he gives her, even when he doesn't know the self-doubt racing through her mind, assures her more than anything that she made the right choice apologizing to old friends and mending those bridges because without having done so, she wouldn't be with Duncan Elias.

She leans in and plants a quick kiss on his lips before hopping out of bed. Gathering her clothes they threw around the bedroom, she pieces together enough to begin getting dressed. "I'm in The Nation or whatever. I think if you leave with me and we play it cool, nothing bad will happen."

A smirk creeps across Duncan's face. "This can't be a good idea. I mean, I'm not afraid of getting yelled at, but he had his reasons for me going MIA."

"A little snack at Manic Mondays won't end the world, and I definitely don't think that will be the event that outs all us Legends to the Normal world," Bri jokes, zipping up her jeans.

Duncan thinks about her words for a moment. "At a place like that, I think we could say anything we wanted to someone. As long as we are drinking at the bar, whatever we say will be brushed aside as the rambling of two drunk kids."

"Unless I go all *Zombieland* on everyone." She cocks a shoulder high and stumbles a few steps, mimicking a Ramero-style zombie.

Duncan points at her antics. "That would definitely land us in boiling water with The Nation."

Bri searches her room for her wallet. "Well, I'm going." She continues looking around but can't find it. "Once I find my wallet, that is."

"Front room table."

Bri smacks her palm against her forehead. "Duh. Totally forgot. After I grab my wallet, all I'll need are my keys. You sure you don't want to come with?"

"I don't think I should," Duncan says, looking around the room for his shirt, pants, boxer shorts, and socks.

"Fine. I'll bring you home some cold fries. But no complaints that microwaved fries suck." Bri exits the bedroom to grab her wallet and keys.

"And that onion thingy. That reheats okay," Duncan yells as he starts putting his clothes back on.

He hears her drop her shoes at her feet to put them on.

"Onion blossom and cold cheese fries, coming right up!" Bri finishes tying her shoes and opens the door. "Last chance, love! You sure you don't wanna play rock star and go out all hoodie and sunglasses?!"

She hesitates for a moment before opening the door, but there's no answer either way from Duncan. She opens the door and the screen door, standing between the two. "Have fun, babe! See you in a bit!"

Before she can close the storm door, Duncan calls out, "Wait! Let me get a hoodie on."

"Sunglasses, too!" Bri shouts back in a reminder.

"In the car," he says, turning down the hallway and pulling a hoodie over his head.

Bri smiles, sure that this little outing is just what they need.

Holding onto a letterman jacket while walking up the driveway to the Petrovsky residence, the silhouette of a large man shrinks into that of a young man. Bishop swings the letterman onto his Connor-self. The last name across the back of the letterman reads DeSalvo. His knock on the door is answered a short time later.

Puffing away on his cigar, Vistrus states an obvious observation. "Mr. DeSalvo, where is everyone?"

Standing in the doorway, jacket hanging open and doing its best to conceal the plain gray T-shirt that is far from the Coma Noir shirt the real Connor wore a short time ago, he searches for words to keep this encounter heading where he wants it to. "We need to talk…" Simple words that steer any encounter in the speaker's course.

Noting Connor's pale tone, he puffs his cigar. "You do not look well." Blowing out the smoke, he peeks outside from where he stands. "What is going on? Where is my daughter?"

Eyes darting to the ceiling in search of a simple reply that will not raise any alarms, Connor says, "She's still out with everyone else. I just had to talk to you."

Dissatisfaction with Connor's answer presses between Vistrus's tightened lips. He, however, does not want to press matters that might be brought up in the following moments, so he lets it rest. "Then let us talk. Come sit."

Puffing his cigar as they move to the living room, Vistrus turns off the television before reaching into the humidor for a cigar to offer Connor. "You look very ill, unlike earlier this evening, but I am not your father." He threw on those last words to gauge Connor's reaction.

Unsure how the real Connor would properly react, Bishop opts for one that discredits Ken DeSalvo from the equation. "Must have been something I ate. I'll be fine." Before reaching for the cigar, he adds, "I am my own man."

Vistrus extends a match to light Connor's cigar. They both puff a few times before the Connor impostor begins. "You know your daughter's interests are lying on more than just … me?"

He watches as Vistrus raises an eyebrow, possibly pondering Connor's endgame. So, the impostor waits, controlling his breathing and keeping calm, knowing Vistrus can hear his beating heart.

"Trouble in your heart?" Vistrus chooses careful words.

Glancing toward the ceiling once more to bait the words that will fish out what Vistrus knows, he says, "It's everything that's happened." Vague words for an open-ended response. Now Vistrus must respond with some knowledge of the topic at hand. He'll have to show a card, so to speak, giving Bishop something to play off of or against.

"We had this talk, Mr. DeSalvo. She killed another human. You cannot be that forgetful."

The impostor notes the obvious suspicion painted on Vistrus's face. Staying the course will be a delicate nature. Again, he chooses vague words to remain steering the wheel. "Not that, no. I mean with Brianna."

"You better not have betrayed my daughter." Pointed words provide the evidence Bishop needs to sow however much discontent he can.

If he can play it right, broad strokes may also give him the justification he has been seeking for centuries. "Not I, no. But it seems Allison's feelings betray me. Not the other way around."

This man watches Vistrus chew his words, trying to put a finger on their flavor. Bishop can't help but notice that while Vistrus thinks, he stares at his face. He is not looking him in the eye or even searching for some well-guarded expression. It is as if he is looking at his skin, studying its complexion.

Finally relenting whatever thoughts are running through his mind, Vistrus puffs his cigar. *"She has feelings for Bri..."* Vistrus exhales, watching the smoke rise above Connor, *"...as she does for you."*

Double tapping the side of his nose, as if some giant got-ya has been revealed, the false Connor adds, *"There's the rub."* But what rub exactly is it? For a moment, this man pretending to be someone else thinks that is all he ever does—pretends. And for what? For an endgame he has held onto since the day he was told to walk away. His heart aches, and it aches for her. Why drag college-age kids into this? It seemed like the right thing to do. It seemed like a means to an end. For a moment, he forgets the means. Freezing in place, he hopes to remember where it all started.

But a *"Hmmm"* from Vistrus brings his wandering mind back to the moment.

Knowing he must respond, he plays to the common knowledge about Vistrus. *"For a man of choice words, that seems a little too choice."* Puffing his cigar, letting the *silence thicken a moment, he exhales and adds, "Grandma … Eleanor … told me of someone she once loved." Watching Vistrus raise a brow in interest, he continues, "She said that perhaps in another life, they could have been together."*

"What does that have to do with my daughter?" Unimpressed by Connor's words, Vistrus keeps his words low and quiet.

The means to his end start returning to his mind. "We only have but one life, as long as it might be, but what if it were to change?"

Hopes that Vistrus will give him the justification he has been eternally seeking get dashed away in a quick response. "Where are you going with this? I love my daughter. It should not matter who she loves."

But a thought comes to his mind that may give him the justification he seeks. "Exactly. We can't let obstacles stand in the way, then. That would be wrong." Leading words to lead Vistrus to give this impostor his green light.

"That is a decision she has to make. The obstacles are hers to overcome."

Bishop sees his justification pulling further out of reach, so he says the first thing that comes to mind. "We could remove them. Make the path for what should have been easier."

Vistrus stirs, tossing over to the other side. Murmurs break the silence in sleep until his dream pulls him back in.

Satisfied with his remark, he leans forward in his seat. For what reply could be said that argues against protecting a child at all costs?

"A parent's job is not to remove the obstacles in their children's way but to teach them how to navigate and overcome.

Simply removing the obstacles teaches them nothing about how to live life. Only that others will do the work for you."

Of all the responses he could have given, Vistrus had to form the one that was hardest to refute. But refute Bishop must try. Leaning closer as Connor, he continues, "It doesn't have to be like that."

Calming his frustration, Vistrus says through partially gritted teeth, "We cannot simply go through life leaving young adults in the innocence and naivety of childhood. They must learn that the universe does not care. Knowing this gives us purpose and teaches them to be critically thinking adults."

"But she should end up with…" Catching the slip-up in his words, Connor calms himself and his heartbeat, hoping Vistrus's suspicion has not risen. "…me."

Kicking the blankets off him, Vistrus tosses and turns. His murmurs turn into pleas. "No. No. Not right." Still, he cannot wake.

The impostor sees Vistrus calm himself amidst his own cooldown. "Again, Mr. DeSalvo, that is a choice she will have to make. We cannot choose it for her. All we can do is support her decision and accept whatever she chooses. That is something you should have known by now."

Vistrus pauses, and the impostor knows he must speak but is not sure how to respond to such a guided remark. Opting for stoic silence, he hopes Vistrus will speak.

Picking back up, Vistrus adds, "If you want to be on the Council, you have much to learn about life. Life, as in politics, is helping people understand the weight of their actions."

All hope for justifying Bishop's means has abandoned him. He sits, stewing in his loss, feeling old anger roil up around him. "But," he snaps.

Before he can say another syllable, Vistrus cuts in, "But they are their actions to make. Only when their actions hurt others can we intercede. If they choose to hurt themselves, that is on them."

This impostor sits, unsure what else can be said, or if anything can be said. But the lack of response does not seem to sit well with Vistrus, who pipes back up. "Do not make me think I was wrong for presenting you the path to the Council."

"You are not wrong. Nor am I. True love will be unhindered. Whatever needs to be done will be. Imagine how different life would have been for Eleanor if she had ended up with that other man. It shouldn't be different for Allison."

His pleas turn to incomprehensible yells—garbled words of a sleeping mind. Tossing farther in his bed, he rolls close enough to the side that one arm and leg hang off the bed. Still, he does not wake.

The dream replays the moments over and over that his mind cannot move on from. His shouts persist, muffled by the pillow he buries his face in. More and more, his mind tries to snap him from this dreaming state until he rolls back over to the middle and his eyes shoot open.

Patience worn through, Vistrus stands and snuffs out his cigar. "You should leave. I have much to think about, the least of which is my daughter's love life. That is hers and hers alone. What I do need is to take time and reconsider if you have a future with the Council. You may be in The Nation, that is a birthright, but a seat on the Council must be earned. Perhaps I gave you too much credit for being Ken's son."

A thought floats through his mind; a way to make his end—of holding a recognized seat on the Council, even if it is disguised as another. Not wanting to add further fuel to the fire, he follows Vistrus's lead and takes his leave. He exits, hoping the real Connor can mend any fences that this one has fallen.

Vistrus lies in bed, the memory of the dream still replaying itself while he sits in the darkness of late night. He turns to his clock to check the time: 3:50. Nothing unusual about that, but a sense of something akin to déjà vu hits him, stealing his sleep from returning while he searches the recesses of his mind for why it lingers. After a few moments, the sensation fades, but the memory of the dream has not, and the disturbing view laid out in his mind keeps him from sleep.

Pouring a glass of single malt, Egyptian whiskey, neat, he pontificates on this newfound ability to manipulate memories and change the events that occurred when they first formed. *Perhaps that is how they happened? Could I be wrong? My memory has never betrayed me before. Why would it do so now?*

He tightens the belt on his robe before sitting in his riveted, red, crushed velvet chair. Reaching over, he grabs his dulcimer from its stand and begins strumming.

Chords ring out in a melancholy rhythm; to him, it is a mindless task to occupy his hands while he thinks. The sad tones carrying through the Petrovsky residence at this late hour could be a simple coincidence, but something nags at the furthest recesses of his mind that there is more at play here. While he strums away, thinking about the dream, he keeps searching in the back burner of his mind for the meaning of his melancholy waltz.

But the dream is why he sits, drinking whiskey, and strumming away. Thinking about the differences between the dream and the memory from that encounter he holds while awake.

What does it mean?

Having time to wake up and adjust to the sudden shift from sleep, he knows what happened and that his dream changed the events. The meaning of it eludes him.

Could it be a sign? If so, from who and why?

Vistrus sits, nursing his Egyptian whiskey while strumming away, mulling over the variances his dream presented from the reality he knows. And while he sits strumming until dawn, the meaning of the restless event stays as elusive as when he first woke. The only salvageable remnants from the night hint that the differences came as some form of message. Whether his mind couriered the message or someone else did remain an irksome mystery.

Scarlett stops and looks up at the lichgate sign that reads, as it always has, West Haven Cemetery. This time, though, she steps over the threshold to visit neither her parents nor Jack. This visit is dedicated to Allison. Her eyes tighten, pulling up the muscles around her cheekbones. Not in some moment while a smile crosses her face, but more in disbelief that a sunny, cloudless sky sets the backdrop to her visit here. The whistle of passing cars provides only an underscore to the main soundtrack of distant laughter and playing children. She turns to the rows of townhouses across the street behind her, searching for the source of the innocent laughter, if only to relive such naivety for a moment, but she finds no romping children. No adults sit in lawn chairs drinking beer and White Claw as their children splash in their backyard plastic pools. She sees nothing but empty lawns past the cars buzzing by.

Turning back to the cemetery gates, Scarlett thinks that her mind betrays her. But, delude herself as she may, the distant sound of laughter stays unwavering. She crosses the threshold only to realize Mr. Petrovsky never told them where he buried his only daughter.

For a moment, she thinks of walking to Allison's house to ask her father where he interned her, but the thought of seeing her house without her sends tremors through Scarlett. Even the thought of having to speak with her father makes her a little nauseous. Her only savior is the off-white brick building in the distance—the columbarium or the main facility for the cemetery.

The sight of Jack's grave, as she treks to the columbarium, causes her legs to tense and steps to tighten. Her willpower seeps out, and a growing desire to lie on his grave weighs down on her. Struggle as she may, she knows she must prove everyone wrong. She must show them all that Allison is in the Waiting and will one day come back to them.

The tinted window on the door dims the interior enough that she thinks they might be closed. A speaker built into the wall next to the door sits silent, with no button to alert anyone who might be inside. The loneliness of her surroundings stirs up horror movie scenarios about opening the door. She reaches out, trying to ignore the paranoia cursing her thoughts, but Scarlett cannot bring herself to grab the handle. Perhaps a monster waits on the other side of the door, or maybe finding Allison's grave will cement the reality of it, and coping with yet another loss is something beyond her abilities.

But before she has a chance to walk away, the speaker next to her blares to life. "May I help you?"

Scarlett jumps back, startled by the speaker's crackling and the man's piercing words. She hears laughter from within, though not through the speaker.

"No need to laugh," she mutters to herself.

"I'm not laughing at you, little miss. Just a little humorous is all. You can come in, ya know."

Stepping inside, small interment chambers holding the ashes of the deceased fill the back wall. A voice to her right grabs her attention.

"First time here, huh?"

Scarlett turns to see a groundskeeper she does not recognize.

Looking back at the numerous slots and contemplating the lives they could have lived, she utters, "In here … no. Just come to visit my parents."

"And what brings you here today?"

She turns back to the man, finally studying his lithe, malnourished appearance. He turns from an outdated security monitor to her. As he turns in a chair that should have been replaced over a decade ago, a high-pitched squeak pierces the air with such force that Scarlett thinks the dead may rise.

He adds before she can recover from the painful assault on her ears, "Forget where they are buried?"

Shaking her head, Scarlett says, "You don't forget a thing like that." She glances back at the wall as if the ashes might reanimate themselves.

Inside this building, her ears hear no laughter or whizzing of cars on the main road. Only the whooshing sound of her blood coursing through her ears and whatever sound the keeper's ill-kept equipment disrupts the air with.

"Then who might I help you find?" He stands, letting Scarlett see a frame that appears far too frail to carry a shovel, let alone upkeep an entire cemetery.

Still unsure of the situation she got herself into, she mumbles, "Al." He squints an eye at her, sucking his cheeks in, giving the illusion that he may implode. "Petrovsky, Allison," Scarlett squeaks out.

Plopping back into his chair and swiveling back to the monitor, he taps away at the keys while reading the monitor.

"Not a plot, dear," he says, looking back up at Scarlett. "She's right over there." He points at the internment wall. "Fifth column from the right, one row from the top." He turns back to the monitor, reading a bit more.

Words flow from his mouth, but Scarlett dismisses anything else he adds to the conversation. Her thoughts focus on the spot a few feet away from her. She stares at the tiny 6x10 panel barricading her from seeing her friend's remains.

"But he said she was going to be buried," she whispers to herself. "He said that exact word, buried. This can't be right." Shaking her head in disbelief, she turns back to the desk the groundskeeper was seated at, but finds no one there. "Hello?! I think you made a mistake!"

No one replies. Scarlett finds herself with more questions than she started with and with no one to whom she wants to ask them. She stares at the only connection to Allison she knows right now—a small marble cover over a spot that seems too cramped to hold anyone.

Bri sits in a corner booth at Manic Mondays, noshing on cheese fries, cheese sticks, and light beer while flipping pages through wedding magazines and rubbernecking for potential onlookers. A notebook next to Duncan waits for him to scribble notes about their nuptials. Not wanting to hide forever at home, he wears a hoodie (hood on), a baseball cap under that, and sunglasses to finish off the hiding from the paparazzi look.

"We've been sitting here unnoticed for the last half hour. The only thing attracting attention is your constant scanning of the crowd like you expect the fuzz to bust down the door," he chides.

"Well, if you weren't sitting here all Unabomber-chic, maybe I could relax," she scolds back.

He laughs at her choice of words. "You're the one who thought we could pull this off. Maybe we should leave. You seem stressed, and I wanted to talk about something, but not if it's gonna freak you out."

Forcing herself to relax, she leans against the booth back. Taking a few calming breaths, she turns to her betrothed. "I won't spaz out. What's on your mind?"

He deliberates a moment on not if she'll freak out, but how badly she'll freak. Unable to decide where she'll fall, he starts, "While Halloween is still months away, I'm starting to question if we set the date too soon," Duncan says, chugging some beer.

Bri shuts the magazines, turning to him as cheese drips off a fry and onto an issue of *Madame Bride* before landing in her mouth. "But Halloween sounds so much fun. You got me all excited about it and now I want to be married on Halloween." Her tone bears more petulant whining than anything.

An ear-to-ear smile crosses Duncan. Gazing into her eyes, he cups her head in his hands, pulls her in, and plants a big kiss on her lips.

She reciprocates for a moment before pulling back. "I'm still chewing my fry," she says, wiping her lips.

Duncan laughs, adding, "I think I may have gotten some of it."

They both share a much-needed laugh as the heaviness of life's events weighs them down. Settling back into their respective seats, Duncan continues to stare at his bride-to-be, wondering what he did to deserve such a great woman.

"I think Halloween works, but with getting your house ready to sell while looking for one to buy, coupled with planning a wedding, all topped with everything going on with … you know WHO, I just think Halloween might come sooner and less prepared than expected." Though his words are meant to calm her, he is unsure if they did anything besides upset her.

Turning her stare to the half-eaten plates of food and almost empty beer, Bri decides to finish off the last few drinks before signaling for another round. After a short deliberation between another fry or a cheese stick, the stick wins. After dipping it into the marinara sauce, Bri chomps half of it in one bite.

"I don't like when you are right, babe," she relents. "This is all a bit overwhelming."

"And it doesn't help that my parents don't have much to help with," he piles on.

She waves that notion off. "Money is not the issue. It's the planning and knowing how to plan. But we've already set up appointments to try cake. And I want to eat cake."

Chuckling, he interjects, "And you will, my love. We can eat cake now and still postpone. It's not like our big plan has changed. Only the timeline."

Deliberating his rationalized words against her irrational impulses for a moment, she turns back to him as the bartender sets down the round she ordered. "So, what are you proposing?"

"Change the date," he says without thinking she will devolve into a freakout.

"But you said Halloween could still work." Confusion coats her words.

"I never said, 'change the day.' I said, 'change the date.'" He smiles, hoping she picks up what he's dropping.

"I don't get it." She does not pick up what he dropped.

"Next year. Same day … Halloween. But one year off," he says, not realizing the chronological span between said dates and the effect it will have.

Five-alarm-fire sirens ring in her head, having missed his point. "Are you thinking of calling off the wedding? You better not be!"

He throws up his hands in defense against her, having done what she said she wouldn't. "Woah. Not what I said, Bri. I said push it back a year. Why would I want to call off the wedding?"

Still trying to silence the alarms, Bri blurts, "I don't know. I just hear that, you know, like, you want to postpone the wedding and all I can hear is, 'He's having second doubts.' You said 'postpone.'"

His head cocks a little, and he scrunches his lips. "Second thoughts, not doubts. Second doubts would assume I had first doubts. Which I never had. I've had zero. Less than one. Also, not why I proposed the idea."

He sees the wheels turning in her head as the siren's blare fades away. She tries to piece together why this is a better idea than getting married this Halloween, but she seems to stop short of the station.

Elaborating on his explanation, he says, "I have a mental list that goes: One, it still might feel too soon after Allison's…" he lets the word trail off but does not let the beat slow down. "Two, it'll give the house thing time to settle so that won't be on our minds. Three, we'll have more time to more properly vet venues, should the top choice not be available. And it will give us plenty of time to add a few pounds of cake-tasting weight to our waistlines. And that's fun if there ever was."

She lets a smile escape her as she thinks about the plethora of cake samples they could fit in between now and next Halloween. "I accept the change. But I think it's time we leave before someone sees us, makes you, and things end in a bad way."

Duncan signals for the check and they polish off the last round of beer.

"Every great society has its secrets. The Nation, as it is now called, is no different," Bishop says to the Council, sans Vistrus, as he stands before the other Council members.

"Then why does it feel different?" asks a member, exchanging glances with the others.

Bishop offers a smile, hoping to placate their fears before speaking. "Because we are at the center of it. We are not on the outside looking in or studying it in some history books. We are the history that one day, future members of the new Council read about. But secrecy cannot be taken lightly. This is not something you share with your spouse or children. This isn't even spoken amongst each other outside this room."

Bishop watches their expressions, reading their faces and deciding where to take his speech. Before he moves on, he lets his words marinate in their minds for a moment.

"This is not some plan that will manifest in a year. Like any great thing, it will take time. And the longer it takes, the harder it may become to trust it is working, but it will work," Bishop offers further vague assurances.

"What is the ultimate end goal of this?" another member asks.

Bishop paces back and forth, plotting his next oration. He raises a finger as if an idea has struck him to his core, stopping him.

"Protection. A way to ensure we and the ones we love will not have to worry about subjugation from an outside enemy. To ensure that the government of this nation or any other shall not impinge on our way of life."

A councilman interrupts at Bishop's break, his voice a bit more meek than normal. "Isn't that what we do already?"

A collective round of agreement utters from the others.

Bishop responds, "The Nation has an agenda, sure. And it paints the picture of what it wants us to see. But what it shows us and what it does behind closed doors are not the same." Making sure he has captured the attention again, he continues, "The interests of The Nation and the

High Council … are not necessarily what I would consider being your best interests. What I want from you … it's a lot to ask. That's why I gave everyone time to consider the weight of this. What I need from you … first and foremost is trust. A trust in me that I am placing in you. A level of trust that what we do is for the best of all Legends as individuals and not some metaphorical entity known as The Nation."

He watches their faces turn from uncertainty to solidarity in this secrecy.

"In this trust, we will ensure that The Nation and its people shall not perish from this earth. That all Legends shall be protected from all enemies outside of The Nation. That what the governments of the world know about us shall be protected from Normal eyes and that we shall remain a people unto ourselves and free from the prying eyes and probing hands of scientists, whose motives for their curiosity are more often rooted in professional gain and selfish motives than just cause to better mankind. We are mankind of a higher level, yet we are the vulnerable ones. We, who could be easily exploited for what makes us different, persecuted for those differences, those things that make us Legend instead of celebrated for it."

He looks out at the four sets of eyes glued on him, as if hearing those words for the first time, their mouths agape.

"But our success lies in secrecy. For we are the keepers of the righteous. We are the ones who will persevere when all else fails. All of which rely on one thing. One five-letter word that will mean more to the five of us in this room than it will for anyone else we will ever know."

All their heads bob up and down unconsciously, agreeing with every word he says. Seeing this, he smiles.

"That one word is trust. Trust in a better future. Trust in a better society. Trust in a better nation. And all of that begins with trust in each other, and trust in me."

Their heads bob more in agreement. No one dares speak and break his rhythm.

"As for Vistrus, he still does not need to know." Bishop pauses for effect. "There may never be a need to bring him in. He was sent here from Russia, home of the High Council. And therefore, he may be looking out for their best interests and not ours. But, here's the rub … he must be treated as an equal in all other matters. He can never suspect what we have and what our mission is. Is that clear?"

Again, he watches as the members nod their heads in understanding. He cups his hand behind his ear, tilting it to them, demanding an audible confirmation.

"Yes," they all say in unison.

"Good." He lets the camaraderie of the moment linger a second before moving on. "For obvious reasons, I cannot be present during closed-door meetings, and for the sake of the mission, open-door meetings will not find me present either. I will need to be kept informed of all meetings. When given the opportunity, delay acting on broached topics until I can provide input. There is a long road ahead of us and many unseen challenges to overcome. I look forward to our journey together."

A member whose head has been nodding nonstop stands up and turns to everyone. In a tone that offers a new, pre-game war cry, he says, "Trust."

Another member stands and repeats, "Trust."

The third and fourth follow suit.

Bishop closes the distance and leans in, repeating the word to further ingrain it into their minds, "Trust."

CHAPTER 13

*"Dreams tell us what our conscious mind
does not want to acknowledge.
Maybe."*
~A. Petrovsky~

Sitting against her parents' tombstones, Scarlett feels a loss of connection never felt in previous visits. Trying to speak, no words form in her mind to exit her mouth. She leans against her mother's gravestone, looking at the clouds above. Watching two birds fly way overhead, she imagines what it must be like to soar so high above all the chaos on the ground. Scarlett leans forward, imagining the birds are she and Allison, flying together and away from the daily grind in West Haven—flying to wherever their hearts fancy. But as she leans back, the feel of carved stone sends its harsh reminder that she lacks wings. Her attention shifts to the reality at ground level.

Shaking her head, she studies the weather-worn tombstones, trying to wonder how many more years would have gone by without knowing the truth had none of this ever happened. She studies the rounded edge that once was square, thinking about how she fits into the prophecy she still does not wholly believe.

"What's it matter? It's not like you two are in there. I've been talking to empty graves since I was a little girl. What a fool. I come here talking to you guys like you can hear me."

She stops, realizing that she is talking to them as if they are buried, even though the premise of her speech is that they are not. Shaking her head, she inhales. Unsure how to continue, she turns to the cemetery road leading past the stones.

"In a town like this, I wonder how many of the marked graves are empty? Hell, how many unmarked graves are filled?"

The image of Allison's interment spot flashes in her mind. The tiny 6x10, or could it have been a little larger, panel that forever keeps her ashes. Ashes that should have been buried. Again, her mind thinks of Allison's funeral and the words Mr. Petrovsky spoke. He said Allison was going to be buried.

"Buried in the ground, not cremated. Dressed to the occasion in a coffin covered in dirt. Not in some vase or plastic bag, sitting in a hole in the wall." Her anger grows as she speaks to herself about Mr. Petrovsky's hypocrisy about Allison. "He owes me an explanation. If not for me, then because Al would want to know." *Or, at least, Al would want me to know.*

She stands, ready to trounce off to Allison's, but a wave of exhaustion hits her, sending her back to the ground.

Maybe a quick rest first.

She lays her head against the tombstone, staring out into the setting sun. The brightness of it forces her to squint her eyes, which turn to closed eyes. And closed eyes lead to shut-eye. Before she notices herself falling asleep, she is out.

Scarlett's eyes open to darkening skies and gathering storm clouds. Scanning her surroundings, Scarlett feels raindrops pelt all over. Thick, dark clouds block out all light, and the rain obscures any light that manages to break through.

Standing, Scarlett sees Allison approach. The rain beats down heavier and heavier, reducing clear visibility to mere inches.

"Allison! You're alive!" Scarlett's exasperated shout dies in the rain.

Running toward each other, a bolt of lightning strikes a field nearby, illuminating the stormy sky as the raindrops turn crimson, but neither of them seems to notice.

As they embrace in a hug only best friends can share, Scarlett repeats, "You're alive!"

"Either that or we're both dead," Allison jokes.

A joke it may be, Scarlett does not take it as such.

"Why? Why would you say that?!" Scarlett scolds.

"I'm not the one who thought I was dead, silly."

Another flash bursts out, blinding Scarlett. As her vision returns, she finds herself carrying Allison through unfamiliar woods. Stopping to gain her bearings, Scarlett turns to her friend's head hanging off her shoulder.

"Where am I taking you?"

Shrugging, Allison answers, "How should I know? I'm not the one doing the carrying."

The torrential crimson rain continues beating down on them, painting them in bloody hues as Scarlett returns to aimlessly walking through the woods.

"Everyone said you were dead, Al. I told them they were crazy."

"No more crazy than carrying your bestie in a rainstorm through the woods."

"Hey, someone's gotta carry you. No one else seems to be doing it."

"I appreciate you, Lil' Lett." Allison points to a clearing in the distance, lit by a break in the clouds. "Is that it?"

"I dunno. Is it?"

"Seems as good a place as any." Allison smacks Scarlett's backside. "Giddy up!"

Scarlett quickens her pace, but the clearing grows no closer.

"Why does everyone think I'm dead?" Allison inquires.

"You don't remember, do you?"

"Remember what, Scar?"

"You did what you said you wouldn't in a way you promised you never would."

As Scarlett finishes her line, she finds them standing facing each other in the middle of the clearing, a shovel in her hands. She hands it to Allison.

"It's your grave, you dig it."

Shrugging and without rebuttal, Allison takes the shovel. "Sounds legit to me."

After a while of digging in stoic silence, Allison asks, "Figure out where we are yet?"

Scarlett scans the clearing, noting some familiarity but still can't place it. "No. But I think I've been here before."

"It's where you woke up." Allison hands the shovel back to Scarlett and climbs down into a fully dug grave.

Looking six feet down at her friend, Scarlett questions, "Woke up?"

"Yeah, dummy. The Waiting." Allison cocks her neck back to see Scarlett, but the rain beats down on her face. "Now pile it on!"

Laying down with a macabre sense of glee, Allison motions for Scarlett to pile the dirt on top of her.

Obeying as if she has no control, Scarlett piles shovels full of dirt on top of her best friend, one after another.

"But you're not dead! Why am I doing this?!" Scarlett shouts above the falling rain.

"I must be! Otherwise, this is a really stupid idea." Allison's ambivalence toward her burial makes Scarlett stop shoveling.

"Maybe I was right. Maybe we are both dead?"

Scarlett slams the shovel spade into the ground, making it stand on its own.

"Why?! Why would you say that?! How could that even be a possibility?"

Scarlett grabs the shovel and continues scooping dirt onto her friend as if on autopilot.

"Maybe everything they tell us is nothing more than fairy tales. Stories to help us sleep better at night." More dirt falls on top of Allison. "The Grey Fairy, The Nation, the strangeness of being a Legend…"

"But I saw it. I saw you transition!"

Allison shakes her head. "I don't think I transitioned. Nope. And you never transitioned. Maybe we imagined it *all! Us both being dead makes more sense than anything we've been told. I mean vampires, werewolves, fairies, and undying? Come on, Scar, how derivative can you get?"*

"But we aren't vampires or anything like that. We have Societies."

"Named after poets. How pretentious is that?!"

Scarlett stops shoveling to ruminate on Allison's words, but Al won't give her the time to.

"Pile it on, Scar!"

"Why are you making me do this?!"

"Cause Allison's gonna do what Allison's gonna do!"

A flash of lightning cuts through the clearing, blinding Scarlett. The world around her fades to black.

Fluttering open, Scarlett's eyes adjust to the bright moon illuminating her city with an unusually bright glow.

"How long have I been asleep?" Scarlett mutters, looking around the darkened cemetery.

Standing, she straightens herself, dropping a folded paper to the ground someone placed on her stomach while she slept. Bending to pick it up, she unfolds and reads it.

> *Just because the graves are empty doesn't mean we can't hear you. We always have. I saw you sleeping and wanted to say hello, but you looked so peaceful. I didn't want to wake you.*

Perhaps soon we will have a
chance to speak face to face.

Love always,
Mom and Dad

"Seriously? I looked too peaceful? What kind of BS is that?" Scarlett scoffs.

A distant flash of lightning in a far-off storm reminds her of the dream and Allison's words of waking up from the Waiting.

She folds the paper and pockets it, opting to keep this one, before hurrying off to where she was once buried.

Again, Vistrus finds himself blinded by the spotlight, playing pawn to The Nation's game of pomp and circumstance to elevate their egos. He does not question the old tradition because he knows the answer they will spout, "Secrecy of The Nation above all else." So, he does what he can do—stand in the light, staring at silhouettes while they decide what to say.

After a few dragged-out moments, the middle man stands and says, "It's been one week. Last time we spoke, you would not tell us why a Normal, accompanied by a Legend, was trespassing in a government building, which resulted in the death of not only a Legend but also of a Council member. Will you tell us now?"

Vistrus takes a stalling, deep breath. Betraying the trust of The Nation's High Council was not on his agenda today, but he knows the corruption runs deep. What Vistrus doesn't know is how deep it runs. He exhales at a snail's pace, stalling further while he decides how to gauge if and who here he can trust.

After a moment, as agitation sets in on the High Council members, choice words sound from Vistrus. "Before I answer that, I must say something."

He sees all their heads nod in unison.

"But any whispers will quiet my words. If you have something to say, say it to me. Understood?"

A few of the darkened faces begin to turn toward one another but stop. The middle man says, "Understood."

Vistrus shifts for a moment, hoping that he might be able to step out of the light and catch a glimpse of their faces, but the spotlight moves with him as he does.

"What was that, Mr. Petrovsky?" a new, feminine voice asks, her Russian accent as thick as the middle man's.

"Shifted for comfort, ankle turned."

Satisfied with his answer, she replies, "Then continue, please."

"West Haven has been compromised. I fear all The Nation has too."

All the High Council members take an audible deep breath, readying themselves to speak, but the middle man holds up a quieting finger. "What makes you think so?"

"I shall answer, but humor me. Are you not the same council that sent my wife, Inessa, and I to the States before they were a country?"

The middle man thinks for a bit as the other four turn to him. He swallows loud enough for Vistrus to hear the gulp. "I was. Two others as well. The other two, no."

"Three of you already know the answer; the other two might not."

A new voice, deeper than the first and whose accent indicates he hails from a more eastern area of Russia, speaks up. "Enlighten us, then. I would like to know."

Vistrus nods. "My wife was sent to cover up a massacre. Not find out who did it. Only to ensure the next Council did not know the previous existed."

"And you did not know about any of this at the time?" the Eastern Russian man asks.

Vistrus shakes his head. "No. I did not find out until long after her murder."

"Murder?" the same man confirms.

"By the hands of the same man who massacred the first West Haven Council."

Before any of the other members can speak, the middle man stands. Vistrus watches as the man reaches under the table and flips a switch, turning off the spotlight. Darkness engulfs the room while Vistrus's eyes adjust. He hears the man step away from the table and past him. After a few more steps, as his eyes begin adjusting to the darkness, the lights turn on. Protests erupt from two other members, who have thus far been silent.

"Enough!" shouts the man who turned on the lights. He stops in front of Vistrus. A face Vistrus has never seen stands before him, his eyes filled with guilt and heavy lines tell of difficult years. Vistrus does not look past him to the others. "I have long been suspecting that things were … still rotten in West Haven. And it is on me that I never had anyone look further into it. After your wife's passing, all was quiet. I figured that would be the last we heard of it. Naïve of me to think that. For that, I apologize, Mr. Petrovsky."

"Mikhail, we cannot apologize for past mistakes. We must—"

A hand shoots up, silencing the protest. "Enough! This mistake, this mistake *I* will apologize for. Hiding in the shadows from our own while we try to ignore the death we caused. That mistake we shall no longer make."

The other members fall in line, nodding in understanding. The protester falls silent, even in unrest, but does not nod.

"So, Mr. Petrovsky," the man gets back to the topic at hand, "what new wounds are old scars cutting up?"

"Not with that one here." Vistrus gestures to the dissenter.

"Do you not like opposition?" the voice cries out, false confidence fading away with each word.

"On this matter, no," Vistrus says to the nay-sayer before turning to the head member. "Not after all the recent deaths."

The man nods, understanding the subtext in his words. "Ivan, leave this room."

Standing up, but not moving away from the table, he further protests, "I am a member of this *esteemed* council and have every right to be here!"

The lead man looks at the only woman on the High Council and nods toward the dissident. "*If* what he says warrants your knowledge, I will tell you." He turns back to Vistrus, so Vistrus knows he means what he says. "But nothing will get told while you stand here."

The female council member grabs the man's hand and leads him and his petulance out of the room.

Vistrus waits for her to return and take her seat.

"Duncan and Brianna Waldgrave, a member of the Tennyson Society, went into the building on my suggestion." Vistrus slows his words. "They felt the answer to why we are being weaponized while being hunted down lies within."

The head member returns to his chair, motioning for Vistrus to step closer to them.

"What proof did you have they were right?"

Shaking his head, he says, "Only their gut. And I trust these ... young adults with my life. It was Connor who felt I, and many others, were wrong when his friend, Jack Taylor, went missing."

"And?"

"Connor found Jack alive after we presumed the worst."

"While commendable, I do not see how that warrants what you condoned."

Vistrus nods his head, inhaling as he gathers his memories for what he's about to say. "These kids have been through more in the past few years than some members of The Nation go through in their lives. They all transitioned without any adult guidance. We were too busy dealing with our own issues to see the struggle our children were going through. And they all handled it better than we could have hoped … except my little girl. And that reflects more on my failings than hers."

"Did they find the answers they were seeking?"

Vistrus squints at the double-edged question. "Yes, but they were unable to leave with said answer."

The man turns to the remaining council members. "Any questions so far?"

A thin man, too frail for his own health, sits upright before saying, "What does this have to do with your wife's untimely passing?"

"I do not feel comfortable telling you at this moment." The members accept Vistrus's honesty. "But if we can get back in and get what they could not the first time, then we should be able to confirm everything."

"And that is why you need us to protect a Normal, even at the life of a Legend."

"Protect the Normal, protect The Nation."

Mikhail adds, "Perhaps, but if he and his fiancée keep making public appearances before we can do what we need, protection will be the least of his concerns."

Vistrus nods, keeping eye contact with him. "Understood. For too long, though, The Nation has protected its own. Guarding every little detail as if it were sacred. We hide behind tradition and policy not knowing, or forgetting, why either was implemented to begin. These children, these young adults in West Haven, do not see from our obscured view. They may hold on to some naïveté, but you admitted to having done as much. I think the time has come that instead of holding onto the mistakes and misguided wisdom of our elders, we listen to our younger generations."

Mikhail answers, "So be it. We shall protect the Normal. But even we can only do so much before he faces consequences beyond our control." He watches Vistrus's reaction before speaking further. "As for the rest of what you spoke … there is another matter we must discuss. One which involves you abandoning your seat on the Council, yet still having the audacity to show up here, demanding what you did. First, you must speak with the West Haven Police, clear up this mess, and keep The Nation hidden. Consider it penance for your abandonment and audacity."

Vistrus suppresses a smile that tries to escape. "Courage."

Mikhail cocks his head. "Excuse me."

"Courage," Vistrus repeats. "It would only be audacious if you disagreed with my reasonings."

Mikhail shakes his head, smiling at Vistrus's words. "Then that leads us to the second thing we must discuss."

Darkness blankets the forest Scarlett attempts to navigate, returning to where she was once buried. The paths leading back now look unfamiliar, having been tread upon by forest-dwelling animals and city folk alike. Doubt sets in that navigating fairly unfamiliar woods at night is a wise choice. But she treads on, convincing herself that should she find Allison, uncovering a buried body during the day would somehow be more suspicious than at night. If not that, she further convinces herself that night holds less of a chance of being caught by a wandering bystander.

Reasons to walk onward continue to tick off, one by one, in her mind as she sidesteps uprooted and fallen trees, large branches, and the more-than-occasional mud patch. But as many reasons as she can think of to find her friend, she never considers the simple explanation that Vistrus may have changed his mind. A small change in plans that went from him wanting to bury his daughter to cremating her. If Scarlett's dream told her lies and The Nation is real, meaning their 21 grams are real, and Allison's decision wasn't a cry for help and she released her 21 grams, then the only thing left for Scarlett to do is face the truth: Allison's death is permanent. No convalescence in the Waiting for the young Petrovsky. No coming back with different hair or eye color or a birthmark she never had before. No new name to call her by. Nothing.

Scarlett trudges onward, determined to find where she was once buried because she has convinced herself that a graveside dream holds more truth than the attempts at consolation from those still alive. So, she runs through her reasons, again and again, remembering more and more of the path she took the day she woke from her Waiting until she finds a clearing.

Looking around, a certainty in her mind convinces her this is the place, but something about it feels off. She feels like the trees are taller or that she is shorter. For a moment, doubt sets in until she realizes she was shorter, about three feet in the ground shorter.

She squats to take another look at the clearing. This time, things start to feel more familiar. She even spies the reflective eyes of a nursery of raccoons. A smile crosses her, having found the area again. Even the hooting of owls rings in her ears. Whether they started suddenly or she wasn't paying attention before does not matter to her. Scarlett has found the spot where she was once buried and tingles run through her spine, causing her arms and legs to shake. Every fiber of her being screams to her that Allison must be close by.

She spins around, trying to find an area of recently disturbed dirt, but the recent rain obscures the grounds, dashing any hopes of making this an easy process. Relenting to getting dirty, she gets on her hands and knees, feeling the ground next to her for any sign of someone or something buried beneath it.

Minutes turn to hours and Scarlett's excitement dwindles, turning into disappointment. Dirt covers her legs, arms, and shirt. Matted hair from having been brushed away by mud-covered hands sticks out in all directions.

The adrenaline surge from earlier excitement takes its toll. A big yawn warning of low energy reserves escapes her. She looks around, having been undisturbed for a while, and lays down on top of where she once lay.

"Just a little rest before getting back to it," she tells herself, lying on the ground with her hands behind her head, providing a most uncomfortable pillow. But as uncomfortable as her hands may be, a tired head takes what it will to rest. Before the thought of resuming her search has a chance to enter her mind, sleep takes over.

Restless sleep plagues her. Thoughts of defeat and Allison's permanent departure from her life infect her dreams. Deep sleep makes way for disturbing notions of failure as both a friend and a human. As much as she tosses and turns on the muddy earth, Scarlett cannot stir herself from the self-doubt that haunts her, imprisoning her in sleep.

CHAPTER 14

*"Faith is nothing more than hoping
that something we know nothing about
will work in our favor."*
~S. McAllister~

The doors to the West Haven Police Department slide open as Vistrus approaches. The lobby sits empty, save the receptionist, who's busy tapping away on her phone as he approaches.

Standing at the reception desk, Vistrus watches the officer continue tapping away, either ignoring him or unaware of his presence. After a moment of standing unacknowledged, he clears his throat. Without looking up, the officer holds up a finger, telling him it will be just one more second.

After another moment of her escalating tapping, it abruptly ends, and the disappointment painted on her face tells Vistrus it did not go as well as she hoped.

"How may I help you today?" Her tone does not hide her irritation at Vistrus's uninvited disruption.

"Officer Marino expects me." Vistrus tries to keep his interruption brief.

Her gaze turns to the computer screen as her fingers give her phone a reprieve, turning to the keyboard. A few uncomfortable seconds pass before her saccharine smile turns back to Vistrus.

"Looks like he's pulling into the station now. I'll let him know you're waiting," she offers, but Vistrus hears the doors slide open as Officer Marino enters.

Vistrus nods to the receptionist before turning to the officer.

"Officer Marino," Vistrus addresses the man.

He turns and smiles while continuing to walk past Vistrus, waving him to follow as he does.

"Vistrus, let's find some place a little more private."

A few doorways and turns down halls later, the two men find themselves in an interrogation room. Lights illuminate the room beyond the two-way mirror, assuring their privacy.

The officer closes the door and, turning to Vistrus, says, "Quite the predicament I find myself in."

Vistrus nods, remaining silent.

"First, I get your daughter out of a DUI, and now I find myself unsure what to do about a Normal wanted for murdering a Legend. Of course, it's not like others know. No, they just think it's a kid wanted for murder," Officer Marino continues, motioning for Vistrus to take a seat. "Something's happening in The Nation and I'll do my part, but you gotta give me something that lets me know what's going on."

"I shall." Vistrus keeps his break in the silence short before moving on. "Then The Nation remains hidden?"

The cop nods his affirmation as he sits. "But I'm having a hard time delaying bringing the kid in on a favor for you. Especially when he thinks that sunglasses and a hoodie will protect him while having a dinner date with his fiancée at some local restaurant. Like I said, you gotta give me something because from where I stand, even knowing what I know, it's hard to justify your request to delay."

Surprise mixed with disappointment pours across Vistrus's face. "I will handle that transgression. Youthful naivety comes for us all, though mine is far behind me. I do not know about yours."

Catching Vistrus's drift, Marino smiles and nods. "Farther than some. Not as far as others." He nods to Vistrus as he says his last words.

Continuing his thought, Vistrus says, "Mr. Elias knew better. He could have put not only himself at risk, but his betrothed as well. For that, I apologize."

Sensing the rising heart rates of the other man, both Vistrus and Officer Marino take a moment to calm themselves before speaking.

"Any chance his fiancée could have spurred his decision?" Officer Marino asks after taking a moment to calm the air.

Vistrus exhales, not wanting to say what he must. "Her mother was…" He stops himself, not wanting to continue. Reorganizing his thoughts, he continues, "Possibly. I would not put it past her."

"Then let's put a pin in that for the moment." Officer Marino inhales, not wanting to needlessly treat Vistrus like a suspect or criminal. "The Council wants answers, and they aren't too happy with you."

Vistrus offers an apologetic smile. "That is why I am here. Penance."

"Just penance?" Disbelief covers Officer Marino's face, but his cop nature waits for Vistrus to say what's hidden beneath.

"Duncan should not be charged," Vistrus finalizes.

Pushing himself away from the table, playing to dramatics, the officer says, "That's something I never thought I'd hear a Legend say." Calming his role a bit and pulling himself to the table, he continues, "So, protect a Normal. Why?"

"I will lay it all out, and it will make sense. Big things are simmering. When they come to a boil…" Vistrus pauses, unsure where to start. "How far back should I start?"

"How much do you want to protect this Duncan?"

"He is a true friend to The Nation and is engaged to a Legend, well-knowing all about her condition. Imagine what a loyal Normal could do for The Nation as things progress to where hiding is no longer an option?"

"Why would hiding no longer be an option?"

"As I said, things are coming to a boil, and we can use all the goodwill we can muster." Vistrus pauses, waiting for a reply, but Officer Marino sits in stunned silence. "So, you want to know how much I want to protect Duncan? With everything we have."

"Then I say you best tell me everything from the beginning."

Vistrus raises an eyebrow. "The beginning?"

Officer Marino nods. "You heard me."

Vistrus nods back. "How much time do you have?"

"As long as you need."

Vistrus straightens himself, getting a bit more comfortable. Officer Marino follows suit, sensing this is going to take more than five minutes.

As they both settle in for a long story, Vistrus begins his tale.

An unseasonably chill breeze serpentines through the houses and into the street as Brianna skips up Connor's driveway. Her cornflower blue, bohemian chic dress makes a long-needed appearance. She hums an upbeat tune about people hearing her roar as she stops in front of the door. Taking a deep breath in, preparing for the conversation ahead, she knocks loudly and rings the bell for good measure.

As she belts out the last line of the chorus, Connor opens the door, smiling at her moment of relaxed enjoyment.

"I heard you roaring before you knocked," Connor says, greeting her. He scans the driveway for Duncan, but no one else is around. "What up?"

"Hey, Con," Bri says, smiling. "How ya been?"

"Fine," he answers, still unsure about her visit. "So?"

"So what?" Bri steps back so the screen door can swing open. She gestures, asking if she can come inside.

Connor opens the door, asking again, "What's going on? You seem awfully chipper today."

Shutting the door behind her, she looks past Connor. "Nothing's ruining my mood today. Where's Scarlett? Need to ask her something."

"Not home," Connor answers, looking down at his watch. "I don't think she came home last night. Try calling her?"

"Did that, dummy. Like, why would I have come otherwise?" She looks Connor up and down, trying to read something on him.

"Want me to give her a message? What'd you want to ask? Maybe I know the answer."

Shaking her head, Bri replies with a laugh, "Don't think so. But I left a voicemail and thought maybe I'd catch her here."

Connor steps away from the foyer into the living room. "What do you need? I might be able to help."

Looking him up and down again, she asks, "Have you talked with Duncan yet?"

"About what? What is going on?" Connor's confusion over this whole encounter grows with each passing second.

"Stuff is going on, I can't tell ya. Girl stuff, wedding stuff. It wouldn't be right to tell you before speaking with her. Just chat with Duncan." Bri turns toward the door, grabbing the handle. She stops to speak, but Connor gets the jump on that.

"What the hell is going on?! I don't think I've ever been so confused about something so vague in my entire life." He throws up his arms in defeat. "You need a drink or something?"

Bri turns the handle, opens the door, and turns to Connor, smiling. "No worries, hon'. It's not that serious. Talk with Duncan. It'll all make sense." Before he can close his slack-jawed mouth, Bri leaves him standing there, gobsmacked.

"I have been pulling out my hair trying to figure out how this all fits together," Vistrus says, running his hand through his hair, making sure he still speaks in metaphor. Assured his hair remains lush and thick, he sips a steaming espresso.

Pulling out a chair to join him at the kitchen table, Eleanor chuckles, sipping her fresh espresso. "Silly man. What is there to figure out?"

Vistrus thinks, trying to pinpoint the eye of his storm. "All of it. Any of it." He sips his caffeine, stalling to think. "There was this prophecy. Ken and Tracy were supposed to be the ones who brought about the Grey Fairy. Then they were murdered."

Eleanor nods, following his train of thought.

"In the diner, you said prophecies mean nothing. Why have them then?"

Eleanor waits, ensuring Vistrus gives her room to talk, then says, "To connect dots that we otherwise could not connect. To make sense of things beyond our understanding. Sometimes, things just are."

Vistrus shakes his head. He picks up his cup to sip but places it back down. "Nothing you said answered my question."

"And prophecies answer too many. It all balances." She turns to a cabinet. "Shortbread cookies?"

Without hesitation, Vistrus answers, "Sure. But balance does not make sense of everything."

Eleanor grabs a box of shortbread cookies from the cabinet and brings them to the table. Pulling out a sleeve, she opens it, and they whittle it down while talking.

"The symbol for The Nation," she says, biting off a piece of cookie.

"What about it?"

"Balance. The all-encompassing circle. The points. The house. The equal sign."

Vistrus swallows a large bite. "It is a pentacle."

"Come on, Vistrus. You know it's more than that. Besides the points for each of the houses, there's the house in the middle, uniting them all. The equal sign for the balance of power."

"And the all-encompassing circle that we must stay in to protect ourselves." He huffs at himself for having let the meaning slip from his mind.

"I knew you weren't that dense," she teases, downing another cookie. "Balance."

Thinking about the meaning of the symbol, the wheels in his mind come to a stop, trying to connect them to the prophecy.

"How does the prophecy connect it all? Perhaps if I could figure out how it all began, I can tie it all together."

"I was in Éire the first time whispers of the prophecy hit my ears. It was centuries ago. After a while, it becomes another memory lost to the pages of time. But I'll tell you what I can." An unsettling tone comes over her voice. "I fear I may be more involved than I ever wanted to admit."

The elevator door opens to the basement level of the West Haven Historical Society. Raymond and December step out, looking down the hallway to the room where the Council holds their sessions.

Looking at each other, they nod and start walking. Kids and camp counselors spending the day indoors coloring and preparing craft projects to hang on their parents' refrigerators fill the rooms in this hall that aren't used for storage. The room where the Council holds their late-night meetings sits unoccupied. An open binder on the table indicates someone was here recently and that someone might be returning soon.

Raymond chimes in December's mind, "It's not here. Nor any clue to its whereabouts."

December shakes her head, responding, "We aren't looking for the amulet this time."

"Then what are we looking for?" Raymond asks, glancing at the open binder whose lesson-planning contents are unrelated to their task.

"Whoever is pulling the strings."

Raymond turns his full attention to December. "Why do you think we will find anything here?"

Shaking her head again, she picks open a locked drawer in a filing cabinet. "I don't."

Making his way to help her search the drawer, he adds, "But we might find something that leads up somewhere that does lead us to whomever it is behind all of this."

December gives a quick double tap on her nose, then points at him. "The what of what we might find is the question."

A smooth voice from behind them sounds. "That is not yours to rifle through."

Raymond and December turn around to greet the interruption, but do not close the drawer.

The pale woman from the woods stands in the doorway, blocking their exit. A familiarity strikes both Raymond and December upon seeing her.

December looks her up and down, trying to figure out how she knows her. December points at her mouth and closes her pointer finger and thumb together, signing "No." She proceeds to fumble her way through basic sign language, making up what she doesn't know.

"I don't know sign language," the woman says. "What are you looking for?"

A smile breaks out across Raymond's face. He turns to December. "Inessa."

Her eyes grow big, knowing not only the impossibility of the woman standing before her but also that this person is Bishop, the Adeirrig.

December sounds her voice in the false woman's head. "Pasha, it's been a long time."

The woman's smile contorts as her face begins to shift, distorting her features. Crunching bones and popping joints chime out in a macabre melody as his skeletal structure reshapes itself, growing and thickening. Gurgling emanates from within him as his proportions thicken his frame.

As fast as the guttural sounds drown out everything else, they fade. Before them stands Bishop. The feminine clothes he wore moments ago are tattered and stretched on his frame.

"You have our 21 grams," December continues as his shape finishes forming.

"Give me the Grey Fairy and you can have them back," he says with a sly smile.

Fields of emerald grass fill the countryside. A small, cyclopean stone cottage rests in the field. An old wooden bench nearing the onset of decay holds Aoife before she was called Eleanor. Next to her sits Easpag before he started calling himself Bishop. He buries his head in her shoulder, soaking in the moment that he knows must come to an end. She holds his hand, rubbing the top of it with her fingers without letting go.

Distant storm clouds inch across the sky, closing in. Aoife looks up at the sky, trying to estimate how long until the storm rains down on them. She continues rubbing the top of his hand with her fingers from the hand that holds it. Her other hand sits at her side as if wondering what it should be doing.

Lifting his head off her shoulder, he watches her watch the sky. He pulls his hand away, knowing that hers will never belong to him. The field before them calls to him like a whispering specter, wanting to tell her all his secrets without revealing the reasons behind them. A distant clap of thunder fills him with a sense of urgency, reminding him that, while their time on this planet may be more than most can comprehend, their time together closes in.

Easpag turns his head skyward, watching with her as the clouds continue creeping closer. "The sky will tear asunder when we no longer listen. A spirit splits in two when we turn our attention. Light and dark become grey at the prophesized birth. Bringing together all the Legends of this separated earth."

Aoife continues staring skyward, but instead of looking straight up, she turns to the distant sky where the storm already took hold. "Cryptic words are better spent on youthful flights of existential fancy. They will not sway me."

Joining her in viewing the distant storm, he furrows his brow in thought. "It's … a prophecy."

"I can tell since it used the word 'prophesized.' Any reason you mention it now?"

"The moment felt right. The coming storm is not one we will want to weather alone. But it seems at least one of us must."

Aoife turns her attention to the field surrounding them. "He is not here. This may be a storm we weather together."

"If…" he starts before being cut off.

"If nothing, Easpag. You said you would leave it. Your heart will heal just as this storm will pass. But this storm, we will weather as a final farewell."

Consternation contorts his face, wanting to speak but not wanting to ruin the moment. Opting for a more civil response, he allows his face to relax before nodding.

Aoife turns her gaze to him, though he continues looking outward. "I've never heard that quatrain before. Where did you read that?"

He shakes his head with deliberate motions, dragging out each turn from left to right and right to left, as if needing to concentrate all his energy on the muscle movements. "I … I don't know. It … appeared in my head as if from a dream."

"It came to you in a dream?! Quite the fanciful one, aren't we?"

Though her words hold the animosity of a purring kitten, they tear him like a swipe from a tiger's claw. "I cannot help where things come to me, but it came. It's not like I simply made it up to fill the silence."

Realizing the harsh sting of her words, she chuckles, hoping it calms the air, if not the storm. "I did not mean… What do you think they mean?"

Inhaling to calm himself, he thinks about the lines of the quatrain. "Well, if we take it line by line, we might more easily dissect it."

Nodding at his reasoning, Aoife looks at the approaching storm and the clouds frozen in their approach.

"Give me the first line again, Easpag."

"The sky tears asunder when we no longer listen. What do you think that could mean?" His wonder sounds sincere. Looking out at the emerald grass, he sees woodland creatures scurry in the distance.

Aoife thinks about the line, wrinkling her nose before her words form. "If we take the literal translation, it means the sky tears in two if we stop listening. But listen to what?"

He shrugs, thinking about her literal take on the words. "What about metaphorical?"

Scratching her temple, she says, "That, I'm not so sure. The sky could be anything bigger than the individual. It could be our lives, our homes. If we take in the word referring to Legends, it could be that something splits us. But the second half about listening might be harder to decipher on a metaphorical level. What's the next line?"

Thinking through the quatrain, trying to remember the proper words, he fumbles them, saying, "A spirit splits ... in two when we ... turn our attention. But the sky split in two." His attention turns to the distant clouds once again, noticing the delineation between the dark storm clouds and the clear sky above them. "Where they meet. Maybe the sky tearing asunder is a literal storm."

"And the spirit splitting is a spiritual one. A storm within one's self. Or within our society."

"Perhaps a Legend itself will split." The wheels in his head turn, churning new ideas from the brief conversation. "It speaks of light and dark. Could that be something?"

A distant thunderclap turns her attention to the clouds, now inching closer again. "Perhaps. Maybe one of the Societies will split somehow. If we take a philosophical approach to light and dark, maybe it means their condition will become two. One side represents the good of it all and the other, the darkness we carry."

They think about the possibilities of what it might mean for a while, sitting in comfortable silence as the clouds continue inching ever closer. Aoife looks straight overhead, the white clouds from moments ago darken as she watches them. "That last line, though. A grey from light and dark. A prophetic birth."

A realization washes over Easpag upon seeing dread overcome Aoife. "Don't think on it too much, dear. It was just, it felt right at the moment. It could mean so many things. We may never know."

The clouds overhead begin to cry. A droplet of water hits her face. The space before when another one hits is long enough to not cause concern.

"We may never know. You're right, Easpag. But now I know the verse. And the power lies in knowing it."

Lightning flashes across the horizon and the clouds overhead weep harder, making it impossible for Aoife and Easpag to avoid the teardrops. Standing and looking at the cottage, Aoife says, "We should go inside." She begins walking to the cottage.

"When will Nioclás be back?" Easpag inquires, the undertone of his meaning not lost on her.

"Why should that matter, Easpag?" She stops, letting the rain soak her further as she weighs the pros and cons of going inside with him. "Perhaps sitting in a storm could be a good send-off."

"You never could do simple," Easpag says, laughing as he sits back down in the now pouring rain.

"Perhaps one day I will. But today is not that day."

"And what better way to say goodbye to a tumultuous relationship, whatever kind it may have been, than sitting in what looks like it will be a raging storm?"

A roaring, rolling thunder follows his words, trying to add its thoughts on the subject, but Aoife speaks over it. "And you never could let a metaphor go unspoken."

They sit on opposite ends of the bench, soaking in the rain as they watch the distant lightning. She knows this storm should be the end of whatever relationship they held, but her heart of hearts knows that any relationship, no matter how big or small, never truly ends; they are only delayed for a while.

"Why are you only telling me about this now?" Vistrus's voice rises for a few words, then calms down. "We have been blindly piecing together this puzzle long enough."

Eleanor nods. Her lowered eyes tell him of her shame.

"We could have used a hint at the picture long ago, Eleanor." Mixed emotions bubble to the surface; a feeling Vistrus usually evades, though not foreign to him altogether. Taking a deep breath to calm down, he adds, "I wonder how many lives could have been spared?"

Eleanor hesitates an answer, only parting her lips as if she desires to speak, but the words won't sound. Closing her mouth, she squints, trying to form an answer Vistrus will find acceptable, but she comes up empty.

Vistrus's eyes grow big as a thought enters his mind. "Would my little Allison not be gone were it not for your silence?"

Betrayal splashes across Eleanor's face as she tries to comprehend the accusation he levied.

"No. The events are peripheral to her actions. And don't dare say her actions weren't peripheral to the events at hand. Everyone involved in her life missed the signs. The blame does not fall on me."

"No. It falls on me for every time she asked to see a therapist and I said, 'No.' It falls on me for turning a blind eye to teenage drinking."

"Many teens drink. They don't all lead to the same destination," Eleanor offers.

"But not all teens end up at a police station for driving under the influence." Tears well in his eyes, thinking about that night.

"I had no idea." Eleanor reaches out, placing a hand on his arm.

"The officer changed the charge. Said it was a diabetic insulin reaction. I did not question."

Without needing to ask, Eleanor knows why the charge was changed. "It's nice to have friends."

"I could have been a better friend to my daughter instead of a constant father."

"It is not our job to befriend our children. Ours is to teach them how to live in this world."

"And I failed."

Eleanor does not have a response to salve the wound. "It appears I have as well."

Silence falls over them while they stew in the moment's turmoil. Neither make eye contact. Eleanor opts to stare at the walls, plotting out a plan of attack to clean the scuff marks off them. Vistrus stares out the window with the forlorn expression of a marooned sailor yearning to sail the sea.

After distracting herself long enough to finalize a plan of attack on cleaning the kitchen walls, she turns to Vistrus, still lost in thought. "Nobody does something thinking it's the wrong thing. We do what we do because we believe it is right."

CHAPTER 14

Turning to her, he adds, "Only after can we see how wrong we were."

His words linger in Eleanor's ears. She wants to speak but holds back her words, unsure what further damage they might inflict.

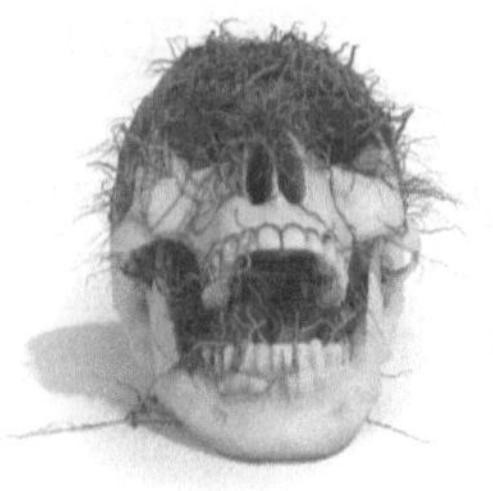

CHAPTER 15

"Pithy quotes do little to solve life's problems."
~J. McAllister~

A loud, repeating thud against the door wakes Brianna. Wiping the drool from her mouth, she looks around, realizing she and Duncan fell asleep watching television last night. The bowl of now-stale popcorn sits half-empty on the side table. Hearing another thud on the door, she lifts herself off Duncan, who remains asleep.

"Coming!" she shouts toward the door. Nudging her man, she says, "Get up! Someone's here."

She leaves him to wake and opens the door to see Vistrus standing there.

"Mr. Petrovsky?"

Cutting past any pretense, he responds, "Yes, it is. May I?" He motions toward the indoors.

Shaking off the rest of her sleep, she finds her manners. "Yeah, for sure." She moves aside to let him in and shut the door.

"Is Mr. Elias arou…" he begins before seeing Duncan still rubbing the sleep from his eyes on the couch. "Yes, he is. Good."

Extending his arms above his head in a ludicrously long stretch, Duncan jokes, "I'm around wherever I look."

Vistrus gives a half-smile and appreciative nod at Duncan's humor. "Well done, but we must set aside the comedy." The serious turn in his voice scares away any drowsiness lingering over Bri and Duncan.

Duncan stands next to Bri as Vistrus strides into the living room.

"Can I get you something to drink? Coffee, vodka, water?" Bri rattles off the list.

He waves a dismissive hand. "No, thank you. I want to get to the point."

Bri waves for him to take a seat. She and Duncan take seats on opposite sides of the couch, but Vistrus remains standing.

"You," he starts, his gaze locking on Duncan, "do not know how to listen."

Duncan shoots his hands out in defense. "Woah. What are you talking about?"

"I told you to stay indoors until things settle. Lie low."

Duncan nods, admitting his digression. "I took precautions."

"I am not asking for excuses for why you … digressed. Nor am I saying that you did." Vistrus relaxes his stern tone, letting them stew in the scolding while he thinks that reason might hold water. "Why did you risk exposing yourself?"

A smile crosses Duncan as he holds in immature laughter. Vistrus realizes his choice of words might have been better.

"I didn't think I exposed myself," Duncan says, trying to hold in laughter coming to a boil.

Vistrus grows irksome at their incomprehension of the seriousness of the risk they took. "Do you think what you did is funny? Or are you so immature that my choice of words amuses you?"

The poke in his words disperses the growing laughter. Duncan straightens himself, focusing on the subject at hand.

"She wanted some cheese fries, and we were working on wedding plans," Duncan says. "No one saw us."

"Someone did; otherwise, I would not know," Vistrus corrects Duncan, "but that is the point. Had it not been a Legend who was an off-duty officer, things could have ended far worse than a lecture from me."

Brianna adjusts herself on the couch and clears her throat. "We shouldn't have to hide. He did nothing wrong."

"If the officer was not In, then the same thing that first happened to Mr. Taylor could have happened to Mr. Elias." Vistrus lays out a possibility. "While what you did was justifiable by our standards, breaking and entering, starting a fire, setting off sprinkler systems, and killing a human are still wrong. I had to smooth things over and while the B&E was easy, the murder was not." Vistrus struggles to keep his voice controlled.

"He wore a hoodie, a hat, and sunglasses," she says. "We were careful. He shouldn't have to be, like, some hermit or something for doing the right thing."

"Sometimes, Ms. Waldgrave, we need to put aside our cravings for cheese fries until it is safe to eat them in public. Everything happening in West Haven holds far more importance to the future of The Nation than one night out for appetizers and beer will ever."

Duncan and Bri nod their heads, feeling the gravity of their actions.

"Soooooooooooo … what now?" Bri says.

"Now. You may both walk as you wish."

Duncan tenses up. "You just came here to bust my balls about a covert night out when you could have skipped the lecture?"

"Life has consequences, and what you did could have had far worse consequences than any you would want to imagine. I lecture because you are adults now, and yet you still acted oblivious to what could be." Anger coats his frustrated tone.

"Mr. Petrovsky, I am sorry," Bri pleads.

"Sorry does not cut it. You already have to hide who you are. Legends struggle with the transition and the physical differences. I had to mourn my daughter because she could not cope with it." His anger diminishes as longing sets in. "Life does not care. We must be the ones who do. Part of caring is being careful. I cannot express enough the magnitude of what lies ahead."

Bri and Duncan hang their heads as they begin to understand the seriousness their night out may have held.

Vistrus continues, "It is hard enough being a Legend. Having to deal with everything life throws at us. What makes you think that had something happened, had Duncan been spotted and apprehended, that had you been exposed, that life would have been easier for you?" Vistrus takes a deep breath, trying to let his words sink in. "Are cheese fries worth it?"

Neither respond. They continue to sit, the gravity of their current situation keeps them from speaking.

"As I said, things are smooth. Now, we must figure out what comes next."

Pressed against the trunk of a large tree, Bishop's Paul Bunyan-like proportions camouflage with bark-like skin and ivy-esque hair wrapping around it while he listens to the conversation taking place inside Eleanor DeSalvo's kitchen as Eleanor, Connor, and Scarlett exchange words of Allison's growing sexual identity conundrum. Words that offer little interest as he purses his lips in boredom. Taking a deep breath, he exhales away impatience and urgency, knowing that sometimes patience brings things to those who wait.

Inside, the conversation presses on in blissful ignorance of the outside presence. Connor confesses Allison's emotional distance and unwillingness to open up. Outside, Bishop empathizes with Connor's words. Not with Connor, but that Allison won't open up. Having done so in the past, he knows too well that being open and honest will only lead to pain in the end. A suffering that has led to this moment and all previous events between the pain and now. So, yes, Connor's words make for a sympathetic Bishop.

All words that, while interesting, still offer no useful information for his endgame. But as their conversation continues, Eleanor brings home a point that plants the seeds of an idea in his mind. Find the back door—a different way in.

Satisfied with what was overheard, Bishop walks away from the tree and the house. As he does, the vines and bark-skin recess and disappear, morphing into human skin and features. The large stature stays the same, but the setting sun silhouettes him, hiding Bishop from Eleanor and her grandchildren. A coincidence in his favor not unnoticed by him as a smile crosses his face.

Walking away, the seeds of this new idea begin to sprout. Ways he can infiltrate Eleanor's life without being suspected take root. The early adult years are ofttimes confusing, making a great way to work himself in. But how he can exploit a girl's newfound feelings against her boyfriend to ultimately win Eleanor over has yet to solidify. For now, the idea molds itself and begins taking shape.

A light morning rain provides a cool atmosphere on this unusually warm start to the day. The quiet soaks in what water it can. In the clearing lies Scarlett, still sound asleep as the raindrops patter on her face, slowly stirring her awake.

Her eyes clench shut, fighting against the light of day and the realization that she slept in a dirt hole. Pulling out her cell phone, she finds the battery drained, making her wonder how long she slept. It could have been days for all she knows. The dreams play fresh in her mind, more like memories being remembered than a dream fading from consciousness. Her sleep had been so deep that each dream made her feel like she was there, wherever there was, and away from the world she has come to despise.

But clench her eyes shut as she may, the tapping drops against her skin force her to face her grim reality once again. As her eyes flutter open, the morning light assaults them, and pain pierces through to their center. She controls her eyelids, letting her eyes adjust to the sunlight, minimizing the pain the light causes as well as her existential pain.

Looking around the silent forest, save the rain hitting tree leaves and a few birds singing, she wonders how no one crossed paths with her while she slept. She ponders that perhaps they did but left her in her slumber. As depression can do, it plants a somber thought in her mind that maybe no one even went looking for her. While the others handle Allison's loss in their way, as cavalier as it seems to Scarlett, she wonders if her handling of it has pushed them far enough away that they don't notice her absence.

"Hmm. Their loss, I guess," she utters, raising her arms above her head in a stretch so deep that her vision whitens for a moment. *Could it be my loss?*

That thought dances around her while she brushes the dirt and leaves that were last night's bed off her clothes; she knows it could be her loss. There's no reason why they wouldn't want her back. The logical side of her brain shouts for her to return, to rejoin the world of Connor, Bri, Duncan, and all who are still around to care. But the other half of her brain, the half that taunts and teases her, says she has work to do. Work that will prove them wrong. Except, after everything she has done to prove herself right, she feels that any further dive down this rabbit hole will only continue proving her wrong.

Standing in the clearing, looking at the numerous paths she can take, not remembering which she took to arrive here, the metaphorical fork in the road, while lost, does not pass over her head. She knows Allison might be in the Waiting, but, after everything, it looks as if she did end up six feet under, or in the case proving true, a small hole in the wall. At the end of it all, Scarlett wonders if it really matters what path she takes.

A raccoon scurries past her close by, catching her attention. She watches the lone creature pitter-patter about, looking for something. She assumes it's hungry for food, but she could be wrong. It could be searching for its friends or family, lost much like she is, alone in the woods and not knowing which way to go.

"Psst. Psst," Scarlett calls to the raccoon. "Come here, little guy."

For a moment, the raccoon stops and looks in her direction, as if it understood what she said, and now contemplates some decision. But it decides to continue on its journey, disappearing into the forest, leaving Scarlett alone once more. While the critter's fading into the forest is the obvious cue for Scarlett to quit procrastinating and return home, a voice in her head tells her there's no reason to. That even at home, there is no Allison. No best friend forever to share the day's events with. No one to whisper secrets to. No ride or die waiting because, as the label states, "ride or die," and in Allison's case, the latter half is where things rest.

Relenting to the likely fact of Allison's demise, Scarlett lays back down on the ground where she slept, taking time to understand the true nature of how things are sans Allison and does so by watching the clouds float by.

But even in acceptance, Scarlett knows that life must go on. Sitting and wasting away in a forest preserve, as tempting as it sounds at the moment, is not a feasible choice. But right now, watching the cotton candy clouds shapeshift in the sky seems like the perfect place to be. So, she gives herself this time, trying to heal and find acceptance of learning to live without her confidant and tries to exist in this moment. But she cannot find the peace she needs. If only Scarlett could grab a moment for herself to be alone with thoughts and memories of a dearly departed friend that didn't sink her deeper into a desire to never leave these woods.

As the clouds shift from one abstract shape to another, Scarlett wonders how long this deepening depression will last and if acceptance will ever be just around the corner or forever out of reach. She tries to imagine what it will be like to move on and exist without Allison, but each time she does, a dizziness overtakes her. Nausea roils in the pit of her stomach when she plays out how each day will be with no one to call. She imagines the looks that her cousin will give her, knowing what she said and how she acted. Wondering if Connor, Bri, and Duncan will allow her to move on or be a constant reminder of her inability to handle the loss from the onset with the aplomb that they have: always being treated like an outcast, unable to conform to the societal standards laid out in some secret manual of handling the death of a loved one. Some outcast black sheep because god-forbid death affects her more severely than the others. Or perhaps she lacks the metaphorical tools needed to cope with such tragedy that others were given. Maybe she was absent from school that day.

Her thoughts drift in and out from happy to melancholy to depressing, thinking of everything she can in desperation to hold on to the memory of her friend. As her thoughts drift, she finds fleeting solace in scarce moments and, in others, despair. But the time in these woods is hers alone, and she will take all she needs. Everything else, be damned.

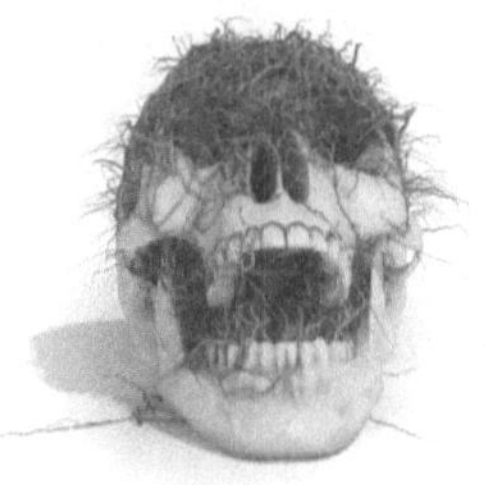

CHAPTER 16

"Sometimes, the worst response you can give
is the only one to be said."
~C. DeSalvo~

A knock on his bedroom door stirs Connor from sleep. The grogginess of waking has his mind searching for both the source of the sound and a shirt when another knock taps against the door. This time, his mind wraps around the sound as he picks up a band T-shirt off the floor.

"Come in," he says with the excitement of someone about to get an un-anesthetized wisdom tooth extraction.

The door creaks open, and Scarlett peeks her head inside. "May I come in?"

Seeing his cousin for the first time in days washes away most of the lingering sleep. He rubs his eyes, yawning away any sleep still fighting to take control.

"We've been worried about you. It's been a hot minute since anyone's seen you," he says, rising from bed. He steps to her, embracing her in a welcoming hug.

"Been busy." She embraces him back but cuts it short. "Can we talk?"

"Everything okay?" He plops back down on his bed, motioning for her to take a seat on his desk chair.

Scarlett's eyes study the floor, as if the words she's searching for hide under the pile of his clothes. After a moment, she turns back to him. "You need to clean a little."

He chuckles. "Yeah, I gotta do laundry soon, but I'm pretty sure that's not what you came in here for."

She scratches behind her right ear. "No. It's … I know you all are sick of me talking about it and wish I could just get over it like you all have."

Connor's hand shoots up to stop her.

Keeping his voice calm, he interjects, "No one is over it, and no one wishes you were over it. This has been one of the hardest things to deal with in my life."

"Then why are you and Bri and Duncan all acting like nothing has changed while I am over here falling apart? Am I the only one who can't keep it together, or am I the only one who's absolutely devastated by her death?"

The word death rolls off her tongue, but it stings a bit too much. It is as if even saying the word makes it true, pushing Allison further away from memory. Scarlett feels that saying the word somehow admits that she is wrong and cements in the fact, pushing away any remaining hope for Allison's return. It stings and stings hard.

"Don't you dare say that you're the only one devastated by the loss." His stern tone drives home his point. Taking a moment to soften his words, he continues,

"We all are. But we can't let our lives fall apart because she is gone. It sucks. It's a sad reality that no one, her father most of all, wants to admit, but it's reality, and wallowing in the fictitious doesn't do you any good, and it's not what Allison would want."

"Wouldn't she, though?" Scarlett asks, slinking down in her chair. "I mean, wouldn't anyone want others to wallow in the loss? It means you care."

"No. The whole 'the more you suffer, the more it shows you care' thing is asinine. Allison knows what it is like to suffer. She did it silently and look where it led. Do you think that knowing where it led for her, she'd want anyone, most of all you, to feel the same way?" he poses his question, but he wonders why he hasn't thought that before.

Scarlett tilts her head side to side while she ponders his words. Allison was her best friend. Why didn't she reach out to her for help? Perhaps she did, and Scarlett did not notice the cues and missed the warning signs. They all must have missed them; otherwise, Allison would still be here, and Scarlett would not be having this conversation. But that doesn't matter anymore. What matters is if Connor is right. Would Allison want Scarlett to feel the despair she felt before taking her life?

"No? I don't think so. She may have been a tiny ball of angry energy, but she was our tiny ball. She was my yang to my yin or whatever. How do I handle this? How do I act like her ... passing hasn't left me completely void? Tell me, Connor. How do I be like you?"

Those last words sting Connor, but he knows that is not how she meant them. He scoots closer to her.

"If I had those answers, I'd have shared them with you already, Cos'."

He holds back tears. Watching his cousin spiral further into depression chips away at the waning strength he musters to put on a happy face. He might fool Scarlett, Bri, Duncan, and anyone else he sees, but he can't fool himself. Watching his cousin be so vulnerable makes him feel that, maybe, she holds more answers than she realizes.

"How do I know that I'm not still in the Waiting or even dead? Every day gets worse and worse, and it's harder for me to hold on to the belief that crawling out of the dirt led me back home." She tries to look him in the eye while speaking, but can't bring herself to do so.

"I promise, this is as real as it gets," Connor says, shrugging his shoulders in acceptance of this dismal presence they share.

"But that's the thing, Con." Scarlett waves a pointed finger. "If I were dead, and being punished or tortured or whatever, you would say that. So how do I know that you're not just saying that to trick me?"

Connor grabs her hand, pulling it down to his lap. "It's hard to disprove something that can't be proven."

"Exactly. Anything anyone says to me just sounds like someone trying to convince a crazy person they're not crazy by playing into their delusion. Like, a long time ago, I was watching some show, and this guy was nuts, and they called his psychiatrist to the scene. She said to play into the delusion and let it play out, so when it ends, he'll come back to reality." Tears start falling down her cheeks.

"That's heavy. But I promise you, Scarlett, there's nothing delusional here. You're alive, and most of our friends and family are not. If this were some fugue state, would they have ever died, or would you have chosen one where they are still deceased?"

Scarlett opens her lips to speak but stops herself. Adjusting herself in the chair, she wipes away her tears. "It's too much, Con. Nothing makes sense."

"I know. Death is a hard thing to make sense of."

She shakes her head. "It's not that. While, I mean, it is that, but not only that."

He hesitates at opening another can of worms but decides to see what else he can add to the mix of emotions today.

"Then what is it?"

She fixes her gaze on him.

"Allison's not buried."

"What?"

"I'll tell you everything I've discovered, but you better buckle up."

She proceeds to tell him about the lack of a cemetery plot and the small interment she found instead. Filling him in on all the details between her time at the cemetery and in the forest.

After she finishes her story, Connor finds himself scooched back on his bed, leaning against the wall.

"That's a lot to take in," he says, stalling for time to think of something to say. "Vistrus could have changed his mind. He may have found cremation a more suitable situation."

She shakes her head. "No. No parent wants to bury a child, let alone burn them to ashes."

"It's a lot of coincidental elements you are linking together. There's no proof, no hard evidence," he says, offering a softened blow.

"It's too many coincidences, Con."

"How many more random elements until you find yourself so far down a rabbit hole you can't or won't come back from? How much more until you become the crazy conspiracy theorist people avoid?"

"Now you want to avoid me?"

"Not what I'm saying. I'm saying how far are you willing to go? Do you not remember what almost happened to me when searching for Jack?"

"Yeah. And you were right."

"But this is different."

"How?"

"Because you're wrong."

Still in disbelief, she looks around his room as if it still hides what she is searching for. "Am I? I mean, okay, work with me on this. We're in our twenties, but Legends have been around for centuries. And if they have their vials, they basically can't die." She waves her hands at the generalities of her words. "I mean, they can, but you know what I mean. So, how many Legends out there had to die and come back as someone else? How many of us no longer go by the names our parents gave us or live another life as someone else because we can't be who we are for too long, because of how we age? I've talked with Vistrus and Raymond and December. If word got out that I had died, I wouldn't be Scarlett anymore. I'd have to change my name to Violet or Rose or some other color."

"What are you getting at? Do you want us to call you Rose?"

"No. If I ever have to change my name, I want to be called Dorothy, but that's not the point."

"Then what is the point?"

"That all this evidence I found could be what's needed to make Allison look dead when she's not. No body left to ever dig up, no proof that she's not alive and living as someone else."

"If she were still alive, she'd have come back to you by now, whatever her name might be and whatever she looks like."

"But that's the thing. She could still be in the Waiting. She still could be effervescing."

"Convalescing, not effervescing."

"What's the difference?"

"Big difference. I'll explain later," he says, but before she has a chance to speak again, he continues. "Here's the thing, Scar. She's not in the Waiting. There's nothing to recover from. She opened her vial. Her 21 grams were in her when she passed."

"What?! How do you know?"

"After we left, Vistrus found the vials. She opened hers."

"I refuse to accept that." Scarlett's denial creeps back in.

"I wish it wasn't so, but it is. I am so sorry."

Memories of the last few days flood her mind, thinking of the cemetery, the forest, and everything that still doesn't make sense to her.

Shaking her head, Scarlett throws up her hands, waving them. "No. It's not true. It can't be. I know she's still with us. Even if you, Bri, Duncan, and her father have given up, I refuse to let go. You were right before, and I am right now."

"Except she's not missing. She's dead. Nobody wants it to be this way, but it is what it is, Scarlett. The sooner you come to accept the facts, the sooner you can heal."

Scarlett sits in stunned silence, trying to wrap her head around everything crumbling around her.

Connor stands up and moves to the window, pushing aside the shade and curtain to look outside. Darkness suffocates the backyard, but in his emotionally heightened state, he can see it as if it is midday.

He puts on a pair of jeans, patting the back pocket to make sure he has his wallet. He picks up a pair of socks off the floor, giving them a good sniff. Shrugging at the minimal smell, he puts them on.

He turns to Scarlett and grabs his cell phone off his desk but doesn't pocket it. "Take your time. Sit. Do what you need. I have to go do something. If you need, call."

She turns to him, an emptiness in her eyes stares past him. "I don't think I need anyone anymore."

At a loss for how to respond to such a statement, he leaves her alone in his room, closing the door behind him as he lights up his cell phone.

Connor pulls up to Bri's house. He sees front room lights shining through the curtains, but at this hour, he still feels his dropping by is more intrusion than welcome. After pulling out his cell phone, he sends her a text.

[Still cool?]

It doesn't take more than a moment before his phone chimes.

[Duncan says get your ass in here.]

He can't help but smile, hearing Duncan say this to her to tell him, as he turns off the ignition and exits.

Both Bri and Duncan stand at the door with smiles on their faces to greet Connor.

"What is this? Some Stepford suburban thing goin' on?" Connor chuckles.

Without responding, Bri plays into his comments. "Come inside. I'll start some tea and plate some cookies."

Furrowing his eyebrows, confused at her comment, he says, "No thanks. Not hungry?"

Duncan laughs, shaking his head.

Bri joins in the laughter, saying, "I was kidding. Stepford. You said it." Taking a beat to calm the moment back to a more serious note, she sits in the living room.

Connor snatches a spot on the reclining chair but doesn't start.

Duncan leans forward in his seat next to Bri. "Don't think ya came over for silent reverie."

Nodding his head and searching for how to start, all Connor musters is, "Yeah. I think I need your help."

He looks at both Duncan and Bri to make sure they know he meant both, but by now, he doesn't need to make Duncan feel included. He knows he is.

"Help with what? We breakin' back in?" Duncan says with a little too much excitement.

"No, yeah. I mean, yeah, eventually. But no, not now. Now…" Connor slumps in his chair. He tilts his head side to side, contorting his lips, not wanting to say anything bad or negative about his cousin. "Scarlett needs help."

"Like mental?" blurts Bri with undertones of sarcasm.

Duncan pats her on the shoulder. "Yes. I do believe that's what he means. But we don't joke about that." His eyes shoot wide, trying to remind her of recent events.

She looks down at her feet, realizing how she said it. "I didn't mean it like that. It just came out."

Connor waves it off. "We're friends. Under normal circumstances, you'd be fine, almost funny. But right now, I think you might be right."

Connor watches Bri's and Duncan's expressions turn completely serious and, from the weight on Bri's face, overwhelmed.

"When are things ever going to let up around here?" Bri says, exasperated.

Putting a pin in her question for a moment, Duncan turns from her to Connor, asking, "What's goin' on?"

"The short of it, she's not doing too hot with Al's passing." His mouth cringes at the last word. No hesitation in saying it; it feels wrong to him how it rolled so naturally off his tongue.

Duncan gives a short couple of nods of understanding. "What can we do?"

Connor's face winces at the question, telling of more that weighs on him.

"What is it?" Duncan asks in response to his wince. "What else you not tellin' us?"

"The pale woman I met. Something's not sitting right with the last time I saw her," Connor says, while trying to connect the thoughts. "It's probably nothing."

"But…" Duncan prods.

"But I just can't shake it."

Bri jumps in, saying, "Spill it, Con. Whatever it is, we can't help Scar if your mind is all bogged down with thoughts of another female."

"It ain't like that, Bri," Connor says, managing a chuckle.

Bri laughs along with him. "However it is, it needs to be figured out. So, spill."

Connor and the pale woman walk side by side through the forest preserves. The cloudy sky and heavy tree cover make the woods pitch dark. The minimal light illuminating the woods only paints highlights on their surroundings.

"Why are we strolling through the woods?" asks Connor, a little uncertain of her intentions.

"Because I still can't seem to convince you that the answers I have are the answers you seek," the pale woman responds. A small smile inchworms onto her face.

"And our jaunt will somehow assure me?" The scrunched look on his face screams of skepticism.

"In the end, we can lead the thirsty to water, but we cannot make them drink." She stops for a moment to turn to Connor and offer a saccharine smile. "If you do not want what I offer, then I offer, at the very least, my friendship."

"So, this is just two friends taking an after-hours stroll through a forest preserve?" He tightens up at her attempts to ease his suspicion.

She shrugs, turning her palms skyward. "If that's all you want, yes. If you decide to ask questions, then I shall answer."

She continues her stroll, and he keeps pace. He studies her expression while they walk in silence, though he gleans nothing useful. Relenting to her lack of tells, he finally breaks the silence.

"You've already told me the why of why me," he begins.

She gives a deliberate nod that urges him to continue.

"You've even told me a bit of why The Nation," he continues before pausing.

Her eyebrow raises in curiosity as to where his thought is leading.

"But ... why does it ... matter to you specifically?" he stumbles over his words, almost as if they were not what he wanted to say but all that his mind would allow his lips to utter.

A dog-sly smile paints itself across her face. She struggles to wipe it off, but cannot. Something hidden under that expression sets Connor's alarm bells ablaze. He watches her try to hide the joy she feels, knowing that joy, generally, does not need hiding. But she tries, and it's her attempt to do so that makes him think of a slimy used car salesman knowing the car he's about to sell has damage that will cost more than the price tag. The smile hides secrets she will never reveal. A smile that sends shivers down his spine and a voice inside his head telling him that if he ever found them out, he would not live to tell anyone.

She looks at the canopy above, trying to see the night sky beyond. She stops and inhales as if experiencing the smell of night-blooming jasmine for the first time. After a moment for herself, she turns to him.

"My reasons run deeper than the waters they live in. I am not sure you'd understand." She stops for a moment to study him. "But you seem to trust me. Or at least, you trust me enough to walk the woods with me while no one else is around for, well, they are far enough away." Again, she pauses, but Connor does not offer words. "Those with faith need no explanation."

Connor breaks his silence. "And those with an explanation have no need for faith. So, which is it going to be? A need for faith on my end or an explanation on yours?"

She turns back to the woods, continuing her stroll. Connor does not follow, opting to wait and see if she'll urge him along. After a few yards, she turns back to him, waving him to her.

"Faith and trust go hand in hand. Without one, you cannot have the other. And, as I've pointed out, here you are, alone with me. That points to a level of trust, which has me asking myself, 'What have I done to this poor boy that he has no faith in what I want from him?' And for that

answer, I would turn to you, but I do not think your brain has formulated that answer yet."

She pauses to see if Connor will try to respond, but he does not. Choosing silence as a momentary companion, they both walk for a few minutes, letting the night sink into them. Connor spends his time alternating between watching the forest floor so he doesn't trip and studying her expression to find a kernel of truth in her words. But all his eyes can see are the blurred lies hidden by her smile and squinted eyes.

"You say faith and trust go hand in hand, but they don't. I trust a train barreling toward me on the tracks will try to stop if he sees me. But I do not have faith that the train will be able to stop, no matter how hard he pulls the brakes. I also have faith that I can prove my innocence in my grandfather's murder. But I do not trust that I can do it alone. So no, they do not go hand in hand." He takes a deep breath, annoyed that she still will not tell her reasons, nor does she offer them now. Continuing, he says, "However, if you have the answers and will not share, then yes, faith and trust do go hand in hand in that I have neither in you."

She nods her head as another smile etches on her face. This smile is not one he has seen before. Malice and contempt sculpt this smile, and a fire in her eyes does not call for Connor to come warm by it. This fire calls for him to roast on it. But, as he feels the heat of her newfound, growing wrath, it dissipates.

"Perhaps you are not the man I thought you were."

"Perhaps I'm not."

She huffs. "I had a vision for us. A vision where we led The Nation beyond West Haven."

"Beyond West Haven?"

"The Nation is not some Chicago suburb organization for a few Legends with nowhere else to turn. There are councils all over the United States. Outside every major city lies at least one council. In every state, Legends are trying to live their best life, encumbered only by the fear of how the Normals will treat them. Every country on this planet has its members."

She shakes her head, trying to embrace his naiveté for a moment. A part of her wants to revert to that innocence of becoming an adult and knowing you're supposed to know while knowing that you don't know all the answers. In this fleeting moment, she longs to be who she once was and can never be again.

"Did you really think that the West Haven Council, that the confines of The Nation, lie within the greater Chicagoland area? Did you think them as some locally owned company with a service range? This is worldwide, and you and I could be at the top. But we cannot get there without starting where we are."

Calming herself from her empathic speech, she looks him in the eye, impressing her urgency on him. His eyes, however, fight off any attempt to be overtaken by the sadness in her. But that's what he sees; a desperate sadness that rages against whatever it is she will not tell him. To Connor, it is what she will not tell him that causes his resistance.

"You have the opportunity to use your current … dilemma to your advantage. A moment where you can come out on top and in control of not only your life but the life of the West Haven Council. I believe I can get them to understand your side and welcome you. But you have to have faith in me. You have to trust that what I do is for the best, and that means supporting every action I take, unwavering

and without question. If you can do that, I can offer you everything."

Connor steps away from her, putting distance between them. He scans the forest for anyone else, listening for heartbeats, footsteps, and whatever else might give away the presence of someone else. Nothing. It is only them. Even the sound of passing cars is too distant to be of help, should things head where they might.

"If you can offer me everything, then you can offer me nothing. The man who sold the world sold back to us what we already possessed. I will not be sold what is already mine. Without the truth, which you so willingly conceal, your offerings hold no temptation. I cannot stand by someone who appeals to base human desires and no clear path to arrive there because they have no clear motives to offer."

The pale woman stands shocked, but the shock only slows the growth of her anger. Noticing her anger causes his heart rate to rise and his muscles to ripple with the need to transition into his Legendary state. He feels his skull start to stretch as he speaks.

"I never wanted the world, only what was mine. The world belongs to no one man, and anyone who thinks it does has nothing to offer that he doesn't intend to take back."

Connor pauses, watching the pale woman's skin start to cover itself in bark. He waits, seeing if she steps toward him, but she does not.

Nodding, she says, "I am sorry you feel that way. I did not bring you out here to fight." She steps farther away from him. "Think about what I said. If you change your mind, I'm sure you'll see me again."

She turns away from Connor, disappearing into the woods around them.

Connor stands still for a long while, listening to her heart pump blood through her body as her skin crunches and crackles, turning from bark back to flesh. Even after all the noises from her transition have long faded, he stands, listening to the sounds of the night, ensuring that when he moves, it is safe to do so.

"You tool," Bri says as Connor finishes telling the story.

"Tool?" Connor replies with a hint of indignation.

"Yeah, tool. As in, the answer is right in front of you, and you're, like, too much of a tool to think critically enough to see it." Bri smiles at her own observation.

Duncan sits, opting for the role of silent spectator while quiet chuckles escape his lungs.

Connor leans forward in his seat. "I think, like, an explanation is in order," he says, mocking her use of the word "like."

"You're so caught up in, like, the memory of the experience and, like, the adrenaline at the end that you missed the reason it keeps, like, running through that thick skull of yours," she says, adding an extra emphasis on the numerous "likes," knowing it annoys Connor.

Running his hand through his hair, Connor sinks back into his seat, thinking that she might have a point. The running hand turns into a head scratch as he cannot put a pin in where the point lies.

"Fine, Bri. Tell this tool where his sentience fell short."

Bri purses her lips, as if the thought in her mind inflicts pain. "Your sentence … what does a short sentence have to do with anything?"

An uncontrollable laugh escapes Connor and Duncan. Both catch it before it continues, though more laughter tries to break free.

"Not sentence, love," Duncan chimes in from the proverbial stands. "Sentience. As in, intelligent creature capable of abstract thought."

Bri's finger shoots into the air before tapping herself on the forehead in recognition of her momentary lapse of intelligence. "I knew that. Must have been a blonde moment."

"So?" Connor urges her back to the topic at hand.

Shaking her head clear, she responds, "Yeah, so it wasn't the end that stuck with you, since that's where you and her split ways."

"Love, what was it then?" Duncan steers her to the point.

"It was earlier, like way earlier, when she talked about being thirsty for water." A big smile crosses her face, proud of her moment.

"Then why'd you let me tell the whole damn story?" Connor asks, tossing a dismissive hand toward her.

"'Cause, it's, like, rude to interrupt." She laughs. "But the water is the point. Not the weird shit at the end."

Relenting to Bri's point, he sighs. "Fine. What's the point of the water in all this?"

Bri beams with pride, knowing she figured out something Connor didn't. "Scarlett needs help. Yeah?"

Connor shrugs, nodding his head. "Yeah."

Continuing, Bri says, "Just like a thirsty person needs to drink water."

"Okay," he continues, trying to predict where she is going with this.

"But if Scarlett knows the help is there but isn't taking it, it's not our job to walk away from her." Bri's hand tries to goad Connor to arrive at her conclusion before she says it, but he's still not catching on.

She continues, "Then we don't abandon her with help she cannot utilize. We walk with her through the woods until she decides she either a) wants our help, or b) walks away altogether."

"But I don't want her to completely walk away from us." Connor's words hold an undertone of desperation.

Duncan raises a quick finger to chime in. "But we already have. Instead of listening to what she has to say and figuring out if she's right, we keep forcing this idea on her that her friend is gone."

"But she is," Connor interjects.

"Yeah, she is. But think about it from her side. She was, too, and now she's back. She's holding onto this hope that will never diminish because she experienced it firsthand. And until she has concrete evidence, there's probably going to be no convincing her otherwise."

Connor runs his hand through his hair, sighing at the thought of what lies ahead.

"So, what do we do?" Connor lays out the question to end it all.

"We listen." Duncan keeps it simple.

"We listen?" Connor repeats.

"Yeah, we listen and be there for her. We don't tell her over and over, hoping she finally understands. We have the evidence. Use it to disprove her theory, and then she will have to see the truth."

Connor takes a deep breath, holding it for a moment to try to calm himself. Upon exhaling, he realizes the stress of it all became a thousand times heavier with Duncan's words.

Duncan notices Connor's hesitation, as does Bri.

"What up, Con? You don't seem convinced," Bri says, joining back in.

Connor shakes his head. "No. I'm convinced. It's just that … if we show up and provide all the evidence, that might push her farther away from us. I don't know…"

A laugh escapes Duncan. "We don't just barge in with a box full of dirt and a lock of hair and be all, 'See, now you can't deny it.' That sort of strong-arm tactic never works on someone so caught up in their own theories."

"What?" Bri asks, her face rife with confusion.

"You can't disprove something that doesn't exist. It goes back to walking through the forest." Duncan brings it back to the beginning.

Bri's eyes light up. "We walk with her. Let her talk it out with us and we just, like, listen."

Duncan taps his finger to his nose, then points it at her. "Exactly. Once she has said all she can say about it, we go with her, still listening and waiting until she proves herself wrong. Then, and only then, can we say what we need."

"This sounds like a lot of tiptoeing," Bri observes.

"Yeah, it is. But I think Duncan's onto something," Connor says, finally coming around to seeing the bigger picture. "Had I believed the pale lady, she would have shown me more. But what she said didn't play to my needs."

Duncan smiles. "All we have to do is play to hers."

"Yeah, but how?" Connor's growing skepticism doesn't quell his current anxiety. "I mean, we can't literally walk in a forest. I get the metaphor you painted plain enough now. But the execution…"

"That's a completely different monster," Duncan finishes Connor's thought.

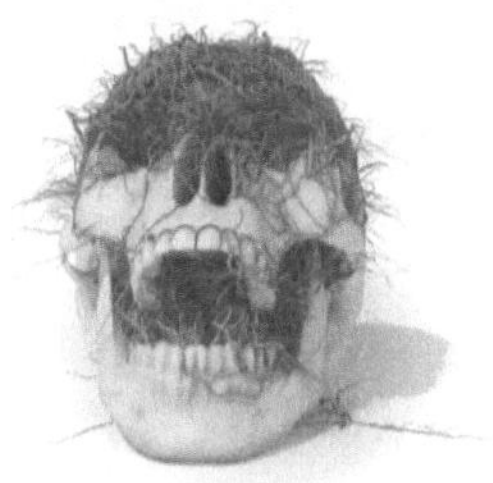

CHAPTER 17

*"There's something to be said for
keeping one's mouth shut."*
~E. DeSalvo~

Late-night strolls always provide Vistrus a certain sense of peace, even if he uses said strolls to try to track down a wanted man. Tonight is no different. The West Haven alleyways lack any signs of life. Even the rodents seem as if they are vacationing elsewhere. While he hopes that his time defending his beloved city from the Adeirrig will end in finding out his whereabouts, he knows the night might be best spent uneventful.

The night presses on with a near-full moon gracing the sky. Turning down a sidewalk to a side road for one last look before calling it a night, Vistrus spots a familiar figure down the block. He rubs his eyes, shaking his head in disbelief. A familiarity in the silhouetted outline stops him dead in his tracks. His ears pick up a racing heartbeat, causing him to check his surroundings for a moment before realizing the heart he hears is his. Try as he may to calm himself, a plethora of emotions roil below the surface while tears well in his eyes. He watches the figure walk in his direction, getting ever closer. His eyes find no need to struggle in the darkness, but she stands too far in the distance to be certain. Though he shouldn't be uncertain. The figure making her way to him has been deceased for nearly twenty years. But as she walks with a delicate grace he hasn't seen in as many years, he no longer believes his eyes.

"Inessa," he whispers to himself.

His heart yearns to run to her and embrace her in his arms. A feeling he has longed for every day since her passing. But his mind croaks the impossibility of it all to himself, leaving him to stand, unable to move as the evidence of her being grows more undeniable with every step she takes.

His well of tears breaks the dam and falls down his cheeks. The uncertainty of it all being made more and more certain each time the light catches her face, painting a smile on him from ear to ear. Even the pounding thump-thump of his heart overwhelms his ears.

As she walks closer, he notices her demeanor differs from his memory. She seems almost lost—out of place. His newfound joy turns to concern. He smells something rotten in West Haven.

"Inessa? Love, is that you?" he calls out in a whisper loud enough that a soft shout would have sufficed.

She stops herself, finally seeing him as if for the first time. Looking around all shifty-eyed, she turns to him. Recognizing Vistrus, a smile creeps across her face. "Of course, it's me."

Vistrus also does a quick scan, finding nobody. "Yes. You are my beloved."

Her smile twists with scheming thoughts. "Of course I am. As you are mine."

He stares at a face he hasn't seen in so many years, feeling like something does not add up. Her bone structure remains as his memory recalls. Her eyes and hair are both as before. But something seems less than what he remembers. Perhaps the way the moonlight and shadows hit her face distorts the memory he holds so dear.

"How have you returned to me? Where have you been all these years?" he asks, his heart pounding in anticipation of the answer as any rational thought evades him.

She shrugs, looking around for others as if they lurk in the shadows. Turning back to him, her face scrunches, searching for an answer. "I don't remember."

His yearning for a storybook reuniting of lost love turns to concern that this woman, be it his long-thought-deceased Inessa or some imposter, is neither healthy nor safe.

"Where are you going?" Vistrus asks.

She stares down the street, looking for an answer to his question. He tries to see what caught her attention, but all he can see are driveways leading to the street, with cars parked in a few of them. Following her line of sight, she appears to stare at a driveway finished with large pavers instead of concrete. But as soon as he turns back to her, her focus shifts farther down.

"Is that where you are headed?" Vistrus asks, pointing down the road to the paved driveway.

She waves her head around, lost in her thoughts that leave wanting eyes gleaming in the streetlights.

"Where are you coming from?" he asks, changing course.

Head tilted to the side, she turns back to him. "A long way from home."

"And where is home?" Hope grows in his heart like a bad fungal infection he knows should not be there.

Those words jostle something in her mind, clearing it and causing her to focus on him. "With you, Vistrus."

The hope he thought should not be there grows even more. To hear her say his name again brings an indescribable joy he never knew existed. All fears wash away at the sound of her words. A sanctuary from all that troubles him surrounds the two of them right now. He did not realize that he could feel such feelings.

He smiles as a couple of joy-filled tears fall. Extending his arms out to embrace her, he says, "Inessa, my love. I never thought I would see you again. You look as beautiful as you did all those years ago. How … is this possible?"

She enters his warm embrace, wrapping her arms around him. Resting his head on her shoulder, he stares off into the distance, letting this moment overtake him. Tightening his squeeze on her for a moment, he inhales her scent. However, it does not trigger any memories of her. No undertones of what he knew as her carry in her scent. Something sets off his internal alarm. An unnamed, unnerving feeling about the way she feels in her arms. This woman in his arms looks and sounds like Inessa, but she feels like someone else. Still, he holds onto her and the hope that those misgivings are wrong.

In the far distance, away from Inessa's line of sight, Vistrus sees someone turn onto their sidewalk. He struggles to see so far away, but again, an air of familiarity lies in that person. While concentrating on figuring out the new person and why, for two people in a row, he thinks he knows them, Inessa pulls away a few inches. As she backs away, a stabbing pain engulfs his abdomen.

Fighting against the agony and warm blood flowing down his hands, he falls to the ground. His muscles tense and his heartbeat quickens, but no skin stretches, no muscles grow, and no hair thins. Try as he may, he cannot find it within himself to transition to his Legendary state.

Tears fill his eyes, blurring his vision as he looks up at Inessa. He coughs, and a little spittle of blood flies out of his mouth.

"Why?" is the only word he manages before she turns and walks away.

Tears blur the image of Inessa as she walks farther and farther away. He cries, wondering why this happened, thinking over and over about what he could have done to deserve this punishment. As thoughts swirl in his brain, mixing the reasons why with excruciating pain, he hears fast-approaching footsteps behind him.

As they get closer, he hears a woman call out, "Mr. P!?"

His thoughts settle down for a moment, recognizing Scarlett's voice. She stops next to him, squatting down. He turns his head, nodding to the woman in the distance.

"What do I do?" A frantic shaking takes control of her words. "How do I stop the bleeding? Help!" Her words come out faster and faster, raising in pitch. "Mr. P, I don't know what to do. You're bleeding so much! How can I stop it?!"

The pitch of her voice raises so high that it becomes inaudible to her. Clearing her throat, she rephrases her last sentence. "I need to stop this bleeding!" But again, she cannot hear herself.

"Apply pressure," he says, still maintaining some strength.

"How?" her dog's-ears-only, panicked voice asks.

"Press hard with one hand. Like I am."

She presses down with one hand, pulling her cell phone out with the other. "Who do I call?"

"Call your grandmother. Find out who took over for Dr. Wong."

Her thumbs struggle to wrap around the phone to tap the screen open. The more she struggles, the more her breathing intensifies. After a few frustrating fails, she manages to unlock the phone and dial her grandmother.

Each passing ring increases her panic and rate of breathing. Staring with helpless eyes down at Vistrus, he meets her gaze with wide eyes, and a smile trying to stifle itself.

After the fourth ring, Eleanor picks up. Still higher-pitched than usual, but within the human range of hearing, Scarlett says, "Dr. Wong needs to take over!"

Confused by the unexpected, high-pitched greeting, but sensing Scarlett's panic, Eleanor asks, "Scarlett, is that you? Is everything all right?"

"Dr. Wong! Who took him over?!" Scarlett's anxiety grows with each passing moment. She does not realize the changes in her appearance Vistrus sees.

"Dr. Quinn. Why? What happened?" Eleanor asks, trying to come up to speed on the events.

"I don't know. Mr. Petrovsky's been stabbed. I'm holding his wound shut. Pressure. Send help. Send Dr. Quinn." Scarlett calms down a few notches, and while still bordering on panic, she controls her breathing.

Coughing, Vistrus says, "Tell her to hurry. Something is not right."

On the phone, Eleanor says, "I heard him. Where are you?"

"On Olcott, between Kedzie and Monroe. Hurry. He doesn't look too hot!" She hangs up the phone, turning back to Mr. Petrovsky. "Sorry I said that. You look fine."

She turns her attention to the wound, seeing her arm for the first time since her freak-out. While no new blood leaks out onto her crimson-stained hand, her arm appears far more pale than she has ever been. Even in the streetlights, she stares at veins and arteries not normally visible. While it might be shadows cast by the moonlight and street lamps, she thinks she can see the muscle tissue beneath her circulatory system.

"This isn't real," she mutters to herself. Her hand starts to pull off the wound.

"Keep applying pressure," he urges, reminding her of the current predicament. "I assure you, this is one hundred percent real."

"Nope. I'm not here. I'm still lying under that pile of dirt and this is my mind somehow seeing my body decay," she deludes herself.

"Scarlett," he begins, ensuring her attention focuses on him, "you are not buried. You are witnessing your first transition into your Legendary state. Albeit a partial transition, a transition nonetheless."

Keeping pressure on the wound, Scarlett examines her other arm to find the same translucency. "Does my face also look like something out of Hellraiser Jr.?"

"Do not belittle yourself. Use your phone's camera," he suggests.

Still applying pressure to his wound, she uses her free hand to fumble the phone camera open. Her thumb hovers over the reverse camera button, debating the pros and cons of seeing herself in even a partially Legendary state at this moment.

Watching her face, Vistrus knows she still holds no knowledge of her appearance. "Look already. It is very interesting."

"Always what a girl wants to hear," she says, laughing at the unintended moment of levity. Approaching sirens warn them that she does not have much time before she needs to look like her Normal self again. In her morbid curiosity, she switches the camera to the front view, but the image is blurry, like the camera won't focus. She presses the screen on where her face should be, but it only scrambles like an old analog signal. She pockets the phone in frustration, leaving only Vistrus to see her veins and arteries push blood through her circulatory system. Vistrus concentrates on the striations of her jaw and facial muscles moving with every furrow of her brow, and each time she opens and closes her mouth in some attempt to make sense of this situation. He must concentrate and stay alert.

The sirens push every closer, working her up into visible anxiety. Turning to Vistrus, she says, "Make me, me again. They can't see me like this."

Shaking his head, he responds, "No, they cannot. Breathe slowly. In and out as if you are meditating. In and out. One breath at a time. Slow and deep." He watches her follow his commands. "Close your eyes. Forget the sirens. Forget my wound, but keep pressure on it. Only think about your breathing. In … out … in … out."

She does as she's told and slowly her body returns to what she prefers seeing in the mirror. As she opens her eyes, the ambulance turns the corner. With her free arm, she waves them down. The ambulance stops and the back doors open. Two EMTs and a female doctor, all in mid-conversation, exit the back of the ambulance.

"We are trained professionals, Dr. Quinn. I still hold that we did not need a doctor's assistance," the EMT says.

"Trained professionals or not, this call specifically requested me. So, let's do what we're here to do," Dr. Quinn returns the volley. Turning to Vistrus, she asks, "How are you holding up?"

"Not as good as I should, considering…" Vistrus's words hold an ominous tone.

Dr. Quinn nods. "I think I understand. In that case, we need to get you taken care of quick." Turning to Scarlett, she adds, "On the count of three, you are going to let go, and I'll take your place." She waits for Scarlett's confirming nod. "One … two … three." Scarlett removes her hand and the doctor presses down. "Good job, miss."

Scarlett nods. "Who do you need me to call?" she asks Vistrus, while looking at the paramedics start their job.

"Go home and wash up. The doctor has me from here. Fill in Eleanor and Connor. Tell the others if you want, but Eleanor and Connor are a must," Vistrus says as the paramedics work away on him. "Scarlett…" She turns her gaze to him. "You did well."

The paramedics lift him onto the gurney and raise it before pushing him into the ambulance.

"We'll get to the hospital after I tell Grams," she shouts as they shut the door.

Scarlett stands in the middle of a residential road, half-covered in her deceased best friend's father's blood as the ambulance carries him away.

"It's not abandoning her," Duncan assures, opening a box of Rosati's pizza. "You want mushroom and onion or pepperoni and sausage?"

"Both, please," Bri says from the kitchen as she grabs glasses and a two-liter of soda. "Well, she thinks it is."

"And she's wrong. Going through stuff or not right now, the house is fifteen minutes down the road. It's barely moving." He plates up a square slice of each for her and a few of each for himself. "Either way, I am not sure *that* house is really what we want, even if the area is."

"I thought it was … charming." Bri enters the living room with the glasses and soda. She sits on the couch next to Duncan. "At least no one I know has died there."

Taking a bite of his pizza, Duncan chuckles. "While a noble item on the list of pros, I don't think that's a great reason to say yes to a house you think is *charming*. We should pass. Keep looking."

Bri flips through channels with the remote. "Yeah, you're right. I never envisioned myself living at home at this age."

"A good house isn't cheap, and the last thing you want to buy is a money pit. Good bones only go so far." He spies a good John Hughes flick on the television. "Stop. Let's watch this."

She sets the remote on the couch arm. "I can't argue that. Moving was supposed to be the fix we needed."

"What fix? I didn't realize we were broken."

Bri slouches in her spot, gingerly tearing a bite off her slice of pizza. "*We're* not. *I* am."

"But you're not. Never have been." He sets down his plate of pizza and clears his mouth out with a drink of soda. The movie drones in the background as a red-headed teen yells at his father about not going to college and spending his college money on a pair of earrings. Continuing, Duncan says, "I know you love makin' sure you look as beautiful as you can all the time. Presenting yourself in the best light helps boost self-image issues you'd rather not admit to."

Bri raises her hands to object, but Duncan throws up a finger and scrunches his face, signaling he's not finished.

"And being in … whatever Society it is that you're in doesn't help when you don't like what you see in the mirror normally, let alone when you are in your Legendary form. But that image you see, the one that makes you doubt yourself, makes you doubt your self-worth, only exists in your head. What everyone else around you saw, even what Allison saw, was only ever the beautiful and well-meaning, if perhaps a little misguided, woman that I see right now. No one out there thinks you're better off any other way."

A smile creeps across Bri's face. She looks down at her hands that now hold his, rubbing her thumbs over his hands while staying intertwined. His words ring true. A fundamental truth of who she sees versus who everyone else sees will never be the same person. If she is ever to overcome her self-doubt, she knows she'll need someone by her side. She lifts her head to meet his waiting gaze.

"So, like, now what?" Meek words fall from her lips. Her eyes gaze into his, but only a blurry picture paints itself on the canvas of his eyes.

"Now we keep looking. We don't rush into anything. We have a place, and while it's not one we want to stay in, it's secure and, except for a few tragic and traumatic events, is filled with a lifetime of memories. As for the other wounded hand, before we offer any help, we need to assess how bad she is right now."

"Like…" Bri starts a thought that flees before she can grasp it. "…I lost it. Like, what does that mean?"

"It means, if we are to help Scarlett somehow, we need to figure out where she's at, mentally or otherwise. We need to disprove her belief that Allison is in the Waiting without breaking her further. It means we need to find a way to help her heal without making the pain worse; otherwise, we could push her farther away, and she may never properly heal."

He leans in and kisses her forehead.

"What was that for?" she asks.

"Thinking about what she's going through and that it could have easily been you another time makes me glad you are as strong as you are, whether you realize it or not. And I love you for that and many other reasons."

Bri leans in, planting a big kiss square on the lips.

"I hope that one day I can believe in myself as much as you believe in me."

"You will. But things take time."

"I ain't got nothing but," she quips. "So, Scarlett, how exactly are we going to do everything you said and help her heal? I don't think this is something we can bring to a guy who smacks her on the forehead, causing her to fall over, having a semi-seizure, before she gets up all cured."

A huff escapes Duncan. "Me neither, but we need something."

"Something indeed. You're the idea man. Any ideas?" Bri raises an eyebrow, hoping to conjure something from the depths of his mind.

But Duncan only shakes his head. "Nothing. I think we may need Connor to help carve a path through these unknown woods."

"You're big idea is Connor? Man, I had much higher hopes for you with all the big talk on how to help her." She chuckles.

"Hey," he says, grinning, "at least I had a start of an idea. You couldn't even complete yours. But you're right. I'll need something to bring to Connor. Let's head over and see what he thinks."

Bri picks up her empty plate. "Can the great Scarlett intervention convention wait until after we finish eating? I'm still famished."

Duncan nods. "Me too. Let's eat."

Scarlett's brisk pace carries her down West Haven side streets toward her grandmother's house. Cell phone in hand, she hits send, hoping Grandma Eleanor answers; it only takes two rings before she does.

"Hello?"

"Grandma, hey. Something happened to Vistrus."

Before Scarlett elaborates any further, Eleanor cuts her off. "Not on the phone. Come over. I'll put on some tea."

As she slips her phone into her pocket, it rings. Looking at the name, expecting it to be Grandma asking what kind of tea she'd enjoy, surprise greets her with the name Brianna.

"Bad timing, Bri," Scarlett starts.

"No hello? Bad timing, for sure. What's up?" Bri's tone turns serious.

Scarlett's pace quickens in proportion to her growing anxiety. "Can you come to Grams's?"

"Like, now?" Bri asks, surprised by Scarlett's request at this time of night.

"Yeah, like now." Scarlett's urgency knocks any nonchalance out of Bri.

"Of course. Duncan?" Worry creeps into Bri.

"Sure." While Scarlett may not have intended to sound dismissive of Duncan with one word, it rang that way.

"We'll … be right there." Bri holds back her urge to poke at the bear that was Scarlett's last reply.

"One more thing." Scarlett's tone turns apologetic.

"What?"

"Can you pick me up? I'm out."

"Where?"

"Olcott and Kedzie. Hurry." Scarlett hangs up.

Looking around, waiting for her ride, she can't help thinking about each passing car and the obliviousness they possess to recent events. But as she thinks about their ignorance of what transpired, she thinks about what their lives must be like. How their lives were probably very similar a few years ago. Walking around thinking that the world was far more simple than it is now. But nostalgia for simpler times does not wash over her. Scarlett does not don rose-colored glasses; she knows that some of those passing cars live lives as complicated as her. Whether it is on the same level is a different story, but complicated is complicated. Each passing car holds a life as full as hers. The distance between their lives keeps them safe from each other. No Legends to impact the Normals. No Normals seeking death to the Legends they fear. But the separation of those lives may only be a temporary state. Even if the separation is one-sided. So, for the moments she waits for Bri to pick her up, Scarlett ponders the sonder she feels about each passing car.

Eleanor hangs up the kitchen phone and walks into the dining room. She pours tea into three fancy porcelain cups from a matching teapot, saying nothing of her phone call with Scarlett. Passing out the cups to Raymond and December, she then takes a sip before sitting at the dining room table with them. While family and those she considers family gather around the kitchen table, and the two guests could be considered friends, their visit's urgency makes Eleanor think the dining room a more proper place.

The three of them enjoy a sip of tea. Raymond and December sit, contemplating the phone call they overheard while waiting for Eleanor to prompt the reason for their visit. Eleanor notes their curiosity.

"Some news about Vistrus, since I can tell you are wondering. Our time is limited right now, so I'll get right to it. From what I understand, your watch as Sentinels came to an abrupt, if voluntary, end," Eleanor begins, sipping her tea.

Raymond smiles, but it fades just as fast. His voice chimes in Eleanor's mind, "The Council led us to believe it knew more about our concerns than it did."

"And finding that leaves us with nothing to give them," December adds to Eleanor's mind. "It was an agreement of mutual accord. Deception does not find a wanting subject."

Eleanor nods, setting down her glass. "Understood. So, our little Council here in West Haven proves quite the conundrum. Is that why you're here?"

December and Raymond share a look, but neither says anything that Eleanor hears in her head. December sips her tea, looking down at the liquid before speaking in Eleanor's mind. "Delicious. Irish Breakfast?"

Eleanor shakes her head. "Scottish Breakfast. Similar, but a tad smoother." A chuckle escapes her. "It's nice having company over the age of twenty-one, but you didn't come here to talk tea."

Raymond sets down his glass after taking a long drink. The words in Eleanor's head sound softer than he usually lets on, betraying a need for something he has never spoken of before. "We are looking for something that belongs to December. We would like it back."

Eleanor, out of habit, reaches to clutch her necklace hiding beneath her blouse. She grabs it once before letting go, almost in some unconscious need to ensure its safety. "Whatever I can do to help. What is it you are looking for?"

December notices Eleanor grab something under her blouse, but decides not to ask, instead sipping tea as her words sink into Eleanor's brain. "A charcoal portrait I drew many … many years ago." December pauses, gauging Eleanor's reaction, but reads nothing. "In fact, I had given it originally to someone else for safekeeping, but that person's time has passed."

Raymond chimes in, "Now we only seek to procure what is rightfully hers." His head nods to December.

Eleanor nods; her first reaction since the reason for their visit has come to light. "A portrait? Like a self-portrait?" she asks, keeping her motives close to her chest.

December straightens herself to speak but glances at Raymond first. A slight nod from him indicates she shares his want.

"Not a self-portrait. It was … just a face I imagined. No monetary value. However, it is mine, and I feel that it might be safer in my hands than anyone else's. I hope that makes sense." Her words float through Eleanor as if a songbird sang them.

"Who did you give it to that they cannot give it back?" Eleanor asks, prying for information they may not otherwise concede.

Raymond shakes his head. "I gave it to an old friend, someone who passed from this world almost twenty years ago. Their name does not matter. What does are the whispers we hear. Having acted as Sentinels, the watchmen of West Haven, we hear things. Rumors, facts, or otherwise. But the birds whisper that might know what we seek."

Playing into his metaphor, Eleanor adds, "This whispering bird, a split-tongue raven, I presume, or African Gray, if words are literal. What did it kaw?"

"That its resting spot has been disturbed. That this portrait I sketched," December chimes in Eleanor, "has more to do with recent events than I can explain."

A fading smile on Eleanor emphasizes her words. "As I said, dear, if I can help, I'll help. What do you need from me?"

"Whoever has it, it is mine, and we will do whatever it takes to get it back. We would like you to let us know if you know of its whereabouts." December ends her thought with a smile, finishing her cup of tea.

"If I find anything, I'll let you know. I wouldn't want to keep something too invaluable to someone away from them, especially if they are the rightful owner."

Raymond stands, finishing his tea. Pushing in his chair, his thought sounds in Eleanor. "We appreciate your time. If this matter can be handled with finesse, we have more we'd like to discuss."

Eleanor stands, waiting to walk them to the door. "I'd be delighted to help any way I can. Thank you both so much for the visit. I can't wait to do it again."

Raymond and December walk in front of Eleanor, who sees them out.

Watching them drive off, Eleanor formulates a plan to keep Scarlett safe and the portrait away from

Raymond and December until she figures out why they want it back so badly.

Scarlett enters the backseat of Bri's car, shutting the door behind her. Before she has a chance to buckle in, Bri pulls away from the curb. "Grams's, huh?" Bri asks for confirmation.

Setting the buckle in its latch, Scarlett turns back to Bri. "Yeah." Pulling out her cell phone, she types up a text to Connor.

[Get to Grams's.]

She hits send, setting her phone on her lap. Glancing out the window for a moment, she turns back to her phone, lighting up the screen in case she missed a response.

Duncan pulls down the passenger vanity mirror to sneak a peek at Scarlett. He watches for a moment, trying to decide what to say and when to interrupt her, while Scarlett mentally wanders, lost in consternation. After the third time she checks her phone, he decides to break the silence. "Are you gonna tell us why we had to pick you up and why we are going to your grandma's?"

She checks her phone one more time, but still no response from Connor. "I was waiting for Connor, but yeah, so ... something happened."

By the time they arrive at Grandma Eleanor's house, Scarlett finishes filling them in on the happenings of her transition and Vistrus's stabbing.

Duncan holds back a smile wanting to creep out. To him, her transition sounds like the coolest thing ever, but he also knows that the circumstances prompting it are nothing he should smile at. So he sits, trying for a cool nonchalance, but he can feel the corners of his mouth curl up a little.

Putting the car in park, Bri turns back and stares at Scarlett. They both remain silent, knowing the flood of sensations that accompany a transition. The stare they share holds unspoken feelings of everything they must hide while wanting to shout it from the top of their lungs because this thing they possess embodies their truest state so uniquely, and they must live knowing the rest of the world will never know them for all they can be. And that shared state of fear and uncertainty is why neither of them sees Duncan holding back his grin. It's why neither turns to share in this silence with him because he can never understand the fear they feel. A fear that, while Brianna has known for a few years, Scarlett has known for a couple of hours.

"Allison would have thought you looked cool," Duncan says, breaking the silence.

Both ladies turn to him, unsure they heard him properly.

He throws his hands up in apology. "I know I have no right to speak on what you went through. I can't do that. But you have to admit, Allison would have liked it."

For a fleeting moment, Scarlett's eyes lighten from the burden of her guilt. The weight on her eyelids seems to lift and the muscles surrounding them relax, causing her mind to clear, though there is nothing beyond the fog. As quickly as the moment of relaxation came, she tightens up again. Her eyes weigh down, trying to close on her. The fog settles back in her mind, and her anger returns.

"She would have, but she's not here," Scarlett snaps at Duncan. "Let's go tell Grams."

Not waiting for any confirmation from the other two, she exits the car and strides to the door, reaching it before either Bri or Duncan has a chance to exit the car.

"He's at the hospital now?" Eleanor asks.

Scarlett nods. "He wanted me to fill you in, but I need to tell Connor. He said you and him were a must-know, but I can't find him. He's not picking up and hasn't called me back." Her words quicken as she speaks. "I have to get to the hospital and make sure he's all right. Dr. Quinn has him, but I should be there."

Eleanor extends her arm, resting a hand on Scarlett's shoulder. "Breathe, Scarlett, breathe."

Scarlett nods, forcing herself to calm down.

"Good. Slow breaths. You don't need to work yourself back up into a transition. Not if you want to go out in public," Eleanor says, encouraging her to stay calm. "You three head to the hospital. I'll see if I can find my grandson."

Before anyone has a chance to say anything more, they hear the front door open.

"Hey," Connor says, entering.

"What took you so long? Why didn't you answer?" Scarlett's words hold the frantic worry from earlier.

Connor enters the kitchen, his hair wet and unkempt. "I was in the shower, thinking about things."

"I think you're a little old to use that excuse any-more," Bri jokes.

"Dear," Duncan says to Bri in a reminder of Eleanor's presence, "he probably meant thinking, not doing what you shouldn't be imagining him doing."

Scarlett catches on to the meaning of Bri's joke. "Eww. Gross. And Why? Why would you say that?"

"I was thinking. Got lost in thought." Connor turns to Duncan and Bri, continuing, "But I came up with something of an idea from what we talked about last week."

Duncan nods in understanding. While Bri opens her mouth to say something, Duncan starts first. "He'll fill us in later, love. We have to get to the hos-pital and check on Mr. Petrovsky."

Connor takes a step back, waving his hands in front of him. "You said nothing about that in the text. Just to get here. What happened to Vistrus?"

Elanor stands to walk them all to the door. "Scarlett will explain on the way." Turning to her granddaughter, she adds, "Dr. Quinn did show with the ambulance?"

Scarlett nods.

"Good. Go see him and figure out why this happened. Tell him I'll be by later."

The emergency room doors slide open as the group approaches. The harsh waiting room lights shine down on waiting patients: some doubled over in pain, a few keeping pressure on non-threatening wounds. All with concerned family members by their sides. Looking past the waiting area and beyond the reception desk, they scan for signs of Vistrus, but none of them sees him.

Stopping at the reception desk, Scarlett waves a meek hand, hoping to grab the nurse's attention. The nurse finishes entering something into the computer, then looks up at the group before her. "How may I help you?"

A sense of relief washes over Scarlett, hoping this person can help. "Hi. We're looking for a man who was brought in an hour ago, give or take."

"Name?" the nurse asks, hands at the ready on her keyboard.

"Scarlett McAllister," Scarlett says, unsure why the nurse wants her name.

Connor steps forward, looking at his cousin. "She means the patient's name." Turning to the nurse, he says, "Vistrus Petrovsky. P-E-T-R-O-V-S-K-Y."

The nurse nods at the screen before looking at Connor. "He's already been admitted."

"What room number?" Connor asks.

"Are you all family? Family only." The nurse lays out the rules.

Before anyone can speak, Duncan chimes in, "Yes. Son, daughter, and nephew and fiancée." He gestures to Scarlett, Connor, himself, and Brianna respectively.

"Technically, it's immediate family only. But I'm not the visitor police," she says, double-checking the screen for the room number. "Room 1051. Floor ten."

Duncan offers a sincere smile to the nurse as Scarlett and Connor already start off.

As they wait for the elevator, a tangible shift in mood silences them in thought; the ride up continues the silence. Connor wants to tell the others that Vistrus will be all right. That when his father was assaulted, he was not terribly injured. He wants to remind the others that Vistrus is a Legend, after all, and Legends heal. Then reality slaps Connor across the face because, for a split second, he was back in the elevator, riding up to his father's hospital room, able to talk with him and have Ken tell his son that everything will be all right. But he can't have calming words with his father. No more can he think of his dad as unstoppable. He decides to keep his thoughts to himself as they ride in silence. No elevator music to calm the worries of families on their way to help loved ones recover or to say one final goodbye. No idle conversation to calm nerves. Not even another hospital employee makes the elevator stop on their way up. Only uncomfortable silence.

The ding signaling the tenth floor releases some of the tension. Stepping out, the friends read the signs telling them which rooms are which way. An arrow points them to room 1051 at the very end of a long hall on what a casual observer may think is a forgotten floor. The lights, though on, barely illuminate the hallways. No heart rate beeping dots the airwaves. Even the nurse's station monitors sit silent and the chairs rest empty, absent of nurses. The shut patient room doors betray no sounds from inside.

As they approach room 1051, sounds ping their ears. No pulse rate monitors nor any typical noise produced by hospital equipment emanates from the room. Connor stops, with Bri and Duncan following suit.

"Can you hear that?" Connor asks, pointing at the room still half a hallway down.

Duncan shakes his head. "I don't hear anything. Like absolutely nothing."

Bri cocks her head, listening. "No, babe. Like, whispering."

Connor nods. "Yeah. And more than a few whispers. What's it sound like, Bri?"

She shakes her head, trying to decipher the words. "Sh ph ma one," she whispers as if chanting some spell.

"Shifamaone?" Duncan asks.

Scarlett listens to the whispers, keeping her thoughts to herself.

"Yeah. As in, I have no clue. It's all muddled whispers. Nothing more than heavily breathed sounds. You seriously can't hear that?" Bri asks Duncan.

Duncan shrugs. "Not at all. But he's there, and we came to see him." Duncan continues to the room, with the others following.

As they get closer, the whispering grows, but the words remain muddled, almost foreign. With four rooms to pass, they notice a gray-blue smoke seep out from under the door. It does not permeate into the hallway. It holds on the other side of the door, climbing the outside of the door. Stopping two doors down as a bright light diffuses in the thick smoke, the group of four watches as the light intensifies and the smoke thickens. They inch closer, curiosity getting the best of them. The whispers in the room turn to chants and the smoke crawls down the door, holding itself at the bottom as if deliberating on entering the room.

Scarlett, Connor, Bri, and Duncan stand on the other side of the door, unsure if knocking would be the best idea, though none feel like entering uninvited would be the wisest move either. As they stand there, unsure of the events unfolding, a whooshing sound grows on the other side of the door. A sound akin to a mix of a flushing toilet mixed with the moment an airplane begins acceleration for take-off. Just as the sound grows loud enough that the four look to each other for their next move, it silences. Some unknown force sucks in the smoke from the door's bottom and the light disappears. All chanting ceases and foot-steps approach.

Frozen in the uncertainty of what to do next, the four young adults stand there as the door opens. An adult male rushes past, glancing at Scarlett and meeting her gaze.

"Dad?!" Scarlett's words usher forth, unable to contain themselves.

The man quickens his pace, but she catches up.

As the second person exits the room, Connor notices their attempt to conceal a slip of something in a satchel. Connor tries to see the person's face, but they have already passed.

Bri and Duncan both stand unsure of what to do or if they should go after Scarlett or into Vistrus's room.

Before Connor, Bri, or Duncan decide their next move, a voice calls to them from the room, weakened but familiar: "Enter."

A wave of relief washes over them upon hearing Vistrus's voice.

Entering the room, all seems normal. No smoke lingers nor any light bulb seems the source of brightness that emanated under the door. The machines monitoring Vistrus are functional but silenced. A smile on him tells the young adults that everything will be all right.

"Eleanor sent you here, no doubt," he says, pressing on his wound.

Connor nods. "After Scarlett filled everyone in. She did well."

"Better than she knew." Vistrus looks outside the door, listening. "She saw her father, I take it?"

Nodding, Connor says, "Talking with him now."

"So I hear." Looking at the consternation on their faces, he continues, "While I appreciate the check-in, I sense another reason you came."

"Scarlett's not doing so hot, Mr. P," Bri offers up.

"What do you mean, 'you can't talk'?" Scarlett huffs, standing next to her father.

James looks down at his daughter, trying to hold back years of unstated emotions. "We have to take care of something right now." He motions to the second person from the room, passing them as they speak. "Time is of the essence. Believe me when I say I want nothing more than to spend much overdue time with you. Now, though, is not the time."

He starts walking off when Scarlett asks, "When then?"

"Soon. I promise." He walks off, disappearing around a corner.

Scarlett stands, unsure of what to do as rejection weighs her down. Her logical brain knows that her father speaks the truth, or at least, she hopes he does, but her emotional side screams to her that he wants nothing to do with her and will forever avoid any interaction he can.

Looking back at the hospital room, she hears muddled speech. Unable to make out any words, she decides to chase after her father, but by the time she rounds the corner he turned, he is gone. No trace of anyone there.

Dejected, she leaves the hospital alone and disillusioned.

The moonlight illuminates the forest floor, inviting Connor, Scarlett, and Bri farther into the woods. Bri clings to Connor closer than either of them feels comfortable with while Scarlett trudges ahead, unsure exactly what they hope to accomplish.

"Wouldn't you feel better clinging to your fiancé instead?" Connor asks, trying to pull his arm free.

"I would, but he's not here. He had to work, and I don't feel comfortable trotting through the woods at night. There are bears, lions, blood-sucking bats, or worse … zombies," Bri babbles.

Connor chuckles at her paranoia. "First, there are no bears or lions in the Chicagoland area, let alone West Haven. And any bats around here eat fruit. Vampire bats are found in Africa. I think we're safe."

She pulls away from him. "Yeah, well, what about zombies … or other bad things?"

Keeping an eye on Scarlett, Connor continues, "Well … the closest thing we have to zombies are Undying. You got that base covered. I think we're kosher."

Realizing she is the thing she's fearing, she straightens herself. "Well, look at you, Mr. Logic. Maybe the dark plays tricks on people and we get caught up in our thoughts."

"That's all it is. Between you and me, we have Undying and werewolves covered," he says, quickening his pace to catch up with Scarlett.

Keeping up with Connor, Bri asks, "I thought you weren't supposed to call yourself a werewolf."

"We're not. But you aren't supposed to call yourself a zombie. Times change."

As they catch up with Scarlett, they come to the same clearing Scarlett found herself napping in not too long ago.

Scarlett turns back to them with a long-unseen grin on her face. "This is it. She's here. We just have to find her."

Connor takes a deep breath, turning to Bri, who seems more deflated than enthused. "We have to help her through this; otherwise, she'll never heal." Nodding, Bri steps into the clearing.

Scarlett runs back to where she slept before, trying to find the exact location again. She stops, turning about over and over. "I was here. Somewhere. But this is close."

"And did you find any evidence that Allison is buried here?" Connor asks, hoping to break the cycle.

"Not evidence, per se. More of a feeling. But she's here. I know it." She kneels down, clawing away at fallen leaves and dirt, digging what she can to find Allison in the Waiting.

"What do we do now?" Bri whispers to Connor.

"Hope," he musters.

"I could have hoped at home," Bri lashes out. "At least there I have my television and temperature control."

A chuckle escapes Connor, causing Scarlett to turn to them. "Are you going to help or not?"

Taking a deep breath, thinking about her words, Connor turns to Bri. "It might be the only way to break her from this obsession."

"So helping her means digging holes? Not my idea of fun, but whatever helps our friend deal with all her loss, right?"

"Exactly. Let's dig in."

Their enthusiasm wanes as time passes and no evidence reveals itself that Allison heals in the Waiting. Connor and Bri watch Scarlett fight against the unarguable reality she butts against.

"She's here. She has to be. There's no reason she should be anywhere else."

"But she's, like, not here," Bri points out the obvious. "We've been digging for days—"

"Almost three hours," Connor corrects.

"Fine, whatever, three hours, Scarlett. We haven't found her because she's not here."

Placing a hand on her shoulder, Connor whispers, "We need to be gentle with her."

"We've been gentle with her," Bri mocks, her voice not any quieter than when she last spoke. "That didn't work. We need to be real. Touch love and all."

"Tough love, Bri. Touch love is a very different kinda love," Connor clarifies.

"Whatever." She turns to Scarlett. "We love you, Scarlett, but Allison isn't here. Yeah, it sucks. But what do you want us to do? We've already dug up half this clearing for nothing."

Her harsh words sink in as Scarlett's head drops. "What now?"

"Nothing, Scar. Now you heal. Now you learn to live and move on, keeping her memory alive. No one can take away the memories you have of her or Jack or your family."

"That feels like a crappy consolation."

"It is."

"Then no."

"No?"

"What do you mean, 'no'?" Bri seeks some clarification.

"I mean, you two may have given up, but not me." Scarlett turns back to the ground, digging again, trying to find her friend.

"Scarlett, come on. We can't stay here all night," Connor tries to reason, taking a few steps away, hoping it convinces her to stop.

She doesn't look up or acknowledge him, continuing to dig a deeper hole.

Bri takes a few cautious steps, stopping next to her. "Come on, Scar. You can't continue doing this." She reaches down to pull Scarlett up, but she yanks her arm away.

"You can't stay here, but I can and will. Go. Give up on your love, Connor. Give up on your friend, but I refuse to accept such a crappy consolation prize for a lifelong friend. I've already accepted Jack's not coming back. I know most of my family is gone. I won't accept Al, too. There's got to be more."

"There isn't," he begins. "Sometimes life sucks. Sometimes things happen, and there's nothing we can do but try to live. Try to keep their memories alive by remembering, not dwelling. Yes, it hurts right now. It probably hurts worse than anything you've felt before. I mean, maybe not as bad as getting your throat ripped open, but bad. But it gets to be something you can live with. It becomes a part of you."

As Scarlett continues to dig, her ears absorbing Connor's words, her skin pales, turning translucent. She does not take notice, though Connor and Bri do.

Continuing, he says, "And as it becomes part of you, it becomes okay to live without them. I still miss my mom and dad and grandpa and Jack. I still wish I could call them or have dinner with them. But I've come to accept that time has passed. Now, they live in my memories … in the times we had. I promise, Scar, it will happen for you too, eventually."

His words seem to fall on listening, though unresponsive, ears. Scarlett's now transparent skin shows muscle fibers and her circulatory system, like some reference image poster hanging in a college-level biology classroom, as she continues digging deeper and deeper until she hits something.

A surge of anticipatory adrenaline courses through her as she claws away at the dirt to pull up a skull. Turning to show Connor and Bri her discovery, she holds up the skull. "See! Things are buried here! She must be close!"

Connor takes a closer look at the skull in her hands. "It's an animal skull. Probably died right there."

Turning the skull to her, disappointment overwhelms her. The skull drops through her hands, though she never lets go. Neither Connor nor Bri notice the moment, and Scarlett's distracted dejection keeps her from witnessing it.

Turning to Connor, Bri motions the way they came. "I gotta jet. You coming or you gonna make me walk eight miles home?"

"We can't just leave her here looking like this."

"We can't stay here all night either."

"Hold on, Bri." Turning to his cousin, seeing her transition back to her Normal form, he tries convincing her one more time. "Scarlett, I gotta get her home. You can't stay here all night again. It's not safe."

"Go. Give up and accept that she's nothing more than a memory. Until I see her body, I refuse to accept it." She turns her back to them, now digging in a different spot.

"Grief is the hardest thing to deal with, Scar. You won't find your answers here."

Connor turns, leaving Scarlett in the woods. As Connor and Brianna walk back to the car, distant sounds of frustrated digging haunt their ears.

Back at the hospital, Vistrus sits upright in bed, watching a daytime documentary about Vlad the Impaler on the History Channel when Connor walks in, shielding his eyes.

"Do they have magnifiers in those windows?"

Vistrus huffs. "Just a sunny day. Close them, if you would like."

Giving his eyes a moment to adjust, he says, "It seems brighter than when I was outside, like five minutes ago."

"Cloud cover must have moved. What brings you here today, Mr. DeSalvo?" Vistrus uses his business voice.

"You look a hundred times better than the other night."

"I feel it. The little perks of being a Legend. You still have not answered my question."

"Scarlett. She went digging and we couldn't pull her away."

"Did she ever make it home?"

"She's been hibernating in her room, trying to figure things out."

Vistrus turns off the television, motioning for Connor to close the door.

Shutting it, Connor says, "She transitioned."

Vistrus nods. "I know. She did in front of me."

"Some stressor it took for her to finally do it."

"Stress, time … different triggers for different folks. How did she handle it?"

"The transition? Didn't seem to notice. Allison's death, everyone's death finally catching up to her, and not finding anything to prove us wrong, not so well."

Connor takes a seat in a heather blue chair with chipped, brown framework.

"What can I do?" Vistrus asks matter-of-factly.

Staring out the window, Connor thinks for a moment before responding. "I feel like this is going to kill her. There's nothing we can do?"

"No. She must heal. She must learn that things die, even Legends. It will take time, but she will get there."

"Don't you think losing her parents, grandfather, and Jack was loss enough to learn?"

"She was young. Her life was always lived without parents, at least what she remembers. This is different." Vistrus pauses, contemplating. "You said she is hibernating?"

"Staring at some picture Grams gave her."

"What picture?"

"Not a picture. Some charcoal drawing. I'm guessing she had it commissioned. I don't know. Why?"

Connor stares at Vistrus, watching the wheels turn in his head, face scrunched as if he's trying to solve some complex mathematical equation. After a few long moments, Vistrus snaps from his thoughts. "Nothing. Yes, it was a commissioned piece." An uncomfortable shiver shifts Vistrus in his seat.

"Everything okay?" Connor notices Vistrus, suspecting he might not have heard the entire truth just now, but knows better than to push it. But a young man in his early twenties doesn't always rest on doing the right thing. "Is there something more to this than you're telling me?"

Vistrus hits Connor with an evil eye, hoping to dissuade him from continuing this line of questioning, but Connor remains stalwart.

"There is something more," Connor observes. "If you are going to ever trust me to be on the Council, how can keeping things from me help?"

"It is not about keeping them from you as much as it is keeping you out of harm's way." A pang of relief paints a smile on Vistrus.

"Keeping me safe is not your job. That … responsibility for someone ended with my parents' passing. Your job is to prep me for a seat. You can't do that and protect me at the same time." Connor stops, taking a moment to revel in the wisdom he didn't know he had.

Vistrus looks out the tenth-floor window at the city of West Haven, staring into the distance beyond the town to the hidden underbelly of it all. "You know, Connor, we used to feel comfortable here. The Council made members of The Nation feel safe. Like West Haven was a town they would want to live in."

Connor points out the obvious naming scheme. "Like a haven of sorts."

A hearty laugh escapes Vistrus, causing him to grab at his still-healing wound. "Yes. It was founded a long time ago. Clever was different back then." Turning back to stare at his hometown, he continues, "Things are changing, and you are right. I cannot protect you if I am to prepare you." Checking the door to ensure it is still closed, he looks at the space under the door for any shadows betraying any would-be eavesdroppers. Seeing none, he focuses his ears for a moment, confirming what his eyes tell him. "That portrait was no commission."

"Figured as much," Connor interjects, still focused on trying to see what entranced Vistrus in the West Haven skyline.

"I found that, locked away with a glove."

"A glove?"

"A white glove."

"Why a white glove?"

"Now you are asking the right questions." Vistrus's tone carries a sense of pride.

"On that same note, what do a glove and portrait have to do with the other?"

Nodding, Vistrus continues, "Again, a good question. What, indeed?"

"Well?" Connor asks, pulling back as if he fears the answer.

"The prophecy of the Grey Fairy."

Frustration rushes through Connor as he turns toward Vistrus. "Yeah. I was told all about how my parents were killed because she got pregnant, even though she shouldn't have been able to. I know the whole thing. But now you're telling me some sketch of Scarlett has to do with it and my parents' deaths were what … for nothing?"

Vistrus reaches out a hand to calm Connor. "No, your parents' deaths were incidental to the prophecy. They were killed for the same reason the others were killed."

"And why was that?"

"That is the answer we seek."

"Where do we find that?"

Vistrus slows a moment. "It will not provide closure to their deaths. No answer you find will make their deaths okay."

"I know. But knowing why can't hurt."

"It might. But I do not think telling you that will stop you, anyway."

"So? You are stalling. Where do you think the answer lies?"

"In the WHO building. That notebook Bri and Duncan found."

"Then it's time we break back in."

"Tread lightly. Should anyone resort to killing, I cannot save them this time."

Bishop, disguised as Connor, watches from afar while Scarlett talks to her parents' tombstones, as if they were alive and listening. His pale, gaunt features have eluded everyone so far. Now he must decide how to deal with Scarlett. Years of yearning turned into an obsession with every waking thought centered on what steps he could take to win his heart's desire. Having killed Nick DeSalvo, the main obstacle to his goal, only Scarlett remains. He leans against a tree, contemplating how to deal with the young McAllister. Blood lust lingers in his veins, thirsting for more. Still unsure how he can get Scarlett to help him with his cause, he walks toward her, sun to his back.

His mind races with the possibilities of everything he can do to finally sway the fortunes in his favor. Nick is gone. Ken and Tracy are gone. If there are any witnesses to the crimes, Connor will be the one who is blamed. While motivation for the crimes might seem lacking, misplaced anger over his girlfriend's undecided sexuality will be blamed. With all the rest taken care of, it leaves only Scarlett.

He sees her turn from the tombstones to look at him for a moment. The sun behind him shadows his sickly features, for she turns back to her parents. He looks around the cemetery, seeing no one in sight. In a flash, he is back in the old days when it was only Eleanor and himself. No one else around. No one standing in their way or coming between them. The days when he was courting her, and Nick was not yet in the picture. Days when the future looked so bright and certain. When even the uncertainty of things to come held optimism and hope. A time when the sounds of birds singing and kids playing was a welcome sound and didn't grate against his nerves. The days before it all went so wrong.

Step after step, anger rises in the entirety of his being as he stares down at the last remaining reminder of what is and never should have been. He stares at the back of her head, listening to her whisper some pointless words to parents thought long dead. His lip curls at thoughts of the Grey Fairy—thoughts of the beginning of it all. He thinks back to a former life when hope sprang eternal and life seemed worth living. A memory plays out in his mind of Desanka holding charcoal, sketching out a then-unfamiliar face. A face he stares at now ... or the back of her head, at least. His growing confusion over how someone was able to draw her from nothing but imagination over a century ago fuels his ever-growing anger. Thoughts of her being so close to someone he feels is rightfully his drive him further into madness. Everything he has ever wanted and been denied kneels, facing away from him, embodied in this young woman who knows not what could have been, who says the same parting words she has said every time she has visited their graves, "One day." Two simple words that mean nothing to the impostor behind her, but somehow drive his rage beyond control.

As she leverages herself against the stones to stand, he lashes out a clawed hand. Long hair and thickened, gray, claw-like nails rip through Scarlett's throat, sending flesh and blood flying about. He watches her collapse to the ground before she ever finishes standing. He watches her struggle to push her dangling esophagus, trachea, muscle, sinew, and blood-spewing veins back inside her exposed throat as crimson spatters the stones and stains the grass.

The smile on his face highlights the insanity in his eyes as he watches her gasp for breath, flailing around in a futile attempt to hold on to life. But something dampens his joy in the destruction of the symbol of his life's setback. In all of her writhing, she never breaks eye contact. He sees her stare at his hypertrophic muscles, bulging veins, sharpened teeth, and claws. He knows she knows that somehow it is not Connor who stands before her. It is this ability, even when fading from breath, to see what is not truly there that dampens his delight in this moment. He transitions from Legendary form back to Connor. Scarlett's eyes widen as he does, but only for a moment. As her breaths weaken and strength fades away, the look of disbelief never strays from her face. Even now, he cannot fool her.

It is in this moment that he knows nothing more stands between him and the Council, him and his love. There is only what once was—Bishop and Eleanor. "You will never lead The Nation. It is not yours to control."

He watches confusion wash over her as Scarlett holds strong to her last breaths. He walks into the sunset as a car crawls down the cemetery road. Walking past the car's open window, he hears a female voice call out, "Connor?" He stops, taking a moment to register the name being called out as his. The female continues, "Baby? Did you see Scarlett?"

Stepping back to the open window, he peers inside. "Yeah. Up at the grave. Said she wanted time."

He waits as she looks him over. She raises an eyebrow at something. Perhaps she sees through his facade. "You holding up okay? You don't look so well."

He smells the alcohol on her breath, relaxing with the thought of one less body to explain. "Just feeling a bit ill." He figures a dismissive answer will force her to drop the subject. He stares off in the direction he is heading. A clear indication he wants to be on his way.

"Did Rex make it to a hospital?" Desperation coats her voice in a clear attempt to keep the conversation going.

"Who?" His mind has no recollection of this name. After his recent killing, his mind can't place the face before him, let alone a name he is unfamiliar with.

He sees something switch in her expression like a light being turned on in a darkened room. Readying himself, he awaits her reply. "Poor baby. You must be taking it hard. I'll call you later. Go rest."

Taking the cue and opportunity, he heads away as she drives off toward Scarlett.

Walking off, he can't help but wonder if she ignored the blood on his clothes or, if for some reason, she did not notice. Perhaps the sun cast a shadow on it or she mistook it for sweat. Either way, it is one less person to worry about and one more situation that can be traced back to Connor, should any suspicions arise. With the car behind him, he transitions into his Normal form, taking his leave.

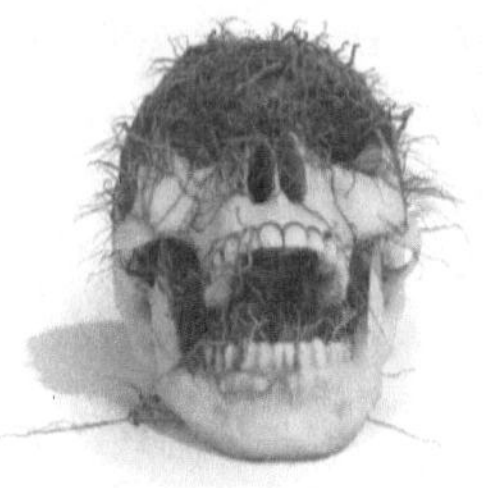

CHAPTER 18

"There's no place for anger
when making decisions."
~S. McAllister~

Duncan sits next to his betrothed, setting a bottle of Dragon's Milk stout next to their wedding binder. Bri sneaks a sip of beer as he settles in.

"We've gone over all these details countless times, love. There's not much more we can do."

"But every time we look, something changes," she whines.

"And they always will." Duncan stops himself from continuing, grabbing a drink to force himself to think. "No matter how many times we look at the plans, the details, the everything about our wedding, we will find something we think we can improve on. Something that we think will make it better."

"Don't we want to have the best wedding we can?" Bri asks, defeat setting in. "I know I do."

"A wedding is one day. An over-priced party where guests give you a gift so you pay for their dinner."

CHAPTER 18

Her eyes go wide. "That was a really over-simplified definition."

"Yes. It was. Purposely so. Point is, a wedding is one day. Our marriage is a lifetime. When we are old, or at least when I am old and gray, we won't remember the details of the wedding except through pictures and videos. What we will remember is the life we shared, the moments after the wedding."

"So, you're saying the wedding is pointless?"

Laughing, he says, "Not at all. I've been to some weddings that still stick out in my mind for one reason or another. What I am saying is at the end of the day, we could fudge the details around forever, or we could be happy with what we've chosen, knowing that no matter what we choose, countless options would make us just as happy."

"So be happy with the choices we've made?"

"Exactly. The wedding is important, but it's only one day. We are forever."

Taking a deep breath and settling herself, Bri exhales, breaking into a smile. "Fine. I can deal. But speaking of forever, what about the housing sitch?

Duncan looks around her house. "You've done a good job of making it yours. Yeah, this house has seen its fair share of tragedy, but wounds heal and scars are cool. This isn't the same house it was before."

"You mean like when my mom was killed or the latest trauma in the Waldgrave home?" Her words are pointed but land softly.

"I get your point. All I'm saying is rushing into a decision based on trauma never ends as well as we hope."

Before either can respond, a knock at the front door interrupts their conversation.

"I got it," Duncan says, grabbing his beer and hopping up.

Opening the door, Connor greets him with an eager energy. Seeing the beer in Duncan's hand, Connor asks, "Got another?"

Duncan cocks his head in an invitation for Connor to enter. "In the fridge. Help yourself. Glad you stopped by, though. Need to ask you something."

As they enter the kitchen, Bri greets him. "What brings you by?"

"I need to do something. I could use your help … again?" Connor says, cracking open a beer.

"Again?" Bri reiterates.

Connor takes a long swig before speaking. "We need to get back into the WHO."

"Yeah, we know," Duncan says, knowing it needs to happen.

"That notebook might be more than we thought. We need to get it."

"Sign me up," Duncan says, smiling.

"If he's going, I'm going," Bri says.

"But no killing this time," Connor says, eyeing Duncan.

"Not like I meant to. It was us or him, and it wasn't going to be us," Duncan defends, finishing with a sip.

"Understood. But Vistrus can't protect us again. We go in, find it, and get out."

"Yeah, but, like, it's not going to be sitting out in the open, waiting for us. How are we going to find out where they keep it so we know where to go?" The intelligence behind Bri's question surprises them all.

"Leave that to me. You guys just be ready." Connor cops a squat next to them, noticing the binder. "Still hashing out the details?"

Bri shakes her head.

"Just talking about moving," Duncan says, frustration coating his words.

"Might not be happening for a while," Bri admits. "Might have to see how things play out here first."

Finishing off his beer, Connor turns to Duncan, "You said there was something you wanted to ask?"

Duncan shoots a glance at Brianna. "Did you ask Scarlett yet?"

"Haven't exactly had a good moment yet," Bri responds, turning her attention to Connor.

"Well, the wedding is a while off, but there's stuff that isn't finalized yet," Duncan starts as an uncharacteristic hesitation sets in. "But we were wondering..."

Connor tries to be patient but his paused silence lingers too long. "What's wrong? Are you guys not getting married? Is she pregnant?"

"No, we're fine, and she's not pregnant ... I think," Duncan says, turning his attention to Bri.

"God no! I'm not pregnant. Ew," she defends.

"Whew. Well, what then?" Connor's relief settles in.

"Best man. Wanna do it?" Duncan blurts out.

"Yup. That's a great way to ask." Connor's laughter off-puts Duncan.

"Look, sorry, bro. Just never asked anyone before," Duncan's defenses raise.

Connor waves off his laughter, trying to calm Duncan. "It was perfect, brother. Of course. I'd be honored." Connor turns to Bri. "I assume his asking if you asked her…"

"Yeah, but don't say anything. Got it?" she mocks sternness.

"Of course." Connor throws up his hands in surrender.

"So, two questions," Bri says, changing subjects. "One, how are we going to get Miss Drowns-In-Sorrow to join us, and two, when's the second great break-in happening?"

"I do not know what to do, Ammar. There has to be something, somewhere that explains why she appeared on a tablet made centuries before we were."

A breeze blows through the clearing of the forest preserve as they stand by a small pond, staring into it as if trying to recapture a childhood long since passed.

Ammar lets out a hearty laugh, half-forced, half-real. "Vistrus, we've been friends for many lifetimes. What, in your experience, makes you think that life so neatly wraps up everything in simple explanations?"

Realizing the naiveté of his words, Vistrus smiles in spite of himself.

"Knowing you, you never asked her about it. Did you, Vistrus?" Ammar calls him out.

"There are certain doors that should remain closed. Certain questions you do not ask. As I always said…"

"…Never ask a question you do not want an honest answer to," Ammar finishes for his friend. "And this not asking, where did that get you?"

Vistrus stands, turning his attention to the water and the fish tapping the surface in search of food. Before answering, he takes a deep breath of fresh air, turns, and starts walking toward the trees.

Ammar keeps pace. "Not answering me is fine, but don't delude yourself, Vistrus. It's only a disservice to yourself."

"Perhaps you have a point, Ammar, but what good will it do now to reflect on your words?"

They walk for a bit, enjoying the chill autumn air. Ammar waits for some revelation from Vistrus that never comes.

"I hate to say this, Vistrus, but if you want answers—concrete answers—you may need to read her diaries."

Vistrus stops, snapping his head to his friend, though the fury in his eyes screams they are anything but friends. "How many times have I told you her diaries are private thoughts meant only for her eyes?" He calms himself, taking a moment before continuing their walk.

"And I respect that, Vistrus, more than you think. But that sort of respect is reserved for the living. That time has passed."

"Not as passed as I would like it to be."

"Didn't you tell me that Allison even said she wanted to read them?"

"For different reasons."

"But reasons with a reason of reasoning."

"That was not as meaningful as you wanted it to sound."

"But it got my point across," Ammar pauses, reflecting on his and Vistrus's previous words. "She is no longer with us. She would not care if you read them now. Again, promises of such privacy are for the living."

Vistrus stays silent in admitted defeat. He contemplates the idea of reading his wife's private thoughts, something he had never considered before.

"What if I do not find the answers I seek?" Vistrus breaks their extended silence.

"What if you do?" Ammar offers.

"That is not helpful. If I do, then I will know there was far more to my Inessa than I ever thought." The words sink as they leave his mouth.

"And if you don't," Ammar begins, "then you knew her as well as you always thought you did." A pause fills the air, almost suffocating them, before Ammar continues, "Either that or you come away with more questions than you went in with."

"What good will that do anyone?"

"Vistrus, anything you learn from her diaries—anything—will only paint a more detailed image of the woman you loved and who loved you. There was never a moment where she came off as anything less than loving. The more you find out, the more beautiful the picture will be."

Vistrus nods. "Perhaps you are right."

"Besides, it might provide insight into why she ... declined." Ammar chooses his last word carefully, as if cherry-picking the least poisonous berry from a lethal batch.

"That, Ammar, is something many would like answered."

Ammar smiles in self-satisfaction. He enjoys a few steps in silence before saying, "Then the only one stopping you from finding everything you need is yourself."

Nodding in subconscious agreement, Vistrus responds, "That is why we have been friends for so many years. You always do say what needs to be said."

Sitting at the Council table in the basement of the West Haven Historical Museum, Vistrus, Raymond, and December thumb through old tomes whose bindings crack from decades of neglect.

"Wasn't anyone in charge of caring for these?" Raymond's voice chimes in Vistrus's mind.

Without looking up from his book, Vistrus responds out loud, "Yes, but much like others on this Council, they have a different agenda."

December flips through a tome, stopping to chime in with, "Their agenda never sat well with us, Vistrus."

The words echo in his head. Words that, had they been spoken out loud, may have resounded a little more, but now, after all past events, they ring loud enough. "Perhaps my listening skills could have used a little polishing."

"As long as you don't say, 'better late than never,'" Raymond chimes in.

Vistrus stops thumbing to look up at him. "I would never. But, that said, there is something I should have brought to your attention sooner."

December shoots him a scolding stare. "And why didn't you?"

Vistrus never could get over that the voice projected into his mind never sounded mean enough.

If looks could kill, she'd kill them all, but no matter how much she tried, her voice always came across as pleasant to him. He, however, did not miss the point.

"Until recently, I was not sure who I could trust. And the one person I trusted with the information paid with his life." Vistrus's voice carries a melancholy tone.

"And now?" Raymond goads.

"Now, I know the Council cannot be trusted, but you two, well, you are here," Vistrus says, stalling.

"Get on with it, Vistrus," Raymond continues his goading.

Vistrus stands from the table, walks to the door, and peeks down the hallway, checking for anyone else before closing and locking the door. Returning to the table, he takes his seat, sitting upright to grab their attention from the texts.

"I found something a while ago. Something that should not have existed," he begins with the vagueness of a campfire story to gauge their reaction and interest. "From what I can deduce from Inessa's diaries, you had something to do with it."

He watches the last remnants of disinterest wash away. If he did not capture their full attention a moment ago, he has it now.

"I do not exactly know how it ties into all that has happened the past few years, but it does. Of that, I am positive."

Raymond and December share knowing and eager looks. The long pause of their exchange leads Vistrus to believe they share a private conversation, one which he is the subject of. Before he can interject, they turn to him.

December extends a hand to grab his attention. "What makes you think we hold any responsibility for these past events?"

Vistrus opens his mouth to answer, but their lack of specificity holds him back. Chewing over his words for a moment, he says, "I never said you were responsible, only that you are connected to them. If we keep holding onto suspicion, we will never advance."

"Can you give us a clue?" Raymond's goading turns to a plea.

Playing a round of *Super Password* is not Vistrus's idea of fun, but he will do what he must to maintain safety for those he loves while not burning bridges.

"Portrait." Only one word passes his lips, but it sends Raymond and December to sit straighter than they have ever sat before. The bug eyes staring at him betray the importance of this to them. Continuing, he says, "Clearly, you know what I am talking about. Why is this so important?"

December holds up a finger before chiming into Vistrus's head. "The portrait belongs to me. It was something that I drew many years ago; it was present when we first were changed. I would like it back."

Vistrus shakes his head. "This is not some painting stolen by the British to display in their museum and claim as their own. It is safe and unsuspecting." He watches December hold back words her mouth cannot say. "I feel there is more to your wanting than you let on."

Raymond shifts in his seat. "Trust must be given."

"Yes, and I have given you something. Now it is your turn," Vistrus says with the compassion of a teacher giving a student a life lesson.

"Fine," Raymond begins. "When we first transitioned, there was a third with us. We were the first, or so we thought."

"Who was the third?" Vistrus inquires.

"His name was Pasha," December chimes in. "He was a charlatan, but we did not know. We were ill, and he promised us health."

Raymond takes the floor. "When we transitioned, there was war, plague, death. Lots of it. But we could speak. We could laugh. Then we drank his snake oil and everything was changed. As I said, we were the first."

Vistrus interrupts, "What does this have to do with a portrait?"

"It was there." Desperation coats December's mind voice. "So was my amulet and a pair of gloves."

"If you thought you were the firsts, where are your 21-gram vials?" Vistrus asks before realizing the answer to his question.

Raymond and December both widen their eyes, offering a slow nod.

"They must be safe. You have survived this long without them," Vistrus offers.

Raymond shakes his head. "It is not about being safe, Vistrus. It is about not going against nature. Normals do not have such luxuries, neither should Legends."

"Vistrus," December interjects, "do you have any idea what it is like never being able to laugh or hear your voice out loud? It has been centuries since I enjoyed those simple things most take for granted."

Raymond continues, "We, like you, have lived long enough to see death for countless lifetimes. Living and dying is one thing. Not being able to have control over either is another."

"The portrait, the amulet, and a pair of gloves are four things. Vials for your 21 grams would be two of those."

A mixture of deep-seated embarrassment and frustration wash over Raymond and December as they both contort their faces while thinking of what to say. Raymond relaxes first, chiming with, "That's the thing, Vistrus. We aren't sure which of those are our vials."

December brightens for a moment, echoing, "We are fairly sure it is the amulet. I got a glance at it after the explosion, and I saw some sort of mists floating in the amber. I think we share the vial."

Vistrus thinks on the implications of this before saying, "What does this have to do with said Pasha?"

Raymond stands, pacing back and forth, working up the courage to say words he never previously uttered.

"It was stolen … by this Pasha." His words come slow and deliberate. "As well as her drawing."

Vistrus watches Raymond pace, trying to understand the gravity of their situation. After a moment, he turns to December, asking, "But how did you draw Scarlett?"

A smile creeps across her face as she huffs and shakes her head. "I didn't." Her voice resonates through Vistrus's mind. "Again, I was just drawing what came to mind. There was no guiding voice from the cosmos telling me that this was some prophetic piece of art. It was what it was."

"But everything I have read in my wife's diaries, even the little in old texts, all point to her and your portrait as the Grey Fairy. You must have known something." Vistrus's trademark stoicism turns to pleading by the end.

December taps the side of her nose, pointing it at him. "There's the rub. I drew it, and I didn't know. So how did someone else?"

Raymond takes a seat, ideas swirling through his mind. Vistrus sinks into his chair, lost in the expanse of it all. December watches them as all three try to figure out the entirety of it and piece together what they've been missing.

Silence fills the room, adding an uncomfortable tension to their mystery, weighing it down more and more, until it becomes suffocating. Finally, December pipes up in everyone's minds, "If her diaries led you this far, maybe there's more in them? Perhaps you haven't found it yet."

Vistrus can't help but nod his head at her words. A silent and unconscious acknowledgment of the merit of her suggestion.

Connor and Duncan sit in the front seats, driving through West Haven with a begrudging Scarlett in the back seat next to Bri. The radio plays commercial after commercial, filling the background with noise while Scarlett thinks up another excuse for not wanting to be part of tonight's activities.

"You don't need me," Scarlett whines. "I could be doing anything else with my life."

Bri turns to her, brow crossed, and eyes squinted. "Shut up, already! We all understand your issues. None of us are happy about it, but we can't, like, dwell in our misery. No one wants that, especially Allison."

"She can't want anything. She's gone, remember?" Scarlett snaps.

"Then she wouldn't want it. Whatever. Don't be pedantic," Bri returns the volley before turning to Duncan. "Same entry plan as last time?"

Duncan nods his head. "Figured it worked well last time…"

"And you don't think they'd have upped their security since the last time we broke in?" Scarlett interrupts.

Connor looks at his cousin through the rearview mirror. "Doesn't matter. We can't go through the front. Back's the only way."

"And why do you need me?" Scarlett asks, crossing her arms. "It's not like you're listening to a damn thing I say."

"You know what, Scar. We hear what you say. We just aren't responding to it because you've been acting like a twat-waffle ever since she died," Bri snaps, releasing simmering frustration.

"Sorry I haven't gotten over her suicide as quickly as you all have," Scarlett says through gritted teeth.

"You all just brushed all these deaths off your shoulders. Steel bones and all you are made of."

Her derision causes Connor to pull onto the shoulder, slamming the brakes. He turns back to her. "You know what, Scar? I loved her, too. She was my girlfriend. My love. And yes, you loved her, too. We all did in some way or another. And none of us are happy about it. None of us wants to be doing this. It's not like we wanted to be committing another felony, let alone a first. I am sure Bri and Duncan would rather be putting together a wedding registry or watching a movie while snuggling, or, hell, even grocery shopping. There's not a person here who hasn't struggled in some way with all the loss. Our parents were brutally murdered. Don't think for a moment that I 'just brush it off.' Every night when I close my eyes to sleep, I see their bodies. I don't get to think of fond memories of prom. No. I get Mom and Dad dismembered and covered in blood. Those are my memories of prom with Al. So you don't say we brush shit off."

"Duncan already did our registry," Bri interjects, completely missing the point.

"Point missed but still stands, Bri. Hell, I would rather be doing any of those things with Allison. But we are not Normals. We do not have the luxury of blissful ignorance. We are trying to stop the WHO from curing a condition that needs no cure. What we are trying to do is break into a government building to steal some book, which we have no idea where it is."

"So? What do you want from me?" Scarlett asks, remaining belligerent.

Connor snaps, "We want you to shut the fuck up. Stop wallowing for one night and help the people who need you to be there. Help the people you still can help and be a part of this family and team."

Scarlett breaks down in tears. "How can I help anyone? I couldn't even help my best friend."

Duncan turns off the droning radio. The mood in the car quiets as the boiling anger subsides, making way for the pain, regret, and helplessness breaking through the surface. Emotions that run wild in heavy silence.

For a moment, Scarlett's weeping dominates the space. An audible reminder that healing takes time and self-realization. Bri, Duncan, and Connor exchange looks, all of which say the same thing: They've all been an ass.

"Why haven't you said anything about how you feel?" Bri asks, putting her hand on Scarlett's shoulder.

"I've tried … in so many ways. I've shown you where I thought she was buried and what didn't add up to me in this whole thing. The exact words of whatever I just blurted out may not've been said, but I tried." Scarlett lays it out for them, trying to control her sobs.

"But you didn't say what was on your mind," Bri rebuttals.

"Dear, she used subtext," Duncan says, trying to keep the situation from blowing back up.

Scarlett keeps her head down, but points at Duncan, flinging her finger in his direction. "What he said."

Bri quiets her voice. "Sorry we missed it."

Connor turns back to the road but remains idling on the shoulder. "We've been busy and none of us have had proper time to mourn. I am sorry we all missed the signs."

"Me, too," Scarlett says, wiping her tears away.

"When this is all over, then we can face our feelings head-on. No suppression while dealing with more … time-sensitive issues," Connor offers.

"Promise?" Scarlett asks, a light of hope in her eyes.

"Promise, but I need you to be with us tonight. One hundred percent with us," Connor says, looking at her in the rearview mirror again.

A wave of calm washes over Scarlett. All the anxiety simmering beneath the surface subsides, leaving only still waters. Everyone feels it, the days since Allison's passing, all building up and waiting to boil and finally spilling over, dissipates, leaving only the calm after the storm.

She meets his mirrored gaze, wiping away more tears. Shaking her head, she says, "One hundred."

The heavy air in the car lifts, lightening the mood. Connor pulls back onto the road, heading toward the WHO building.

In the newfound silence of awkwardness after settled arguments, a chuckle escapes Scarlett. "Twatwaffle. Such language, Bri."

"Well, you needed to hear it," she says, laughing.

"I guess I did. So, the plan… Do we have our walkies?" Scarlett brings the conversation back to the task at hand.

The parking lot sits empty, save a few cars. From their previous entry point at the broken fence, they watch, waiting to time the patrol car, but none ever comes. It seems that outside security took the night off, or is no longer required. Even the windows of the upper floors illuminate less than before.

"Half the staff taking the night off?" Bri whispers in earnest.

Duncan shakes his head. "Something feels wrong."

Nodding in agreement, Connor whispers, "There's no turning back. We need to do this. We need to find that book. If it's still there and we don't get it tonight, they won't be stupid enough to leave it around for a third attempt."

Scarlett chimes in soft tones, "Would *we* be stupid enough for a third attempt?"

"Let's not make that something we need to find out," Duncan says, heavy gravity in his voice.

"Do we split up again?" Bri asks in a quivering tone.

Connor and Duncan exchange a look, trying to figure it out in silence, but Scarlett speaks first. "No. This time we remain strong in numbers, or whatever the saying is."

"Close enough," Duncan says. "I agree."

A half-smile crosses Connor as his head nods back. "Good. Me too." Turning to Duncan, "You lead. You know where the room is."

Shaking his head, Duncan throws up his hands. "Hell, no. Of the four of us, I'm the only one without some sort of super smeller or 'roid strength. Bri leads. She knows the way, has strength, and is more capable."

"Plus, I can always beat people with whatever body part falls off me," Bri quips, causing them to all smack their faces.

"Let's hope it doesn't come to that," Scarlett says.

"Wait. Do we need our walkies if we're all staying together?" Duncan asks. "Why bring extra stuff if we don't need?"

"In case something happens," Scarlett offers. "Better not need and have than need and not have."

Duncan offers a nod in agreement. "Where are the earbuds? We had earbuds last time."

"Couldn't find them. Must've lost them somewhere. It'll be fine." He surveys his friends one last time before heading in. "All right? Let's do this," Connor says, holding the fence hole open wider for the others to fit through.

They stop outside the back entrance. "That was easy," Bri says, smiling.

"Why you gotta go and say that?" Connor says in all seriousness.

"What?" Bri asks, lost as to why he responded that way. "It was easy. Easier than last time."

"Yeah," Connor starts. "But saying that jinxes things. Now things are gonna get tough."

"Don't be superstitious, Con. We're fine. Now, let's go inside before our stalling proves you right."

Duncan tries the back door to find it unlocked. "Too easy?"

"There's only one way to find out. Bri with me, then Duncan, then Scarlett. We need the strength on the ends."

"I still have no strengths," Scarlett reminds them.

"Fine. You and Bri first, then Duncan, then me. When we feel safe, Bri takes us to where you two saw the book."

Bri throws a double thumbs-up. "Overthink things much?" Sarcastic words to lighten the moment before she heads in.

Inside, empty hallways greet them. They stand, waiting, while Bri tries to get her bearings from their last time here. They all bounce and sway, overflowing with anticipation as an idea hits Connor.

"Cameras," Connor says.

"Not a great time for pictures, but I have my phone," Bri offers.

Connor puts up a hand, stopping both her from continuing and himself from saying something mean. "Security cameras." He points to the corner of the halls. "I'll head to the security office and keep watch. You three head up."

"Walkie on channel three, Con," Duncan says, turning his on.

Connor nods, adjusting his walkie as well, and runs off.

The hallways to the security office lack any signs of life. No uniformed detail patrolling the halls nor any badged employees. Any office doors left open reveal empty rooms, not even a desk chair remains. Connor's heart sinks as he approaches the security office. Thoughts of doubt flood his mind, thinking that if the bottom offices are vacant, there must not be anything left upstairs. Those thoughts lead to him wondering, if the building is being vacated, what the need for security cameras would be.

Before that train of thought travels too far down the tracks, he finds himself standing outside the security office. He stops and listens, ear pointed to the closed door. Ignoring the thumping of his heart and the whoosh of blood rushing through his veins, Connor concentrates on every other sound he hears, discerning if it presents a threat. The air conditioner drones in the background of what remains, but he still needs to know what lies beyond the door. Pushing the sound of the AC unit aside, he hears the hum of solid-state electronics and computer fans on the other side, but no heartbeat, no breathing, nor any sounds of other activity.

With great caution, he turns the knob and opens the door enough to peek inside. Nothing but a few monitors and their computers. A sense of relief fills him as he enters, taking a seat at the desk to watch over his friends.

It only takes a minute to find them on camera. While some of the monitors are turned off or playing static, the others show empty rooms of a building seemingly devoid of any other people.

The power buttons on the off monitors either turn on to static, blank screens or have lost function-ality, leaving potential blind spots for Connor to keep watch over while the others snoop around for *The Grey Fairy Anomaly*. Blind spots fill the stairwell, but no movement shows on the covered areas, leaving Connor a little calmer than before.

As they stop outside the door leading to where they need to go, Connor checks the available monitors for that floor. Seeing no one, he presses the talk button on the walkie, saying, "Looks all clear past the door. You should be good to go."

Duncan responds with a thumbs up at the camera, his head pointed at Bri, who's saying something to him, but Connor can't read her lips.

Into the walkie, Connor asks, "What is she saying?"

Turning to the camera, Duncan presses the talk button on his walkie, "She's asking why we didn't just use earbuds and our phones."

Without thought to his response, Connor says, "Because I grew up watching too many action movies, so the logical approach didn't come to me. Plus, phones can be interfered with; walkies can't. Why didn't you suggest it before, Bri?"

She turns to the camera, shrugs, and says into the walkie, "Just thought of it now." She turns away, then turns back to Duncan's walkie. "Well, are they?"

"Are they what?" Connor responds, irritated.

"Are they interfered with? Do you have full bars?" Bri asks.

Scarlett pats herself down, checking for her phone before remembering she left it at home.

Checking his phone, he sees full bars. "Yeah, but no earbuds, so let's stop talking about this and continue," Connor suggests.

Scarlett opens the door to the hallway, peeking left, right, left, then right again before signaling for the other two to enter. Connor keeps an eye on their position among the monitors while watching the others.

Bri and Scarlett switch positions, keeping Duncan in the middle, so Bri can lead them to the room. As they skulk down the hallway, Scarlett's agitation builds, causing her to fidget again. Movement in an adjacent monitor labeled "Archives" catches Connor's eye. The monitor, though, shows the doorway leading into it from the hall, not the inside of the office itself. Now, whatever he thought he saw has passed. From the position of the monitor in the overall layout, Connor assumes it's on the same floor.

"Careful," he says into the walkie. "I think I saw something somewhere on your floor. Like someone went into a room."

Duncan clicks the talk button and whispers, "Heard." Before he can put away the walkie, Bri whispers something to him. "Hey, texting doesn't require earbuds. I'll keep my phone on vibrate. That way there's less noise."

Connor picks up his phone and texts Duncan.

⌈Good idea. Tell Bri thanks.⌉

The three of them find themselves standing in front of the laboratory Duncan and Bri were in during their last visit. The windows to the room show the extent of damage still remaining. Scarlett sways back and forth, shifting her weight between her legs as if she needs to use the restroom.

⌈Connor: What's up with Scar?⌉

Connor watches Scarlett become more agitated as she whispers to Duncan. Her shifting weight between her feet turns to shifting weight and fidgeting hands. Bri grabs Scarlett's hand, leading her into the laboratory. The monitor outside the room flickers and scrambles for a moment as Scarlett walks off-screen. Before Connor can begin watching them on the monitor within the room, it scrambles and blurs like an old television playing HBO for a non-subscriber.

Connor taps the monitor, hoping to give it an old-fashioned fix, but to no avail. He looks at the other monitors, hoping for a view into the room but none supply relief.

[Connor: Monitors went out.]

He sits, waiting for a response. After a moment, his phone buzzes.

[Duncan: All of them?]

[Connor: Inside the lab]

No response comes back. Connor waits for Duncan to say something, but nothing comes.

[Connor: Status?]

The three dots blink on his phone as Duncan types his response.

[Duncan: Does the hall camera work?]

[Connor: Yeah.]

[Duncan: Then make sure no one comes in.]

Connor watches the other monitors, ensuring they remain clear of any threat to their mission. The monitor inside the lab remains scrambled, flashing static every so often. The monitor outside the lab scrambles as the one inside returns to normal. Connor watches Bri and Duncan but sees no Scarlett.

[Connor: Where's Scarlett?]

[Duncan: Stepped out. She's freaking out. IDK.]

As he watches the blurred monitor, the news footage of them outside Officer Max Espinoza's house flashes in his mind.

[Duncan: I'll get her]

Duncan leaves the lab, leaving only Bri in there to search. The scrambled monitor turns to full static as the monitor inside the lab scrambles, rendering Connor's station useless.

[Connor: OMW Monitors down.]

Abandoning the monitors, Connor runs up the stairs to meet up with the others. Turning the corner, he sees Duncan and Bri standing over Scarlett, covering her. As he approaches, spying what he can of his cousin, his heart races, wondering why she is lying on the floor. Stopping next to them, he sees his cousin, head between her knees.

"Scar, what happened? Are you all right?" Connor asks, trying to get a look at her.

"It hurts so bad!" she cries, lifting her head from between her knees.

Her hands, covered in translucent skin, hold the sides of her head as she rocks in pain. Even the skin on her face shows her veins and muscle tissue.

"Something's not right, Connor! It didn't hurt this bad before." Tears fall from her eyes as her translucent skin fades further. The veins and muscle tissue turn translucent as well, showing her organs and skeletal structure beneath.

Turning to Duncan, he asks, "What happened to her?"

Duncan shrugs. "I dunno, man. She saw the fire damage from last time, mentioned the smell, and she got worse. I thought she was just freakin' out about doing this again."

"I think she is freakin' out," Connor says, squatting to be next to his cousin.

"I think she looks like those glass frogs or like she's turning into a ghost," Bri observes.

Scarlett holds her arms out, both looking like a skeleton being held together by sinew. "Hideous."

"I dunno, Scar. I think it's cool. Halloween-chic," Bri tries to lighten the mood and calm her down.

But both Connor and Duncan turn to her, jaws dropped by her words.

"What?" Bri turns out her hands, shrugging. "She kinda looks … IDK … hauntingly beautiful."

Duncan takes a deep breath, knowing he needs to stop her but unsure what to say to get her to shut up. Connor stares, too appalled to speak.

"I mean, moreso beautiful when she had muscles and veins. All-Scarletor is more Halloween-chic. Plus, if anyone can comment on her looks, it's me: Miss I-use-my-jawbone-to-beat-people-with. But the pain will pass, Scar. Always does."

Ducan leans into Bri, whispering, "Scarletor?"

Nodding with a smile, she says, "Yeah, Scarlett and Skeletor. You know? He-Man?"

Duncan turns back to the conversation at hand, and he and Connor both realize the validity of her point, turning their attention back to Scarlett, whose skeletal features turn a bit transparent as well.

"Well, did you at least get the book?" Connor asks.

Bri shakes her head. "Not in there."

"I think they realized we'd be back," Duncan admits.

Thinking about the remaining possibilities, Connor says, "Archives seem like as good a place as any if it's still in the building."

"Yeah, archives. Like we know where that is." Sarcasm coats Bri's words.

"Well, just so happens, Miss Jawbone, I do," Connor says, matching her sarcasm. "Scar, can you walk?"

She stands up, slowly, but without pain. Opening her mouth to speak, only a breathy wind emanates. Trying to speak again, the same windy exhale accompanies her.

"And I thought I was creepy in my Legendary form," Bri quips.

Scarlett goes to slap Bri on the shoulder, but her hand passes through her. A gesture that was noticed by everyone.

"What the hell was that?" Connor asks, staring at Bri and Scar.

Scar shrugs, knowing her voice is out of commission.

"Hit her again," Connor commands.

Again, she tries to slap Bri's shoulder, but her hand passes through.

"How is she standing on the ground and not falling through?" Duncan points out the obvious.

They stand, thinking for a moment before Bri speaks. "Concentrate, Scar. Really want to hit me! Think of me as the enemy, some villain trying to do something bad."

Scarlett concentrates and swings again, this time connecting harder than Bri would have liked.

"Damn, Scar. That hurt," she scolds, rubbing her shoulder.

Scarlett exhales a long wind in response.

"Good job," Bri congratulates. "But that hurt."

"Is this her mega evolution or did she touch something?" Duncan voices his concern.

"She's not a Pokémon, dude. This is her Legendary form. This is why everything that's happened, happened."

Scarlett stands, trying to regain her Normal form as the others watch her struggle.

"So, now what?" Bri asks.

"We still find that book. It's all about her. Maybe it will have answers," Connor suggests.

Scarlett gives a boney thumbs up, motioning for Connor to lead the way.

An uneventful search of the floor ends with them standing outside the door labeled, "Archives." Duncan reaches for the handle without hesitation, finding it locked. They all exchange looks, hoping someone else expresses some great idea on how to get inside.

"Connor can wolf out and bust it down," Bri suggests in the same manner, as if suggesting IHOP for breakfast.

"As much as I love being compared to a kid's tale, the noise could attract someone," he reminds her.

"He's right, love," Duncan whispers to Bri before turning to Connor. "In her defense, there's no one around and if no one's here, noise won't matter.

"Then why are we all whispering?" Connor asks.

"Point taken," Duncan says, admitting defeat. "But it's not like any of us have lock picks."

Before anyone can respond, the whooshing of wind sounds from Scarlett. They turn to her as she goes to reach through the door as Connor puts up a hand. "Stop."

Scarlett releases a frustrated breath.

"If you have to materialize or whatever to unlock the door, you might materialize in the door and something could happen to your arm," he points out.

"And she can't walk through the door; otherwise, she'd fall through the floor," Duncan points out the other fallacy in her idea.

"Yeah, well, I still think Connor should just Hulk his way through," Bri throws out, growing annoyed.

Wind whooshes from Scarlett, what remains visible of her moves through the door, and after a few seconds of her fumbling around, the door unlocks and opens.

"Sweet," Bri exclaims. "And Connor didn't have to lift a finger."

"Let's find this book and get out of here," Duncan declares.

"We can't," Connor says, pointing at Scarlett. "Scarlett's not exactly dressed for public consumption."

"That sounded way worse than you intended, Con, but yeah, she can't go out like that," Bri adds.

Scarlett moves past them, unable to add her thoughts on this matter. The others take her cue, dropping the matter for the moment, and enter the room.

Filing cabinets labeled like a library's card catalog line the walls of the room. A table in the center hosts one chair. A small, unlit lamp on the table casts a shadow on a book beneath it.

"While I'm no master criminal, something about this seems too easy," Duncan whispers.

Gesturing to the book, Connor adds, "I take it that's it?"

Duncan nods a few times. "Do we just take it?"

"Aaaannnd ruuuunnn," Scarlett adds in a breathy voice, her structure becoming less transparent as she calms herself.

"What if it's booby-trapped like in the movies?" Bri postulates.

The other three turn to her, unsure if her statement holds validity, while also recognizing the absurdity of what it would take to go through all that for one book.

"This isn't Indiana Jones, love. I doubt there are any traps," Duncan says, grabbing everyone's attention. "I highly doubt that even if they were expecting us or someone to come try to rob them, they would go through the setup of booby-trapping a book. The logistics alone would be a nightmare. Not to mention the renovations needed to hide said trap."

A voice from behind them speaks, causing them all to jump back. "He's right. There are no booby traps. But there is me."

The man stands, blocking their exit from the room, and looking each up and down.

Bri's memory from her eyeball in a thermos moment flashes in her mind. "He's on the Council."

Connor steps in front of the group, matching the intensity of this man's glare. "Well, you're not Vistrus, Grandpa, or the guy Duncan took care of. So, what are you, then? Kipling Society? Poe?"

The man shakes his head. "Tsk tsk. You should know the proper way to address this. Are you In? That is what we say."

Stepping a few inches closer, feeling his muscles growing, he adds, "I figured in here, there's no need for the formalities. But since you asked, I am in because of his age and his cunning."

A dog-sly smile breaks across the man's face as his muscles grow to match Connor's. "Because of his grip and his paw."

Their hair thickens in patches, thinning over the surface. Blood drips from their mouths as their canines grow. Veins pulsate as if ready to explode in a low-budget horror movie blood bath.

"You won't win this, boy. Give me the book and leave while you can," he warns.

A warning that only succeeds in kicking Scarlet's anxiety into overdrive. In less than the blink of an eye, she turns completely transparent. The only sign she still stands in the room is the shadow she casts from her wispy, shifting outline, like a living Rorschach drawing drawn in varying shades of near-clear.

Even Bri has gone from her wanna-be beauty queen day look to full fright night, leaving Duncan as the only Normal in the room.

Duncan sinks back behind Scarlett and Bri, sneaking the book off the table and into his waistband. He knows that if there were a prize for the most useless in this battle, he would win.

Connor shakes his head. "Why do you want the book so bad?" Connor fishes for information.

"Because he needs it," comes the man's short reply.

"Who'sh hhh?" Bri asks, causing her jaw to dislocate.

"Yeah," Connor growls. "Who's this he?"

The man steps forward, unbothered by Connor or Bri's presence. He does not seem to even pay any mind to Duncan. "The head of the Council, of course. The one who's always been in charge. You'd best fall in line if you want to make it out alive." He looks at the table, seeing the empty spot where the book had been. His anger at the missing book overtakes him, causing him to shove Connor out of the way as if he were a small child.

Jumping back, Connor growls, "No one ever gets out alive." He lunges at the man, sending them both to the ground. Keeping the man grappled under him, Connor shouts to Bri and Duncan, "Get out of here!"

Connor wraps his arms around the man's head and neck. Duncan sidesteps to the door, grabbing his fiancée by her rotting hand. The man pries Connor's arms off as if he were opening a slice of American cheese. Turning to face him, the man pushes Connor off, sending him into the ceiling. Drywall and dust fall around them as Connor embeds in the ceiling long enough for the man to rise and move before crashing back down. As Connor stands up, the man plants a foot in his chest. A loud ripple of cracking bones sends Connor back to the ground, clutching his chest and gasping for air.

The man turns to Duncan and Bri. "Give me that book!"

But before he can move to them, an unseen force sends him doubling over in pain. Duncan watches as Scarlett starts reappearing behind the man, leaning over him, her hand inside his chest.

"I hope you have your 21 grams in a vial somewhere. Because that pain you feel is my hand squeezing your heart. You people have taken my parents, my family, my boyfriend, and my best friend from me. All we want is something good to come our way. One good thing, but no. We get one lousy book and you want to take that, too."

Duncan and Bri watch, flabbergasted, as the man transitions back to Normal, his face turning purple and his hands clutching his chest.

"No. This life. I never asked for it, and yet it's taken almost everything from me. Understand? You want the book? I'll give you the damned book when you give me back my best friend!"

She squeezes harder. The man's eyes start bulging out of his face, ready to pop.

"Sharleff!" Bri calls out, holding her dislocated jaw in place. "Yer hillin' hi'!"

The meaning of her mispronounced words does not fly over Scarlett. She looks up at Bri, who even in her Legendary form of death and decay, shows mercy in her eyes. Duncan, too, having been in her shoes far too recently, silently pleads to let the man live.

"He'll live," Scarlett screams, anger overtaking every inch of her.

"Only if he has a vial!" Duncan points out.

Scarlett looks at the man, his eyes red and ready to explode. His face passes to a purple so dark, she wonders if it will ever return to normal. But even in all that, she sees a pleading life, not wanting to die. She can't be certain, as maybe it is wishful thinking, but she thinks she sees a pang of regret as well. So, she releases his heart and pulls her hand out of his chest. She transitions back to her Normal state, watching as the deep hues of purples and blues fade from the man and his eyes recede back into their orbital sockets.

She helps Connor up off the floor, and the four of them leave the room and the man behind them. As they approach the stairwell to head home, Bri turns to Scarlett. "You need one good thing?"

Scarlett huffs. "I was mad. Who couldn't use a good thing?"

They descend the stairs in no hurry at all, taking in the events of the evening.

Bri nudges Scarlett. "Would being my maid of honor be a good thing?"

"Yes. Yes, it would," Scarlett says, trying to smile at the good news through the trauma of the night's events.

"Then at least we have that going," Bri says.

Later that night, after their break-in, Scarlett leads Connor, Duncan, and Bri through the woods. "I want to show you guys something," Scarlett says.

"Something like a raging forest kegger?" Duncan jokes.

"No," Scarlett says, laughing. She thinks about her next words while they walk through the quiet forest, stars shining above. "I want to show you what's been eating me. Where I've been."

"Are you sure this is a good idea?" Bri asks.

Scarlett nods. "Look, none of us are carrying shovels, so it's not like we're gonna dig up the forest looking for Allison."

"Why do you want to show us, then?" Connor asks, looking at the night sky above.

As they approach the clearing where she was buried and thought Allison was buried, she turns to them and stops. "Because … you all deserve to know the road I've been down and why." She sees apprehension coat all their faces. "I'm not going to freak out. It's more of a healing thing." She turns to the clearing and steps into it. "Look."

The others step out of the woods and into the clearing as well. Moonlight illuminates the area, giving a surreal, eerie aura. Scarlett walks about halfway across before stopping. She turns to the others who have not followed her and calls out, "Come here. Look."

The three exchange worried glances before giving Scarlett the benefit of the doubt and walk to her. They stop and see nothing unusual—only dirt and leaves. Pointing at the ground, Scarlett says, "This is it."

"What is it?" Duncan asks.

Connor and Bri both know without having to ask. Something in them says that one day, this spot might be theirs as well. Not wanting his cousin to say words she might not be ready for, he turns to Duncan, answering his question. "This is the spot where she was in the Waiting."

Duncan stares at the ground, trying to imagine what it would be like to wake up covered in dirt. Before he can let his imagination run wild, Scarlett breaks the silence. "I wasn't dead. So, don't ask me if I saw some white light. I don't remember that part. But waking up…" She pauses, gathering her courage to speak about it. "Waking up was hard. Suffocating. I thought maybe I was in hell."

The others keep their thoughts to themselves, giving Scarlett all the time she needs to say what she has to.

"It's very jarring and lonely. I figured if Allison was here, I'd find her and wait. Make sure she was taken care of when she woke."

Bri squints, wanting to speak, but holds back her words.

"I know now that she is gone. She was in pain. But she told me she wouldn't do that. She told me. And what I don't understand … what I'll never understand is how she could do this? What did we do to make her think she couldn't talk to us? She may have killed herself, but it's the living who have to deal with the aftermath. The dead don't care. And I'm mad at her for that." Scarlett turns her gaze to the ground where she was buried. "And I hate being mad because I can't tell her that. I can't tell her why I'm mad, and it seems so pointless to even be mad." She pauses again, looking around the forest, taking in the sights as if this is her last time here. "Anger has become pointless." She turns to her friends, who remain silent. "I just thought you should see what's kept me so preoccupied. Thank you for listening, and I'm sorry I've been so angry."

Scarlett doesn't wait for a response from any of them. She walks away, knowing they will follow her out.

As they reach the edge of the clearing, they do not hear the rustling of leaves and dirt moving next to where she gave her speech.

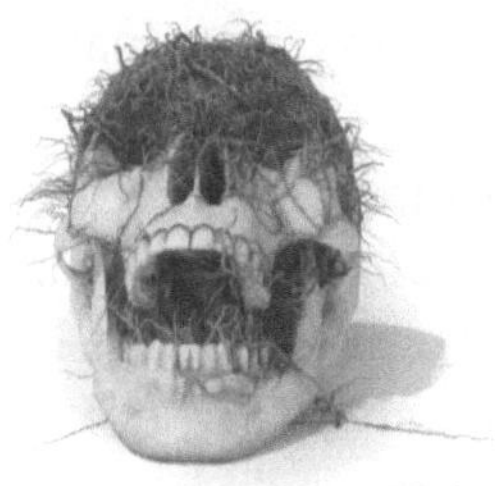

CHAPTER 19

*"Self-ware individuals acknowledge
their shortcomings."*
~J. McAllister~

"Sometimes we learn that things we believed our entire lives were wrong. I don't mean thinking there's a 'the' in front of White Castle or that the castle is plural. I'm talking about big things. Things that we base parts of who we are around, dearie. Seemingly little things sometimes, like all sugar is bad when everyone knows a little sugar makes things a bit sweeter. Big things are what we're talking about. Things that we never knew could be wrong. You following along?" Eleanor looks Scarlett in the eyes, making sure she's still with her.

Scarlett stares, entranced by what her grandmother has to say, listening to the pearls of wisdom she's passing down to the next generation, in hopes that Scarlett and her peers might one day make the world a better place.

"I'm all ears, Grams." Scarlett scooches back in her chair while leaning forward, further planting herself firmly for any information that might try to blow her away.

"Here's what I mean, love. Humans hold on to what they know. If I were to prove that the sky is anything but blue, you'd think me mad. But if you only went outside at dusk when the next morning's weather should be a delight, you'd be convinced the sky is red. Then one day, if you went outside in the morning and it was blue, you'd think blue was the odd color. And it would take a whole lot of convincing to convince you otherwise." Eleanor stops for a moment. "You following along, young lady?"

Scarlett nods, unsure where her grandmother might take this.

"When you first learned you were a Legend, it took some time to fully realize what that entailed, no?"

"Yeah. I mean, yeah. It was hard. Even now that I've transitioned, it's not any less strange," Scarlett admits.

"But you know it's a part of you," Eleanor leads Scarlett.

"Yeah, sure," Scarlett says, shrugging off the seriousness of it all.

"But it took lots of evidence and rearranging of everything you knew to fit that new reality into your life. And this book you have, this *Grey Fairy Anomaly*, this is that thing that disproves so much of what we knew to be true." Eleanor turns her attention from Scarlett to the book sitting next to her on an end table.

Scarlett sits up a bit, glancing at the book. "And you've read it all?"

Eleanor nods. "Of course. I've had it for over a week now. I've read every word, dear. It's one thing to think you know something for a year or two and have that blown apart. It's different when you've been alive the centuries I have. I am not sure how to process this all."

"No one wants to admit they're wrong, Grams. And the longer they've been wrong, the longer they hold on to the falsehood they hold true. It's human nature. I saw it with Allison when she first transitioned. I think… I think that's part of why she did what she did. She never wanted to admit what or who she is. Like there was something inherently wrong with her for being a vampire or Legend or whatever we call it."

Eleanor lets out a little chuckle.

"What's so funny? What did I say?"

Shaking her head, Eleanor stands up. "I'm getting some juice. You want some juice?"

"Sure."

Eleanor steps into the kitchen. "Orange or prune?"

"Orange, thanks. Who likes prune juice?" Scarlett laughs.

"It's not a matter of liking it. More a matter of need. Legend or not, we need fiber."

Scarlett contemplates the pointedness of those words for a moment. "You still have to tell me what was so funny."

"Vampires, Legends, Normals. Words don't matter much. I mean, sure, they matter in some sense. If I started calling you Tom, you'd be a little confused."

"No more so than I am right now," Scarlett interjects.

"If, from the time you were born, we called the color of your copper red hair black, you would think that all things that color family were shades of black."

"What would you call black?"

"Red … anything, really. Point is, we assign a word to something, and that's what we call it."

"Now I'm lost, Grams."

Eleanor comes back into the front room with a glass of orange juice for Scarlett and prune juice for herself. She sits and takes a sip.

"The Nation wasn't always The Nation. The Council wasn't always the Council, and the Societies had different names."

Scarlett's interest grows. "Connor mentioned the Society names, but the others, what were they called?"

"The Council was the Body, but it was the Gaelic word for body. The Nation, I can't remember anymore. It's been so many years."

"Al's mom wrote about the Body and the Mind in her diaries. We never figured out what those meant."

"Not sure it matters much anymore. I know what they mean and I know what the prophecy of the Grey Fairy means," Eleanor says, dejected. She sets down her glass, turning her gaze to the window looking out at the street. She watches as if expecting someone, but not even a car drives by.

"Well, Grams, what's it mean?" Scarlett's interest and growing excitement offset Eleanor's disappointment.

"Nothing. They mean nothing."

"They can't mean nothing," Scarlett says, as if encouraging an answer from an unsure student and she was the teacher.

"It means what we thought was the prophecy, what we thought we needed to do to protect you, protect The Nation, has all been for nothing. The deaths over the past few years … all for something other than a prophecy to unite the Normals and the Legends." Eleanor's dejection turns to wandering curiosity.

"There has to be more," Scarlett prods.

"Years before you were born," Eleanor says, chuckling. "Decades before your parents were born, a man gave me something," she says as her thoughts slip back to when Bishop gave her his glove. "He said it represented me holding his heart in my hands."

"That's sweet," Scarlett adds, sipping her orange juice.

"It was literal. And this necklace I keep tucked away…" She pulls out the amulet from under her blouse. The amber inside the metal casing swirls with mists. "This is what the Sentinels have been searching for. He never knew which was which."

"Bishop?" Scarlett asks, confirming.

Eleanor nods. "Bishop, Easpag. Whatever name he went by. He never knew. And they've been looking for this for far too long."

"You've thrown a lot of info at me, Grams. I'm not sure I understand how this all ties together."

Eleanor turns to her grandchild, the amulet still in hand. Reaching around the back of her neck, she removes the amulet and chain. "Here, child. This was never mine to have."

"Only adding to my confusion," Scarlett informs her.

"Bishop realized the rarity of your kind. The genetics behind how grey fairies were born before genetics was a science. I don't know how, but he did. And he based a story, a prophecy, on it." Eleanor squints, anger growing.

"Why? What's the point of doing so?"

"Because he was an accident. A legend who never should have been. Same with the Sentinels. They weren't born; they were made."

"They told me." A realization hits Scarlett. "Pasha was the third person with them. He stole their amulet. Pasha and Bishop are the same person."

Eleanor turns to her grandchild. "And he gave me his vial and theirs."

"But why?"

"To safeguard it. I loved him. Many lifetimes ago, I loved him. But I was never in love with him. Your grandfather was the only man I ever loved like that."

"What does him loving you have to do with everything that's happened?" Scarlett's mind races, trying to connect all the dots.

"The Nation sent Inessa here, well, the Body, if not The Nation, to investigate the deaths of the old Mind under the guise of working with her husband, Vistrus, at the museum."

The dots start connecting, and Scarlett's eyes grow wide. "And Bishop killed the old Mind. That's what her diaries were trying to say."

Eleanor grabs the book off the end table and hands it to Scarlett, who's still holding the amulet in her hands. "Take the book to Vistrus. Tell him to read it. All of it. If he gives you so much as a raised eyebrow, you tell him I said so. Nobody disobeys a grandma."

Scarlett hops up and dashes to the door. Opening it, she turns back to Eleanor. "Grandma, what do I do with this?" She holds up the amulet.

Eleanor shakes her head. "That's up to you, my child."

"You read the entire book?" Vistrus says, looking up from his cigar.

"I read it, then gave it to Grams," Scarlett replies, wiping away the cigar smoke drifting her way.

"Why would you not give it to me?" Vistrus inquires, puffing away.

Connor puts up a cigar-holding hand to stop Scarlett from answering. "That was my call. There were things in there that I thought she should see first."

A satisfied smile crosses Vistrus. He leans back, puffing again. "I am glad I put my trust in you and the future of the Council, Connor. While I would have liked to read this first, I understand and agree with you."

"What council?" Scarlett asks. "Isn't it all but dead or whatever?"

Vistrus gives a big nod. "Dead? Never. Convalescing and in need of new blood."

"What does that mean, Mr. P ... trovsky?" Scarlett asks, adding in his full surname.

Shaking his head at her, Vistrus says with frustrated words, "It means things are in the works. But now, having read this, it all makes sense."

"There were a few passages we could not decipher. Allison always did that." Connor's voice holds tones of longing.

Nodding a knowing nod, Vistrus leans forward, holding the book in his hands. "They were instructions. Kill all Legends related to Eleanor. Leave Eleanor alone. I cannot believe I never saw it."

"Saw what?" Connor asks. "What did we miss?"

Instead of answering, Vistrus rises from his red, crushed velvet chair, cigar held firmly between his lips, and walks away. Scarlett and Connor stretch their necks, watching him disappear down into his music room.

"Do we follow? Is he coming back?" Scarlett shoots off.

Shrugging, Connor shakes his head. "I'm still trying to piece everything together."

"I talked with Grams after she read the book. She laid out most of it. That guy, Bishop, and her used to be an item. But she fell in love with Gramps. Bishop, who had other names before, never stopped loving her. And all of this somehow ties Bishop, Grams, Mrs. Petrovsky, and all these deaths together."

Waving his hands in disbelief, Connor shakes his head. "So this is all a string of murders based on the oldest motive in the world? Love?"

Vistrus reemerges holding the same briefcase that Ammar gave him. "The lines between love and obsession blur too easily."

Connor points at Vistrus's words. "Obsession. I can believe that."

"Obsession and secrets. Holding either too long will inevitably cause damage. Holding both will lead to madness." He sits back down in his chair, setting his cigar in the ashtray and the briefcase on his lap. He opens it, placing his hands on the stone but leaving it in the case.

"It makes no sense. Grams wasn't tight with Mrs. Waldgrave. And Jack's parents? Jack? No. *This* is madness," Scarlett cries in disbelief.

"That is where the secrets come. If the deceased weren't close to Eleanor, they were close to me." Vistrus pulls the stone from the briefcase and closes it, setting the stone on top, facing up.

"So?" Connor says, defiance coats his tone.

"I was married to Inessa," he states.

"Again, so?" Connor's frustration grows.

He turns the stone, so it faces Scarlett and Connor. "This stone is older than any Legend I have ever known. It rewrites our history, and I do not know the implications that it holds. We may never know."

Scarlett smiles, looking at the picture. "She's pretty."

"She was my wife," he says, pointing to the picture framed above the living room piano.

Both Scarlett and Connor drop their jaws, dumbfounded.

After letting them stew for a moment, Vistrus clears his throat, pulling them back to the moment.

"Tie it all together, Vistrus," Connor says in a tone befitting a maturing young man in need of knowing and not the idle curiosity of a child.

"To make a long story short, we moved here so she could investigate a massacre. She eventually solved it. Bishop found out and killed her; that was the beginning. Bishop's love for Eleanor turned into obsession long ago. His wrath we feel now."

"So it is all about love and jealousy. That's what I said!" Connor proclaims with a little too much excitement.

"No. Obsession and jealousy. They often go hand in hand," Vistrus says.

"What does this have to do with the prophecy that killed my parents?" Connor asks.

Vistrus holds his words for a moment, letting his anger at the situation settle. Taking a long exhale, he says, "There never was a prophecy."

"But I changed," Scarlett says, exasperated.

"And you are who you are. But the prophecy was made up by Bishop for whatever reason. Likely to help him find his 21-gram vials," Vistrus continues.

"Wait a second," Connor interjects, starting to doubt everything. "What about the Council and their dissolvement?"

"Dissolution. Bishop. It is amazing how easily you can control a group of people when you manifest a scapegoat for their problems. Point a finger at a blurred mass and people look. Tell them what they are looking at and people see the image form," Vistrus offers.

"So, they were betraying The Nation?" Scarlett asks.

Nodding his head, Vistrus adds, "Whether they knew it or not is a different story, and I missed all the signs."

"What do we do now?" Scarlett asks.

Connor and Vistrus share a look to which Vistrus nods his chin at him.

Turning to Scarlett, Connor says, "End this by killing Bishop."

"That's all good in theory, but how do we find him?" Scarlett points out the flaw in the plan.

"The same way porcupines mate," Connor adds with a smile.

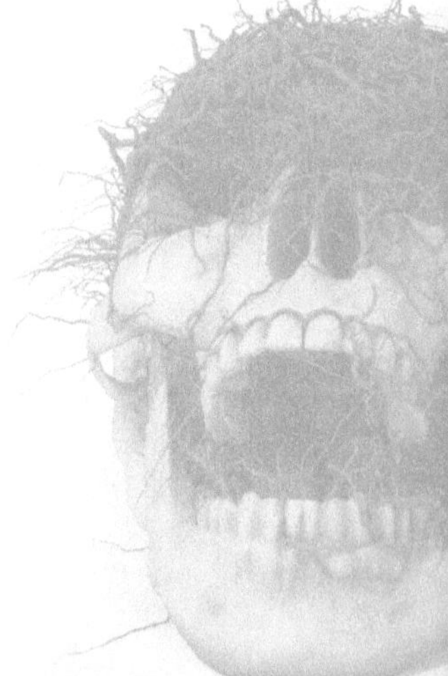

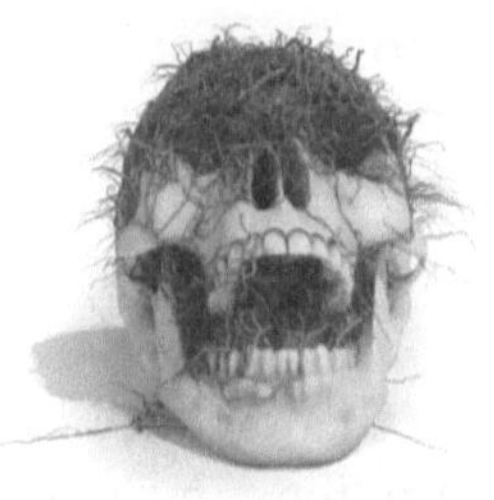

CHAPTER 20

"Some only see the shortcomings in others."
~L. Taylor~

The West Haven Museum always held a particular place of peace for Vistrus. It was the reason he and Inessa moved to the States, even if it was under false pretenses. The nighttime strolls through the displays, whether for work or simply to enjoy the wonderment of times past, the museum was a haven for him.

This evening provides that same feeling as he strolls the Egyptian section filled with unidentified sarcophagi, discussing matters with Eleanor, Raymond, and December.

"Why are we here, Vistrus?" Eleanor asks. "I might be more vivacious than I look, but I do enjoy the comfort of my home."

Nodding, he says, "While you feel safe there, I feel safe here. Important matters call for an important location."

"And this display is safe?" Raymond's voice chimes in everyone's mind, eliciting a chuckle from Eleanor.

"No." Vistrus keeps his reply simple as he stops at a door labeled, "Employees Only." "But it leads to here." He opens the door, motioning for the others to follow.

Without question, they follow him through the back halls to the storage area until it ends at a dead end, made from cyclopean stonework. A different construction than the rest of the area.

Vistrus removes what grout he has rebuilt and opens the secret door.

Raymond, December, and Eleanor all exchange glances, wondering the same two things: Where does this lead, and what are they doing here?

"What's the meaning of this?" Eleanor asks.

Releasing a good huff, Vistrus says, "Nick had a similar tone when I showed him." He steps into the hallway, again motioning for them to follow. "This was once important. I think it is time to recognize its importance again."

At the end of the hall, he again releases a lock on a secret door, opening the way to the old chamber. Stepping inside, he flips the switch, illuminating the serpentine marble, slanted walls, and recessed lighting.

"I half-expected Bishop to jump out from the shadows," December chimes in their minds, laughing.

"I doubt he's hiding in the shadows of some cave. I presume he has a home like anyone else," Raymond responds in their minds.

"But he can change how he appears. We cannot knock on every door in West Haven, hoping he answers as himself," Vistrus points out the obvious.

Eleanor stands a little straighter as an "Ohh!" escapes her. "Pavers."

"Pavers?" Vistrus parrots.

"A while back, I was at the store and ran into him. I didn't think anything of it at the time. I was so silly. But he mentioned he was paving his driveway. That's got to narrow it down a smidge." Eleanor smiles, happy to supply what info she has to help.

"While that helps … somewhat … with tracking him down, what was your purpose in bringing us here, Vistrus?" Raymond chimes, growing irritated.

"This is where it all began for me," Vistrus says, looking around the room, taking in the details of the walls, the dust on the floor, and everything he can. "It is where I found the glove and the portrait of the Grey Fairy. Well, the portrait that became the Grey Fairy."

"Inessa knew about this place, then," December begins. "We gave those to her for safekeeping. She must have locked them in here."

Nodding, Vistrus says, "This is what she kept referring to as the Mind in her diaries. She knew the importance of what you gave her and their connection to the murders of the old Body, Mind, whatever it was called—Council."

"And you want to bring this back for what?" Eleanor asks, looking around, trying to figure out the use for this room.

"The Council cannot stay hidden in the basement of the historical society forever. What better place can you find in West Haven for proper chambers than this?"

The other three exchange questioning looks, unsure how to respond.

"We are too old for timidness," Eleanor snaps, waving off the silence. "With the history connected to this place, why would you want to do such a thing, Vistrus?"

"Honoring the past does not mean embracing the violence that formed its history. It means acknowledging it happened and ensuring it does not happen again. I believe that if anyone can make this place into something of quality, it will be the next Council. It may be their future, but it should be rooted in the past," he offers, arms open to the room.

Raymond and December nod in agreement, but remain wordless.

Eleanor looks around, trying to figure out the logistics of moving items into the room while taking mental measurements for furniture. "You are … or were on the Council. If you think this is a good idea, who am I to say no?" She smiles as they all look around the future of the West Haven Council.

Scarlett walks up to the main entrance of her alma mater, gripping a reusable shopping bag in one hand and a picture frame loosely wrapped in an old bedsheet in the other. The stonework rotunda stares down at her as though welcoming her back once again.

Some lobby attendant or hall monitor, whose identification badge reads Dorris, approaches the door with a smile. "May I help you?"

Smiling back, Scarlett recognizes the hall monitor. "Hi, Dorris! I used to be a student here. You were here, too."

The lady shrugs, shaking her head. "I'm sure you were, but I see so many students. Sorry."

Scarlett nods, understanding the volume of students might make for blank faces after a while.

"Is there a reason you are here today?" the lady reiterates her initial question.

Realizing she still hadn't answered, Scarlett apologizes, "Oh yeah, I am looking for Raymond and December. They work here."

Nodding, the lady unlocks and opens the door. "I know them. Quiet people if ever there were." She pauses, looking Scarlett up and down. "Friends of yours?"

Without hesitation, Scarlett answers, "Family friends. Just came to give them some … gifts."

Pursing her lips, the hall monitor turns to a sign-in sheet. "If you say so. Sign in." She grabs a name tag sticker and permanent marker. "Name here. Put it somewhere visible."

Nodding as she writes her name, Scarlett says, "Of course." Sticking it on the left side of her shirt, she adds, "Have a great day!"

As Scarlett walks away, Dorris pulls out her cell phone and dials a number. As the call connects, she says, "Are you In?" A moment later, she says, "With the breath from their pale faces. You said trust no one. Well, someone came for them."

Walking the halls, Scarlett feels like they have shrunk somehow. No longer holding the menacing feeling of learning to navigate them, making new friends, and surviving the four years. Now, she sees lockers that have been party to decades of countless stories, the floors that innumerable students tread upon, and the sounds of teachers, year after year, teaching the same curriculum only updated to meet the newest standards. Yes, the rose-colored glasses of years gone by have definitely tinted her whimsy as she strolls down to the cafeteria to find December.

At the lunch line, she sees December doling out lunches as she's done every day for who knows how many years. Weaving her way through the lunch line, she waves, calling out, "December!"

Finishing her scoop, December sets it down, turning to Scarlett. She waves her around the counter but does not chime any words into Scarlett's mind.

"We need to talk. When are you free?" Scarlett says, motioning to the bag and wrapped frame.

A held-up finger and scanning head tells Scarlett that December's break might come sooner today than on other days. She turns to someone prepping items for the next period, motioning in question for this person to cover her position for a bit. The prep cook nods, taking up the scoop so December can go converse with Scarlett.

As they walk to the teacher's lounge, Scarlett turns to December. "I think Raymond should be here, too."

Chiming into Scarlett's mind, December says, "Already on his way."

Scarlett looks around, not seeing Raymond, asking, "So can you just, like, chat anywhere? Do you two have long-distance calling?"

December releases a breathy chuckle, shaking her head. "There's a range, but yes, it is longer than a shout would carry."

As they enter the teacher's lounge, they see Raymond sitting at a corner table, a mop bucket resting nearby. Sitting down, Scarlett rests the portrait on top of the table, her bag by her side.

"What's this about?" Raymond chimes to Scarlett.

Scarlett's lips push from side to side as she thinks about how to begin. "Grandma…" she begins out loud and stops right away. Moving the thoughts to her mind, she begins again. "Grandma Eleanor trusted me with something." She pauses again, huffing as if her words lack the importance she strives for. "You once trusted me with a story about you two. How you came to be how you are."

Raymond's eyebrow raises, uncertain Scarlett will take this anywhere good. December rests her hand on his shoulder in a sign to give Scarlett a chance.

"My grandma told me something came to her attention—something you guys might be looking for." She unwraps the portrait, showing December the picture she has been hunting for countless years.

December's eyes light up and an ear-to-ear smile covers her face. Raymond's apprehension dissolves away as well.

"Mr. … Vistrus found where Inessa hid them for safekeeping. I believe it belongs to you, December."

Raymond leans in, chiming with, "Why are you giving this back to us? What do you want?"

"I'm not much for hidden agendas. There's a lot going on. Some guy hunting all Legends, the WHO taking part in some whack experiments … I thought a little goodwill or altruism, or whatever it's called, might be a good thing right now." She nudges the frame in their direction. December wastes no time in taking it and looking it over as if seeing a long-lost child returned home.

After watching December stare at the portrait for a moment, Scarlett continues, "There's more." She pulls up the reusable grocery bag and pulls out the gloves. "I remember you mentioned these were there when you first transitioned."

Raymond squints at the gloves, inspecting them for some unseen element. After a moment, he turns to December. While Scarlett can't hear what he says to her, the expressions on both their faces tell her that this will be useful to them.

As Raymond and December carry on their private conversation, a name tag adorned Vistrus enters the teacher's lounge. "Raymond, December, Dorris called," he calls out, not seeing Scarlett, whose back is turned to him. "Someone is looking…" As he says this, Scarlett turns around, causing him to pause. Realizing the false alarm on the call, he calms down and walks over to them, seeing the portrait and gloves.

"What are you doing, Scarlett?" Vistrus asks, sitting next to her.

"Returning things," she says, "What's it look like?"

"Are you sure about this?" he asks his question, but the tone holds more curiosity about her character than about the potential consequences of her actions.

Nodding, she says, "Why wouldn't I be?" Continuing as if the interruption never happened, she says, "I also have this. If it is what I think it is, or, I should say, holds what I think it holds, I can't think of anyone else who should have it." Scarlett pulls out the amulet, the mists inside the amber swirling about, and places it in December's hands.

A teary-eyed Raymond turns from staring at the amulet to Scarlett, saying, "Thank you."

"When Grandma gave them to me, she told me to do with them what I think is right. They aren't mine to decide what is right."

With her words, Vistrus's head knocks back, blown away by her words. He brings it forward into a knowing nod and a sense of peace washes over him. "You are going to be great, kid," he says under his breath, watching the long-lost items return to their rightful owners.

"Thank you so much for throwing me a wedding shower," Bri says, hugging Eleanor.

"My pleasure, dearie. Every couple deserves a nice shower, I think," Eleanor says, smiling.

"It means a lot. I think my mom would totally approve," Bri responds, looking around at all the guests, chatting and enjoying the hor d'oeuvres.

In the other room, Scarlett, Connor, Duncan, Vistrus, and a few others break out into a chorus of laughter at something said. Bri stares into the room, searching for the joy that has been missing for so long—a heavy look of longing not lost on Eleanor. She puts a hand on Bri's arm, patting her a few times.

"It will pass," Eleanor says a little above a whisper.

Turning to her elder, Bri's eyes widen. "Why would I want it to pass?"

Smiling and huffing, Eleanor says, "*'It'* being the hard times weighing down your stare. Don't think I didn't see it."

Bri turns back to the festivities. "Didn't realize it showed."

"Be around as long as I have, you learn to read expressions." She adds to herself, "At least you think you do."

"Adulthood isn't all pain and loss? Happier times are waiting? Is that the gist of it?"

Eleanor stands, making her way to the empty buffet. "Want a piece of cake? It's Portillo's."

"Already had one … but what the hell, yeah, bring it on," Bri says, laughing and patting her stomach.

Plating the pieces, Eleanor continues, "Life is what you make of it. Cliche as it sounds, all bad times have a silver lining. It might not be a silver lining for you, but if you can learn to appreciate whatever that silver lining is, it makes life a little more livable."

"So, learn to love the bad. Not the marital advice I thought I'd get, but I'll take what I can get." She takes the plate from Eleanor. "Thank you."

Eleanor sits back down, digging her fork into her piece. "Of course. But that's not what I meant. Being able to appreciate things that are not meant for or do not affect you will give you a … more level outlook when you have your problems to sort out." She shoves the bite of cake into her mouth.

Bri chews her food and thoughts for a moment. "Makes sense, I guess. No wedding night advice?"

Eleanor raises a brow at Bri. "I thought you kids were experienced … beyond needing advice like that?"

Bri tries to retain a smile, but her blushing cheeks betray her. "Eleanor! You naughty woman." They share a good laugh, then Bri adds, "Scarlett mentioned that you met her grandfather at prom? I didn't know prom went back that far."

"Little white lies to hide hard-to-believe truths. I met Nick long before the tradition of senior prom started. I was dating someone else, actually."

"You are naughty!" Bri taps Eleanor on the knee.

"Being in a relationship and feeling satisfied—content—are two different things. You look happy with Duncan. I've seen you two together."

Taking a bite of her cake, Bri beams. "He's the best," she says, covering her mouth. "Not at all who I imagined I'd fall for, but I love him so much."

The two enjoy the moment together as the laughter from the other room continues and someone calls out, "Bri, get in here! This is your shower, and these gifts aren't going to open themselves!"

Eleanor and Bri stand, setting down their plates.

"Who was this other guy? The one you were dating when you met your husband?"

Before Eleanor can answer, the doorbell rings. "Go. Enjoy your shower, sweetie. I got the door."

Bri grabs what is left of her cake and heads off to the other room.

The door opens to show Bishop and a West Haven Council member covered in bruises, breathing heavily, standing there.

"Completely inappropriate, Bishop." Her tone holds no love for the man. "I see you brought what's left of the Council. Some show of force?"

The councilman turns to Bishop, a look on his face of disbelief, but remains silent. Bishop shakes his head at him, then turns to Eleanor. "I'm done playing games. I want what's mine."

Scarlett and Bri skip to the door. "Who's here, Grams?" They both stop and see the two outside. "Oh." Then to the councilman, they add, "Did our first encounter not leave a lasting enough impression?"

The councilman offers a fading smirk, opting for a silent response.

"Are you not going to invite me in?" Bishop asks, pretending all is well between them.

"You are not welcome. This is a joyous occasion and not meant for you," Eleanor says through gritted teeth.

Bishop looks around at the decorations he can see from where he stands. "A wedding shower, I see. I was hoping one day we could have shared in one of these."

Realization hits Bri, causing her to blurt out, "Is this the DB you were dating when you met your hubby?"

Eleanor nods, keeping her stare on Bishop. "Not sure what a DB is, young lady, but yes, this is him."

"Douchebag, Grams, douchebag," Scarlett answers. "Connor! Get over here!" The urgency in her voice summons him before she finishes her brief sentence.

Staring down the men at the door, Connor stands guard next to his grandmother. "What do you want?" Connor demands.

"I wanted a happy life with Aoife or Eleanor or whatever name she currently goes by, but no. I wanted to be the one who made her happy. I wanted it all. Do you have any idea how that eats away at you over all these years?" Bishop keeps his stare on Eleanor even as he speaks to Connor.

Connor laughs, saying, "If unhinged had a poster child, you'd be it."

"Quiet, boy," the councilman interjects. "There's so much more going on than you understand."

"Trying to cure us, weaponize us, do anything but protect us. I understand all too well," Connor begins. Gesturing to everyone around him, he continues, "We all understand. The past four years have been nothing but death and pain because of you," he gestures to Bishop, "this assface, and everyone else who thinks that Legends are something other than human."

Confusion washes over the councilman as he turns to Bishop. "You said they were our enemy. That they were trying to cull us. You said there was a war brewing. That they thought we were unnatural and should be cured."

Bishop huffs, shaking his head and turning to the councilman. "Of course, there's a war brewing. There's always something brewing below what we can see. I kept you prepped for it. Yes, we are unnatural. We need to be cured. That's been the plan this whole time."

"What was all that talk in the beginning about trust? It was all just some ploy?" The councilman turns to Eleanor in disbelief and defeat. "I didn't know." He shifts, unsure if stepping to the other side would be welcome or taken as an act of aggression. "He's the last Adeirrig. We couldn't let anyone cure him. This was his war; he told us it was yours."

Bishop scans everyone at the door. "This war can end. Further acts of violence can be avoided. Just give me the Grey Fairy."

"I don't—" Scarlett starts saying before Eleanor holds up a hand, silencing her.

"It's no longer in my possession. Neither is the glove or amulet you gave me." She watches his eyes grow wide. "You know, the ones you say symbolized me holding your heart in my hands."

Bishop's wide eyes and red face fume with anger. "Where are they?"

Vistrus steps into the room, hanging up his cell phone. "Safe and that is all you will get from us."

"I need that parchment. Tell me where it is." The words seethe out of his mouth.

Vistrus steps forward, next to Eleanor, opposite Connor. "Why?"

"Because I was never supposed to be ... this. Because we aren't natural. But mostly, because it's mine." False authority fills his tone.

"Um, no it's not," Scarlett says. "And yes we are." Her tone turns petulant. "You're unnatural. I'm not unnatural."

He eyes Scarlett, searching for the unspoken words in her short response. "Yes, it is mine. You think this is the course of human nature? Look at your-selves, monsters among men. There's nothing nat-ural about what I've become." He holds defiance in his words. "I'll be able to finally show you, Eleanor, what true love is, and everything I'm willing to do for it, for what should have been my family."

"You have no idea what some are willing to do for their family," Vistrus says, clenching his jaw in restraint. "I suggest you leave before something hap-pens you cannot take back."

"I've done many things I can't take back. What would a few more be?" he scoffs.

"Not at a wedding shower, please," Eleanor pleads. "We'll get you your vial. I'll tell your lackey when we do."

Resisting momentary defeat, he says, "So many avoidable deaths dating back further than the past four years … had you just done what I wanted, Eleanor."

"You can't kill us all," Connor snaps.

"I expect to hear from you within the hour. If not, I'll see if I can't prove this young man wrong." He eyes Vistrus. "This killing has gone on long enough. Don't you think?" Bishop turns and walks away.

"Yes, it has," Vistrus mutters.

After Bishop has moved beyond a Legend's ear-shot, Vistrus turns to Eleanor and Bri. "I hate to have to steal anyone from the party, but Scarlett and Connor need to find December and Raymond, and let them know what is happening. I have a flight to catch. The Head Council needs to know right away."

"Can't you FaceTime them?" Bri asks, bringing the obvious solution to light.

Vistrus shakes his head. "They avoid anything that can be monitored for reasons such as this."

Duncan pops his head from the corner, holding a can of soda. "I know it's not my place, but I think they might make an exception, given the circumstances and all. Call and explain. If nothing else, you spend ten minutes on your drive to the airport. Best case, you save the hours of flight, unable to do anything, and get things moving faster."

Vistrus points at him, looking at Bri. "I like him." Turning back to everyone else, he says, "We all know what to do. Brianna, Duncan, my apologies."

They both wave him off. "Like, go," Bri says.

Sitting in his office, Vistrus sits in front of his laptop monitor. A window on the monitor shows a few irritated and muted faces in a Zoom® meeting, all sitting in low light like suspects being interrogated in old-time mob movies. Only Vistrus and a square labeled Mikhail remain unmuted. A cigar burns away in the ashtray next to a bottle of Scotch.

"I have told you about Bishop before." Vistrus's frustration shines in his words. "We do not have time for me to sit on planes for fifteen hours. This is too important."

"Fine," Mikhail relents. "Then get to the new information."

"Bishop needs to be eliminated. His threats escalated," Vistrus warns.

"Then it looks like the timeline for what we discussed is accelerating. Have you had time to dissolve what we talked about yet?" Mikhail asks, rubbing his chin.

"Not yet," Vistrus says, checking his watch, "but I do not think it will matter soon. There will be no one left."

"Then make your picks and make it official. You have our full support. The West Haven Council must thrive for the benefit of all Legends. I don't want one man deciding to out The Nation because of some long-held obsession."

"Already covered, Mikhail. We have kept The Nation secret this long," he responds.

"And Vistrus ... get your affairs in order. The future of The Nation rests on you."

Connor drives through town with Eleanor in the front seat and Scarlett in the back. The radio is off and tension sits heavy as he weaves through traffic.

"Turn right on Milwaukee," Eleanor instructs. She closes her eyes in concentration.

"You know where they live?" Scarlett asks.

Eleanor opens her eyes, irritated. "I know a lot of things you don't," she replies. "Now, shush, I'm busy." Again, she closes her eyes.

"I had to track them down at school when you could've told me where they live?" Scarlett asks, checking the seatbelt to ensure it's in properly.

"You never asked, dear. Now, quiet." She grabs Connor's arm. "Slow down, dear. We'll get there. Turn right at Main Street." She closes her eyes briefly, smiling as she opens them.

"Well, it would have been nice to know is all I'm saying." Scarlett crosses her arms.

"Am I following the road around to Washington?" Connor asks, slowing his speed on the side streets.

"Yes, Connor. Park when you get to the corner of Monroe and Washington," Eleanor instructs. "Next time you need to know something, Scarlett, just ask."

Connor finds a spot on the street, and he and Scarlett follow Eleanor to a two-story home on the corner, whose brick-and-mortar first level gives way to a siding-lined second level.

"Ringing a bell helps," Scarlett sasses, reaching for it.

But before she can push the button, Raymond opens the door, chiming in everyone's mind, "Come in. We have much to do and little time."

"I was talking to him while you were babbling, Scarlett. Sometimes shushing is about more than shutting you up for a bit," Eleanor says with a smile.

Raymond leads them to an adjoining room with a cyclopean stonework fireplace. December tends to the fire, carefully placing smaller pieces of wood inside an already-lit fire.

"What's going on?" Connor asks. Looking at the amulet, gloves, and portrait resting next to December.

"The time has come," December chimes in their heads. Her words, as cryptic as they sound, hold a peaceful air. "When we first acted as Sentinels for the West Haven Council, it was not out of the kindness of our hearts or a misguided need to belong to something larger than ourselves. We were searching for our vials. Our 21 grams. If ever there was a way to stay informed with events even The Nation finds strange or unusual, being active close to a council was it." She lifts up the amulet, inspecting the mists inside. "All we ever wanted was to be in control of our fates, our time to die when that time came. I have no need to tell you, Eleanor, that waking from the Waiting gets no easier each time it happens."

Scarlett turns to her grandmother, asking, "What is she going to do with all those things?"

Eleanor offers a short smile accompanied by sad eyes.

Decembers chimes in, "Destroy them, Scarlett. It's what we've desired since they were first taken."

"Why?" Connor asks. "You can't come back if you do this."

Raymond chimes in, taking the answer to this question, "Because humans, no matter how special, should not live as long as we have. Forget the power that time and knowledge bring. The pain and longing to leave behind everything you will inevitably lose is beyond explanation. So many loved ones whose faces have been all but forgotten. Friends, Normals or Legends, whose passings blur together."

Scarlett's eyes remain fixed on her grandmother, watching her and seeing the long put-off end that Eleanor has started yearning for.

"Entropy is an inevitable part of existence and no one, not even The Nation or the Legends should be exempt from that experience," Raymond finishes.

"So, how are they going to destroy the vials? Is there some incantation or chemical compound that needs to be mixed—" Scarlett starts asking but is interrupted as December tosses the amulet into the fire, no ceremony, no magic words, no alchemical formula conjured up from medieval England to dissolve it away. An unceremonious toss, as if throwing an overcooked marshmallow into it to watch it expand and burn away to ash.

"Oh, well, that was anticlimactic," Scarlett mutters.

"That's the funny thing about life, dear," Eleanor says, keeping her eyes on the fire. "Most of it passes without us knowing. We are too busy looking for the grandiose to see the wondrous happening in the smaller things."

The amber inside the pendant pops and cracks in the fire, sending out two faint spouts of mists. Each mist floats to either December or Raymond, encircling them in numerous, intertwining rings that contract and expand in a slow waltz before embracing them in an ethereal hug before dissipating.

"Who needs grandiose with things like that?" Scarlett says to the room. "Now what? Are they going to rapidly age and die like the guy who chose poorly in that one movie?"

Raymond laughs a windy, hollow laugh. Chiming in their minds, he says, "This isn't Hollywood. That's it. Now, when we die, whenever that may be, we die. The end. But there's no sudden acceleration to the endpoint."

Eleanor pats her granddaughter on the head. "So much to learn, young one."

"So much time to learn it all," Connor reminds her.

"Indeed, there is," Eleanor concedes.

"So, what's next?" Scarlett asks.

December picks up the gloves sitting next to her. She offers them to Eleanor, chiming in with, "It only makes sense that you be the one to dispose of them."

Eleanor nods, taking the gloves. She stares down at them, imagining the life she never had and remembering the life she did have. A kernel of curiosity floats through her mind, wondering how different the life she had could have been had she handled Easpag's rejection differently. Could her beloved Nioclás still be alive? Would all those who perished by Bishop's hand or command still be alive had she done things differently? As those thoughts drift away, another idea enters her mind. One that brings peace to the guilt now weighing her down. As the newfound peace fills her, she tosses the gloves into the fire.

"Do you have to burn the portrait? I mean, it's so cool," Scarlett says to December.

December offers only a shrug.

After a moment, the gloves combust, burning away the fabric that held another's 21 grams. A mist floats out from the fire, circling the room before dissipating into nothing.

December turns to Scarlett. "It appears I get to keep what has been mine all along."

Connor looks around the room, trying to figure out if he missed something. "I don't get it."

"Get what?" Eleanor asks.

"They have their 21 grams back. I assume that's what the smoke show was. But why can't they talk?"

A knowing smile crosses both Raymond and December, but it is December who answers. "Our voices weren't lost because of our 21 grams. They were lost in the explosion that made us Legend. There is no magic in life. But life is magical. Learning to separate the two will do wonders for your sanity."

"Now," Raymond chimes in, interjecting, "we have to confront Bishop."

"I'm so ready for this," Connor says, rubbing his fist in his hand.

Shaking his head, Raymond continues his thought, "Bishop made us what we are. Swindling poor peasants for quick profit during a plague. He gets his just desserts, and we are to serve it."

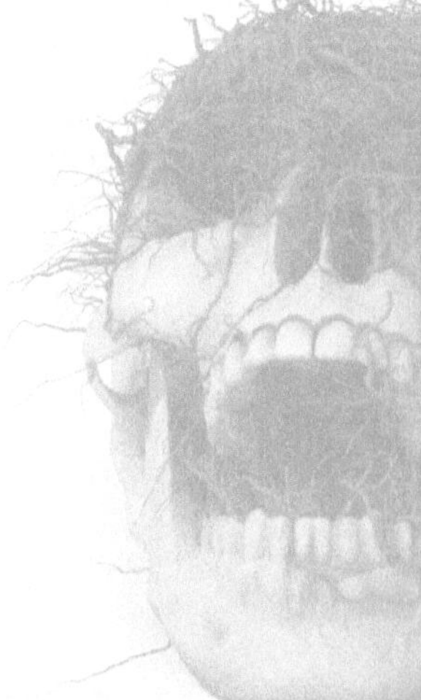

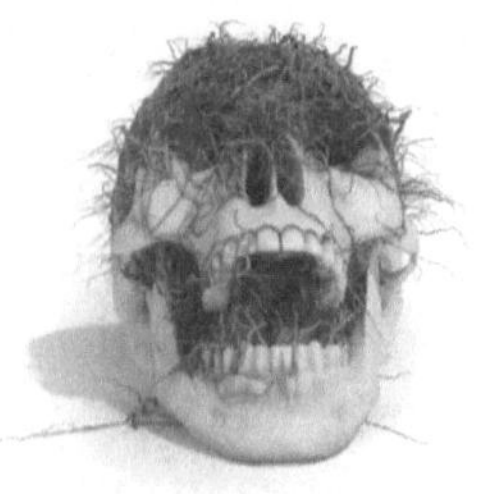

CHAPTER 21

"The end of your story will come one day."
~J. Taylor~

After leaving Raymond's and December's home, Connor pulls up to his house but leaves the engine running and does not exit the car. Scarlett looks around from the back seat, confused.

"I thought we were going to find Bishop and do whatever it is we do?" Scarlett asks Eleanor.

"This is not something you have to be part of," Eleanor starts.

"Like hell, I don't," Scarlett interrupts. "He killed me, remember?"

Scratching her head, Eleanor says, "I do. But your time in the Waiting is on my hands. I realized something before we burned the gloves."

"That I don't need to be where the action is?" Scarlett spits her words.

"That perhaps I could have been more upfront with Easpag when I turned him away. I would not say I led him on, but perhaps, in his eyes, I did. I never meant to.

There was never a part of me that wanted to be with him. I always told him, 'Maybe in another life,' but I now realize that he held onto a false hope he found in those words. There was never any implication of hope on my part, or never any intention of. The deaths, your … time … were not because of me and my actions. At some point, he needed to stop blaming others and take responsibility. He never did. There comes a time when placing blame on past trauma, past pain is no longer an excuse for actions and becomes a crutch, an excuse for current behavior."

"And this is why I am being dropped off at home? Does Connor get to go?" Scarlett asks, unsure what's going on.

Eleanor nods. "He might be needed."

"And I won't?" Scarlett defends. "I have things I can do now."

"There's something else you need to do." Eleanor looks at the house.

"What?" Scarlett's word holds petulance.

"You need to go inside. There are people in there who owe you an explanation." With those words, she exits and pulls the seat forward so Scarlett can exit.

Scarlett exits and looks at her house. Her heart races with uncertainty, pounding in her chest and causing her to feel tremors ripple through her body, uncertain if this is nervousness and excitement or something related to her Legendary state.

Eleanor sits back in the car and closes the door but rolls down the window. "There is so much more for you than confronting an old man. Go."

Scarlett watches as Eleanor turns to Connor, instructing him to drive away and disappear around the corner. Turning to look at the house, she sees movement inside, but the light outside and lighting inside prevent her from making out details of who it is.

With a pounding heart, sweaty palms, and shaking legs, she walks up the driveway to her home. A glimmer of diminishing hope rushes through her that perhaps Allison waits inside. But she knows that is an impossibility. So she walks up the driveway, wondering who it may be.

Windshield wipers swipe back and forth at blinding speeds in vain attempts to clear the downpour off the glass in hopes that James might see the road ahead, if only for a second at a time. Cars zoom by, helping the wind edge the McAllisters' car closer and closer to the riverbank. The light from the street lamp diffuses in the weather while oncoming cars blind them with the unnecessary use of brights in stormy conditions.

A crying infant Scarlett in the back seat adds to the stress of navigating the roads. James McAllister turns to his wife, Hillary, fast asleep in the passenger seat.

He smiles at how peaceful she looks in the storm.

Glancing in the rearview mirror to see his crying child, he sings softly. "Hush little baby, don't you cry. Daddy's gonna buy you a…" The words elude him for a moment, so he makes something up. "A diamond sky. And if that diamond sky don't shine, Daddy's gonna buy you a ... bottle of wine."

He shakes his head at himself, continuing his improvisation. "Daddy really should know the words, but asking that is just ... absurd. Please stop crying. I don't know what's wrong. But I promise I'll stop singing this song."

Scarlett's cries grow louder as another car zips by them, splashing the windshield, momentarily blinding him. The car drifts closer to the shoulder, causing him to readjust a tad too harshly, jostling Hillary from her slumber.

"Go back to sleep, my love," he whispers to her.

The crying continues even as the rain lessens for a moment. Taking advantage of the lighter rain, he reaches back, trying to keep an eye on the road while feeling around Scarlett's car seat, searching for a pacifier, bottle, or other source of her current unpleasant condition.

He keeps the wheel held steady, thinking he holds a straight path on the road, but even in the lighter rain, the conditions are dark and visibility is limited. Finally, he feels something digging into her little thigh and pulls out a squished baby toy.

As he hands it to her, saying, "Here you go, baby girl," a car passes them a little too close for James's comfort. He adjusts the wheel, pulling them right, but over adjusts, sending him onto the shoulder leading down to the river. Pulling the wheel back, the tires grip in the wet mud, sending him farther down to the river. He struggles against gravity, screaming for Hillary to wake up, but it is too late. The car flips on its side, resting a moment as water starts seeping in.

Frantic, he unbuckles, calling for Hillary, who is non-responsive. In the backseat, Scarlett's cries grow *louder and more scared as James shakes his wife, trying to wake her.*

"We'll be okay, Scarlett. I'll make sure you're fine." He moves to crawl into the backseat, but the shifting weight causes the precariously balanced car to flip over, sending him tumbling about as the car lands upright but sinking.

"And that is where we let the story fade," James tells Scarlett as they sit at the dining room table along with Hillary and an even more fair-skinned young adult. "It wasn't a proper bedtime story for a baby, but the more you heard it, the more it became real. I don't know what Ken or Tracy may have varied when they told it to you, but that was the story we came up with."

The story does nothing to alleviate the tension in the room so thick a sharpened knife would dull trying to cut it.

Scarlett's slack jaw, twisted face, and furrowed brow paint a perfect image of disgusted disbelief. "So, now that all this is out in the open, things are hunky dory? Couldn't we have just outed all this when I was an infant and not spent my life thinking your deaths were somehow my fault? Do you know how that weighs on a person?"

Hillary leans over to her estranged daughter, trying to grab her hand, but Scarlett pulls away. "We didn't know. We were told things. Horrible things and were scared. We did what we thought was best. We made mistakes."

"Oh, you think so?!" Scarlett scoffs. "And now I have to accept that I have a sister, too?" She turns to the one with porcelain skin. "You're about my age. Why didn't I see you in school?"

Meek words exit the young woman as she says, "I went to Maine South."

Scarlett throws up her hands in defeat. "So, she gets to have the storybook life while I am led to believe I am an orphan being raised by my aunt and uncle, who, as you know, aren't actually my aunt and uncle because … HORMONES! She didn't have to deal with *any* of what we had to go through these past years."

Her sister stands, pushing in her chair. "I think it's best if I wait outside."

James nods in understanding, though the look on his face pleads she stays. She does not.

He turns to Scarlett. "It was always a means to an end. We never wanted to leave you. You know that. I can't say I'm sorry enough. No one can. But don't take this out on Maeve. She had nothing to do with it."

Scarlett shakes her head, crossing her arms in defiance. "Sure, whatever. But my parents, the ones who raised me and changed my diapers and helped me through homework and first crushes, those parents are six feet under. You left to play family elsewhere. Don't expect this to end in hugs and forgiveness."

Her words end while a thick, heavy silence drowns the room. Even the furnace sounds dampen in the uncomfortableness of the moment. Scarlett keeps tossing glares back and forth between the two of them while James's and Hillary's expressions plead for forgiveness.

Hillary sits upright, wiping her expression clean. "I understand things take time. And forgiveness, how we hope to be forgiven, may never come. But don't take this out on Maeve. She never knew about you, either. She always wanted a sister."

"Did anyone ever stop to think about what I wanted? Did anyone ever ask *that* question?" Scarlett takes a few deep breaths, calming herself. She even holds her pinkies to her thumbs, saying, "Ohm," a few times, hoping a brief moment of channeling serenity will aid her. Sighing, she relents, "Fine. I will give her a chance. See what happens. But don't expect nightly family meals or Scarlett and Maeve's day of fun anytime soon."

Both James and Hillary nod, a glimmer of hope in their eyes.

"Life sucks, you know? I lose damn near everyone close to me. I lose my best friend, but she…" Scarlett waves a dismissive hand to where Maeve departed the conversation, "…she gains a sister."

Consternation covers Hillary as she speaks. "Sometimes, the things in life we think we lost are found again. Sometimes in new ways. Sometimes in the ways we already are familiar with."

Scarlett's expression does nothing to convince Hillary that her words are doing the slightest to convince Scarlett there are good things on the horizon.

Continuing, she says, "Give it time; that is all we can ask. And I think that, at least, is fair."

Scarlett's lingering frustration and anger evaporate as she relaxes for the first time since she walked through the door.

"I'm not sure that is fair, but what choice do I have? What choice have I ever had?"

Connor parks his car near a park. The street sign next to him reads, "N. Oketo Ave." He looks out at the families playing on the swings with their little ones and the groups on the tennis courts playing couple's matches. The evening sun sets, shining its fading light on the park in some cosmic display of Norman Rockwellian ideals even as a storm approaches.

"Why are we here?" Connor asks, staring at the people playing.

From outside the car, a knock on the window grabs his attention, causing him to whip his head around, startled.

"This is where Bishop said to meet. This is where it all ends," Vistrus says through the car window. "Now, come." A command, not a request.

Connor and Eleanor exit, following Vistrus through the park to a set of doors leading to an indoor complex. Outside the doors, Raymond and December stand, waiting.

"Has he shown?" Vistrus asks, looking around.

Raymond shakes his head, chiming, "He will."

"This could be a trap," Connor points out.

"I do not think so," Vistrus replies.

"Why not? It'd be perfect. Getting us all here leaves Scarlett vulnerable." Connor joins the scan of the crowd in search of Bishop.

Vistrus stops scanning to catch Connor's attention. "This is where she was found."

Connor contemplates the "she" in Vistrus's words, assuming he knows but is not one hundred percent sure. "Your wife?"

Vistrus nods. "His doing. He wants to end it here. I am sure."

The sky overhead darkens as thunder booms in the distance. The park patrons gather their young ones and belongings as the rain begins to drizzle. Even the tennis players think better than to play in the rain.

As everyone exits the park, a park employee exits the building, locking the doors behind him.

"Closing a few minutes early. Rain and all," he says. "We'll be open tomorrow." Without waiting for a response, he jogs off, covering himself from the increasing rain.

They huddle under the shallow awning, trying to stay dry while they wait on Bishop.

"My friend Ammar always thought the storm would pass," Vistrus says. "While I hoped, I doubted it would."

Raymond, December, and Eleanor listen to his words, picking up the subtext. Connor follows along, trying to decipher the meaning without asking.

"I think all Legends want the storm to pass. On some level, it has always been our hope. People being able to be themselves without fear of persecution simply for existing." He stops, taking a moment to look up at the falling rain. "But Council after Council has failed to make that dream a reality." He turns to Connor. "I am leaving soon, Mr. DeSalvo."

"Why? Where?" Connor asks as if Vistrus won't tell him otherwise.

"The Nation needs me, but not here. You are needed here. You knew this day was coming," Vistrus says, holding back a smile.

Connor nods. "Didn't expect it so soon. Where will you be?"

"I am going home to Russia. I will be on the Head Council there. You will lead the West Haven Council."

"And who else? It can't be just me!" Connor's exasperation grows with each breath as he struggles to stay calm.

"Whoever you pick. It is your council. One from each society. You represent Kipling. I am sure you have your Poe, Tennyson, and Coleridge."

"The last point in the star represented the Frye. I don't know any Clochnawa," Connor points out.

Eleanor butts in, "They have not been represented in many years. I do not think they'd mind. But Scarlett needs a place. Perhaps Frye can represent her."

Vistrus nods, saying, "I agree. Connor, assuming we make it through this night, the future of West Haven rests on you."

"Great," Connor deadpans.

Before their conversation can continue, a flash of lightning and a clap of thunder pull their attention toward the end of the walkway. Bishop stands there, rain pouring down on him.

"Where is it?" Bishop demands.

December and Raymond walk forward, faces locked on Bishop, but no one hears their exchange of words. Even without words, the rain that picked up into a downpour cannot mask the rising tension between the three of them.

In a flash of lightning, Bishop transitions into a hulking form, hair long but sparse, muscles bulging. A form Connor is most familiar with. Raymond and December, too, both stand transitioned from their Normal selves.

December's skin grows thick and bark-like, her hair into vines. Raymond's form matches that of Bishop.

Raymond and Bishop grapple, vying for the upper hand. Eyes locked on the other, silent words are exchanged, meant only for the other.

While they stand, grappling for dominance, December grabs Bishop's feet, using the slick ground to make him lose balance.

"Are we seriously going to stand here and watch this happen?" Connor asks.

"It is not our fight, Mr. DeSalvo. Not yet," Vistrus says without breaking watch from the battle.

Falling to the ground, Bishop kicks December off of him, sending her flying against the tennis court's chain-link fence. Turning, he mounts Raymond, who, from the bottom, swipes his thickened nails at Bishop, hoping to gash him open.

As Raymond's nails swipe once, drawing first blood, Bishop's muscles recede, his hair thickens, but into long vines as his skin grows bark. As he gains his armor, his lost strength allows Raymond to throw him off, letting him stand.

Raymond's muscles recede halfway, and his hair grows longer. Blood drips from his mouth as his teeth fall to the ground. Raymond pounces on top of Bishop and uses his elongated canines to rip away the bark covering his skin. With each chunk pulled away, blood spatters to the ground, washing away in the rain.

As December shakes off the fall, standing and moving toward them, a bolt of lightning strikes down only a few blocks away, lighting up the sky bright as day and distracting everyone but Bishop.

He transitions again into a hulking form, grabbing Raymond by the neck, squeezing and twisting with such force that the crack of bones echoes above the rain. He stands, dropping his body to the ground. December, shocked at the brutal end to her companion's life, transitions to match Bishop's form. The two forego the grapple session, opting straight for punches and swipes, taking turns ripping into the other's flesh. So much blood mixes with the rain that the ground turns a faint red.

Swipe after swipe releases countless years of pent-up anger and hatred for the other. A twisted moment of release December knows will be her last.

Connor steps forward to intervene, but Vistrus holds him back. "It is not ours to step in." But Connor ignores his words, struggling against the elder Coleridge Society member. The pain filling Connor causes him to start transitioning, and Vistrus transitions, too, to match the younger man's strength.

After countless more swipes, both Bishop and December fall to the ground, tapping out of the fight. Still, whatever words they share are only for the other.

Finally, Vistrus releases Connor, and both crouch down next to December as her last breaths leave her. No words chime into their minds, only a smile on her face as she releases from this world.

A cough from Bishop pulls their attention from December. Blood pours out of his mouth with cough after escalating cough. As his strength wanes, he looks up at Vistrus and Connor. A small chuckle escapes him. "This isn't over. The portrait still holds my 21 grams." He keeps his gaze locked on them and he smiles.

Connor shakes his head. "The portrait never held your 21 grams."

The smile fades as the reality of the situation weighs down on him.

"Those tacky-ass gloves did. And those were burned," Connor finishes.

Vistrus returns the smile Bishop left, adding, "Tell them I say hello." He bends down, offering the same death that Bishop gave Raymond.

After the body stops moving, Vistrus and Connor stand, staring at the carnage before them.

"What do you do now, Mr. DeSalvo?"

"We move Raymond and December. Give them a proper burial," Connor answers.

"And Bishop?"

"Let the storm deal with him." Connor's words leave his mouth, as if said by someone else, but he knows they are his.

Vistrus picks up Raymond, leaving Connor to pick up December. They turn to the awning to find Eleanor crying.

Connor leans into Vistrus. "What should I say?"

Vistrus shakes his head. "Staying awhile?" he shouts to her above the storm.

Eleanor does not look at him, keeping her eyes locked on Bishop, but she nods.

An answer good enough for Vistrus, who starts off with Raymond. Connor follows, leaving Eleanor behind as she walks to Bishop, crouching down to mourn the losses this day.

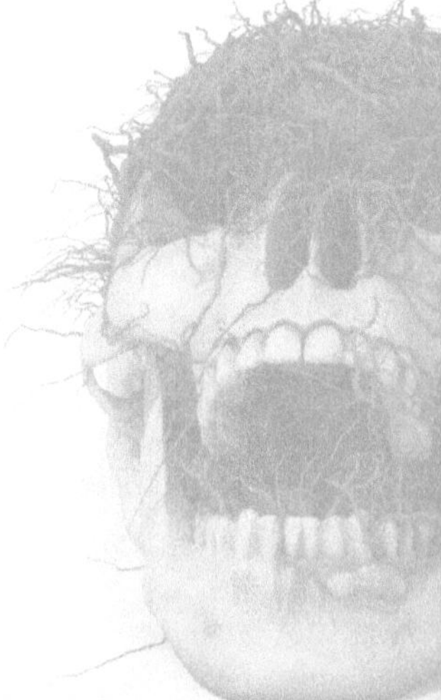

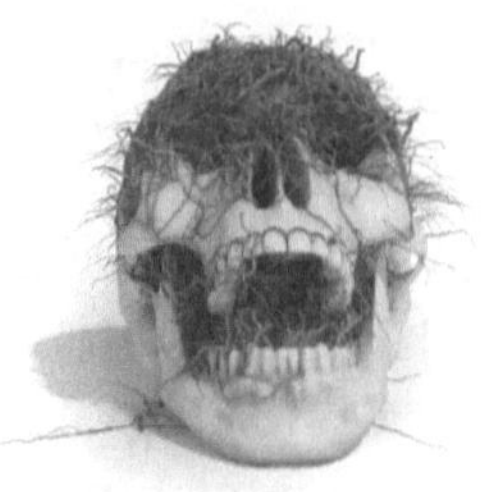

CHAPTER 22

*"The end of one story is the
beginning of another."*
~N. DeSalvo~

"The Grey Fairy? After all the centuries, that's what you're after?" Raymond says in Bishop's head.

Bishop nods. "That is all you can help me with. Anything else I am after is none of your concern." Bishop steps closer. "You hand the Grey Fairy over to me and I'll return your 21 grams." He pauses for only a split second before a hint of contempt washes over him. "And don't pretend to not know what I am talking about."

December holds up a finger before sounding off in Bishop and Raymond's minds. "How do you want us to proceed in obtaining this fairy?"

"Any way you can. All I want is what's mine. Same as you." His face relaxes and softens, almost allowing the corners of his lips to curl up. "The centuries have come and gone. And here we stand in a basement in need of a good renovation. After all this time, wouldn't you have hoped for something more?" A wistful tone seeps into his words. "I *have never strayed from what I desire. But it has taken far longer to get it than I hoped."*

"What is it that you have longed for all these years?" December's words ring through his mind.

A stark pull back to the moment wipes away any hint of wistfulness and reminiscence from Bishop. "The same thing I've always wanted. But sometimes timing is against you. Time, however, is not."

"And after all these years, the Grey Fairy is the key?" Raymond chimes in.

With anger flickering in his eyes, Bishop turns to Raymond. "Funny how things work out. But the details of why and how are none of your concern. You want your 21 grams and I want the Grey Fairy. Bring it to me and you shall have yours."

Bishop pauses to gauge their willingness to help him, but he cannot.

"Do we have a deal?" he reiterates.

Raymond and December turn to each other, reading the other's eyes for a moment before nodding.

"We do," chimes Raymond.

"Good. Bring it to me. Until then…" Bishop trails off for no other reason than dramatic effect.

"How do we find you once we have it?" December's words ring.

"You are the Sentinels of West Haven. I thought you saw everything?" Bishop jabs his words.

Raymond nods. "When we have what you seek, we will be here."

"Good, good," Bishop replies, turning to leave, but after taking a step, he turns back. "Did you find what you were looking for before I came in?"

Raymond shakes his head. "Perhaps we were mistaken."

Satisfied, Bishop steps to the door and waits for them to leave. As the inseparable pair leave the room, Bishop shuts the door behind them, locking it.

They enter the elevator and hit the lobby. Once the door closes, December turns to Raymond. "I, in fact, think we found exactly what we were looking for."

Raymond turns to his companion. "I agree. But he did not need to know that. It would lead to further questions."

"Questions we wouldn't want to answer," December finishes the thought, catching his reasoning for the deception. "What now?"

"Now, we figure out what he wants the Grey Fairy for, find a way to make sure we get what we need, and stop him from ever getting what he seeks." Raymond's words do not end with a suggestion, and December's smile says she couldn't agree more.

"I'm glad throwing her to the wolf was not part of the plan," December adds.

"I never said that it wasn't." Raymond chimes, causing December to turn to him in shock.

The elevator door opens, and they make their way out of the building in silence. December waits until more distance is between them and the West Haven Historical Society.

"There has to be more than that," December pleads.

"If we are to pit predator against prey, make sure the prey is armed."

"Reverse the roles," December chimes, tapping her temple twice and pointing her finger his way. "How do we do that?"

Raymond shakes his head. Before answering, he stops and looks out at the horizon. Nothing unusual lies there, but it captures his gaze, nonetheless. December stops next to him, looking out as well, knowing that this moment is not one to interrupt. Raymond soaks in the sights for a few, striking some long-lost memory that decides to resurface. A car whizzes by, honking and almost causing an accident while it cuts off another car, pulling Raymond out of the moment.

"Of all the things we know we don't know, this is the next thing we must know."

A nursery of raccoons scampers about the nighttime forest clearing Scarlett visited on many occasions. Nearby, the mother raccoon watches her offspring play among the leaves as the dirt beneath them shifts. She cries out for her kits, bringing them in her direction as the dirt continues pushing up and away. All the raccoons scurry into the woods, leaving the mound of dirt the only movement in the clearing.

The dirt continues to push away as a petite hand with black-painted nails emerges from the ground. From the cover of trees, the mother raccoon's eyes shine as she watches with curiosity. Another hand emerges, pulling the dirt away in frantic swipes.

After a short time, a cloth-covered head rises as a torso sits upright. Gasping for breath, the hands pull off the hood, and Allison looks around, confused and scared.

In the distance, she sees the glowing eyes of the mother raccoon and the smaller eyes of her kits floating like monsters from some cosmic horror novel. She sits and cries, trying to understand the unfolding events. The raccoons' curiosity gets the best of them, and they emerge from the tree line. Allison squints, seeing the group of raccoons bob their heads, trying to understand the event.

Smiling at the animals through her tears, Allison looks around the clearing with a strange sense of familiarity. She looks down at the hood that covered her head. A crinkling from inside the hood seems off since the hood is cloth. Inside, she finds a plastic zipper-lock bag with a piece of paper inside.

She opens it while keeping an eye on the raccoons for fear of some strange mob attack. As cute as her mind may find that, she does not want to be scratched to death by trash pandas. But the raccoons must have similar thoughts, as they keep to the tree line.

The paper inside the bag is a note from her father.

Allison,

I do not envy your position. It has been many years since I was in the Waiting. First, I want you to know I am not mad. Nobody is. We only want you to come home and be safe. Please come home first. I have some explaining and many apologies.

Love,
Dad

"This test, Mr. DeSalvo, is one of trust and secrecy." Vistrus pauses, waiting for a response.

After a moment of careful consideration, Connor speaks. "While I do not think you would put me in a compromising situation and will accept regardless, can you humor me with how a test concerning secrets can also be about trust?"

Vistrus smiles. "While secrecy and trust rarely go hand in hand, this will make sense. Before I can begin, I need to know if you accept."

Connor takes a deep breath of uncertainty about what comes next. "I accept."

"Life can be cruel." Vistrus stops for a moment to see if Connor will interrupt, but he does not. A smile rises to the surface but drowns just as fast. "Legends see cruelty in many forms. There is a granted certainty that we will out-live any Normal we meet. Legends can die of old age. I have just never known of any who has. Legends face untold discrimination by any who find out and do not or will not understand." Again, he pauses to puff his cigar, letting his preamble sink into Connor's consciousness. "You have experienced such cruelty. As has Ms. Waldgrave, Ms. McAllister, and Mr. Taylor before his passing. Cruelty is unfair." He puffs and immediately exhales, watching the smoke dance upward. "As I have said, life can be cruel. It is a lesson best learned and quick."

Vistrus watches Connor nod with narrowed eyes. He sees Connor's impatience push its way onto his face through tightened lips.

"I shall get to my point. What I am about to tell you must not leave the confines of you and me. No one else may know. Not Scarlett or Brianna. Not even Duncan. Eleanor neither. Do you understand the importance of this?"

Connor waits for permission to speak.

"I need you to respond," Vistrus urges.

"I understand."

"This I say because lessons learned that can be taken back ease the blow when the lesson cannot."

"What lesson? What is going on?"

"Allison is not dead."

"And I can't tell Scarlett? This is killing her."

"It may be, but she will heal. She knew before anyone else. But life can be cruel. She will have many years ahead of her to learn that. Starting with training wheels will make it easier to navigate when they inevitably come off."

Taking a deeper breath than his last, Connor sits with those words for a while, contemplating the implications. Vistrus relaxes back into his chair, giving Connor the time and space he needs. With not much left to their cigars, Vistrus finishes his off, while Connor milks his for every puff it's worth. After snuffing out the cigar, Vistrus grabs both of their glasses before walking into the kitchen to top them off. Returning with another round, he hands Connor his whiskey.

Taking the glass and looking Vistrus in the eye, Connor finally responds with, "So Allison is in the Waiting, which means she's not dead-dead. But I can't tell her best friend, who happens to be my cousin, because this is a test and to pad the blow for when it does happen with no coming back. Even though we've all already gone through this with Mom, Dad, Grandpa, Jack, Mrs. Waldgrave, Jack's parents...?"

"Correct."

"How will this help?"

"Because now, for the first time, they have the chance to deal with loss and not have it be final without pending doom. To mourn and accept and have it return."

"Why not just do this when Scar was down for the count?"

"Timing did not present itself. Life does not always work in a timely manner. Now, I have the chance."

"And being in the Waiting is not a timed event. As in, no one knows how long she'll be buried?"

"Also correct."

"And the only people who know and can know are me and you?"

Vistrus nods in affirmation.

"This sucks, Mr. Petrovsky ... big time."

Sitting back in his chair and taking a sip, Vistrus offers a simple response, "It does indeed."

Vistrus plates some beer brats and coleslaw, passing out the plates to the others. Scarlett, Connor, Bri, Duncan, and Eleanor fill his kitchen with long-needed laughter, however apprehensive it might be. As Vistrus joins them at the table, Scarlett lifts her glass, grabbing everyone's attention.

"First, I'd like to thank Vistrus for wanting to have everyone over. It's been too long since we've laughed in this house." Scarlett turns to Vistrus, who offers an appreciative nod. "But I would like to take this opportunity to talk about something. And I don't want to do it dragging down the mood, making everyone all sad and moody."

She watches as Duncan chomps on his brat, but otherwise, all attention is on her. Bri wipes some coleslaw from her mouth. Everyone eats, keeping the mood light and attention on her.

"Healing takes time, and sometimes that means talking. It's been hard for me since, well, coming back or waking up or whatever. Waking up covered in dirt is … not fun, to say the least," Scarlett continues.

Both Eleanor and Vistrus nod in an unspoken understanding. Bri has stopped eating, though her fingers keep stretching for the food.

"Eat, Bri. This isn't sad. Just is what it is. But yeah, it's not fun. No one prepared me for it. There was no one to do it." She notices Eleanor looks sad, almost disappointed. "No one should have thought I would have needed to know when I did. But here's the thing…" She stops and takes a giant chunk of her bratwurst. "These are really good, Mr. Petrovsky."

"Thank you. The secret is PBR. But Scarlett…" He waits for her to meet his gaze. "You can call me Vistrus. We are all adults."

She nods with a head tilt and a smile before continuing. "Where was I?"

"About to say a thing," Bri offers.

She waves a finger at Bri. "That's right. The thing is, no matter what kind of prep you give, waking up like that is something no amount of preparation can prepare you for. I know that waking up like I did, did not make dealing with Allison's death any easier on me … or you guys. But, I wanted to say thank you for not giving up on me. I know she's gone and I'll make peace with that one day."

A voice from the front door speaks. "Don't make peace with that too soon. Let me die first."

They all turn to see a dirt-covered Allison leaning against the wall.

"Got an extra brat? I'm starving." She stumbles into the kitchen, leaving a patch of dirt on the wall where she leaned. "I'll clean that later, Dad."

"No worries. Glad to have you home." Vistrus's eyes well with tears as he rises from his seat.

"I got your note," she says, tears falling as she collapses into him.

Wrapping his arms around his daughter, he says, "I am so sorry, Allison. I should have seen the signs. Been a better father." Tears flow from him, a mixture of relief and regret, happiness and sorrow.

"I'm sorry, too, Dad." Allison returns the tears.

Eleanor watches with a smile that tries to eke out as Scarlett, Bri, and Duncan all sit in shock. Connor watches with relief, seeing his love return to him.

As they sit in the sobbing embrace, Scarlett finally cries out, "I KNEW IT!"

Allison pulls away from her father, stepping to Scarlett. She leans down, hugging her friend, who is still too shocked to stand or hug back.

She holds her hug for a while, unsure if Scarlett can't or won't hug her back. Right now, she doesn't care about the reason, only that she can hug her again. Letting go, she turns to Connor.

"Connor, babe, I'm not sure what to say. What I must have put you through," she turns to the others, "all of you through, I can't imagine." She turns back to Connor. "There was a lot going through my head."

She faces her father for a moment before turning back to Connor. "I know I'm still working things out with my attraction to women, but I still love you."

"I love you, too," he says. "That never changed. Never would."

Scarlett, still in shock and unaware of the current conversation, shouts, "I KNEW IT! You all doubted me and I told you!"

Vistrus and Connor exchange a look that does not pass Scarlett by.

"What? What was that look?" she demands.

Silence falls as all eating comes to a halt. Duncan grabs Bri's hand under the table, giving it a squeeze.

"I'm with her," Bri interjects. "There was definitely a look."

Connor opens his mouth, but Vistrus holds up a hand so he can speak first. "It had to be done this way."

Scarlett's confusion twists on her face to anger. "Had to be done this way?!"

Vistrus takes a deep breath. "Learning to deal with loss is a part of life. I thought it best to do so, knowing that it was only temporary."

"That's pretty messed up, Dad," Allison interjects. "How did you know I'd be back?"

"You opened my vial, not yours." Turning to Scarlett, he continues, "Loss is not always temporary. Learning it now will help you deal with it when it is permanent."

Shocked, Scarlett shakes her head. "I'm not sure that was your call to make on my behalf."

He raises his brows, doubting his actions, saying, "Perhaps you are correct. But that debate is moot. There are bigger things at play."

"Bigger things?" Scarlett asks, her words dripping with sarcastic doubt.

"Yeah, Scar," Connor interjects. "Bigger than I ever imagined. I recognize that what was done was not all on the up-and-up, but this isn't about you or me or any one individual here. It's about all of us."

Duncan raises his hand, unsure if he can speak. Vistrus motions for him to ask his question.

"Um, what bigger things are at play?" Duncan asks, looking around at everyone as they all turn their attention to Vistrus.

"As audacious or courageous as you and your claims might be, I have to admit that ... sometimes we hold on to power long after our relevance and reason for holding it has passed." Mikhail steps out from behind the table, stopping next to Vistrus. "You will not always agree with the others, Vistrus. Sometimes, patience and silence are your only ally."

Vistrus turns toward him while keeping a side-eye on the others. "They can make a great team."

"Like vodka and ice." Mikhail laughs a small, awkward laugh, as if it's his first time laughing. He stifles it, but it tries creeping back out.

Vistrus does not join the laughter, contributing a smile to the moment instead. "Where are you going with this?"

Mikhail straightens himself, tugging on his button-down shirt. "You have been grooming Connor for a seat on the West Haven Council, no?"

Vistrus nods.

Continuing, Mikhail says, "Do you think The Nation, given what you say you feel is true, can benefit from you staying on the West Haven Council for as long as you wish to serve?"

Vistrus raises a brow, unsure of what Mikhail means. "I wish to serve as long as I can do good for not only The Nation but all mankind."

Mikhail nods. "That is what we thought." He turns to his Council members, looking them over, gauging their reactions. "We think that the time has come to redistribute responsibility and power to those better suited to wield it."

Vistrus squints an unsure eye at him. "You think me?"

"We do. Your words gave us a lot to think about. And while in the moment, words can sway, reflecting on those words can shove."

"I understand."

"It's not fun anymore, Vistrus. After centuries of fighting the same battles, the same war, the passion leaves you. It slinks away in the night while you sleep like some mistress leaving before the wife comes home."

Vistrus cocks his head, wondering about Mikhail's reasons to use such a colorful simile.

"One day, you will wake up and the joy will be gone. Don't do what I did and hold on to it, hoping that it may return. It won't. I know because it never did. It's been countless years since I enjoyed leading The Nation. Countless years since I forgot why we do what we do."

Vistrus nods, listening in silent patience as Mikhail continues talking.

"It's not about money. We have what we need for more than our lifetime. I think I held onto it because of tradition ... because I wanted to preserve what once was. That is a fool's game. Change is the only constant in an ever-changing world. It took me far too long to realize that, and it was you who made me see it."

"You are welcome?" *Vistrus asks tentatively. Unsure if the response was warranted.*

Mikhail nods. "Thank you. We have always had odd numbers, so when voting, ties would not happen. Five members. I am leaving this behind."

"For what?" *Vistrus asks before he can stop himself.*

"A hammock and a pile of books. Anything other than this. But not only myself. Ivan, too, partially in protest but more so in understanding. And one other." *He turns to a member who has yet to speak in front of Vistrus.* "We are the remaining three from when Inessa was sent to the colonies."

"That leaves two members. An even number," *Vistrus says, pointing out the math.*

"And you make three," *Mikhail says.* "Until you tire of this, too."

"What about the other two seats? One for each society? Not just odd numbers, Mikhail."

Mikhail shrugs. "That's for you and the others to decide. That won't be my problem."

"But until it becomes not your problem, there's the matter back home of the West Haven Council to deal with. My seat, Connor's grooming," *Vistrus points out the flaws in Mikhail's plan.*

"The corruption you speak of has been fooling us for too long. Dissolve the Council. Form a new one. Whatever you decide is yours to do. When you are ready, Mother Russia calls you home."

Vistrus leads Scarlett, Connor, Allison, and Bri down the hallways of the museum. The crowds exit as the minutes count down to closing. One by one, the lights dim, signaling time for all patrons to leave for the day.

"You excited for your bachelorette party next week?" Scarlett squeaks.

"I still can't believe you're getting married," Allison says, feigning disbelief.

"You're coming, right, Al?" Bri asks, tugging on her arm.

"Wouldn't miss it for anything." Allison laughs. "But I have to make an appearance at Duncan's bachelor party."

"I thought that was guys only?" Scarlett asks.

"Hey, Connor asked. Who am I to say no?"

Connor throws up his hands. "I'm staying out of all this."

Vistrus turns to them without breaking stride. "You are about to step into something big and all you can talk about are parties?"

The four of them try to act serious, but the mood is anything but. As they approach the auditorium, Duncan stands outside the door, waiting to hold it open for them. The chatter from inside brushes away the ease they felt and the situation before them sinks in.

They all turn to each other, gulping and tensing up.

Duncan opens the door to reveal an auditorium filled with Legends, all in Legendary form. From where they stand, they see the stage—four podiums mic'd up and waiting for them.

Vistrus watches as the four young adults stare past the doors, looking at a room filled with people like them. People who feel the same fears, share the same problems, and have the same desires. He continues watching as all four of them gather up the confidence they not only didn't know they had, but never knew they would need.

"This is your future in there. Those are your people you will lead." Vistrus pauses, letting those words sink in.

The four start to take cautious steps forward, listening to what Vistrus says as Duncan holds an open arm, pointing the way.

"You are in The Nation. You know the Legends exist. You help decide if we are to remain campfire stories and scary movies, or if we shall see the storm pass."

The four of them cross the threshold into the auditorium. The chatter quiets down as they approach the stage. Vistrus enters as Duncan shuts the door behind them, still whispering to the leaders he helped groom. "So, you have to stop and really ask yourself, are you In?"

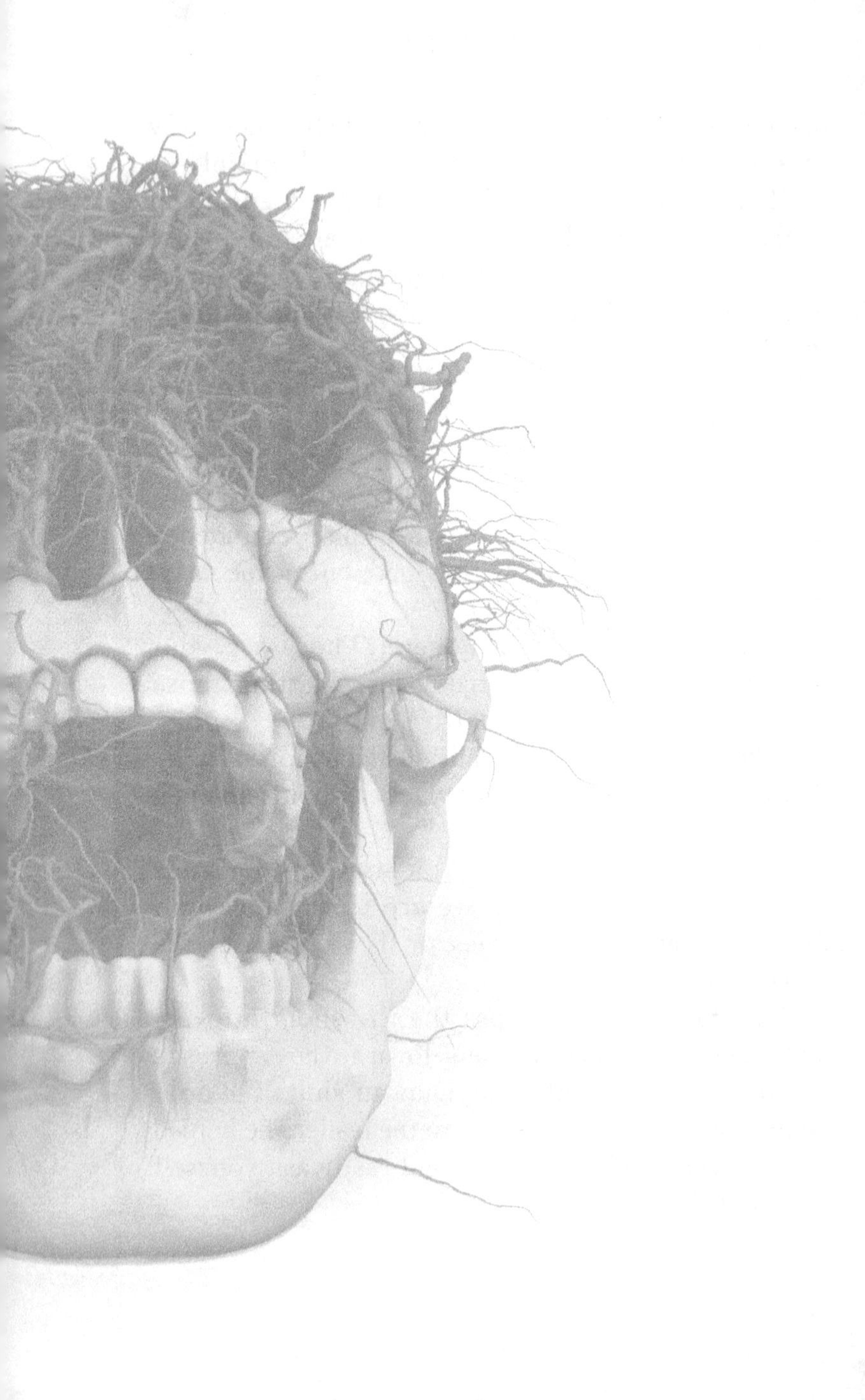

BOOK CLUB QUESTIONS:

1. Who was your favorite character throughout the series?

2. Do you feel knowing about Bishop's past made his actions any more justifiable?

3. What was your favorite storyline throughout the series?

4. Which book was your favorite?

5. What do you think happens to the characters as time passes?

6. Do you think Bri and Duncan have their happily ever after?

7. Would you like to meet any of the characters in real life?

8. Would you want to live in West Haven?

9. If you were a Legend, would you feel comfortable coming out to the world?

10. Are you In?

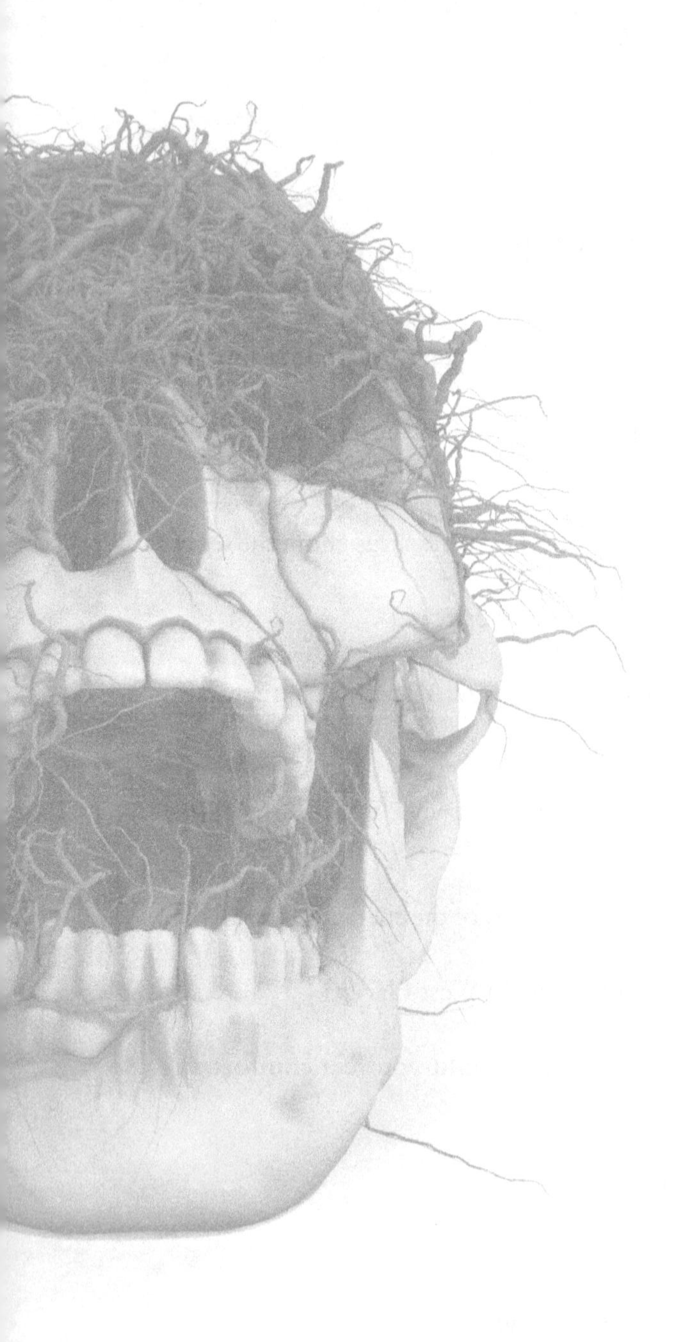

AUTHOR BIO

Nick Savage is the author of *The West Haven Undead Series* and *The Fairlane Series*, writing both contemporary fantasy and modern romance. He strives for realism and relatable characters that people will want to read time and again. He lives in the Orlando area with his wife and two Maine Coons.

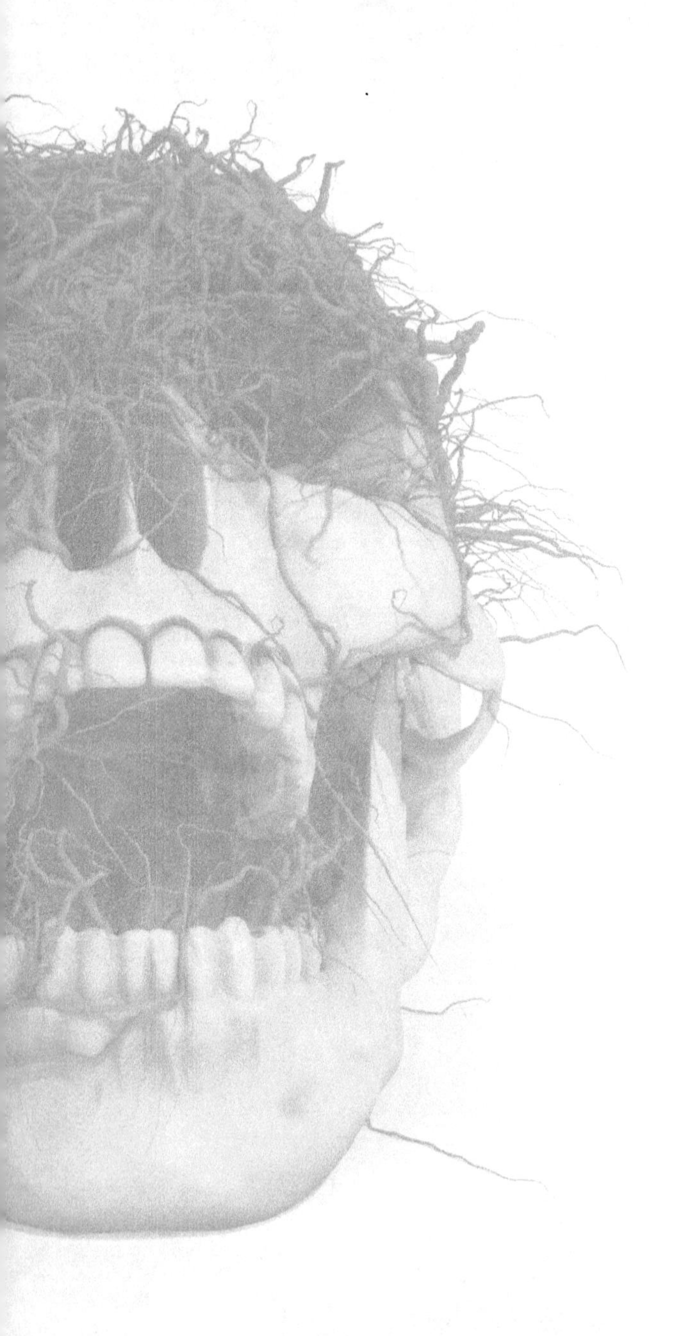

Discover more at
4HorsemenPublications.com

10% off using HORSEMEN10